PRAISE FOR ~~ONCE~~

"Diane Sawatzki's ~~...~~ history and culture ~~...~~ librarian, then told ~~...~~ truly fascinating stor~~...~~ ~~...~~story-loving friends and I thoroughly enjoyed Diane's last book, *Once Upon Another Time*. Knowing her literary skill and attention to historical detail based on sound research, we can't wait to get our hands on the sequel!" - John Anderson, author of *Ute Indian Prayer Trees of the Pikes Peak Region*

"*Once Upon Another Time* is a creative journey to another time. As an avid hiker living near the Palmer Divide, I delighted in the descriptions of Colorado life in the 1860s. Sawatzki is a talented author who has crafted an engaging tale about a young widow lost in a time warp, and the Ute native who befriends her. This is a must-read for local book clubs!" - Sharon Gerdes, author of *Back in Six Weeks*

"The Colorado of *Once Upon Another Time* contains grizzly bears and raucous saloons, a 15-year-old illiterate prostitute and Mexicans who befriend the Utes, as well as those who contribute to the banditry and general lawlessness Kate discovers. Kate and Victor become real to us, though the circumstances of their meeting are fantastic, in the fantasy sense of the word. *Once Upon Another Time*, as its name suggests, is a kind of fairy tale, one in which adults with a fascination for the Old West will delight." - Annie Dawid, *Colorado Central Magazine*, author of Rubery award-winning *York Ferry*

"Kate MacKenzie isn't the only time traveler in this book. A Ute Indian named Victor did it first, only in the opposite direction. He has been living in the modern world alone—learning, adapting, and yearning for his own time. Between extensive research and writing, Sawatzki took about six years to craft this well-written, action-packed novel." - Norma Engelberg, *The Tri-Lakes Tribune*

"*Once Upon Another Time* hooked me with its time-traveling fantasy, but as a biographer what transported me all the way to a satisfying conclusion was Sawatzki's use of well-researched, well-depicted historical events, characters, and Colorado settings." - John Stansfield, storyteller and author of the award-winning *Writers of the American West* and *Enos Mills: Rocky Mountain Naturalist*, among other works.

"In Diane Sawatzki's novel *Once Upon Another Time*, the author captured all the ingredients which make a book enjoyable. Not only was the writing and story excellent, but it draws the reader into an unexpected world that keeps you engaged with the characters until the very end." - Robert Cronk, author of *Decrypt – The Lori Merchant Trilogy Book One*

Photo courtesy of Pixabay.com.

MANYHORSES TRAVELING

*****

DIANE SAWATZKI

Author of
Once Upon Another Time

Published by:

DIANE SAWATZKI
pdpmark@pcisys.net

PALMER DIVIDE PRODUCTIONS LLC
PO BOX 42
PALMER LAKE, CO 80133

www.palmerdivideproductions.com

JimandDiane@PalmerDivideProductions.com

©Copyright 2017

Printed in the United States of America
ISBN-13: 978-1978480001
ISBN-10: 1978480008

This is a work of fiction. All of the characters, organizations, and events portrayed in this novel are either products of the author's imagination or are used fictitiously.

Dedication

To Roger, Harriet, and Cathy for helping
me navigate the vast river of words.

LIST of CHARACTERS

Major Characters

Kate MacKenzie - young widow who travels back in time, returns to present, loves Victor

Victor Manyhorses – Ute Indian widower from 1863 who travels to present, loves Kate

Little Eagle – Victor's parentless granddaughter, 3 months old at beginning of book

Bear – shapeshifting grizzly, accompanies Victor and Kate

Doozie – 16-year-old former prostitute from 1863 who Kate takes under her wing

Colorado – present time

Lily – Kate's grandmother

Ivan – Kate's grandfather

Luis – Victor's friend at homeless shelter

Seattle – present time

Mark – Kate's fellow teacher and friend

Alex – Kate's best friend

Adele – Swinomish Indian artist

1863 characters

Buster P. Carmody – wagon-freighter

Doozie Chastity Harwood – saloon-owner and friend

Blackstone – cruel circuit judge who killed Doozie's husband

Bridgette – prostitute, Doozie's right-hand woman

Mexican bandits – Mexican brothers who murder and terrorize white settlers

1863 Utes

Rising Moon – Victor's best friend and brother-in-law

Prairie Flower – Rising Moon's wife

Badger Woman – widow who Victor rescued from the Arapaho

Mourning Dove – Victor's mother-in-law

Ouray – Victor's close boyhood friend, influential chief of another Ute tribal band

Laughing Brook – boy whose life Kate saved previously, horse-tender

Running Deer – war chief of Victor's band, Laughing Brook's father

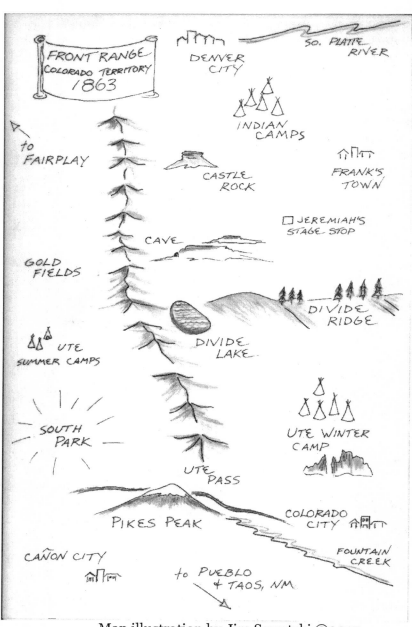

Map illustration by Jim Sawatzki ©2017

CHAPTER ONE

Pikes Peak Region—present day

Afternoon sunlight streamed in through the windows of Lily's living room as Kate sat in a rocker by the fire, trying to puzzle things out. Lily snored in a rocker beside her. Little Eagle snored between them in an antique cradle.

Kate and the baby had been back from 1863 for two days, and Victor still hadn't joined them. Although Kate's headache was gone, and the gash on her forehead was healing, she was still exhausted from the time travel and worried about Victor. Was he still alive, or was he lying somewhere in the past, wounded or dying?

She glanced down at the baby sleeping in her cradle. *It's a miracle we both made it back alive.* Kate looked over at Little Eagle's discarded cradleboard, caked with dirt and dried blood, and remembered the day she'd found it pinned beneath Victor's dead daughter, her crying baby trapped inside it. *I'm caring for her baby now.*

"Lily," Kate said, shaking her shoulder.

Her grandmother awoke with a snort. "What?"

"I've got to go back up to the mesa. I've got to go look for Victor."

Lily sat up straighter and shook her head. "No, honey, don't. You've been through so much already."

Kate got up and peered out the window at the crystalline snow. "I have to, Lily. If he's alive, he could be lying up there, wounded. I promise I'll be back by evening." Hurrying into the kitchen, she threw on a jacket and boots. She went out onto the porch, strapped on Lily's snowshoes, and set off through the forest.

————————

A breeze sighed through the ponderosas as Kate stood beneath them on her snowshoes, catching her breath after trudging up onto the mesa. She'd come up here to search for Victor but feared she wouldn't find him. As Kate rested, she was aware of the sun on her skin, the snow dripping off the trees, and the serene stillness of the forest. She heard a voice, and her heart leapt. She spied Bear and dared to hope. She saw Victor emerge from the trees, and their eyes locked.

He grinned and ran toward her.

"Thank God," she whispered, feeling his arms around her. "I thought I'd lost you." She inhaled the scent of him, the scent of leather and horses and wood smoke.

Bear caught up with them and lunged at Kate, knocking her into a snow bank and dislodging one of her snowshoes. "Hey!" she said, laughing as the massive grizzly licked her face. She rubbed Bear's head until the animal groaned with pleasure.

Victor reached down and pulled her up. "Are you okay?"

"I'm fine," Kate said, brushing off the snow. Sinking down onto a rock, she removed her pack and the other snowshoe.

Leaning his rifle against the rock, Victor shed his pack and sat down beside her. He clasped her face in his hands and kissed her.

After a minute, Kate drew back and smiled. "I knew you weren't dead because I'd feel it if you died, but I was really getting worried. What happened?"

He touched her cheek. "I'm sorry, Kate. I was delayed, and there was no way to get in touch with you. How's Little Eagle?"

"She's safe at home with Lily."

"I'm glad to hear that," he said. "I have a monster headache," he added, rubbing his forehead. "Do you have any ibuprofen?"

"Of course," she said, reaching into her pack. "After our last trip, I always carry it." She dug out several tablets and handed them over with her water bottle.

"Thanks," he said, and downed the pills. "Time travel's exhausting."

"No kidding. I've been back for two days, and I'm still tired. My headache's finally gone, though."

"I'm dizzy, too. How long were we gone this time?"

She laughed. "Only two days. Can you believe it?"

He shook his head. "That's incredible. We were in the past for three months."

"What took you so long? What happened to you after you left me and Doozie?"

"I had Blackstone and Charlie trapped in a canyon south of here, but they slipped away during the night. Did you ride back to Jeremiah's like you promised?"

Kate shook her head. "No. We meant to, but we built a fire to keep warm, and we were so exhausted we fell asleep. I shouldn't have let Doozie talk me into building that fire." *Poor Doozie*, she thought, *dead at sixteen.*

"You're safe now, Kate, that's all that matters. By the time I made it back to the cave, you and Little Eagle were gone and the passage had sealed again."

"I'm sure it opened because of the solstice. I must've passed out after I came through because I don't remember anything after that. Bear must've followed us through and brought us back to Lily's. Her paw prints were all over the porch."

Victor nodded. "She must've returned for me after she took you home."

"So she *does* influence when the passage opens," Kate said.

"I think she does. Do you have any food? I'm starving."

"I brought apples." She pulled two Jonathans from her pack and handed him one.

"Thanks," he said, biting into it.

As they ate, Bear sat on her haunches a few feet away, watching two squirrels chase each other through the trees.

"Since I'm here," Kate said, "I should go to the cave and look for the penny that I lost."

He laughed. "Why? It's just a penny."

She swallowed a bite of apple. "Lily gave it to me, and it's dated 1863, so it might be valuable. Plus, I'm attached to it. Before I came through the first time, I flipped it to help me decide whether to move back to Colorado or stay in Seattle."

"Like a heads or tails type of thing?"

"You got it. If it landed heads up, that would mean I should move back here; if it landed tails up, that meant I should stay in Seattle. But I didn't see how it landed because Bear scared me and I bolted for the back of the cave, then fell down the passage."

He took a penny from his pocket and held it out to her. "Is this it?"

"Yeah!" she said, reaching for it. "Which side did it land on?"

"Hold on. Did you decide whether to move back here?"

"I did," she said, nodding. "There's no place I'd rather be."

"Good, then you can take it." He tossed his apple core to Bear, who snapped it up.

Kate tucked the penny into her pocket. The sun was sinking, and it was snowing now, big flakes blanketing the forest. "We should get back," she said, throwing Bear her apple core. "It's getting late, and Lily might be worried."

He shrugged into his pack and shouldered his rifle. "Does Lily know about me?"

"Yes, I told her everything."

"Was she shocked to hear you're in love with an Indian?"

"Not that in particular, but of course she was shocked to hear my story. She didn't believe me at first about the time travel, but I had Eagle as proof, so she finally had to. So, how *did* my penny land?"

"Heads up, which means you should move back here."

"That's great because I'm going to." She strapped on her snowshoes, put on her pack, and held out her hand. "Let's go home."

"Home," he said, clasping her hand. "I've never had a real home here."

"Well, you do now, and believe me—after being stuck in 1863 for all that time, it's a pleasure to have hot showers, flush toilets, and comfortable beds."

"Can we can sleep together at your grandma's?"

"I sure hope so."

They trudged off through the gathering shadows. Bear plodded along behind them.

———————

The snow came down steadily as Lily's two-story house came into view, its windows full of welcoming light.

"I can't wait for you to meet her," Kate said, forging ahead on her snowshoes.

"I'm looking forward to it," Victor said, following behind her, "but it'll be strange being in her house again." His head was pounding, and he was dizzy with weariness.

Kate stopped and peered over her shoulder. "What do you mean, *again*?"

"Remember, I told you I sometimes slipped inside there."

"I think I would've remembered *that*. You broke into their house?"

He shot her a thin smile. "I never broke in, exactly, but I often snuck in when they were gone. Remember, I showed you that Ute book I borrowed from their library?"

Kate nodded. "Okay, I do remember now. Why did you sneak into their house?"

"After I came through the passage, I was trapped in this time for years, and I was lonely. I only slipped in when they were gone, so they never knew I was there. I didn't want to scare them."

"That makes sense, I guess, but it's still a little creepy. What did you do in there?"

"I took a shower sometimes, made myself a sandwich, browsed the bookshelves, and read by the fire." His head was really pounding now, and his legs were shaking as he stood there. He had to get inside and rest.

"How many times did you sneak in?"

"Ten or fifteen, I guess."

Kate's eyebrows arched. "Ten or fifteen! And they never saw you?"

He shook his head. "No. Like I said, I only snuck in when they were gone, except for that last time. I even peeked through the window that night and saw you sitting by the fire, all alone and crying."

"It must've been the night after Ivan's surgery. We'd just found out he was going to be okay, so I must've been crying because I was so relieved. You said you only snuck in when they were gone, except for that last time. What happened then?"

"I'd left my pack inside, so I came back to find it. How's Ivan doing?"

"I haven't seen him since I've been back, but Lily says he's doing great. Let's get going." She turned around and set off as the snow came down even harder.

When they reached the back porch, Kate took off her snowshoes and leaned them against the house as Victor peered through the window into the kitchen. Stomping the snow off her boots, she unzipped her gaiters, untied her boots, and kicked them off. "Put your boots on this mat to keep the floor clean," she said as she opened the door.

"Okay," he said, kicking the snow off his boots. As he stepped inside, he noticed a pie cooling on the table, a fire burning in the woodstove, and the enticing aroma of baking bread. *It's like coming home.*

Kate removed her pack and pointed to a small room next to the kitchen. "You can put your pack and rifle over there in that storeroom. Here, hand me your rifle."

After handing it to her, he eased his pack off and rested it against the table, untied his boots and set them on the mat. He hauled his pack into the storeroom and unhooked a small accessory pack. "I have a gift here for your grandma."

Kate grinned. "Really? That's nice. What is it?"

He shot her a grin. "You'll find out."

"Come on," Kate said, grabbing his hand and pulling him through the kitchen. As they entered the living room, Victor spied a silver-haired woman in overalls sitting by the fire, rocking Little

Eagle back and forth in a cradle. *My granddaughter, alive and well.*

"Look who I found on the mesa," Kate said. "Lily, this is Victor. Victor, Lily."

Lily rose from her rocker and stared at him, her blue eyes wide with wonder. "I don't believe it. So, you really *do* exist!"

Victor nodded. "I do." *My granddaughter, right there in the cradle.*

Lily continued to stare. "Sorry, it's just...I'm very glad to meet you, Victor."

"I'm very glad to meet you, too," he said, holding up his little pack. "I brought you a gift from the past."

"For me?" she asked, smiling. "What is it?"

He unzipped the pack and held it out for her to look inside.

Lily peered in, but drew back. "You brought me...uh...mice? Why?"

Victor's heart fell, but he pressed on. "Kate said if they found this species of mouse back in that meadow, developers couldn't build there. We had plenty in the past, so I brought a pair back for you."

Lily gasped. "These are Preble's jumping mice? How wonderful! Thank you!"

"You're welcome," he said, handing her the pack. "They're hibernating now, plus they're probably groggy from the time travel. We can put them in the meadow."

Kate leaned forward to look at the mice. "Hi, guys. Welcome to the future."

"Amazing," Lily said. "How'd you know what they looked like?"

"Kate showed me a picture from a report she had. Excuse me." He slipped past Lily and snatched up Little Eagle. *She feels soft and precious, like a basket full of smiles.*

"That's incredible," Lily said. "You just came through the passage from 1863, and you had the presence of mind to bring me mice? How do you feel?"

"Exhausted," he said, collapsing into a rocker. "Dizzy. And I've got a headache."

"I imagine so," Lily said. "Kate slept a whole day after she returned." She studied the mice. "Cute little cusses, aren't they? I'll go put them in the storeroom. You two just rest here by the fire while I get dinner ready. We're having beef stew and apple pie."

"That sounds delicious," Kate said, slumping into the rocker next to Victor. "But I have to warn you—be careful about going out on the kitchen porch without us."

"Why's that?" Lily asked.

"Bear followed us here," Kate said. "She's off hunting now, but when she comes back, I'll bet she'll sleep on that porch to be near us."

Lily laughed. "So, I've got a Ute in my living room, his granddaughter in my cradle, mice in my storeroom, and a grizzly on my porch. Incredible." She ambled off.

Feeling exhaustion wash over him, Victor closed his eyes and settled into his rocker. He felt Kate lift Little Eagle from his arms.

"Rest now," she whispered. "I've got her. You made it through, and you're safe."

He heard the fire crackle as he drifted off.

CHAPTER TWO

"**W**ake up, honey," a voice whispered.
As Kate opened her eyes, she saw Lily hovering above her. Little Eagle slept nearby in her cradle, and Victor dozed in the rocker beside her. *So the miracle is real. He's come back to me.*

"Dinner's ready," Lily said. "Come and get it." She turned and left the room.

Kate nudged Victor's shoulder. "Wake up sleepyhead."

He snorted and looked around. "Where are we?"

"We're at Lily's. Dinner's ready. Are you hungry?"

"Ravenous," he said, glancing over at the baby. "Should we bring her?"

"No, let her sleep," she said, rising from her rocker and taking his hand. "We'll come get her if she cries. Come on." She led him from the living room.

In the kitchen strains of Mozart wafted from the speakers, a fire roared in the woodstove, and a feast graced the table. There was a Dutch oven steaming with stew, fresh-baked bread on a cutting board, bowls of salad, a pie, and a bottle of Merlot.

"Smells wonderful, Lily," Kate said, pulling out a chair. "This is quite a spread!"

"Thanks, honey," Lily said. "Would you care for some wine, Victor?"

"I would," he said, sitting next to Kate. "Merlot's one of my favorites."

Lily poured them each a glass. Setting the bottle down, she picked up a ladle, dished out the stew, and set their bowls down in front of them. "Alex called when you were up on the mesa, Katie. She said Cisco misses you, so she's giving him lots of attention, and she's still planning on picking you up at the airport Friday evening."

Victor dug in. "This stew's delicious, Lily. Who are Alex and Cisco?"

"Thanks," Lily said. "Alex is Katie's best friend, and Cisco is Katie's kitty."

Kate buttered a piece of bread and bit into it, savoring its rich flavor. "So much has happened since I've been gone, I'm not sure I even *want* to go back to Seattle."

He frowned. "But you said you were moving back here."

"I am, but I can't move before school's out, or I won't get a good reference."

Victor grabbed a piece of bread, slathered it with butter, and took a bite. "I see. Couldn't you move back now and do something else for a living?"

"As I matter of fact," Lily said, "she's considering taking over our antique business, but she needs to keep her options open. Right, honey?"

"Right," Kate said. "If I miss teaching, I'll never get another job if I quit before the end of the school year. Besides, if I'm moving back, I need to sell my house first."

He sipped his wine. "If you feel you must go, I could take Little Eagle to the reservation and live there while you're gone. I'd miss you, though. We just found each other again." He reached over and touched her cheek.

"I'd miss you, too," she said, her heart sinking. "Fly back to Seattle with me."

He choked on his wine. "On a plane?"

Lily snorted and tucked into her stew.

Kate stared at him. "That's how most people fly, silly."

"I'm afraid to," he said, frowning. "I don't know how those things stay up there."

"It's simple aerodynamics," Kate said. "I can Google it and show it to you."

"I've never been away from Colorado. Our Shining Mountains are sacred to us."

Kate sighed. "But I'll miss you and Eagle."

"Listen, Victor," Lily said. "Maybe it's none of my business, but I think you should go to Seattle to see how Katie lives. She went to *your* world and saw how *you* lived."

Victor considered this. "What would I do all day while she's off teaching?"

"You could do your artwork," Kate said, her spirits lifting. "Seattle has lots of museums and galleries you could visit for inspiration, and I could teach you to use the buses. Maybe you could meet some of the local Indians and study Northwestern art."

He nodded. "That would be useful. Do you *know* any local Indians?"

"Well, no," Kate said, "but I'll bet we could find some. It'll be an adventure! I'll be off every weekend, so we could explore together. I could take you to see the ocean."

"Now, there's a thought," he said. "I've always wanted to see the ocean."

Something niggled at Kate's brain. "Wait. Do you have a driver's license?"

"I have one," he said, "but it's not really mine. When my friend's uncle died, he sold me his car and threw in the license. Why, is that a problem?"

"It could be. TSA's really strict in Denver. Do you have any other I.D.?"

"No. What's TSA?"

"Airport security. Does the uncle look anything like you?"

He shrugged. "I don't think so, but don't us Indians all look alike to you Anglos?"

Kate cuffed his shoulder. "You don't all look alike to us, and they really study those I.D.s. You might be able to bluff your way through, but what about Eagle?"

He speared a forkful of salad and shot her a sly look. "She doesn't have a driver's license either."

Kate laughed. "Very funny. Couldn't we get her some other kind of I.D?"

"I doubt it. She was born in 1863. How would she get one?"

Kate turned to Lily and asked, "Do babies need an I.D. to get on a plane?"

Lily reached for her water. "I really don't know, honey, you'd have to check with the airline. We can look on their website after dinner. Maybe Victor could get her one at the reservation. Don't all Native Americans have to be registered or something?"

"Beats me," he said. "*I* never have. *Native American* sounds so formal, Lily. Just call me an Indian."

"Okay," she said, smiling. "I wasn't sure which term to use."

He scraped his bowl clean with a piece of bread. "Can I have more stew?"

"Of course," Lily said. "Help yourself."

He dished out a second helping. "We call ourselves Indians, Native Americans, or Natives, but we often identify ourselves by which tribe we're from. For example, I'm a Ute from the Tabeguache band of Utes, but you can just call me Victor."

"I'll do that," Lily said.

Victor swallowed a mouthful of stew and washed it down with a gulp of water. "As you know, my granddaughter's full name is Little Eagle, but we just call her Eagle most of the time. Many of us have lived around Spanish people, so we often have Spanish names as well as Ute ones. I go by Victor around Spanish people and Anglos; I go by my traditional names around Utes. My full name is Victor Manyhorses Traveling."

"You have such cool names," Kate said. "You should go by them here."

"You don't think they're too *Native*?" he asked.

Kate sipped her wine. "No, they're ethnic. You should use them."

"Your English is excellent," Lily said. "Did many Utes speak it in your time?"

"No. Some of the chiefs did, and those who traded with the Anglos, like my friend Rising Moon. He and his wife traded pelts with some of the shopkeepers."

Kate held up the bottle of Merlot. "More wine?"

"No," he said. "My headache's creeping back, so I'd better stick to water."

"Okay," Kate said. "More wine, Lily?"

Lily waved her off. "No."

Kate refilled her glass. "Victor speaks several languages, but he didn't become fluent in English until he time-traveled the first time and got trapped here for four years."

"I see," Lily said. "How many languages do you speak besides Ute and English?"

"Spanish, Arapaho, and Cheyenne," he said, buttering another piece of bread.

"My goodness," Lily said. "You're quite the linguist."

"And you're quite the baker. This bread's wonderful."

"Thank you. It's whole wheat with raisins and sunflower seeds. Will you miss being back in the past?"

He paused before answering. "I'll miss the wildness of it, the freedom to ride among the Shining Mountains. I'll miss my people, but according to white man's history, the tribes will be forced onto reservations in 1880. After we rescued Eagle, Kate tried to talk me into bringing her to the future, but I resisted. I wanted her to live with Utes and learn our culture, but I suspected she'd have a better life here."

Kate noticed the sadness in his voice. *He's left so much behind to come here.*

Lily nodded. "We all want the best for our granddaughters, don't we?"

"We do," he said, "so I was torn. But fate made the decision for me of coming to the future. After we left Jeremiah's and headed for Colorado City with Doozie and Homer, we got ambushed by Blackstone and Charlie. Did Kate tell you any of this?"

"Part of it," Lily said. "The part where you led Blackstone and Charlie off after they killed Doozie's husband. That was a brave thing to do." Looking at Kate, she continued, "So, tell me the rest of it."

Kate's pulse quickened as she related the story. "After they rode off, we took the baby to the cave and hid all day and all night. When those bastards showed up the next morning, Doozie killed Charlie, but Blackstone shot her. When the passage began to open, we started climbing, but Doozie lagged behind, so she insisted we leave without her while she covered us. As we left her, Blackstone shot her again, and she plunged down the passage. I never should've let her talk me into building that damn fire."

Victor frowned. "You mentioned that earlier. Why's the fire so important?"

"Because if we hadn't built it, we wouldn't have gotten so comfortable that we fell asleep. We would've returned to Jeremiah's, and Doozie might still be alive."

"But she *is* alive," he said.

"*What?*"

"I didn't realize you thought she was dead."

"That's wonderful! You saw her?"

"Yes, in the cave. Right before I came here."

"She's alive! How was she?"

He shrugged. "Not bad, considering. She had a nasty shoulder wound, but we patched her up well enough to travel. Another bullet grazed her temple, but the scrape was superficial."

"Who's *we*?" Kate asked. "Who patched her up?"

"Rising Moon and Running Deer were hunting nearby and heard the shots, so they rushed to the cave. They arrived just before I did." He took another bite of stew.

Kate's head was swimming. "What about Blackstone? Did you see him?"

"No, he must've fled before we got there. Doozie passed out after he shot her, so she didn't remember anything after that."

"That's strange," Kate said, sipping her wine. "Wonder why he didn't kill her?"

"She was off to one side, partly buried under some rocks and dirt, so I bet he didn't see her."

"Poor Doozie. Just sixteen and already a widow. I'm glad she's alive, but I wish I could've said goodbye to her. Didn't she want to come with you?"

Victor shook his head. "No. I offered to bring her, but she said, and I quote, 'A tart like me don't belong in the future with decent folks. I'm gonna head back home, give Homer a proper burial, and run that saloon. Tell my sister Kate I'll never forget her.'"

Kate felt the tears begin to come. "I'll never forget her either."

"Okay," Lily said, "explain something to me. If the passage only opens on solstices and equinoxes, how did Victor get through if the solstice was over?"

"I can explain," he said. "Bear's presence also causes it to open. She came back to guide me through."

Lily stared at him. "How's that work?"

Victor shrugged. "She's magical."

"A magical bear," Lily said, rising from the table. "Now I've heard everything."

"It's a lot to take in," Kate told him. "Give her time. Want some pie à la mode?"

"Maybe. What is it?"

She squeezed his hand. "It's pie smothered in ice cream."

He kissed her cheek. "You bet. I love pie, and I love ice cream, so I'll take some."

"Don't get used to it," she said, rising to help Lily. "I'm not as fine a baker as Lily, so don't expect pie this good if you come to Seattle. Finished with your dishes?"

He sopped up his remaining stew with his bread and handed his bowl to her. "I can help with the cooking if I come. I cooked when we were traveling, remember?"

"Sure I do," she said, carrying the dishes to the sink, "but we were camping in the wilderness then. My neighbors might frown on cooking wild game on a spit in my backyard." She loaded the dishes in the dishwasher.

"I can cook other things besides game," he said. "Like eggs, burritos, and steak."

Kate laughed. "We'll see."

"Don't discourage him, honey," Lily said, setting a carton of ice cream on the table. "When a man offers to cook, you should say 'thank you' and let him." She cut three slices of pie, set them on plates, and covered each slice with a generous scoop of ice cream. "Here you go, kids. Dig in."

Victor did. "Um-m-m-m. This is terrific pie, Lily."

She put the carton of ice cream back in the freezer. "Thank you," she said as she sat down. "It's Dutch apple with French vanilla, Katie's favorite."

"I'm pretty sure it's my favorite now, too," he said.

They savored their desserts for a while as wind buffeted the house and snow pelted the windows. Kate braced herself and asked, "Can Victor and I sleep together?"

Lily stared at her. "You mean, while you're here in my house?"

"Yes," she said, feeling her stomach twisting into knots.

"*Have* you been sleeping together?"

"Yes, for some time now."

"Do you love him?" Lily asked.

Kate turned to Victor. "Yes, with all my heart."

"And do you love her, Victor?"

"Absolutely."

"Then of course you can sleep together," Lily said, reaching across the table to squeeze their hands. "You belong together. I don't have the right to keep you apart."

Kate blew out a sigh. "Good, I'm glad that's settled. I was starting to feel like a guilty teenager sneaking in after curfew."

"But you'd better be good to her, Victor," Lily added, "or you'll catch hell from me and Ivan!"

"Don't worry," he said, "I'll be good to her."

"Speaking of Ivan," Lily added. "His doctor says he should be getting out of the hospital soon."

"That's great," Katie said. Hearing a thump out on the porch, she got up and hurried to the window. Bear was out there in the pelting snow, sitting on her haunches and peering in. "Lily, come here. I want to show you something."

"Okay." Lily finished her last bite of pie, picked up her plate, and ambled to the window. "That bear's huge!" she cried, shrinking back. "And why's she staring in at us like that?"

"She wants to see if we're in here, so she can make sure we're okay."

Lily stared at Kate. "You're kidding."

"No, it's true. Bear's very protective."

Lily looked out. "Will she break inside and ransack my kitchen for food?"

"No," Kate said. "At least, I doubt it. She's got plenty of prey out there to hunt."

"Mercy," Lily said. "A magical grizzly who's protective. I'll have to warn Ivan."

Kate patted Lily's shoulder. "She'll behave, you'll see. If you want to keep on her good side, you can give her chocolate. She likes the dark kind, with nuts and raisins."

"I'm not feeding her," Lily muttered. "Besides, animals aren't supposed to have chocolate. Isn't it bad for them?"

"Supposedly, but she seems to tolerate it just fine."

Bear huffed against the window and slumped down into a grizzled ball of fur. Just then, the baby's cry came from the living room.

"Eagle's awake," Victor said, jumping up from the table. "I'll go get her." He hurried out.

"He really loves that little one, doesn't he?" Lily asked, watching him go.

"He's nuts about her," Kate said. "She's his past, present, and future."

"Katie," Lily said, touching her arm. "Be careful. Victor seems like a good man, but you barely know him, and he's got a child. That's a lot of baggage."

Kate drew in a breath and let it out. "I know. I didn't intend to fall in love with him, but I couldn't help it. He makes me feel alive. As for the baby, you know I've wanted one since Jon and I lost ours. I deserve to be happy again, Lily."

Lily turned those bright blue eyes on her. "I agree, but you're a teacher and he's an Indian from another century. How would he ever make a living here?"

Kate shrugged. "I don't know. We haven't gotten that far. But he's a good artist."

"That's nice, dear, but it's hard to make a living as an artist these days."

"He could help me run your antique business."

Lily's eyebrows arched. "Does he know anything about antiques?"

Kate laughed. "I doubt it, except for those he's seen in the past, but he can learn, can't he?"

"I suppose. Where would the three of you live? Here?"

"Why not? You said you were planning on moving. I could buy you out."

Lily sighed. "Maybe. I'll have to talk to Ivan. We're not ready to move yet."

Kate stared out at the falling snow. "When I was in the past, I forgot what Jon looked like, and I felt guilty. Then I fell in love with Victor, and felt even guiltier."

"Don't feel guilty," Lily said as she hugged her. "Just be careful. Jon's only been gone a year now, and you're still vulnerable."

"I was so lonely back there in the past, and Victor helped me. He understood what it was like because he'd time-traveled, too. He saved my life in so many ways."

"I know, dear, and there's a lot to be said for that, but..."

Victor sauntered in carrying Little Eagle. "She really stinks."

Kate smiled. "Lily, could you fix her bottle while I go upstairs and change her?"

"I'll get right on it," she said, "and bring it up when it's ready."

"Victor, follow me." Crossing the room, Kate led him through the kitchen, up the stairs, and into her bedroom. He took in the queen-size bed with its flowery comforter, the framed wedding photo of Kate and Jon on the nightstand, the card table with baby supplies, and the large wicker basket on the floor where Little Eagle slept.

"Nice room," he said.

"Thanks. I grew up here, so it's always been mine. My dad died when my mom was pregnant with me, so she moved back in with Lily and Ivan, and they helped her raise me. It's a little tight, with all this baby stuff, but it'll do."

Victor nodded, looking around. "Where'd all this baby stuff come from?"

"We bought most of it, but Lily's been stockpiling baby clothes for years in hopes I'd have a child" She patted the card table. "Put Eagle right here."

"Okay," he said, laying the baby down. She giggled and reached for Kate.

"Phooof!" Kate said, unsnapping Little Eagle's pajama bottoms "You're really loaded."

"What's that weird thing she's wearing?" he asked.

"It's a disposable diaper. You throw it away when it's dirty. It's not ecological, and I feel bad about it, but that's what people use these days." She took it off, folded it up, and tossed it in the plastic receptacle.

"And she sleeps down there, in that basket on the floor?"

"Yeah, just like at Jeremiah's. It's safe, there's no place to fall if she rolls out, and she likes it."

"Can I take a shower and get more ibuprofen? My headache's getting worse."

"Sure," she said. "I'm sorry your headache's back, but it'll pass. The ibuprofen's in the medicine chest in the hall bathroom. Just grab a towel from the closet in there."

"Okay," he said, and hurried out.

"Hi, sweetie," she cooed to Little Eagle. "Let's get you cleaned up." She wiped off her bottom and waved it dry, rubbed on some ointment, and wrapped her in a fresh diaper. "There," she said, "doesn't that feel better?" After cleaning her hands with a wet wipe, she settled into the rocker with Little Eagle as Lily came in.

"Here, honey," Lily said, handing Kate the baby's bottle.

"Thanks," she said. "I never thought such a tiny person could take so much energy. I'm wiped out." She eased the bottle into the baby's mouth.

Lily smiled. "You're doing fine. I'm glad we switched her to formula because that cow's milk was bothering her tummy. Is water running in the hall bathroom?"

"Yes. Victor's taking a shower."

"Okay," she said, turning to leave. "I'm off to bed. 'Night."

"'Night," Kate said. As she rocked back and forth, she watched the baby pull on her bottle. *I've wanted a child for years. Now I have one. And I also have Victor.*

She smiled and drifted off.

CHAPTER THREE

Victor snapped awake. *Where am I?* Moonlight streamed through a gap in the curtains, revealing Kate lying beside him. They'd both passed out fully clothed, too exhausted to undress. Easing out of bed, he drew the curtain aside and looked out into the yard. Ponderosas stood flocked with snow; Bear prowled between them in the moonlight.

Kate turned over and whispered, "What's wrong?"

"Nothing. A dream woke me. Go back to sleep."

"Come back to bed," she groaned, reaching for him.

"In a minute." Bear was out there hunting, a dark shape against the luminous snow.

Kate got up and joined him. "Why's she punching at the snow like that?"

"She does that sometimes when she's frustrated. Maybe her prey escaped."

She yawned. "She's such a character. What was your dream about?"

He grasped at the receding memory. "It was confusing, like many dreams, but I remember Growling Thunder and I were shooting at each other. He called you a witch, and cursed us both."

"That crusty old pig, he doesn't deserve to be a medicine man. It was just a dream. Try to forget it."

He stripped off his jeans. "Don't worry, it's already fading. Want to fool around? We've got this great bed here."

She nodded and took off his shirt.

Victor peeled off her blouse, ran his fingers around her nipples, and felt them stiffen. He pulled her down onto the bed and covered her chest with tiny kisses. Tugging off her jeans, he gripped her buttocks and slipped inside her. Waves of pleasure surged through him as she moaned and wrapped her legs around him. When they finally finished, they lay there caressing each other, their bodies bathed in silvery moonlight. After a time they crawled under the covers and slept.

———————

Little Eagle's cries woke Kate from a deep sleep. Tossing off the covers, she threw on her robe and hurried to the baby's basket. "Okay, little girl," she said, yawning as she picked her up, "let's get that wet diaper off." She clicked on a nightlight and got to work. When she was done, she shoved her feet into her slippers and carried the baby downstairs.

Down in the kitchen, she took a bottle from the fridge and set it in the microwave to heat. She paced as she waited, jiggling Little Eagle to keep her quiet. When the timer dinged, Kate retrieved the bottle and squirted formula onto her wrist, sunk into a chair, and eased the nipple into the baby's mouth. Little Eagle grunted as she tugged on her formula.

"You're a ravenous little wolf pup, aren't you?"

A fire thrummed in the woodstove as wind hurled snow against the windows. As Kate fed Little Eagle, she tried to imagine how hard it would be to work fulltime and take care of a baby. Even if Victor could come back with her, her teaching job was so demanding. Maybe she should just stay here in Colorado. Maybe she should call her principal, try to wheedle out of her contract, and postpone teaching until Little Eagle got older.

The baby dozed off. In a fog of weariness, Kate carried her upstairs, laid her in her basket, and crawled back into bed. When she awoke, dawn was lighting the eastern sky. She snuggled next to Victor and slept again.

———————

"Rise and shine, kids!" Lily cried out in the hall, stomping past their bedroom on her way downstairs. "We're having pancakes for breakfast, then we'll go visit Ivan!".

Victor groaned. "She's such a dynamo. How old is she anyway?"

"Seventy-six," Kate said, and yawned. "Hard to believe, isn't it?"

"She's a force of nature. Hope you inherited some of her energy so you can take care of me when I get old."

"It's not going to work like that, Tonto. *You'll* be taking care of *me*."

"I don't think so. It's not the years, it's the mileage, and I've traveled through time a lot more than you have. And don't call me Tonto, sweetheart."

"Fine, but don't call me *sweetheart*, sweetheart."

"Fair enough."

Little Eagle woke up and started crying. "Oh, no," Kate muttered. "She's *your* granddaughter, so you should help me take care of her like you did at Jeremiah's."

In my own time, men don't take care of babies, but we're no longer in my own time. "I'll make you a deal. I'll feed her if you change her."

"Deal, but I have to pee first. Be right back." Lunging out of bed, she put on a robe and hurried out.

Victor got up, opened the curtains, and pulled on his jeans. "Hi, little one," he said, picking up the baby. "How are you this fine morning?"

She giggled.

"*We're* having pancakes for breakfast, but *you* aren't because you're too little."

She giggled again and kicked her legs.

Kate returned and walked to the changing table. "Just put her on here."

"Got it," he said, laying the baby down.

"Okay, honey," Kate said, bending to change her. "I'm here." She unsnapped Little Eagle's pajama bottoms and slipped them off.

Victor watched Kate peel the diaper off and stuff it into a container. "There," she said as she finished. "We're done. Think you could possibly learn to do that?"

"I could, but you're so good at it."

"That's because I always *do* it. Let's go have breakfast."

Down in the kitchen, the aroma of strong coffee filled the air. Lily scurried around, frying bacon and cooking pancakes. She snatched Little Eagle's bottle from the microwave and handed it to Kate. "I warmed it up for you."

"Here," Kate said, passing the bottle to Victor. "You got off easy this time. I usually pre-mix the formula, keep some bottles of it in the fridge, and nuke them in the microwave. I'll show you how to mix the formula some other time."

He sat down at the table and slipped the nipple into Little Eagle's mouth.

Lily put a pitcher of syrup in the microwave and punched the timer. "Would you keep an eye on breakfast, Katie? I need to pack up some things to take with me today."

"Sure," she said, draining grease off the bacon as Lily went into the living room.

As Victor fed the baby, he spotted a book on the table titled *The Grizzly*. It had a bear on its cover, staring up at the surrounding mountains. "Who's Enos Mills?"

"He was an early conservationist who helped establish Rocky Mountain National Park. If he'd had his way, the park would've extended all the way to Pikes Peak."

"I'd like to meet him," Victor said. "Sounds like he knows bears."

"You can't," she said, flipping the pancakes. "He's dead. He died almost a hundred years ago. His writing style's a little dated, but you should read his book."

"Maybe I will." He noticed the baby had drifted off.

Lily returned with a box and set it on a chair. "Here's that book," she said, picking up *The Grizzly*. "I want to take this to the hospital today and start rereading it."

"Can I borrow it when you're finished?" Victor asked.

"Of course," she said, tucking it into the box. "How're those pancakes coming?"

"They're done," Kate said, carrying a platter of food to the table. "I can't wait for Victor and Eagle to meet Ivan," she said as she sat down.

"Eagle can't go, honey," Lily said, buttering her pancakes. "They don't allow babies in hospitals."

"Why not?" Kate asked.

Lily shrugged. "Because they might catch something, or give the patients something. We'll have to take turns watching her if we all want to go visit Ivan."

"I don't need to," Victor said, rising from the table. He laid Little Eagle in her cradle and sat back down. "I can meet Ivan later, but I'd like to get my car back from a friend today. I'd also like to go to the gallery in town where I show my artwork to see if I've sold any."

"Your work's in a gallery?" Lily asked, smiling at him. "Young man, you continue to amaze me. I'll lend Kate my car so she can drive you around."

Victor buttered his pancakes, doused them with hot maple syrup, and dug in. "These are delicious, Kate. What do you mean you can't cook?"

"I never said I couldn't cook; I said I didn't have *time* to cook. Besides, Lily made the batter."

"Well, you cooked them just right. And this bacon's crispy, just the way I like it."

"Thanks," she said, sipping her coffee. "I'm thinking of calling my principal to try to get out of my contract. Maybe there's a way I can do it and still get a good reference."

Lily frowned. "But you love teaching, honey."

"I do, but even if Victor could come to Seattle, I can't teach and take care of Eagle, too. I was up in the middle of the night feeding her."

"You were?" he asked. "I didn't hear you."

"That's because I was quiet as a mouse."

Lily turned to Victor. "I still think you should find a way to go with her."

"Remember, I can't take a plane. Speaking of mice, where'd you put the ones I gave you?"

"They're in a cloth-covered cage in the storeroom," Lily answered, pointing across the kitchen. "Since they're hibernating, I thought it should be dark, and it's cooler in there, too."

"Good idea," he said, "but they can't stay inside forever."

"I know," Lily said, reaching for some bacon, "but I'd like to keep them 'til Ivan comes home in a few days. I'm sure he'd like to see them. Speaking of Ivan, I want to catch his doctor on her morning rounds, so we should leave right after breakfast."

"Okay," Victor said. "But first I need more pancakes."

———————

When Kate and Lily peeked into Ivan's room, he was sitting in a chair joking with his nurse, his eyes bright and his cheeks rosy.

"And that was just for openers!" he said. "Guess what the fool did then?"

"Beats me, Ivan," the nurse said, removing his blood pressure cuff. "One-twenty over eighty, that's excellent. Look, you have visitors." She smiled and hurried out.

"Good morning, dear," Lily said as she walked in.

"Hi, Lily," he said. "And Katie, I haven't seen you in days!"

She bent down to hug him. "Sorry it's been so long. You look great."

"That's all right, honey. Lily told me about your adventures. Where's this Victor fellow I've been hearing about, and his little granddaughter?"

"They couldn't come in. You'll have to wait 'til you come home to meet them."

"Too bad," Ivan said. "Sit down beside me and tell me all about your travels."

"Okay," she said, pulling up a chair. "But it might take a while."
"I've got all day, Katie. Let her rip."

————————

After leaving the hospital, Kate drove south on Cascade Avenue a few blocks, turned right at Penrose library, drove down a hill past a park, and pulled into a parking space in front of the Depot building. "This looks nice. I like the old part of town."

"Me, too," Victor said, unhooking his seatbelt. He gathered up the baby, opened the door, and crossed the sidewalk to a gallery. Kate could see the artwork in the front window was tastefully arranged, with regional landscapes, silver jewelry, and Native American pots.

"What do you think?" he asked, shifting Little Eagle in his arms.

"Very impressive," she said, studying the display. "This should be a good venue for you, with all this Southwestern art." A large oil painting featured a snow-dusted Garden of the Gods with Pikes Peak rising behind it. Three small watercolors depicted Indians skinning hides, tending horses, and sitting around campfires. A small sign beside them said *Victor Manyhorses*.

"These are yours?" she asked. "You're pretty good! And your work's in the front window!"

He grinned. "Don't sound so surprised. I'm lucky I got in here. Stephen gave an opening for me and some of the other artists, with wine and food and lots of artsy people. I sold four sketches that night. Come on, let's go in."

Inside, he led her past walls hung with more large landscapes, past glass cases filled with exquisite turquoise and silver jewelry, past tables laden with contemporary Indian pottery. A sign on an easel leading to another room stated *Artwork by Victor Manyhorses*.

"You have your own *room*?" she asked, gripping his arm.

Victor shrugged. "Like I said, I was lucky to get in here."

"I think talent has a lot to do with it. So, show me your work." As they strolled through the room, she saw watercolors and sketches of regional landscapes and wildlife, even one of Victor's horse, Milagro. He was running flat-out, his mane flowing behind him. "This one's great," she said. "You've really captured him."

"No one can capture Milagro. I've never had such a magnificent horse."

Kate watched sadness cloud his face. "You really miss him, don't you?"

"Of course I do. Don't you miss Lady Grey?"

She nodded. "Next to Doozie, I miss her the most. It's bizarre, isn't it? There's a whole world going on back there without us. All those people living out their lives."

"We chose to come here, Kate. We need to forget about that other world. Take your time looking around while I see if Stephen's in his office. Here, take Eagle." He handed her the baby and hurried out.

As Kate studied Victor's artwork, she felt it pulling her back into the world they'd left behind—a world of danger and hardship, of wildness and stunning beauty. She saw sketches of Prairie Flower cooking over a campfire, Laughing Brook tending his tribe's horses, and Rising Moon fashioning arrows. Suddenly, Bear lunged at her from a large painting—fierce and huge and terrible. Victor had captured her, too.

He returned, grinning, holding up a handful of bills. "Stephen's not here, but his secretary Amy gave me my money. I sold three more sketches, a painting, and a courting flute."

"He pays you in cash?" she asked, glancing at the bills.

"Of course; I don't have a bank account. I've been thinking about going with you out to Seattle. Will six hundred and seventy bucks be enough to get us there?"

"More than enough," she said. "But how can you go? You can't fly out."

"No, I can't. But I can get my car back and drive out. Would you like that?"

"I'd love it!" she said, and hugged him. "What made you change your mind?"

"Something that Lily said, about how I should see where you live. And I could take care of Eagle while you're off teaching."

"Now *that's* a serious commitment since you'd have to learn to change her."

"I realize that, but like you pointed out—she *is* my granddaughter."

"Okay, then. I'll trade in my ticket and drive out with you. We'll need to buy a car seat, though. It's illegal to hold her on our laps like we've been doing, and it's not safe. Now, let me think—if Ivan comes home tomorrow like we're hoping, we can spend two days with him, leave early on Friday, and still have three days to drive back. So, it's doable—barely. I'll call Alex and ask her to watch Cisco a little longer."

Victor turned to study his painting of Bear. "This is one of my favorites."

"Mine, too," she said. "Wish we could take it with us."

"Maybe we could entice her spirit into the painting and take it with us."

Kate laughed. "Could we? Bear *is* magical."

"I doubt it, but we could take the painting if you want."

"Let's do it. It'd be nice to have a reminder of her."

He took the painting off the wall. "I need to tell Amy I'm taking this. Come with me and meet her, then we'll visit my friend and get my car. Are you ready?"

"I guess so," she said, "but it's hard to leave all this great artwork."

"Come on," he said, turning to leave. "I can always do more."

"Okay," she said, following behind him. "How far away is your friend?"

"Not far. He works just a few blocks from here."

———————

"Here it is," Victor said, pointing to a stark concrete-block of a building.

"Your friend works at a homeless shelter?" she asked, parking at the curb.

"Yes," he said, clutching Little Eagle and opening the door. "He's getting his masters in social work. I often stayed here when I was passing through town. That's how we met."

As Kate followed Victor into the shelter, she noticed an office where a young Hispanic man was working at a battered wooden desk.

"*Buenos dias*, Luis!" Victor said as they entered the office.

"Victor!" he said, leaping up and clasping his shoulder. "*Como esta, amigo?*"

"*Muy bueno*. Luis, this is Kate. Kate, Luis."

"I'm glad to meet you, Kate," he said, shaking her hand.

"Glad to meet you, too," she said. Luis was slender and trim, slightly shorter than her, in his late twenties or early thirties. "Victor says you're working on your masters."

Luis shrugged. "I'm trying, but it's hard when you work fulltime. I'm about halfway through the program. Who's this little one?" he asked, glancing at the baby.

"This is my granddaughter, Little Eagle," Victor said.

His eyebrows arched. "Your granddaughter? I didn't even know you had kids!"

"I've been watching her for my daughter," he said, shooting Kate a warning look.

True enough, Kate thought, even though his daughter was dead.

"So many changes in your life," Luis said. "Do you need a place to stay tonight?"

"No," Victor said. "We've been staying with Kate's grandmother."

"I see," Luis said, glancing back and forth between them. He was obviously trying to figure out their relationship. "So, you two are..."

"Living together," Victor said, smiling at Kate.

"*Muy bueno, amigo.* And how did you meet this lovely lady?"

"It's a long story," he answered, "but I promise to tell you some other time. Listen, Luis, the reason we came by is to get my car back. Are you finished with it?"

"Yes, of course." Luis opened a drawer, removed a set of keys, and handed them to Victor. "If I'd known you were coming, I would've driven it to work today, but you can pick it up at my house. Thanks for the loan."

"You're welcome," Victor said. "Think it'll make it out to Seattle?"

"Absolutely. I had my cousin tune it up for you. What's in Seattle?"

"My teaching job," Kate said. "I'm on spring break now, visiting my grandparents, but I have to get back out there by Monday."

Luis nodded. "So, you're a teacher. Excellent. What do you teach?"

"High school earth science and biology."

He shuddered. "I was terrible at science. Would you like a tour of our shelter?"

"Just a short one," she said. "I promised my grandma I'd return her car soon."

"Okay," Luis said, beckoning to a woman who was stapling flyers to a nearby bulletin board. "Trudy, could you watch the desk while I show these guys around?"

"Sure," she said, coming into the office.

"Follow me." Luis led them down a hallway into a warehouse-sized room crammed with cots. "This is our main sleeping area, for women and children residents."

As they walked through the facility, Kate's heart ached for its residents. She saw women sitting on cots with mismatched bedding, cardboard boxes overflowing with clothing, children playing with toys on the floor. "How many people usually stay here?"

Luis shrugged. "It depends. We can accommodate two hundred and forty when we're full, and we've been full all winter. They're predicting a storm tonight, so I'm sure we'll be full again. *Buenos dias*, Eva," he said as they passed a woman dressing a toddler.

"*Buenos dias*, Luis," she answered, smiling.

"We have a separate room for men," he added as they continued walking. "We also have a few private rooms for families, but they go fast." He stopped in front of a bathroom. "We have a bathroom for women and children, and another one for men."

"Do you serve meals?" Kate asked.

"Only breakfast," he said. "It's usually just cereal and milk, but sometimes we get lucky and local businesses donate doughnuts or bagels. But residents can get lunch and dinner at a nearby soup kitchen." Luis gestured toward the back of the sleeping area. "Our dining room's beside the rec room, and we have a learning center, too."

"How do people end up here?" Kate asked.

"It varies," Luis answered. "Some barely have been hanging on financially, so if they lose their jobs they lose their home or apartment. Others get divorced and can't support themselves; others miss a car payment and can't get to work, so they get fired."

"That's horrible," Kate said. "I don't think I could stand the lack of privacy."

"You could if you were homeless," Victor said. "This shelter's a godsend if you need a place to stay. It's like an Indian encampment without the privacy of tepees."

Luis chuckled. "I never thought of it that way, but I guess you're right."

As they reached the office, Kate faced Luis and smiled. "Thanks for the tour. It was nice meeting you."

"My pleasure," he said, shaking her hand. "Have a safe trip, you two."

"Thanks," Victor said, and nudged the front door open.

Out on the sidewalk she asked Victor, "You stayed here many times?"

"Yes."

"I can't imagine living here. It's heartbreaking."

"Yes," he explained, "but to me it was a refuge."

They got into the car and drove off.

CHAPTER FOUR

Lily rushed into the living room the next morning and beamed at Kate and Victor. "Guess what? Ivan's being released, so I'm driving into town to get him. Do you need me to pick up anything?"

"I don't think so," Kate said, scanning the items she'd laid out on the table. "We bought that car seat yesterday, and we have enough baby clothes, formula, and bottles."

"Do you need anything, Victor?"

"No," he said, glancing up from feeding Little Eagle. "I bought two pairs of jeans, some shirts, and drawing paper yesterday."

"Okay," Lily said, turning to leave. "See you later."

"See you," Kate said.

"Bye, Lily." Victor got up from his rocker, shifted the baby onto his shoulder, and patted her back to coax out a burp. "Listen, Kate. I have an idea."

"What's that?" she asked, packing baby clothes into a large rubber tub.

"With Lily gone, we'll be alone in the house for hours." Little Eagle belched and snuggled against him. "And the baby will be asleep in minutes."

Kate snapped the tub closed and stared at it. "Hold on. Did I pack my nipples in there?"

"I don't know," he said, slipping his arm around her. "Take off your blouse and I'll check. I'd hate for you to lose such luscious nipples."

"You're shameless," she said, kissing his cheek

"Let's make love right here by the fire. Eagle can sleep in her cradle."

Kate glanced at the sleeping baby and back at him. "You're on."

———————

He rode Milagro through a sea of golden grasses. He felt his horse's muscles ripple beneath him, heard him whinny with the joy of running. They plunged through the grasses, lunged up a hillside, and shot across a prairie.

"Wake up!" Kate said, shaking him. "They're home! Get dressed!"

Emerging from his dream, Victor squinted at the sunlight streaming through the living room windows. "What happened?"

"We fell asleep!" She tossed off their blanket and wriggled into her pants.

"Damn!" he said, hearing the kitchen door slam. He leapt up, grabbed his jeans, tangled his feet in the blanket, and fell down. "Shit!"

"Hurry!" she snapped, struggling into her clothes.

"I *am* hurrying!" He tugged on his jeans and sweatshirt.

"We're home!" Lily called from the kitchen.

"In here!" Kate cried, zipping her jeans. "Your sweatshirt's on inside out," she added to Victor.

"Crap, too late." He pulled on his socks as Lily and Ivan walked in.

"Welcome home!" Kate said, rushing to hug her grandfather.

"Thanks, honey," Ivan said. "It's great to be home." He glanced down at her bare feet. "Aren't your tootsies cold?"

"Oh, no, it's warm here by the fire. Ivan, this is Victor."

"I'm glad to meet you," he said, shaking Victor's hand. "Katie tells me you're from the past."

"Yes, sir. I'm from 1863."

"Amazing," Ivan said, studying him. "How old are you?"

"Thirty-four." With his rosy cheeks, bushy white eyebrows, and brilliant green eyes, Victor thought Ivan resembled Santa Claus.

"Incredible. The same age as our Katie." Ambling over to the cradle, Ivan peered down at the sleeping baby. "And this is your little granddaughter?"

"Yes. Her name's Little Eagle, but we just call her Eagle."

"I see." Ivan stared at Victor's sweatshirt. "Is this the new style?"

"No. I spilled milk on it, so I turned it inside out." Glancing down, Victor noticed he was wearing one of his red socks and one of Kate's blue ones. *Crap.*

As Ivan scanned the room, he saw Victor's mismatched socks, Kate's disheveled hair, and the rumpled blanket on the floor. "Well," he said, raising an eyebrow as he looked from Victor to Kate. He turned to Lily. "Could a hungry old man get some lunch around here?"

Lily grabbed his arm. "Come on, dear," she said, steering him from the room as she winked at Kate. "I've got some nice ham and Swiss for sandwiches, and that tomato basil soup you like."

When they left, Kate snatched up the remaining socks. "Damn. They *know*."

Victor stripped off Kate's blue sock, handed it to her, and put his other red one on. "What difference does it make? Lily already knows we're sleeping together."

"*She* does, but I don't think she's told Ivan. It's embarrassing getting caught like this, in their living room in the middle of the day."

"They didn't really catch us doing anything."

Kate laughed. "You're right, and it was fun doing it by the fire, wasn't it?"

"It was," he said as Little Eagle awoke and started fussing. "She's stinky," he said, picking her up. "You need to change her."

"No, I don't," she said, tugging on her socks. "You've watched me do it, and now it's your turn. Go up and change her while I help Lily with lunch."

"Fine," he muttered, and headed upstairs with the baby.

— — — — — — —

The day passed swiftly. After dinner, Kate and Lily were cleaning up the kitchen while Victor and Ivan perused the library in the living room.

Ivan pulled out a weathered volume. "This book's important because it documents Colorado's territorial days, but I don't care for the author's views."

"I've read it," Victor said, glancing at the title, "and I agree with you. He got his facts straight, but the man was a racist."

"How could you have read it? It's been out of print for decades."

Victor hesitated, considering his options. If he told Ivan he'd read it at the library, he'd be lying. If he wanted to forge an honest relationship with Kate's grandfather, he should tell him the truth. He took a deep breath and answered, "I read it right here in your living room. I often slipped inside when you were gone."

Ivan's eyes narrowed. "Katie told me that, and I understand why, but I still find it a bit disconcerting." He put the book back and chose another. "How about this one? It's worn, but it's an excellent history of the Ute people. You're Ute, aren't you?"

"Yes, and I've read it. In fact, I just bought a new copy of it to give you."

"Why would you give me another copy?"

"I accidentally borrowed it, and it got beat up during my travels, so I bought a new one to replace it."

Ivan frowned. "How do you *accidentally* borrow a book?"

Victor shrugged. "I didn't accidentally borrow it. I borrowed it on purpose, but it was in my backpack when I traveled back in time, and I accidentally took it with me. Kate just returned it. I'm sorry, Ivan."

"That's all right," he said, sliding the worn book back on the shelf. "Keep your new copy. Feel free to borrow any of my books, but please return them in a timely fashion. I can see you like reading. Katie says you can't get enough of it."

"Thank you," he said, impressed by Ivan's generosity.

"You're welcome." Ivan shuffled across the room to a rocker and eased down into it. "Come sit with me. We need to talk."

Uh-oh, here it comes, Victor thought. He settled into an adjacent rocker and braced himself. He took in a breath, blew it out, and waited.

Ivan stared at the fire for a long time, rocking and rocking.

Victor waited. He was good at waiting. He would out-wait Ivan.

"Katie claims she loves you," Ivan said. "I choose to believe her, but I'm concerned. Her husband died just a year ago, and I don't want her to get hurt."

"I'd never hurt her," Victor said. "I love her."

Ivan leaned across the arm of his rocker, his face inches from Victor's. "Maybe you do, but if you hurt her, I'll find a way to destroy you. Understood?"

There it is: the threat I've been waiting for. "Understood."

"I'm serious, Victor. I may be old, but I'll hunt you down and do it."

"I believe you. I promise to be good to her."

"Good," Ivan said, leaning back in his rocker. "Glad that's settled."

Victor looked away into the crackling flames. *Me, too, Ivan. Me, too.*

———————

After breakfast the next day they set off to relocate the mice, with Lily and Kate on snowshoes and Victor trudging along in their tracks. As they emerged from the forest into the meadow, he pointed to a boulder beside the ice-rimmed creek. "See that sunny bare spot next to the boulder? When those shrub willows leaf out, the mice will have leaves to eat and a good supply of water."

"Looks good," Kate said, snowshoeing toward it. "Let's dig them a burrow there."

When they reached the spot, Victor set down the mice's cage and took a trowel from his pack. Digging into the moist earth, he fashioned a burrow beside the boulder and lined it with pine needles from a fallen branch. "Want to do the honors, Lily?"

"I'd love to." Opening the cage, she slid the sleeping mice into the burrow, set twigs against the entrance, and spread her arms in a benediction. "Sleep well, little ones, and when you wake in the spring, go forth and breed like crazy!"

"Amen," Kate said.

"Let's go home and make hot chocolate to celebrate," Lily said.

"I'll drink to that," Kate said. "Then I need to grade some papers. I have a few more to do before we leave on Friday."

With a last look at the burrow, they turned and headed back.

———————

That afternoon Victor sat at the living room table, sketching Kate as she graded papers beside him. Ivan snored on the couch while Little Eagle snored in her cradle. Lily sat in a rocker reading her weathered copy of *The Grizzly*. As Victor sketched, he was acutely aware of the tranquility of the moment, with the fire crackling in the woodstove and dust motes streaming through the golden light.

"Mr. Enos Mills seems to respect grizzlies," Lily said, glancing up from her book, "but he doesn't seem to especially fear them."

"That's unusual," Victor said, "since most whites fear grizzlies and want to exterminate them. Natives are taught to respect Earth's creatures, and we Utes have a rich tradition of bears in our culture. In the old days, many creatures spoke to us, but either they've lost that ability, or we've lost the ability to hear them."

Ivan snorted himself awake. "Let's go for a walk. I need some exercise."

"Great," Lily said, closing her book. "Then we'll have an early dinner."

Ivan rose from the couch. "After that, I'll whip your butts at Scrabble."

———————

Victor laid down *cradle* for a triple word score.

"Your first time playing Scrabble and you're trouncing me?" Kate said. "Unbelievable."

He shrugged and drew more letters. "You knew I was good at languages."

"You're phenomenal," Ivan said. "Here's *bullion*, for a double word."

Lily laid down her letters to spell *braille*.

Kate added *board* to *cradle*, making *cradleboard*.

"Speaking of cradleboards," Lily said. "I assume you won't be taking Eagle's—the one that you brought from the past."

"No," Kate said, getting up to lift the baby from her cradle. "It's too fragile. I'd love to take my old cradle, but we won't have room."

"I need a break," Ivan said, rising from the table and stretching.

"Me, too," Kate said. "I need to call Alex before it gets too late."

Lily nodded. "Okay. I'll go fix us some ice cream."

————————

Kate closed the door to her room and punched Alex's number.

She answered on the first ring. "Kate! How are you?"

"I'm well," she said, lying back against the pillows. "Sorry I haven't called in a while, but I've been kind of busy."

"That's okay. How's Ivan?"

"He's doing great. He came home yesterday, feisty as ever. We're in the middle of a killer Scrabble game, so I can't talk long, but I wanted to tell you I'm not flying in tomorrow. So don't go pick me up at Sea-Tac."

"Okay. Why?"

Kate paused, trying to decide how much to tell her. *Should I say I traveled back in time, fell in love with an Indian from another century, and brought him home? Not on the phone.* "I've decided to drive out with a friend. I should be home this Sunday night, so could you watch Cisco for a little longer?"

"Of course, but that's a long way to drive. Who's the friend?"

"His name's Victor. You'll like him."

"A guy, huh? You've never mentioned him. Have I ever met him?"

"No, he's from a long time ago. You'll meet him when we get there."

"But, how…?" Alex started to ask.

"Katie!" Lily called from downstairs. "Dessert's ready! Come on!"

"I have to go, they're waiting for me. I'll call when I get back."

"Okay. Have a safe trip. Love you."

"Love you back. Bye."

Kate hung up and sighed. She hadn't lied to Alex, but she hadn't exactly told her the whole truth, either. She'd have to find a way to do it when she got home.

———————

After they'd eaten hot fudge sundaes and finished playing Scrabble, they turned their chairs toward the living room windows and watched the evening unfold. Dusk had fallen, and a gauzy curtain of snow fell through the dimness.

"Look, Ivan," Lily said, pointing outside. "There's Katie's grizzly."

Emerging from the forest, Bear crept up the steps, padded across the snowy deck, and stared at them through the glass.

"She's huge," Ivan said. "And she follows you around?"

Kate shrugged. "Bear does what she wants. She'll probably hang around here for a while until she realizes we're gone, so be careful when you go outside."

"We will," Ivan said. "You've had quite the adventure, with your Indians, time travel, and bears." He paused. "What was it like in the past, honey?"

"It might be easier to show you." Getting up to cross the room, she sat at the piano and began to play. "This is 'Lorena,' one of the Civil War tunes I played in a saloon where I worked. Now, try to imagine you're surrounded by boisterous drunks, desperate whores, lonely miners, and rowdy gamblers."

Ivan closed his eyes, smiling as he listened to the mournful ballad. "I can picture it, Katie, but how could a pretty woman like you work in such a place without getting pestered by all those men?"

"I disguised myself as a man," Kate said, smiling as she remembered.

"Fascinating," Ivan said, opening his eyes.

Over at the window, Bear continued staring.

Kate stopped playing. "Look at this," she said, pulling a drawing from a folder on the piano. "I almost forgot, I want to take this with me. Victor drew it."

"Who is it?" Ivan asked.

"Our good friend, Doozie," Kate said. "She runs the saloon now."

Ivan frowned. "Is she a prostitute?"

"She used to be," Kate said, "but she quit when she married Homer, the saloon-keep. She took over the place when he was murdered."

"What a shame," he said, studying the drawing. "She's so young."

"She's only sixteen. I tried to bring her with me, but she wouldn't come."

"I must admit I'm jealous," Ivan said. "I've studied history in books, but you and Victor have really *lived* it." He sighed and rubbed his eyes.

Lily rose from her chair, turned to Ivan, and gripped his hand. "Come on, dear," she said, pulling him up. "It's time for bed."

"You're right, Lil. It's been a long day, and I'm weary. Goodnight, you two," Ivan added as they headed from the room.

"'Night," Victor said. He went to the cradle and picked up Little Eagle.

"'Night," Kate said as her grandparents left. "We'll be up soon." Rising from the piano bench, she went to the window, placed her hands against the glass, and looked at Bear. Bear looked back. "Think she'll be okay when we're gone?"

"Bear's a wild animal," Victor said. "She'll be fine."

CHAPTER FIVE

The next morning, they bid goodbye to Ivan and Lily and headed north for Denver, with Kate driving her rental car and Victor following in his Subaru. When they approached the Denver airport, Victor was astonished by the conical terminal shaped like an encampment of tepees. Tearing his gaze away, he followed Kate into a parking lot so she could return her vehicle.

Hours later, they were cruising I-80, heading west across southeastern Wyoming. Kate drove, Little Eagle dozed in the back seat, and Victor studied the roadmap.

"Could you pass me a sandwich?" she asked.

"Sure," he said, turning around to reach in the cooler. "Turkey or ham?"

"Ham, and one of those cans of apple juice, please."

"Here," he said, handing them over. "Do you feel alert?"

"Alert enough. If I get sleepy, I'll have some of that tea Lily gave us."

"Let me know. The thermos is right here." Victor bit into his sandwich and watched the barren scenery whiz by—rolling hills and sagebrush, boulders and cattle, ranches and outbuildings. From what he could see of Wyoming, it was rugged country. "Too bad we're so far south of Yellowstone. I'd like to see it."

"Sorry, but we're really pressed for time. Maybe we could go there on our way back this summer."

"Okay." As he watched the landscape, he imagined Yellowstone's wonders—its bison herds, thermal springs, and spouting geysers.

Another hour passed as Kate drove and Victor read Lily's copy of *The Grizzly*. When Kate grew weary, he took over driving while she dozed beside him. As the sun dipped lower its light gilded the barren landscape. Instead of bleak, it became magnificent; instead of empty, it became vast. As Victor watched the hills undulate away from the highway, he realized he knew little of this area's Indians. He knew the Sioux and their allies had attacked Custer along the Little Bighorn north of here, but he didn't know which tribes now lived in this land.

A sudden wind blew across the treeless hills, buffeting the Subaru. It began to snow, icy bits blasting across the windshield. He glanced over at Kate, sleeping soundly with her mouth open.

The wind shrieked. The car ate up the miles.

————————

Victor eased into a rest area, parked the car, and stretched his shoulder muscles. His back throbbed. His head ached. He had to pee.

Kate snapped awake and glanced around. "Where are we?"

"Just outside of Rock Springs. Didn't you book a room there?"

"I did," she said, yawning. "They had a great online rate."

"Be right back," he said, opening his door into an icy blast. He ran across the parking lot into the restroom. After relieving himself, he remembered it was his turn to change the baby. He looked around but didn't see a changing table. "Yes!" he said, pumping his fist. "They wouldn't have one in the men's room!"

When he came out, Kate was leaving her restroom carrying Little Eagle. "I know it was your turn to change her, but I did it anyway. Let's go find the motel."

Half an hour later, Kate talked to a desk clerk as Victor strolled around the lobby jiggling the baby. He was drawn to a glass case housing a stuffed black-and-white animal that looked like a bird, but it was over three feet high.

"We're set," Kate said as she joined him. "Well, look at that."

He grinned. "What a cool place. They've got their own Emperor penguin."

————————

As her people unpacked their car, the creature hid on the floor behind the driver's seat, within the dark recesses of a fluffy sleeping bag. She'd hidden here a long time, ever since they'd left the old couple's house. All day she'd listened to her people talking as the car moved forward at a great speed; she'd often peeked out from her hideaway to watch them. Now they were gone, it was dark, and she was very hungry. Easing from the warmth of the bag, she crept up onto the back seat, wriggled into a paper sack, and munched on the discarded food inside. She discovered bits of meat and bread, a juicy apple core, and a shard of dark chocolate. She savored the chocolate, letting it melt in her mouth as she did with such delicacies. The feast filled her tiny stomach. Being small had its advantages.

Climbing out of the paper sack, she climbed up to the windowsill and peered out at the nearby building where her people had gone. As the wind whipped snow around, the creature felt grateful for the car's warmth, yet she knew it would soon turn cold. These machines grew warm when they growled with life, but cooled when they quieted.

The creature watched a man hurry his dog across a hard, black surface. If she were in a larger form and still hungry, she'd be tempted to hunt the dog, but she was much too small. Now she wanted to explore the car. Turning away from the window, she scurried to the square thing they called *the cooler*. It was aromatic and enticing, but her stomach was already full. If she awoke during the night and felt hungry, she would raid it. Crawling to the top of the back seat, she jumped down into another space.

Back here she saw containers and a flat package wrapped in clear, inedible bubbles. She sniffed the package, detecting something that seemed a part of her, something that seemed alive with her spirit. She remembered that Victor had called this thing a *painting*, and had told Kate they could bring it so they wouldn't miss her. But they needn't miss her since she'd come along with them.

She leapt back over the top of the seat, back onto the floor, back into the folds of the sleeping bag. She needed to sleep now and digest her feast; to dream and replenish her energy. While she'd taken the form of Mouse to make this journey, deep inside she was much bigger. Deep inside she was still Bear.

———————

They set off early after a hearty breakfast, alert and in good spirits after a restful night's sleep. They left Wyoming behind and shot into Utah on I-80, where Victor discovered a spur that bypassed Salt Lake City for Ogden and Brigham City. After that, Kate took over, driving northwest into Idaho as Victor read and Little Eagle dozed. She counted off the miles, feeling a sense of accomplishment as she ticked off the distances. She scanned mileage signs, motel signs, fast food ads, and billboards. Monotony set in. Her butt went numb.

"Hey," Victor said, shaking her shoulder. "You're nodding off. Let me drive."

Kate pulled into a rest stop. She dropped off as Victor started driving.

When she awoke, an hour had passed. Retrieving her tote bag from the back seat, she took out her earth science book and began to plan Monday's lesson. She wondered how it would feel to return to Seattle and teach again. She'd only been gone a short time in reality, but she'd been to another world, faced incredible dangers, and fallen in love with Victor. Her life would be different now, with him and the baby around, and she'd have to figure out what to tell her friends about them. She might have to make up a story.

She glanced at Victor, focused on his driving. He was intelligent and adaptable, but could he handle living in her world? Could he handle taking care of Little Eagle when she was off teaching? She turned around and opened the cooler. "Want some celery sticks?"

"No. Got anything else?"

"Carrot sticks."

"Okay. Any sandwiches left?"

"Only three," she said, turning back with a bag of carrots. "Look, there's a rest stop up ahead. Let's break there for lunch." She handed him some carrots.

He frowned. "But I wanted to make it out of Idaho before I stopped driving."

"Why?" she asked, biting into a carrot.

"Just a goal I set for myself. I suspect you've driven more miles than me."

She laughed. "I do that too, to pass the time. We can keep going if you want."

"No, let's stop," he said, munching a carrot.

"Are you sure? Because I think I *have* driven more than you," she teased.

"No, we should take a break."

At the rest stop, Kate opened the back door to grab the cooler and saw a rush of fur as an animal jumped out. "Look, a mouse was in the car!"

Victor eased out of the car and stretched his arms over his head. "Where?"

"It's over there now," she said, pointing. "We must've picked it up somewhere." She watched the mouse dart across the grass and hide under a bush near a picnic table.

"That's weird. Maybe it jumped in at Lily's when I was packing."

As Kate spread their lunch on the table, the mouse watched them from under its bush; as they ate, it nibbled grass and continued watching; as they strolled around the rest area afterward, it followed them, darting from bush to bush.

"That's really odd," Kate said. "Why would it follow us?"

They heard a dog bark and saw a golden retriever pull away from its owner and lunge for the mouse. The rodent burst from its cover and ran, changing shape as it ran faster and faster. It blurred and grew larger, flying up and up, turning into a red-tailed hawk. As it circled above them, the retriever cocked its head, whined, and slunk away.

"Bad girl!" her owner scolded as he grabbed its leash. "What's gotten into you? You know better than that. Sorry," he added to them as he walked away.

Kate's mouth dropped. "Did you see that? What *is* that?"

"I'm not sure," Victor said, staring upward. "But I have a hunch."

"Whatever it is," Kate said, glancing around, "only the dog seemed to notice it." The hawk flew overhead in a wide arc, shrieking down at them as they watched.

"We should get going," she said. "Do you think she'll follow us?"

"Let's find out," Victor said, heading back toward the picnic table.

The hawk cried out and followed. As Kate gathered up their picnic things, the hawk soared above them. As they loaded the baby into the car, the hawk dipped down and flew closer. As they shoved the cooler into the back seat, the hawk dropped to the ground, blurred into a whirling ball, and got smaller and smaller. In seconds the blurring stopped and the mouse reappeared. She jumped into the car, curled onto the sleeping bag, and watched Kate close the door.

"That's *got* to be Bear," she said.

Victor grinned. "I'm sure of it now."

"Incredible," Kate said, shaking her head. "She wanted to come with us, so she changed into a mouse and stowed away. Wonder what form she'll take in Seattle?"

"Guess we'll find out," Victor said, opening the passenger door.

Kate got back in the Subaru and started driving again. "We should stay the night in Pendleton, so we can cross the Columbia River in daylight. I want you to see it."

"Sounds good," Victor said, settling into his book.

———————

As Kate drove across the Columbia River the next morning, Victor stared down at the water, disappointed. "I was expecting something more exciting. It's so placid."

"The Columbia used to be a wild and raging river, but engineers dammed the hell out of it. I'll take you to the ocean sometime if you want to see exciting water."

"Couldn't we go now?" he asked. "I saw a turnoff for it back there."

"Not now, it'll take too long, but I'll show you something cool north of here."

"Okay, but can we go to the ocean sometime?"

"Yes," she said, squeezing his hand. "I promise."

Kate drove north to Toppenish and pulled into the *Yakama Nation Museum and Cultural Center* parking lot. "This is one of the oldest Native American museums in the country," she said, turning off the car. "And it has wonderful historic photographs."

Victor retrieved Little Eagle from her carrier and followed Kate inside, where they paid their fee and entered a large exhibition hall. As they studied the photographs, they stopped to examine one that showed a group of Natives on wooden scaffolding, poised above a series of falls, hoisting salmon out of a raging river.

"Now *that* was the mighty Columbia," Kate said.

"It's magnificent," he said, trying to imagine perching on such rickety platforms to haul in those huge fish. "Where was this picture taken?"

Kate leaned closer to peer at the caption. "Southwest of here, near a place called Celilo Falls. The falls don't exist anymore; they were flooded when the Dalles Dam was built. When we're finished here, I'll show you something else that's cool. It's a little out of our way, but it's worth it."

"Okay, but let's eat lunch first."

It started raining as they passed through the town of Yakima but began clearing as they turned onto I-90 and headed east. When they got out of the car at a viewing area, Kate handed Victor the binoculars and pointed. "Look up there, on that hill."

He adjusted the binoculars and peered through them. The sun burst through the clouds, highlighting fifteen metal horses skirting a bluff above the Columbia. They galloped along the ridge—frisky, wild, and full of life.

"That's awesome," Victor said, feeling a rush of excitement.

Kate squeezed his arm. "Isn't it? It's called *Grandfather Cuts Loose the Ponies*, and it was created as a tribute to the wild horses that used to roam here."

They stood there admiring the sculptures until Kate eventually glanced at her watch. "We should go. We still have several hours of driving left."

"I'm ready," he said, pulling her into a hug. "Thank you for showing me this. It does my spirit good to see such horses."

It started raining again as he drove west.

––––––––

Victor had been driving for over an hour since they'd left the river, and it had been raining the whole time. Kate and Little Eagle were sleeping; Mouse was sitting on Victor's shoulder staring out the window. He was enjoying the solitude. He'd decided he liked the rain, liked hearing it patter on the roof. As the afternoon light waned, the highway lights began to flicker on. It began raining harder, and the hammering woke Kate.

"Where are we?" she asked.

He nodded to a road sign.

"Good," she said, rubbing her eyes and sitting up straighter. "We're almost to Cle Elum. We'll be gaining elevation as we go over the Cascades. Pull over so I can drive over Snoqualmie Pass."

"I can drive it. I drive passes all the time in Colorado."

"You know about snowy passes, but rainy passes are different. Pull over."

They changed drivers and continued on. As they gained elevation, rain poured down in sheets, slithering across the highway—changing to snow, back to rain, and back to snow again. Vehicles sped past them, flinging slush against their windshield. The wipers slapped back and forth, back and forth, back and forth.

Two hours later Kate pulled into a driveway and turned off the engine. Through a curtain of rain, Victor glimpsed a two-story house, a spacious yard, and several dripping trees.

"We're home," she said.

––––––––

After her people went off to bed, Mouse crawled from her sleeping bag and explored their dwelling. It was homey, with lots of plants, places to hide, and big windows. One window was ajar, so she jumped onto its ledge and inhaled, filling her lungs with fresh air. It was laden with moisture and intriguing scents. Mouse detected aromatic flowers, succulent grasses, and tangy evergreens. She spotted a rabbit nibbling on grass, a raccoon raiding a trash can, a fox skulking through the shadows.

Jumping off the ledge, Mouse trotted into the kitchen and discovered crumbs on the floor from her people's dinner. As she nibbled the tasty bits of cheese and meat, she remembered they'd called this food *pizza*. Mouse was lapping water from a bowl when she sensed another animal approaching, so she darted into a narrow space between two counters.

A cat padded to the bowl, sniffed, and growled. Catching Mouse's scent, it followed it to her hiding place, peered in, and yowled. The cat was too big to squeeze in, so he paced back and forth, yowling. After a time he padded off.

A cat in *her* house! Even though it wasn't truly *her* house, she couldn't allow that! Mouse could change into a wildcat or a bear and drive it off. Easing from her hiding place, she crept into the other room and watched the insolent cat jump onto *her* sleeping bag. As he curled into a ball and closed his eyes, Mouse began to change form, but suddenly stopped. She was tired, so why waste the energy? There must be many places to sleep here, so she should let the creature have this one. Maybe tomorrow, after she'd rested, she'd teach him a lesson.

Mouse gathered her strength and darted past the cat. She crossed the room, climbed the stairs, found Victor and Kate asleep in a bed, and settled in between them. Sleep came quickly.

CHAPTER SIX

Kate strode into her classroom the next day balancing her laptop, a cup of coffee, and a tote bag crammed with graded midterms. Glancing at the stacks of papers her sub had left on her desk, she set down her things and sighed. *More grading. It never stops.*

"Hi, Toad," Kate said, sipping her coffee as her students started coming in.

"Hi," the scrawny boy mumbled, slouching off to his seat.

"Morning," Kate said to Linda as she sauntered in. "I like your hair that way."

"Thanks, Ms. Mac," she said, clutching a cup of coffee and a small bakery bag. "Is your grandpa okay? Your sub said he had to have surgery."

"He's fine, Linda. Thanks for asking."

"Cool," Linda said, pulling a doughnut out of the bag. She bit into it, closed her eyes as she savored it, and chased it down with a sip of coffee.

As her students continued coming, Kate saw Wilber in his fatigues and combat boots, Jenna with her long, dark hair and tan, and Rudi with his smile and sassy attitude.

"You're back!" Rudi blurted out. "Hey, that sub they got for you was lame."

Kate clipped the attendance sheet to the door. "Why's that?"

Rudi grinned. "Cause she wasn't as cool as you, Ms. Mac. We missed you."

"Thanks, Rudi. Hope you had a good spring break."

He shrugged. "Not really, dude. I was stuck at home babysitting my little sisters."

Jenna set a brightly-colored pack on her desk and flashed Rudi a smile. "We went to the Big Island. It was awesome."

"Must be nice," Rudi muttered. "Where's that?"

"It's in Hawai'i," she said, taking a small can out of her pack. "I brought these macadamia nuts back for you guys." She opened the can and offered it to Rudi.

He took one, popped it into his mouth, and smiled. "Not bad. Thanks."

"I'm addicted to these things," she said. "Want one, Ms. Mac?"

"No thanks, Jenna." As her students took their seats and settled in, Kate handed back their midterms and started going over them. The morning passed.

————————

Later, in the teacher's lounge, Kate's friend Mark set a cafeteria tray on the table across from her and sat down. "Hi, Katydid. Welcome back! How's your grandfather?"

Kate flashed a smile at Mark as she noticed his sun-bleached blond hair and deep tan. "Ivan's well," she said, unwrapping a tuna salad sandwich. "How was Mexico?"

"Incredible," he said, digging into his burrito. "The snorkeling was excellent."

"Sounds like fun," Kate said. "Did your all-inclusive resort have kayaks?"

"Yeah, you would've loved it. You should come down there with me next time."

Is Mark coming on to me? Has he been waiting since Jon died to make his move? She swallowed a bite of her apple. "Come as what, your girlfriend? Come on, Mark, you're like a brother to me."

"Just kidding," he said, blushing. "I meant a bunch of us could go sometime."

Poor Mark. He and my other friends have been so helpful since Jon's death. While he's been waiting for me to heal, I've fallen in love with Victor.

Mark abruptly changed the subject. "I'm having some people over for a T.G.I.F. party on Friday, so you should come. We could go kayaking if the weather clears. It's supposed to get really warm."

As she sipped her water, Kate pictured his house on Lake Washington, with its lawn leading down to the water and two kayaks tied up at the dock. *This could get complicated. If I bring Eagle and Victor to meet my friends, I'll have to explain who they are and where they came from.* "I don't know, Mark. I'll think about it."

"Come on," he urged. "You need to get out and have some fun."

"Maybe I will; thanks for the invite. May I bring someone?"

"I guess," Mark said, reaching for his water glass. "Who?"

She shrugged. "Just an old friend. We drove back together."

"You drove back? I thought you flew. Why'd you drive back?"

"To help my friend with the driving," she said, glancing at the time. "Gotta go. See ya."

"Later," he said, watching her leave.

Hurrying down the hallway, Kate darted upstairs to her classroom, closed the door, and punched in her phone number. She'd taught Victor how to listen to her answering machine and how to pick up the phone if she called.

"Hi," she said when he answered. "How's it going?"

"Okay. I unpacked the car, did some sketching, and took Eagle for a walk around the neighborhood. She's sleeping now, so I think I'll go up and join her."

"Sounds nice," she said, looking out the second-floor window. "I miss you."

"I miss you, too. Come home, and we'll take a nap together."

Kate laughed and watched her students coming in. "I have to go now. Bye."

"Bye."

Kate shut off her phone and turned to face her students.

———————

Mouse perched on a window ledge in the bedroom, guarding Little Eagle while she slept on a thick mat called a *carpet*, surrounded by soft things called *pillows*. From Mouse's perch, she'd watched the cat bolt outside and run across the grass. He was hunched under a tree now, chomping grass and sniffing rain. The cat was foolish to sit outside in such wetness instead of inside a dry house, yet she was relieved he'd gone out. The baby was safer without him.

Throughout the day Mouse had detected loneliness in Victor as he wandered around without Kate. He missed her. He'd fed Little Eagle, changed her soiled clothing, and laid her down to sleep on the carpet. As he worked he'd talked to Mouse, for which she was grateful. It was good to be acknowledged by her people, after coming all this way to be with them. Mouse missed Kate, too, but she was serious about her duties. She must guard the baby from the cat.

Victor trudged into the bedroom. "Hello, Mouse."

She flicked her whiskers in greeting.

Easing off his shoes, he lay down beside the baby and pulled a covering over both of them. He fell asleep and began to snore. Mouse stayed at her post—guarding.

That afternoon after school, Kate took Victor and Little Eagle to a park near her house for a walk. The curtain of rain had lifted, and the sun cast shadows in the sodden forest.

"I'd forgotten how demanding teaching is," Kate said, turning onto a path that followed a stream. "I just got back and already have a ton of grading. I'm swamped."

Victor assumed this meant she had a lot of work to do. "May I help?"

"Could you cook dinner tonight? That would help. We'll have to stop at the store on the way home and buy food, though. Look," she said, pointing into the forest. "Those rhodies are about to bloom."

He stopped and peered at the dense vegetation, searching for something recognizable. "Okay, I'm game. What's a *roadie*?"

"Rhododendrons. See that bush over there with the big buds?"

"Those ones with the pink edges?"

"Yeah," she said. "That's them. They come in shades of pink, red, and lavender, and they're gorgeous when they're blooming. I have some small ones in my backyard."

As Victor breathed in the moist air, he took in the stream gurgling over the moss-covered rocks, the birds flitting through the forest, the wet leaves glistening in the muted sunshine. "It's beautiful here. I'd like to come back and sketch it."

"I almost forgot;" Kate said, "we're invited to a party this Friday. Want to go?"

"Sure. I like parties, and I'd like to meet your friends."

"Good, but do me a favor. Tell them Eagle's your daughter."

"I don't see why," he said, frowning. "She's not my daughter."

"Educated people these days don't expect guys your age to have grandchildren already. Remember how surprised your friend Luis was at the homeless shelter?"

"Yes, I do," he said, adjusting the baby on his back. "But if they're really your friends, we shouldn't have to deceive them. We should tell them the truth."

"Maybe we will eventually," Kate said, "but not all of them, and not yet. I want them to get to know you first before I spring too many surprises on them."

"I'll think about it. So where's this party?"

"It's at another teacher's house a few miles north of here. He lives on a lake, so we might go kayaking if the weather's good. I have to warn you, though, he might be jealous when he figures out we're living together."

"Why? Does he want to date you?"

"I think so. I get the impression he's been waiting for me to get over Jon's death before asking me out."

"Then he's out of luck because I found you first." He pointed to a waxy-leafed shrub with white bell-shaped flowers. "What's this plant called?"

"That's salal. Some Northwest tribes dried its berries and pressed them into cakes, wrapped them in skunk cabbage leaves, and ate them all winter dipped in fish oil."

"Interesting. And what's that one with the yellow flowers?"

"Oregon grape. Do you want me to carry Eagle for a while?"

"No, but I'm getting hungry. Let's go home and make dinner."

It started raining again as they headed back.

———————

The week passed in a blur of teaching, doing chores, and caring for Little Eagle. Kate tried to reach Alex to explain about Victor, but they kept playing phone tag.

"What does Alex do?" Victor asked Thursday night as they were finishing dinner.

Kate reached for a third piece of pizza. "She's a pet-sitter and a substitute teacher. That's how I met her; she subbed at my school. She's pet-sitting at someone's house north of Bellevue this week, but she'll be at the party tomorrow."

"Good, I want to meet her. Do you have time to watch a movie tonight?"

"I've got grading to do, but if you help me, maybe we could watch part of one."

"You're always grading," he muttered.

"True, but I'll only be doing it for another couple of months."

"Okay, I'll help, but I get to pick the movie."

"It's a deal."

———————

The next afternoon, Kate eased into a parking space on Mark's tree-lined street.

"Remember," she said, shutting off the engine, "tell them Eagle's your daughter."

"I still think it's a stupid idea."

"Please, we talked about this. Do it for me."

"Okay, okay. I'll do it."

"Thanks," she said. "I owe you one." As Victor unhooked the baby's car seat and lifted it out, Kate reached in the back for a bag of chips and a container of guacamole. Locking the car, she led Victor across the street and up the walkway to Mark's house. A note on his front door said: "Come on in. We're out on the deck. Grab snacks and join us."

"Big house," he said as he stood beside her on the threshold.

"It is," she said, suddenly nervous.

"Is this an expensive neighborhood?"

"Yes." *Why am I nervous? I'm going to a party with my friends, people I've known and loved for years.*

Victor studied the two-story stone house, the well-tended lawn, and the new SUV in the driveway. "Is Mark rich?"

"You could say that. His parents died in a car crash and left him and his sister a bunch of money. He's a nice guy, though, and an excellent science teacher. I think you'll like him." She inhaled a deep breath, and let it out. "Oddly enough, I'm a little nervous."

He frowned. "Why?"

"Probably because I want them to like you."

"But they're your friends. If I'm with you, why wouldn't they like me?"

"'Cause meeting you might come as a shock to them. When I left on spring break, I was still a grieving widow. Now I'm back two weeks later with a brand new lover."

He nuzzled her cheek. "And what a good lover he is, too."

"Stop it," she said, laughing as she pulled away. "It'll be a lot for them to take in, that's all, and they've been protective of me since Jon died. Okay, I'm ready." Opening the door, she led him through the foyer and down the hallway into the spacious dining room. Taking the lid off her guacamole, she set it down on the table, opened the bag of chips, and put together a plate of food for them to share. "Come on, let's go out."

As they emerged onto the deck, Kate saw her friends spread around the backyard, talking and drinking. Mark hovered by the grill in the sunshine.

"Katie!" he said, breaking into a grin. "Glad you could make it. It's so warm in the sun here, I decided to cook out. Is this your friend?"

"This is Victor and his daughter, Little Eagle. Victor, meet Mark."

"Welcome," Mark said, shaking Victor's hand. "Good to meet you."

"Good to meet you, too."

"Cute baby," Mark said, glancing down at Little Eagle dozing in her carrier. "You didn't tell me you were bringing a baby, but that's cool."

"Yeah, she's a sweetie," Kate said. "We brought guacamole and chips."

"Terrific," Mark said, setting several pieces of chicken on the grill. "You make such awesome guacamole. I'll have some later."

As Kate scanned the large yard, she recognized most of the other guests. Down on the grass, the math teacher Jake was playing disc golf with his new girlfriend. From the deck's lower level, Bonnie and her husband raised their drinks to her and smiled. "Is Alex here yet?" Kate asked.

Mark shook his head. "Not yet. She's running late because of the traffic."

"Need any help cooking?"

"Nope," he said, unwrapping a package of hamburger patties. "I've got it covered. There's wine and beer in that cooler over there, and glasses on the table beside it."

"Okay then," Kate said, cuffing Mark's shoulder. "I offered."

"What can I get you?" Kate asked Victor as they walked to the cooler.

"A cold beer would be great." Setting Little Eagle's carrier down on a nearby bench, he stretched his shoulders and looked around. "Nice place."

"Yeah, it's a great spot. I'm glad the weather cleared." Taking a beer from the cooler, Kate twisted the top off and handed it to Victor, then poured herself a glass of wine. As they stood there eating chips and sipping their drinks, they gazed at the lawn extending to the dock with its kayaks, the lake beyond it with dozens of boats, and the snow-capped Olympic Mountains in the distance. Mark's cousin Ben waved to them from the dock, where he was tying up a kayak. The late afternoon sun sparkled on the water.

"Hey, stranger," a familiar voice said behind her.

"Alex!" Kate said, spinning around. "It's so good to see you!"

Alex hugged her. "Welcome back!"

"Thanks," Kate said, pulling away. "This is Victor and his daughter, Little Eagle."

"Hi," Alex said, shaking his hand. "It's great to meet you."

"You, too," he said. "Kate tells me you're a pet-sitter."

"Yep, that's me, have pooper-scooper will travel." She glanced at Kate, and back to Victor. "A baby, huh? That's a surprise. Excuse me, I need to say hi to Mark and get a drink. Be right back." She headed across the deck.

"She seems nice," Victor said, scooping guacamole onto a chip.

"She is nice," Kate said. "But she doesn't need to know everything about us yet, so let me do most of the talking."

"Okay, boss," he said, popping the chip into his mouth.

"So," Alex said when she returned, "did you have a good trip?"

"It was okay," Kate said, "but eleven hundred miles is a lot of driving."

"No kidding, but I'm glad you made it. "How do you like Seattle so far, Victor?"

He shrugged. "It's beautiful when it's not raining."

Alex laughed. "I think it's beautiful all the time, but when it's sunny, it's paradise. Look," she added, pointing into the distance. "Mount Rainier's out. It often hides behind clouds, but when it's out, it's really something."

"It's spectacular," Victor said. "It looks like it's hovering above the horizon."

Alex studied him. "What do you do for a living, Victor?"

Oh-oh, Kate thought, *here come the questions. Alex can be relentless when she wants to find out something.*

"I'm an artist," he answered, "but I don't make my living at it yet. In the past, I've worked on a ranch, leading trail rides and tending horses."

Good, that sounds plausible, and he did do that before we met.

Alex nodded. "I see. Have you known Kate long?"

"No," he said, "just a couple of months."

"Oh, really," she asked, shooting a suspicious look at Kate. "How'd you meet?"

Crap. I told her on the phone Victor was a friend from a long time ago.

He turned to Kate and smiled. "We met at her grandparents' house."

Good boy. This is the story we agreed on, and it wasn't a lie, since he first saw me sitting by the fire in their living room.

"At Lily and Ivan's?" Alex asked. "Nice people. Are you interested in antiques?"

Victor sipped his beer. "Not really, just their Native American stuff. They have some authentic Navaho weavings and Hopi pottery. I'm a Ute, so that kind of thing interests me." Just then Little Eagle woke up, looked around, and started fussing. Setting his beer on the bench, he crouched down so she could see him. "It's okay, little one, I'm here." He picked her up and felt her bottom. "She's wet. Is there a place inside where I can change her?"

"There's a laundry room off the kitchen," Kate said. "Want me to show you?"

"No, I'll find it," he said, grabbing the carrier and turning toward the house. "She's probably hungry, too. Is there a microwave where I can warm her bottle?"

"In the kitchen," Kate said, sipping her wine as she watched him hurry off.

Alex turned to Kate. "You want to tell me what's going on?"

"What do you mean?"

"For one thing, Victor said he met you a couple of months ago, but you told me on the phone he was an old friend."

Kate stared at a passing sailboat, trying to figure out how much to tell her. "I don't know why he said that. He's had a lot on his mind lately."

"Okay. You also failed to mention that he's a Native American."

"So? Is there anything wrong with that?"

"Of course not, but you might've mentioned it. And you know almost nothing about babies, yet you seem to know exactly what his little girl needs."

"I've been traveling with her for days," Kate snapped. "Of course I'd know what she needs."

"And another thing—why's a guy taking care of such a little baby? Where's her mother?"

Kate inhaled a deep breath and let it out. "She was murdered a few months ago."

Alex gasped. "My God, that's awful."

"Victor was there when it happened, and he couldn't save her." As Kate watched the sailboat recede into the distance, she suddenly remembered friends she'd left behind in 1863, friends living out their lives without her. "I'm sorry, Alex. I would've told you more about them if we'd had time to talk this week, but we've both so busy. I promise to tell you more, but not here, and not now."

Alex shook her head and frowned, obviously shaken. "That's okay," she said, touching Kate's arm. "Tell me when you're ready. Are they staying with you?"

"Yes." *I can't tell her Victor's my lover yet.*

"You must trust him, then. And that's quite an adjustment, living with a baby."

Kate nodded. "It is, but she's a good baby, and I like having them around. It's been lonely in my house since Jon died. Victor's a great father, and he really loves her."

"I can see that."

"Food's done!" Mark called from the grill. "Help me carry it in and let's eat!"

They hurried inside.

CHAPTER SEVEN

True to weather predictions Saturday morning turned out warm and sunny, so Kate cleaned off a table in the backyard and they ate breakfast outside.

"Let's go into downtown Seattle today," Kate said as she fed the baby. "We could go for a ferry ride and check out some galleries. I'll pack a lunch if you get Eagle ready."

"Sounds good; I'll bring my sketchbook," Victor answered, sipping his coffee. "But I thought you lived in Seattle."

"I live on the Eastside. Downtown's about a forty-minute drive away."

Soon they were speeding along a freeway and shooting across a bridge spanning Lake Washington. As they whizzed over the water, Victor saw sailboats, power boats, canoes, and kayaks down below. He was beginning to understand this was a place dominated by water, and the people who lived here loved their boats. As they emerged from a tunnel, downtown Seattle loomed ahead in the sunlight, dense with towering skyscrapers and shimmering metal. As the highway funneled them into the city, he glimpsed two stadiums and a railroad station.

"We'll do the ferry first," Kate said, focused on her driving, "if I can find a parking space." She drove past stores and street vendors, homeless people and tourists, and a few policemen on bicycles. Driving under an overpass, she nabbed a parking space and glanced at her watch. "We might make the 12:20 if we hurry. Let's go."

Darting across a busy street, they climbed a flight of stairs into a bustling ferry terminal. They bought their tickets and waited in line, watching the arriving ferry rumble into its berth and disgorge its passengers.

"Come on," Kate said, "follow me." The line of walk-on passengers surged over the gangway to the ferry's upper deck as cars drove on below them. Kate led Victor off to the side so they could stand on the back of the vessel, facing the city skyline. A deep horn sounded. The ferry's idling engines thrummed to life, and the ship pulled away from the dock.

"There's the Space Needle," Kate said, pointing to Seattle's trademark tower. "Are you okay? You look a little wobbly."

"I'm fine." He gripped Little Eagle's carrier in one hand and the railing in the other as he watched greenish waves curl away from the ferry's white wake. "I've never been on a boat before, and suddenly there's water all around me. Is this the ocean?"

"Kind of—it's Puget Sound, but it connects to the ocean. Just relax and enjoy it."

Gradually he did. He watched the skyscrapers shrink in the distance and the other boats pass by. He felt the strong wind on his face and Kate's hand on his arm. Seabirds cried overhead, plunging down into the waves. Another ferry passed, heading back to the city. He released his grip on the railing. "What kind of birds are those?"

"Seagulls," she said. "Want to go inside now and eat our lunch?"

"Not yet," he said, feeling the wind blow his braids back. "I like it out here."

She laughed. "Ten minutes on a ferry and you're hooked. I love it."

The wind shrieked through the railings, creating weird, beautiful harmonics. "Do you hear that?" he asked. "It sounds like the wind's playing steel drums."

Kate nodded. "It does. I've been riding these ferries for years, and I've never heard anything like it. Are you ready yet? I'm getting cold, and I bet Eagle is, too."

"I'm ready," he said, turning toward the doors leading to the ferry's interior.

"There's a snack bar inside," she said, pushing the door open. "We could get some chowder to warm us up."

"Okay. What's *chowder*?"

"It's hearty soup with potatoes and clams in it. You should try it." Kate led him past rows of seated passengers to a large booth. "I'll get the chowder. Be right back."

Putting Little Eagle's carrier down, Victor adjusted her blanket and settled in to watch the other passengers. Some were eating and sipping coffee as they gazed out the windows, others were reading books and newspapers, and others were playing cards or scanning their phones. In the next booth, a girl watched a movie on her iPad while her boyfriend dozed beside her, and a man in a suit worked on his laptop. Kate returned carrying a tray with two bowls of soup and two cups of coffee. As they shared the ham sandwiches she'd brought and ate their soup, Victor discovered he liked chowder. Thirty minutes later they arrived at their island destination.

————————

About three hours later they returned on another ferry to Seattle. After getting off on Bainbridge Island earlier, they'd visited an art museum, walked to a nearby bakery, and devoured two pieces of coconut pineapple pie. On the return trip, they'd spotted more sailboats and seagulls, so Victor felt like a seasoned sailor. He'd decided he liked Seattle, despite its stormy weather. Now they hurried off the ferry, eager to visit galleries.

At the first one they saw abstract paintings with vibrant colors and whimsical shapes; at the second they saw photographs of the Northwest with cloud-covered mountains and ocean scenes. Afterward they took a break from galleries and sat on a bench in Pioneer Square to watch people. A bedraggled woman with unkempt hair sat on an adjacent bench, nursing a cup of coffee against the chill. A young man hawked newspapers on a nearby street corner. A pair of lovers strolled by, hugging each other and nibbling cookies. While Kate fed the baby, Victor pulled out his sketchbook and began to draw a girl sitting by an Oriental carpet store. An attractive Native woman stopped in front of the store and peered in. She set her purse down on a ledge and took out a notebook. A skinny teenager in torn jeans sprinted over from the curb, snatched the purse, and darted off.

"Hey!" the woman cried. "He stole my purse!"

Victor leapt up and tossed his sketchbook aside. He chased the thief past other pedestrians, down a steep sidewalk, and into a deserted alley. The thief spun around, swinging the purse like a weapon. He pulled a knife from his belt and jabbed it at him. "Back off!"

Victor knocked the knife from his hand and slammed him into a dumpster. A cop on a bicycle rushed into the alley.

"What's going on?" the cop asked, braking to a stop.

Victor pointed, catching his breath. "That boy stole this purse."

"Drop it!" the cop demanded as he dismounted. "Put your hands out!" The thief dropped the purse and thrust out his hands. The officer cuffed him to a nearby bicycle stand. As the cop picked up the purse, the Native woman came running into the alley.

"My purse!" she cried. "You got it!"

"*He* got it," the cop said, nodding at Victor.

She flashed him a smile. "Thank you!"

He smiled back. "You're welcome."

The cop opened the purse and plucked out a wallet. "What's your name, miss?"

"Why?"

"I have to make sure this is yours," he said.

"Adele Swiftcurrent," she said. "It's right there on my license."

The cop studied her photo, glanced at her, and back at the license.

Adele sighed. "You'll also find my tribal membership card, insurance and credit cards, about fifty-six dollars and change, a tube of lipstick, and my reading glasses."

As the officer looked through the purse, Victor studied Adele. She was in her late twenties or early thirties, stood about five-three in high heels, with a chubby face and pleasant smile. Her red coat complemented her shoulder-length black hair and dark eyes.

"Okay," the cop said, handing the purse back. "Make sure everything's in there."

Adele grabbed the purse and rifled through it. "Nothing appears to be missing."

"Good," he said. "Do you want to press charges?"

"No," she said, glaring at the thief. "But you're an asshole for stealing, so stop it!"

"Yes ma'am," the teen muttered.

"You're a lucky kid," the officer said, removing the handcuffs. "You're free to go, but don't let me catch you stealing again. Take care, miss," he added to Adele. As he mounted his bicycle and peddled away, the thief snatched up his knife, turned, and bolted down the alley.

Adele rose up on her tip-toes and kissed Victor's cheek. "Thank you so much!"

He shrugged. "You're welcome, but it's nothing. I just happened to be there."

"Believe me, it's something. What's your name?"

"Victor Manyhorses."

She shook his hand. "Glad to meet you. I'm Swinomish. What tribe are you?"

"Tabeguache Ute. I just moved here with my girlfriend and baby daughter."

Adele nodded. "I'd like to talk more, but I'm sorry, I have to go." Reaching into her purse, she pulled out a flyer and handed it to him. "Come to my opening later, if you can, and bring your girlfriend. It's not far, and we can talk there."

Victor smiled as he read the flyer. "You're an artist?"

"Yes, I'm a painter. Please come. There'll be food there."

"I'll try."

"Thanks again, Victor," she said turning to go. "Bye."

"Bye." Victor watched her click away in her heels, turn the corner, and disappear. *Great legs*, he thought as he hurried out of the alley. *Friendly, too*, he thought as he trudged up the steep sidewalk. *Beautiful woman*, he thought as he headed down the street.

"Hey there," he said, walking up to Kate and Little Eagle.

"Victor!" she cried. "I was worried about you! Did you catch that guy?"

"I did, actually, and the lady got her purse back."

"That's great! Sit down and tell me everything!"

"Okay," he said, easing down onto the bench. "I chased the kid into an alley and rammed him into a dumpster. Then a bike cop rode in, and Adele got her purse back."

Kate raised an eyebrow. "Adele, huh? So, you're on a first-name basis?"

"She's nice, Kate, you'd like her. She's also an artist, and she's having an opening later not far from here." He handed her the flyer. "Want to go? There'll be food there."

She skimmed the flyer. "We definitely should go, especially since they'll have food. You got what you were hoping for, Victor, to meet some local Natives."

"I guess I did," he said. "And all I had to do was catch a thief."

———————

When Kate and Victor walked into the gallery later, he saw several paintings with circular patterns, bold colors, and distinctive Northwestern animal designs. As Victor turned a corner, he found tables laden with food and drink, and the lovely Adele in a flowing red dress. "Come on," he said to Kate. "I'll introduce you."

Adele's eyes lit up as they approached. "I'm glad you made it! Welcome."

Victor shifted Little Eagle's carrier. "Adele, this is Kate, my girlfriend. Kate, this is Adele."

"Hi," Kate said, shaking Adele's hand. "Thanks for inviting us."

"Nice to meet you," she said, glancing at the baby. "And this is your daughter?"

"Yes, this is Little Eagle," Victor said. "I'm a painter, too. Are these all yours?"

Adele smiled. "Most of them are, but two other artists are also showing. You told me earlier you just moved here. Did you bring any of your work with you?"

"Not much," he said. "Just one painting and a few sketches."

"Well, that's something. You should show me what you brought."

"I'd like that," he said. "But don't let me keep you from your patrons. I had a show myself recently, and I realize you have to circulate."

Adele laughed. "No kidding. Get some food, and we'll talk later." She eased away into the crowd.

"Okay," Kate said. "Let's eat." She poured them two glasses of white wine and loaded a plate with shrimp, cheeses, tortilla wraps, and fruit. "She seems nice."

"She does," Victor said, loading his own plate. "But she's tough, too. You should've heard her scold that thief." He glanced at some of the people hovering near the table: three college-age girls in jeans and fleece jackets, two silver-haired matrons in long pretty skirts, two prosperous-looking young men in tailored suits.

They wandered around the gallery as they ate, studying Adele's paintings and their accompanying texts. He could see they represented thirteen lunar phases and showed how the various seasons influenced tribal life. The paintings had titles like *Moon When Frog Talks*, *Moon to Put the Paddles Away*, and *Moon of the Windy Time*. The tribe's spring was a time of emergence, similar to his own culture, and April's moon was called *Moon of the Whistling Robins*. It signaled springtime's natural music, as well as a season of harvesting shellfish, building canoes, and digging up fern roots. As Victor continued reading he picked out words like *salmonberry, lingcod, chinook, and sockeye*.

Adele sauntered over. "So, what do you think?"

"Your work is powerful," he said.

She smiled. "Like many of the Coast Salish tribes, we Swinomish recognize thirteen lunar phases in a calendar year, and each moon is named for seasonal events that take place during that time."

"I see," he said. "Like we have a bear dance in the spring to honor our grizzlies."

Adele's eyebrows arched. "You still have grizzlies in Colorado? I'm impressed. There might be some in the mountains north of here, but if there are, they're very reclusive. Excuse me," she added as the young men in suits approached.

"Maybe she can help you get into some galleries here," Kate whispered.

"Maybe," Victor said, biting into a strawberry. "She seems well-connected."

"And beautiful," she added. "I notice you didn't help an ugly woman."

He choked on his strawberry. "Stop it, Kate. You don't need to be jealous."

"Just kidding," she said, sipping her wine. "I'm glad you've found an artist friend. Adele reminds me of Prairie Flower because she's short, pretty, and vivacious."

Victor laughed. "You're right. I knew she reminded me of someone."

They roamed the gallery as the evening wore on. Finally they bid goodbye to Adele and drove home. As they crossed Lake Washington, the sky behind them flared with a vibrant sunset.

———————

The weekend passed, and all the next week. While Kate kept busy with planning and grading, Victor created more artwork. After school and on weekends, they explored the area, seeking out hiking trails, forests, and lakeshores. Bear continued to remain in her mouse form, and Cisco learned to tolerate her. As the rainy days of April unfolded, the neighborhood gardens exploded with grape hyacinths, daffodils, and finally tulips. On a clear Saturday morning, Kate was out in the backyard weeding a flowerbed while Little Eagle watched from her carrier.

Spotting a robin, the baby waved her chubby arms and cried, "Gaaa!"

"Yes, honey," Kate said, "that's a birdie."

Victor came out and set a tray down on a table. "I brought coffee and the blueberry scones you bought at the bakery last night."

"Thanks," she said, rising from her knees. "I need a break." Taking off her gloves, she dunked a scone into her coffee and bit into it. "I could use your help with some chores before I put the house on the market. Are you game?"

Victor groaned. "What kind of chores?"

"We need to clean up the flower beds, paint both bathrooms, organize the garage, shampoo the carpets, and wash the windows. We should be able to finish all that in the next few weeks, put the house on the market, and hopefully sell it by the end of summer. How's that sound?"

"Not too bad. Okay, I'll help you." He nibbled his scone and sipped his coffee.

"Want to ask Alex over for dinner tomorrow? I haven't seen her in a week, and she's not pet-sitting, so it would be a good time for you two to get to know each other."

"Sure," he said, picking up Little Eagle's carrier. "I'll take her in for her nap."

"Okay," Kate said, and returned to her weeding. "I'll be in soon."

———————

On Sunday evening, Alex and Kate strolled around the backyard, admiring the flowers. Golden light shone through the flowering cherry trees, and several red-winged blackbirds were singing. Alex stopped beside a bed of white hyacinths, magenta tulips, and daffodils. "I can see you've been out here weeding. These beds look great."

"Thanks," Kate said. "Listen, Alex, part of the reason I asked you over was to fill you in about Victor."

"I'm listening."

Kate took a deep breath and let it out, trying to decide where to begin. "For one thing, Eagle's his granddaughter, not his daughter."

"Okay, but isn't he a little young to be a grandfather?"

"He is to us, but people in his culture have their children much younger."

"I see. So I'm guessing the baby's mother was Victor's daughter?"

"Yes," Kate said. "Her father's dead, too, so Victor's raising her."

"That's so sad. Where's the rest of the family? Couldn't they help?"

"They're back in Colorado, in a really remote area. He wanted Eagle to have a better life, so he decided to move here and raise her in our culture."

"I don't get it. There aren't many places *that* remote. Doesn't he miss his family?"

"He does, but if I tell you something incredible, will you promise to believe me?"

"I promise to try. How incredible is it?"

Kate smiled. "So incredible it's a fairy tale."

Alex's eyes lit up. "I love fairy tales! Tell me."

"Well," Kate began, "remember I told you that Victor's a friend from a long time ago?"

"Uh, yeah. And what does that mean?"

"It means he's a time-traveler."

Her eyes narrowed. "Come on, Kate. You've got to be kidding me."

"No, I'm serious. He's from 1863."

Alex propped her hands on her hips. "Yeah, right. Then how did *you* meet him?"

"He was stuck in my time for four years, waiting for his time-travel passage to open. I met him in a cave after falling down the same passage."

"You've been reading too many novels. Things like this don't happen in real life."

Kate's heart sank. "You're my best friend. Why don't you believe me?"

Alex threw up her arms. "How can I? This makes no sense! What proof do you have?"

"None," she said, "except for Victor and the baby. Aren't they proof enough?"

"No, they're not," Alex said, grabbing Kate's hand. "If you fell down a passage, did you hit your head? Is this what Victor told you? He could be anybody, some kind of scam artist. You need to stop this, Kate. Maybe you need more counseling."

"I don't need more counseling! I need you to believe me!"

Just then, Victor emerged from the house. Mouse darted out through the open door with Cisco chasing her. Mouse ran under an azalea bush, and as Cisco crept closer, Mouse burst into a flurry of wings. She whirled up and up, a feathery tornado spiraling upward.

Alex's mouth dropped open. "What the hell?"

As Mouse became Hawk, Cisco dropped into a crouch, hissed, and slunk away.

"What just happened?" Alex asked. "What *is* that?"

Victor shrugged. "It's Mouse becoming Hawk. She's been doing that a lot lately."

Alex glared at him. "What are you talking about?"

"She's magical," he said. "You know, like a shapeshifter."

They watched Hawk soaring above them, flying graceful circles in the golden light. She landed in a cedar, settled her feathers, and peered down at them.

Alex's eyes grew wide with wonder. "I don't believe this. This isn't happening."

"Believe it," Kate said. "It's happening. I told you it was a fairy tale."

Alex stared at her. "I could really use a drink right now."

"I understand," Kate said. "It's a lot to take in. Wine or beer? We're having enchiladas for dinner, so maybe you'd like a beer."

"Wine," Alex said. "And plenty of it."

———————

"Who wants this last lonely enchilada?" Kate asked later at dinner.

"Me," Alex said, scooping it onto her plate. "And more wine, please."

Kate refilled all their glasses. "So, are you ready to hear more of our fairy tale?"

Alex shot her a look. "Not really, but I'm as ready as I'll ever be."

"As I told you, we met in a cave," Kate began, "and it wasn't exactly love at first sight."

Victor laughed. "No, it wasn't, but I tried my best to be charming."

"At first I was terrified," Kate continued, sipping her wine. "There I was, trapped with this stranger, and I didn't believe him that we'd traveled back in time."

"I don't believe it either," Alex said, leaning closer. "But tell me what happened."

Kate continued with her story...

———————

"That's an amazing story," Alex said an hour later, "but I need a break."

As Alex headed for the bathroom, Kate got up and started clearing dishes. "Talking about the past makes me think of Doozie," she said to Victor. "She's still back there with all those gamblers, drunks, and whores. And with Blackstone, if he survived." She carried their plates into the kitchen, set them in the sink, and began to rinse them.

Victor followed her in and touched her shoulder. "Don't beat yourself up over it, Kate. She didn't want to come here. She was very clear on that."

Kate stared out the window at the fading sunset, at the silhouette of Hawk perched in the cedar. "She's just a kid, so she doesn't know what she wants, and she doesn't know what it's like here in the future. I should've dragged her up that passage."

"If you had, she would've slowed you down, and Blackstone might've killed you."

She felt her eyes fill with tears. "Or he might not have. He didn't kill *her*, did he?"

"No, he didn't," he said, caressing her cheek. "But he could've."

"I can't believe I just left her there. And she even said she might be pregnant."

Victor hugged her. "You've got to let her go, Kate. We have to let them all go."

"I never should've left her," she whispered.

————————

A lantern illuminated a room with a rocking chair, a small wooden table, and a brass bed covered by a crazy quilt. An evening breeze wafted in through the open window, carrying the sweet scent of lilacs. Doozie stood by the window with tears glistening on her cheeks, her hand resting on her belly, and one shoulder wrapped in a sling. From outside came birdsong and horses neighing. From the next room came men's laughter.

Doozie seemed to be somewhere in the saloon, probably in Homer's old bedroom by the kitchen. She peered out the window and up at the shadowy mountains, as though she longed to fly away. She raised a small glass of whiskey to her lips, sniffed it, and set it back down on the table. Pouring a cup of tea from a flowered teapot, she settled into the rocker and began to read a book. As the light outside faded, the lantern light grew stronger and more golden. Doozie sipped her tea and turned a page.

Kate's eyes flew open. Troubled by her dream, she turned over and hugged Victor, taking comfort from his steady breathing. Easing from the bed, she drew on her robe and slippers and padded from the bedroom to the second-story landing, where a waning moon shone in through a bare window. This same moon could be shining in on Doozie, trapped back there in that saloon, reading a book by lantern light. In the dream she'd rejected the whiskey for the tea and rested her hand on her belly, so maybe she'd discovered she was pregnant. Lots of women did that when they were feeling hopeful; Kate had done it too before she lost her baby. It was only a dream, she told herself, so none of it was real, but Kate was safe here and Doozie wasn't.

She sighed and went downstairs to the kitchen. She poured milk into a pan, turned the burner on, and popped a slice of bread into the toaster. Plucking a folder from a shelf, she drew out Victor's sketch of Doozie and studied it. Her face looked young but weary; her smile looked hopeful but thin. When this was drawn, the girl had been in love with Homer; now she was his widow. She was only sixteen. *How could she run a saloon, handle rough men who'd known her as a whore, and manage whores twice her age?*

Kate poured the warm milk into a mug and buttered the toast. Sliding open the glass door to the deck, she went outside and sat in a chair in the moonlight, gathering her robe against the chilly night. Hawk flew down to perch on the table, her yellow eyes riveted on the toast.

Kate tossed her a morsel. "That's for convincing Alex that magic still happens."

Hawk bolted it down and fluffed up her feathers.

Kate drank her milk, feeling it warm her as she thought of Doozie. "Being a bird of prey suits you, but won't it be weird when you start craving mice?"

Hawk cocked her head and stared.

"Sorry. I was just saying." Kate finished eating and sighed. "I have to let Doozie go, Hawk. She made her choice in that cave, and now she has to live with it. I can't go back there and save her because she doesn't want to be saved, right?"

Hawk screeched.

"I'm glad you agree with me." Kate stared up at the moon, feeling the milk begin to relax her. She loved her backyard, with its cherry trees, stately cedar, and the flower beds she'd planted with her late husband. Leaving her home to move to Colorado would mean leaving part of herself behind. "This is crazy," she said aloud to no one but herself and Hawk. "I'm sitting here at two-thirty in the morning on a school night, sharing a snack with a magical hawk. I'm going to bed now. 'Night." Gathering up her dishes, she went inside and set them in the sink.

As she eased into bed a few minutes later, Victor turned over and moaned.

Kate drifted off.

Within the darkness of his dream came the whispers of his people. Victor heard his best friend Rising Moon asking why he'd left them so soon, and his sister-in-law Prairie Flower wondering where he'd gone now. His mother-in-law scolded him for not bringing her great-granddaughter Little Eagle to her. He heard the war chief Running Deer and his wife Raven, and many others—their voices rising in a cacophony of whispers.

Within the voices came their familiar faces, but they were sorrowful, tearful, even accusing. He'd left them behind, even though he knew what trials the future held for them. Finally, he saw his friend Ouray, surrounded by the ruins of their encampment.

"You have left our people, Victor. Why?"

"I had to make a choice," he said. "I had to follow Eagle and Kate."

Ouray frowned. "Had to? Why?"

"They were in danger, and I had to find them. You know how I love them."

His friend nodded. "I understand the obligations of love, yet was leaving us the only way?"

"The only way I could think of. I swear I did what I had to. Don't judge me."

Ouray sighed. "I won't. Do what you must, but remember you promised to help me with the treaty talks, and you made a commitment to our people. I must go now. Farewell, my friend." He turned away.

"Farewell." Victor watched him disappear.

Victor snapped awake, his heart pounding, his forehead beaded with sweat. He turned to Kate, lying beside him, her face tranquil in her slumber. He curled on his side and tried to sleep, but sleep eluded him.

————————

Colorado City—1863

At dawn, over a hundred years away, Doozie awoke to robins singing outside her window. She stretched her arms over her head and winced at the pain in her wounded left shoulder. She was grateful for this saloon she'd inherited from Homer, but the daily running of it made her weary. She collapsed into bed every morning in the wee hours and awoke a few hours later when the sun rose. She could sometimes return to sleep, but this morning a dream had troubled her.

She'd dreamt of Kate, who'd taught her to read and told her about a future time where girls like her could attend school and fashion better lives. Doozie often found herself wondering if she should've gone there. She'd been feverish and confused when Victor had offered to escort her to the future; now she fretted she'd made the wrong choice. She'd watched him go, then returned to town to bury Homer, like she'd wanted, but now she was stuck here, running a saloon with a gaggle of cantankerous whores.

At first they'd pitied her for losing Homer, and they'd softened for a while, but now they were back to their petty bickering. Who had the best room? Who deserved a new dress? Why did that one get more customers than the others? Doozie suspected they wanted her to return to whoring herself, but she never would, unless she was starving, and maybe not even then. She was determined to make a go of running this damn saloon.

Poor Homer. He'd been old enough to be her father, but she'd loved him. He'd given her his name and his saloon, but with him gone, she had no love in her life. Life without it was bitter and hopeless, yet she had to keep living for this baby who could be growing inside of her. She wasn't sure if there *was* a baby yet, but her menses had ceased, so time would soon tell.

She stretched again, careful of her shoulder. It was healing, but it still pained her and she guarded it, so no lifting heavy trays, hanging sheets on the line, or riding spirited horses. From outside came the sounds of the town waking up—horses neighing in the muddy streets, chickens squawking in their coop, the outhouse door squeaking in the yard. She was tempted to return to her dream world, but she couldn't fetch it from the cobwebs, so she decided to heave herself out of bed, make some breakfast, and begin her sorry day.

———————

After school that Friday, Kate met Alex at a park on Lake Washington to go kayaking, and they hoisted their kayaks off their cars to haul them to the lake. As they pushed off from shore and headed for deeper water, Kate watched the water cascade off her paddle in shimmering droplets, creating a sparkling rainbow in the afternoon sunshine. They soon fell into the steady rhythm of paddling.

"Didn't Victor want to come?" Alex asked. "He could've walked around the park with the baby while we kayaked."

"No," Kate said. "He invited an artist friend over to check out his artwork."

"Really? Who?"

"A Swinomish painter we met a few weeks ago at a gallery opening in Seattle. He's hoping she'll help him get started in the local art scene."

"She sounds like a useful contact. Is her work any good?"

"Yes, it's amazing. She does these wonderful circular paintings depicting the Swinomish seasons. I can take you to the gallery where she exhibits if you want."

"I'll be busy dog-sitting this weekend, but maybe another time. Is she attractive?"

Kate laughed. "Oh, yeah. She's a dark-skinned Native beauty."

"Too bad," Alex said. "It'd be easier on you if she was homely."

"I like her, though, and I know I can trust Victor."

Alex snorted. "I trusted Sean too until he hooked up with that nineteen-year-old barista from Starbucks. I like Victor, and I'm glad you trust him. I haven't seen you this happy since before Jon died, though I can't get my head around this time-travel thing."

"It has its challenges," Kate said, "but we know what we're doing."

"What are you doing, exactly?"

"We're living together," Kate said, feeling a frisson of irritation at the question. "You lived with Sean before you married him, didn't you?"

"Yes," Alex said. "Don't get so defensive. I'm just worried about you. You went off to Colorado for spring break and came back with some Native guy you barely know."

"Here's what I know," Kate said, continuing to paddle. "I know I deserve to be happy again, and being with Victor makes me happy. We're lovers. There, I've said it."

"I suspected as much," Alex said. "It's your life, and you can do what you want, but I'm still worried about you."

Kate stopped paddling, stretched her shoulders, and let her kayak coast. *Am I crazy for shaking up my life by selling my house, quitting my job, and moving? Maybe, but I know Victor and I love each other, and I want to live closer to Ivan and Lily.* "Sorry I snapped at you, Alex, and sorry to spring this on you. I've had a rough week at school, and I haven't been sleeping well."

Alex coasted to come alongside her. "Why not?"

"I dreamed about a teenage prostitute I was teaching to read in 1863. I'm worried about her, and I shouldn't have left her back there, but she didn't want to come here."

Alex frowned. "Do you miss the past?"

Kate sighed. "I miss the adventure of it and the possibility that anything could happen. You don't take anything for granted back there, not even simple things like food and shelter. Life was more precious because you could lose it so easily, and friends were more precious because they could die anytime. Did I tell you Victor saved my life?"

Alex's eyes widened. "No, you didn't. What happened?"

"It's a long story," Kate said. "I'll tell you another time."

They sat there, bobbing in their kayaks, watching sunlight glint off the water. Kate would miss being around so much water when she moved; she'd also miss Alex and her other friends.

"I'm hungry," Alex said, and pointed. "There's an Ivar's cafe over at that dock there. Let's paddle to it and get some chowder."

"You're on," Kate said. She turned her kayak around and started paddling.

———————

As Kate headed in from the garage after kayaking, she heard Victor talking in the backyard through the dining room door, and went to peer out through the screen. He was standing across from Adele, waving his arms and explaining something.

"You'd be wearing a shawl," he said, "and you'd flick it at me, to signify you wanted to dance." He flicked an imaginary shawl and started moving toward Adele.

He's teaching her the steps to Bear Dance, the Ute courtship dance he danced with me in the past when I first realized I loved him.

"You'd go backward as I came toward you," he said. As he took three steps toward Adele, she took three steps backward; as he took three steps backward, she took three steps forward. Back and forth they danced, bound together by the simple rhythm.

"Hey," Kate said as she slid the screen door open and stepped outside.

"Hi," Victor said, suddenly stopping. "I've been teaching Adele the steps to Bear Dance."

"I can see that," she said, walking toward them. "I think she's got it." *Just keep your hands off my ... my what? My boyfriend?*

My live-in lover? We're not married, or even engaged, so what are we to each other, exactly?

"Hi, Kate," Adele said, smiling as she greeted her. She was wearing a green long-sleeved tee-shirt, black fitted jeans, and black boots.

Kate was aware of how bedraggled she must look in her sweatshirt and tights, with her hair tied back in a ponytail. "What do you think of Victor's artwork?"

"It's very good," Adele said, glancing at Victor, "especially the bear painting. When he gets more work done, I'll introduce him to some gallery owners."

"That's great," Kate said, hugging Victor. "See, I said you were good."

"Can Adele stay for dinner?" Victor asked Kate. "We could order a pizza."

"Thanks for the invite," Adele said, "but I'm headed up to my hometown of La Conner to visit my mother for the weekend, and she's expecting me for dinner. Let's do it some other time."

Fat chance, Kate thought, and was immediately ashamed of herself. Adele was Victor's friend and fellow artist, and Kate had nothing to be worried about. "Sure," Kate said as they followed Adele into the house. "We'll get together another time."

Grabbing her purse from the couch, Adele said, "If you wouldn't mind the drive, I'll ask you up to the Swinomish rez when we have a celebration."

"I'd like that," Victor said. "Would you like that, Kate?"

"Of course," she said, forcing a smile.

"Okay then," Adele said, turning to go. "I'd better get going. The traffic on I-5 will be heavy on Friday afternoon."

Kate crossed the living room to open the door for her. "See you."

"I'll call you when I get more artwork together," Victor said.

"Okay, bye," Adele said, and walked to her car.

After Adele drove away, Kate turned to Victor. She knew he was blameless, and he loved her completely, but she still felt an insidious twinge of jealousy.

"What?" he asked, frowning.

"Nothing," she said, and turned to go inside.

CHAPTER EIGHT

"Dammit!" Victor swore as he dropped the brush. Paint spattered his pants, his shoes, and the drop cloth. He'd been working on the upstairs bathroom all morning and was making good progress, but now Little Eagle was awake and crying in the bedroom. His back ached. His arms ached. He was weary of doing chores.

"Come here, little one," he crooned as he picked her up. "You're okay." He held her close and looked out the window into the backyard where Cisco was stalking grasshoppers with Mouse. Since she'd changed back into her mouse form a few days ago, they'd made peace with each other and become friends.

A disagreeable odor wafted up from the baby. "Great," he muttered. Laying Little Eagle on the card table, he undid her dirty diaper and peeled it off. He loved his granddaughter but was tired of changing her all day when Kate was away at work. His days seemed crammed with chores, and he hardly had time to paint pictures anymore, except in the evenings or on weekends—but then Kate was home, and he wanted to spend time with her.

"There," he said, tossing the diaper away. Men didn't do much child care in his culture, but he was certainly doing plenty of it now. He wiped the baby's butt clean and rubbed it with ointment as she giggled and kicked her legs.

The phone rang on the nightstand and the answering machine clicked on.

"Hi, it's Adele," the machine's speaker announced. "Are you there, Victor?"

He reached for the receiver. "Hi, I'm here. I'm always here."

She laughed. "Are you okay? You sound a little frazzled."

"I'm just bored," he said, putting his hand on Little Eagle to keep her from falling.

"Have you been painting?"

He snorted. "Only if you count the upstairs bathroom."

"Too bad; you should be painting. Listen, I'm still up here in La Conner, and we're planning a tribal fundraiser this Saturday. Would you and Kate like to come?"

"Sounds like fun," he said, feeling his spirits rise.

"I apologize for the short notice. We'll have a salmon bake, and take one of our big ocean canoes out on the water."

"I've never been in a canoe before, but I'm willing to try it. I really liked that ferry I rode on."

"This'll be different because you'll be paddling. Think you can make it?"

"I'd like to, but let me ask Kate when she gets home from school."

"Okay, but if Kate can't come, maybe you and Little Eagle could. It's a straight shot, just two hours north on I-5, and a half hour west to the park where we're having it. Call me later when you find out, okay? Bye."

"Bye." *A tribal gathering,* he thought as he hung up. *Cool.*

————————

"This Saturday?" Kate asked later in the living room. "We're going sailing with Mark and the others on Saturday, remember? Can't you take a rain check?"

Must be a Seattle expression, he thought. "I don't know. What is it?"

"It's a colloquialism," she said, kicking off her shoes, "for when you want to do something but can't make it. Couldn't we go up there another time?"

"We could, but I want to go to this. I could drive up there."

"There'll be lots of traffic because of the tulip festival, and you shouldn't go alone since you don't know the area."

"I wouldn't be alone since I could take the baby with me, and Adele said it was a straight shot. She can give me directions when I call her later."

"*Please,*" she pleaded. "I want us to go sailing with my friends."

"I like your friends, Kate, but I want to meet some Native people too, and this is a good opportunity. That's one of the reasons I came out here, remember?"

"Fine," she snapped, turning away. "Do what you want."

Was she angry? She sounded angry. "What's wrong?" he asked.

"Nothing's wrong. Did you at least get the bathroom painted today?"

"I made a good start on it, and I worked on the garage, too. Why?"

"Do you think you could finish it tomorrow?"

"Maybe, if you ask me nicely."

"Okay," she asked turning back to him. "Please finish the bathroom because if you finish that, we can replant some of the flowerbeds on Sunday."

His heart sank. "More chores? Can't we just take the weekend off?"

"Come on, we talked about this. I hate to be a taskmaster, but you know they have to be done before we put the house on the market." She eased closer and touched his arm. "Wouldn't it be nicer if we spent the weekend together?"

"What's wrong with you? You're acting weird."

"No, I'm not. I just don't want you to go up to La Conner without me."

"Why not?"

She shot him a look. "Because I think Adele has the hots for you."

"I doubt that. She's just a friend and a fellow artist."

"No, I think she's smitten, and why wouldn't she be? You're a handsome, single Native guy who's also an artist. You two have a lot in common."

He took both her hands and squeezed them. "But I love *you*, Kate, and we have a lot in common, too. We've traveled through time together, and we've saved each other's lives, remember?"

She nodded. "Of course I remember."

"Don't you trust me?"

"I totally trust you, but I don't trust her."

He pulled her into a hug. "Stop your worrying. There's nothing going on between me and Adele, but I do want to go to this tribal gathering. Can't you understand that?"

"I guess so," she muttered. "Of course I can. I guess I'm just being silly."

He lifted her chin and kissed her. "If you don't trust Adele, you can solve this by coming with me, but you'd have to give up going sailing."

Kate inhaled a breath and blew it out. "To be honest, I think I'm jealous of Adele because I saw you two dancing the Bear Dance together."

"Is that all?" he said, pulling back to study her. "It didn't mean anything. Adele said she liked dancing, and that's the only dance I knew to teach her."

"But that's the *courtship* dance! Don't you get it?"

He shrugged. "Okay, but I still think you're worried about nothing. Actually, I could say I was jealous of Mark, but I trust you, so I'm not."

Kate frowned. "Why would you be jealous of Mark?"

"I've seen the way he looks at you, and don't tell me you haven't noticed. And you said he wanted to date you."

"But we're just friends."

"You got it," he said, smiling. "And Adele and I are just friends, too."

She sighed. "So, the only way to resolve this is for each of us to do what we want. You go to the gathering, and I'll go sailing."

"Great," he said. "I'm glad we cleared that up. Can we go for a walk now? I've been inside all day taking care of the baby, cleaning the garage, and taping and painting the bathroom."

"Okay," she said, bending down to pick up her shoes. "Just give me a few minutes to change out of my school clothes and see if Little Eagle's awake."

He followed her upstairs and into the bedroom, where the baby lay sleeping. "Maybe we should wait," he whispered. "I hate to wake her."

"What can we do while we're waiting?" she whispered as she picked up a jar of cocoa butter from the bedside table.

He smiled. "I'm sure we'll think of something." Taking her hand, he led her across the hall into the spare bedroom. They undressed each other, slowly and lovingly, until they stood naked in the light shining through the sheer curtains.

"Lie on your stomach and I'll give you a massage," she said, pulling the covers back. She dipped her fingers into the cocoa butter and rubbed her hands together to warm them.

Victor settled in and closed his eyes. As Kate sat on his buttocks and began massaging his shoulders, he felt the tension in his muscles loosen. She finished his shoulders and continued down along his back.

He sighed. "Don't stop. That feels great."

"You deserve it. You worked hard today." After several pleasant minutes, Kate lifted off him and began to kiss him—tender kisses on his shoulders, back, and buttocks. He groaned and started trembling.

"Turn over," she said, and he did. Kate kissed his chest and belly and groin until he grew hard. She was hovering above him now, smiling as she straddled him. She eased him inside her and sighed with pleasure, beginning to move with a slow, steady rhythm. He felt a surge and groaned again.

"Not yet," she murmured, devouring him with those green eyes. "Wait."

Victor ran his hands along her strong, lithe body, watching her chest heave and her face flush. He gripped her hands and forced himself to wait.

"Now!" she gasped, closing her eyes and throwing her head back. They surged together, higher and higher, until they finally collapsed.

"I love you, Kate," he said, drawing her in against his shoulder.

"I love you, too," she said, kissing his cheek. She fell quiet for a minute, then added, "Sorry I've been so bitchy lately about the chores. I don't mean to be."

He stroked her long hair. "Apology accepted. Just back off though."

"I will. I've just been so tired from teaching and helping with the baby."

"Shhh," he said. "Don't think about it now. Just rest."

———————

On Saturday morning Victor loaded Little Eagle into the car, made his way to the interstate, and joined the hordes of people driving north. Kate had been right about the traffic—it was bumper to bumper most of the way, and moved at a snail's pace. People were trapped in their cars—inching forward, stalling out, and cutting each other off. After about an hour he stopped for a break at a casino that a sign said was run by the Tulalip tribe, and drove another hour to the town of Mt. Vernon. Leaving the interstate he drove west through acres of brilliant tulips, crossed over a bridge to Fidalgo Island, wound down a two-lane road to Bowman Bay, and spotted a banner reading *Salish Sea Native American Cultural Celebration*. As he emerged from the car and stretched, he saw several whites and Indians strolling through the park. A woman was displaying cedar bark weavings and a man was playing a flute. A large canoe with a high prow was beached facing the shore, and the cobbled beach fringed a picturesque bay. Opening the back door, he unhooked the baby's carrier and lifted it out. "Up you go, little one."

Adele hurried over. "Victor. I'm so glad you came, but I'm sorry Kate couldn't. How was your drive?"

"Traffic sucked on I-5, but your directions were good, and those flower fields were awesome. It's beautiful here," he said, looking around. "Thanks for inviting me."

"You're welcome. Bowman Bay is one of my favorite places. Come on," she said, taking his arm. "Let me show you around."

She led him to an open cooking tent where a young man and an older woman were grilling salmon. "This is my friend Victor," she told them, "and his daughter Little Eagle. They're Utes, and they just moved here from Colorado. Victor, this is my cousin Willie Campbell and my mother Vi Swiftcurrent."

Victor nodded. "Glad to meet you."

"Welcome," Vi said, smiling. "Glad to meet you, too. Do you like salmon?"

He shrugged. "I don't know. I've never tried it."

"You're kidding!" Vi said. "You're in for a treat." Grabbing a pair of tongs, she plucked a chunk of salmon off the grill, slid it onto a plate, and passed it to Willie.

"Corn on the cob?" Willie asked.

"You bet," Victor said, setting Little Eagle's carrier down on the table.

Willie set an ear of foil-wrapped corn on Victor's plate and handed it over.

As Vi wiggled her fingers at the baby, Little Eagle giggled. "Your little girl's precious," she said. "I doubt I'll ever be a grandma since my Adele doesn't want kids."

Adele rolled her eyes. "Mom, I never said that. I said I didn't want to have them with the wrong guy. Besides, I'm too busy being an artist to have kids now."

The silver-haired woman sighed. "I love you, honey, and I know your artwork's important to you, but you're not getting any younger."

"How much do I owe you?" Victor asked.

"Ten bucks," Vi said. "Beverages are included. They're outside on that table."

Taking out his wallet, Victor pulled out a ten, handed it to Vi, and bent to pick up Little Eagle. "Aren't you eating?" he asked Adele.

"I've already eaten, but I could use some coffee. Let's go find a place to sit." She led him to a picnic table. "Would you like coffee, water, or lemonade?"

"Coffee with cream." He set the baby down, sat beside her, and unwrapped his corn.

Adele returned minutes later with two cups of coffee. "I needed more caffeine," she said, handing him a fork and his coffee. "I've been up since 5:30 getting ready for this thing."

"Wow," he said, biting into the succulent salmon. "This is delicious."

"Glad you like it," she said, sipping her coffee. "We caught it ourselves."

"Sounds like your mom's pressuring you to get married and have kids."

"Yeah," Adele said, "but I was already married once. Joseph was an alcoholic and wouldn't stop drinking, so I divorced him. That's him behind us in the forest."

Peering into the woods, Victor saw a tall Indian about thirty feet away, drinking from a paper sack and scowling at them. "That guy looks angry."

"Oh, he is," she muttered. "He's still pissed off at me for divorcing him. He lives here on the reservation, and he stalks me whenever I come up here."

"Too bad," Victor said, reaching for his coffee. "So you're still not free of him."

She sighed. "Not really. I feel much freer when I'm down in Seattle."

"He's moving away now," he said, biting into his corn. "Man, this is good, too."

Victor finished eating and fed Little Eagle from her bottle. "Let's go down to the water," he said, hoisting her carrier. They made their way to the gravel beach, and Adele pointed southward across the bay. "See those mountains? They're the Olympics."

"Very impressive. I like being here on the ocean."

"We're not on the ocean, exactly," she said. "We're on Puget Sound, which is a huge saltwater sea that connects to the Pacific. The Native people call it the Salish Sea, so that's why we call ourselves the Salish Sea First Nations. You probably saw the banner."

"Well, it feels like the ocean to me," he said, catching a whiff of the baby's dirty diaper. "Be right back. I've got to go to the car and change her." Ten minutes later he returned with Little Eagle dozing in her carrier and Mouse tucked in his shirt pocket.

Adele shot him a quizzical look. "Cute mouse, but why'd you bring it?"

"She insisted on coming. She's like a dog when you jiggle the car keys." *Perhaps later I'll tell her that Mouse is a shapeshifter.*

Adele laughed. "Whatever. It looks like Willie and one of the rangers are getting ready to take the canoe out. If you want to go with them, I'd be glad to watch Eagle."

Victor glanced down the beach where two men were passing out life vests and helping several people climb aboard. "Are you sure? Do you know about babies?"

"Of course I do. I take care of my little nieces and nephews all the time."

"Okay," he said, handing the carrier to Adele and turning to go. "Thanks. If she wakes up, give her the rest of that bottle."

As he approached the canoe, he could see it was about twenty feet long and made of wood-hued fiberglass, with a raised black-and-red painted prow. Floating in shallow water, facing the shore, with its prow grounded in the gravel, the canoe already had ten people on board and a park ranger sitting in its stern.

"I'm going with you," he told Willie as he hurried toward him. "Tell me what to do."

"First, you snap this floatation device on," Willie said, handing him a type of vest. "Then you roll up your pants, take off your shoes, wade out into the water, and climb in." Willie kicked off his sandals and waded in.

Victor shrugged into the vest but didn't fasten it, being careful not to squish Mouse. "Here goes." Rolling up his pants, he slipped off his shoes and stepped into the water. "Wow, that's cold!"

Willie steadied the canoe for him. "Sit right here in the middle. We're seating people by weight to keep it stable."

As Victor crawled in, he felt the boat rock beneath him and gripped its side to steady it. He sat down and waved to Adele. She smiled and waved back, but her smile turned to a frown as her ex-husband walked down the beach, waded out, climbed into the canoe, and slumped down beside Victor. Willie took his seat at the front.

"Okay," Willie said, "grab your paddle, and do what I say. We have to get this canoe turned around now."

Fourteen paddles plunged into the water. While others on the beach helped push the canoe off, Willie had people on one side paddle backward while those on the other side paddled forward. As they turned and headed from shore, Victor stroked in sync with the others, and they put their backs into it as they glided to the middle of the bay.

"Good!" Willie cried, setting down his paddle. "Let's rest now and just be on the water."

Victor sat there, feeling the canoe bobbing beneath him like a living creature. He spotted fish swimming in the sparkling water and an eagle perching in a nearby tree.

Willie smiled. "Thanks for coming. Now, if you want to join us, we'll tell each other our names and where we come from. My name's Willie, I'm a member of the Swinomish tribe, and I'm grateful to be out here on the water on such a beautiful day."

"My name's Victor," he said, "and I'm a Tabeguache Ute from Colorado. I've never *seen* so much water, and I'm amazed to be out on it. I'm happy to be here."

"I'm Joseph," Adele's ex-husband said from his seat beside Victor. "I'm Swinomish, and glad to be here."

Others sitting behind Victor spoke, some Native and some white.

"I'm Glen," the park ranger said from the stern. "I'm Irish and German, and also happy to be here."

Just then, another large canoe rounded a point, paddled by several muscular Native men and women. They turned toward them, smiled, and raised their paddles in greeting.

"That's our rowing crew," Willie said, raising his own paddle, "and they're out here practicing for our annual canoe journey when Northwest tribes gather together. Every year, over 100 of our canoes travel from their home territories to a host nation, with stops at indigenous places along the way for cultural sharing and celebration. This year they'll be paddling to some host territories in British Columbia. If you bought our salmon lunch today, you helped us raise money for them, so thank you."

As Victor watched the other canoe head to shore, he felt something nudge his leg.

"Stay away from Adele," Joseph muttered.

"No way," Victor said, keeping his voice low. "She's my friend, and she's not your wife anymore."

"I'm warning you," Joseph added. "Back off."

"Leave me alone," Victor said, turning away to watch the Native crew. Suddenly he felt a shove and saw the water rising toward him. He plunged down into the frigid bay, kicking and thrashing as water rushed into his lungs. His flotation vest slid off. He felt a surge of current and saw a dark shape.

He kicked his legs and burst to the surface. "Help!" he sputtered. "Can't swim!" His chest tightened. His heart pounded. Victor sank back down, his lungs screaming for air, and felt a smooth shape beneath him, nudging him upward. As it lifted him up, he broke through the surface and hands reached out to haul him aboard. While he sputtered and gagged, he saw a huge creature rise above the water nearby and peer at him. Everyone stared. Some gasped. The other canoe's rowers stopped paddling and watched.

"What kind of fish is that?" Victor asked, trying to catch his breath. He stared at the black and white behemoth bobbing vertically in the water.

"It's not a fish," Willie said, clearly astonished. "It's a killer whale, but I've never seen one rescue a person like that. It's spy-hopping to watch you." He glared at Joseph. "Joseph! What's wrong with you? Apologize!"

Joseph turned his bloodshot eyes on Victor and spat out, "*Sorry.*"

"Yeah, right," Victor said, coughing up more water. He gulped in air, trying to calm his pounding heart. He'd been drowning a minute ago, and this whale had somehow saved him. It was studying him now with those dark, intelligent eyes, looking eerily familiar. It blew a plume of spray out its blowhole and slipped down into the sea.

"Are you okay?" Willie asked.

"I'm cold," Victor said, shivering. He felt a blanket envelop his shoulders.

"Let's go," Willie said, snatching up his paddle. "We've got to warm you up."

As the canoe turned to head for shore, Victor caught a glimpse of rushing water alongside and saw a blur splash against him, then felt something warm and furry crawl beneath his blanket. He smiled. *Whale had been Mouse.*

———————

Stillness surrounded him with a hint of whispers. Evening descended with its subtle light. A sea breeze floated through the open window, carrying the scent of fish and the cries of gulls. Victor opened his eyes onto a room painted a comforting blue, with lace curtains wafting inward. Adele sat in a chair beside the bed, sketching him.

"Where am I?" he asked, leaning up on one elbow. "How long was I out?"

Adele put her pencil down and glanced at her watch. "You're at my mom's house on the reservation. You've been asleep almost three hours, and you dropped off right after we fed you. Remember the soup?"

He sat up and stared at the sunset. "I do. Fish soup, wasn't it?"

"Yes," she said, closing her sketchbook. "I made it myself. Feeling better?"

He yawned. "A lot better. I've got to call Kate, though, since she'll be worried."

Adele stood up and stretched. "You're welcome to stay here with us tonight if you don't want to drive home in the dark. The interstate will be bad Saturday night, especially during tulip festival. Actually, it'll be bad tomorrow, too, but at least you'll be rested."

Staying here overnight with Adele might push Kate over the edge, but the offer was tempting. "That's a thought, thanks. Where's Little Eagle?"

"In the living room, watching TV with Mom and Willie. Mom wants to keep her."

He smiled. "She often has that effect on women." He peeked beneath the covers, relieved to see he wasn't naked. "I don't remember putting these sweatpants and tee-shirt on."

"Willie helped you. There's a sweatshirt right beside you if you're cold."

He grabbed the sweatshirt, tugged it on, and eased out of bed. "Thanks for helping me after the...you know."

"The thing with the whale? I saw it from the beach. Everyone's talking about it."

"It was my mouse," he said. "She often shapeshifts into other animals."

Adele's eyebrows arched. "You have a shapeshifting mouse?"

He nodded. "She only does it when we're in danger or when she feels threatened. She must've felt threatened when Joseph pushed us into the water."

"I'm so sorry," Adele said, touching his arm. "He's horribly jealous."

"It's not your fault. Where *is* Mouse, anyway?"

"Hanging out with the others. They fed her some salmon and fixed up a shoebox."

He laughed. "She'll love that. Can I use your phone to call Kate?"

"Sure," she said, pulling out her phone. "Just punch in the number and tap this icon when you're finished. I'll give you some privacy." She handed it to him and left.

After entering her number, he listened to it ring until the machine came on: "Hi, this is Kate," the recording said. "Sorry I missed you. Please leave a message." When the machine beeped, he said, "Kate, I'm still up here on Fidalgo Island with Adele and her family. I fell out of a canoe into the water and got chilled, but I'm okay now. They've invited me to stay here tonight, but I didn't want you to worry. Call me. Bye." He set the phone on the bed, went over to the window, and peered out at the sunset. Why should he rush home if he could stay here, get a good night's sleep, and go back tomorrow? He imagined Kate over at Mark's house and felt a twinge of jealousy.

As the sunset flamed to orange and crimson, he went out to join the others.

———————

They passed the evening sitting around a blazing fire in Vi's backyard, eating popcorn and drinking hot chocolate. Little Eagle dozed in her carrier on one side of Victor with Mouse curled on her lap, and Adele sat on his other side. Vi and Willie sat across from them.

"More popcorn?" Vi asked, passing Victor a large bowl.

"Thanks." He poured popcorn into his own bowl before passing it to Adele.

"I'm glad you decided to stay over," Vi said.

"Me, too," he said, sipping his hot chocolate. "Thanks for putting me up."

Vi smiled. "You're welcome. What happened today with the whale was magical. It reminds me of that time years ago when I saw a seal change into a woman."

"Adele mentioned that, but she also said she didn't believe you before today."

"No, she didn't," Vi said, frowning at Adele. "For an artist, my daughter can be amazingly short on imagination." She glanced at Mouse. "Your little mouse is obviously a powerful shapeshifter. Has she ever changed into other animals?"

Victor nodded. "When we're at home in Colorado she stays a grizzly, but lately she's become a mouse and a hawk. She changes forms to protect herself or her people."

"Her people?" Vi asked. "Who else does she protect?"

"Little Eagle and my girlfriend Kate. She saw Mouse change into a woman once."

Vi studied the fire and munched her popcorn. "I see. Since we're by the ocean, it makes sense she'd become a sea creature. Has Adele told you much about our culture?"

He shrugged. "A little. She explained about the moons in her paintings."

"That's a good start," Vi said. "This month is April, a time of emergence."

"It's the same in my culture," Victor said. "We host our Bear Dance in the springtime, to celebrate the bears emerging from their caves after the long winter."

"April's moon is called Moon of the Whistling Robins," Vi added, "when we celebrate the music of springtime. During this moon we harvest shellfish, build canoes, and weave baskets. Chinook runs begin in April, but their May runs are much stronger."

"Is chinook another name for the whale we saw today?" he asked.

Vi laughed. "No, a chinook is a type of salmon. There are five different kinds."

"I'm beginning to realize you have powerful sea spirits here. Do the Swinomish always stay by the sea, or do they travel with the seasons to follow their game animals?"

"We stay by the sea," she said, "and our game swims to us. There are many different whales, and killer whales frequent our waters at various times of year—some are permanent residents and others migrate up and down the coast. We Northwest tribes paint our animals on our canoes to honor them and to bring us good fortune when we hunt. Did you notice that the prow of the canoe you were in was painted?"

Victor nodded. "Yes. I'm fascinated by your artwork. It's so bold and striking."

"Listen, Victor," Adele said. "When you get more artwork of your own together you could exhibit here at our tribal center. It would be terrific exposure for you."

He turned and studied her, admiring how her dark eyes caught the firelight. She was a true Indian beauty, with ample curves, high cheekbones, and jet-black hair. "How can I exhibit at your tribal center if I'm not Swinomish?"

Willie laughed. "Are you kidding? After what happened today, half of our tribe wants to adopt you. You earned major indigenous points with that whale rescue."

"We're having an all-tribal show in October that you could enter," Adele said. "I'm on the admission's committee, and I'm pretty sure I could get you in."

He stared at the flames, pausing before he spoke. "Unfortunately, Kate and I will probably be gone by then. We're planning to move back to Colorado by fall."

She frowned. "But you just moved here."

He nodded. "I know, but we're determined to live there. Kate's going to quit her teaching job and sell her house so we can go back and run her grandparents' business."

"I didn't know that. Why didn't you tell me?"

"Sorry," he said. "I meant to, but I couldn't find the right words. I thought you wouldn't help me get into galleries if you knew I was moving. I didn't mean to deceive you."

"I see," she said, and sighed. "Well, I'm sorry you're leaving, but you can still apply for that show. We can ship your artwork back to you if it doesn't sell, but based on what I've seen, I think it will. You need to get your name out there among the tribes."

"Thanks," he said, finishing his hot chocolate. "Maybe I'll apply. I'm sorry I didn't tell you we were moving."

She reached over and squeezed his hand. "That's okay, we can still be friends. After all, I owe you one. You helped me get my purse back."

"Okay, I'd like that." *And I also like feeling your hand on mine.*

"I'm going in," Vi said, getting up. She picked up her bowl and turned to go.

"'Night, Mom," Adele said. "I'll finish cleaning up."

"Goodnight all," Vi said, and headed inside.

"'Night, Aunt Vi," Willie said, rising from his chair. "Victor, I'd like to show you my horses. Do you like to ride?"

"Absolutely. I've missed riding since I've come here."

"Good," Willie said. "We could go tomorrow afternoon if the weather holds and you're still here. I'll call you in the morning. 'Night."

"'Night." Victor watched Willie amble off and get into his truck, then looked up at the sky and saw a shooting star. "Look, it's an omen."

Adele followed his gaze. "Maybe it means you won't sell the house for a while, but since places near Seattle are selling like hotcakes, it'll probably sell right away."

They sat there in silence, watching the fire burn down to embers. Clouds sailed across the moon. It began to sprinkle, pattering on their dishes.

"We should go in," Adele said. "It's starting to rain." She gathered up the dishes.

As Victor picked up the baby's carrier and followed Adele into the kitchen, he caught a whiff of her perfume, something light and flowery.

"Do you want to watch a movie?" she asked, setting the dirty dishes in the sink.

"Okay. How about something with Indians?"

"I think I can find something." Going into the living room, she opened a cabinet beneath the TV. "Let's see, we've got *Little Big*

Man, *Last of the Mohicans, Smoke Signals*, and *Dances with Wolves*. Which one sounds good to you?"

"What's *Dances with Wolves* about?"

"You've never seen it? It's a good one, but it's heartbreaking. It's about a white Civil War soldier who falls in love with an Indian woman. No, I forgot, they're both white, but it's still good. The Indian actor Graham Greene's in it, and he's awesome. It shows what happened to the Sioux in the 1860s when the whites started encroaching on their lands."

"Sounds intriguing; let's watch that one. Can we have more popcorn?"

"Sure, I'll make some. Do you want a beer? I'm having one."

"Okay, but first I need to change Eagle and put her to down to sleep."

"Take your time," she said, turning toward the kitchen. "There's a portable crib she can use in the closet in the hall. My niece sleeps in it when she comes to visit. You can change her on the counter in the bathroom."

"Great," he said, heading off. "Come on, little one. Let's get you to bed."

———————

Soldiers were burning their village, killing their warriors, and raping their women. Within the havoc of gunshots and screaming came an odd mechanical jingling.

"Wake up," Adele said, shaking his shoulder. "Here he is, Kate. Bye." She handed him the phone and left the living room.

"Hi," he mumbled, trying to shake off his dream.

"Hi," Kate said. "Is it too late to call?"

"What time is it?" he asked, yawning.

"It's almost ten; sorry. I left my phone at the restaurant where we ate dinner, and I had to go back for it, so I just got your message. Did you have fun at the gathering?"

"I did. Did you have a good time sailing?"

"Yes. So, you fell out of a canoe?"

He yawned again. "Mouse and I both did, actually, since she was in my pocket at the time. She changed into a killer whale and saved me from drowning."

"Wow! Did anyone see it?"

He laughed. "Lots of people. It was awesome."

"I'll bet. You'll have to tell me more about it. Were you asleep when I called?"

"Yeah. Adele and I fell asleep on the couch watching *Dances with Wolves*."

There was a long pause, and she said, "Really. So, it's just you and Adele there?"

"No, it's not, so don't worry. Her mom Vi was with us, but she went to bed. Her cousin Willie came over for a few hours, but he went home. He invited me to go riding tomorrow if the weather's good, so I'm hoping to do that before I come home."

"When do you plan to go?"

"I'm not sure yet, he's going to call in the morning. Sometime in the afternoon."

"But you said you'd help me plant those flowerbeds tomorrow and maybe paint the downstairs bathroom. Dammit, I'm sorry. I promised to back off about doing chores."

He took a deep breath in, and let it out. "I haven't been riding for weeks, Kate."

"You're right, and you should go if you can. Maybe I'll ask Mark to help me."

"Mark?" he said, frowning. "Don't ask him. I'll do it, just maybe not tomorrow."

"I'm glad you're staying over, but what time do you think you'll be home?"

"I don't know exactly, but I want to leave before dark. I miss you."

"I miss you, too. Call me before you leave if you can, so I don't worry."

"Okay, I'll try. See you tomorrow. 'Night."

"'Night," she said, and hung up.

"So," Adele said as she sauntered in. "Is Kate okay with your staying here?"

He nodded. "Yeah, but she wanted me to help her with some chores tomorrow."

"I see. But you'd rather go riding, I guess."

"Uh-huh," he said, picking up the DVD case and studying it. "This was one of the saddest movies I've ever seen. The characters were good, but the Sioux got screwed."

Adele nodded. "At least the Swinomish were allowed to stay in our homelands, and we didn't get shipped off to some godawful desert. What happened to the Utes?"

He got up off the couch and walked to the open window. A steady rain was falling, carrying the scent of flowers. "The Utes got forced onto reservations. The one in southern Colorado isn't bad, but I've heard the one in Utah's a wasteland."

"A lot of tribes got the poorest land," she said, joining him at the window. "If it keeps raining like this, you won't go riding tomorrow. Smells good though, doesn't it?"

"It does." *She's standing much too close.*

"'Night, Victor," she said, leaning closer. "Hope you sleep well." She turned and walked away.

"'Night." He stood at the window a little longer, smelling the rain.

————————

Light filtered through the hole in his tepee, carrying the aroma of wood smoke from the morning's cooking fires. As Victor turned over and stretched, he saw Adele sleeping beside him, naked under their bison robe, her arm across his chest. Feeling a pressure against his back, he turned over to see Kate asleep on his other side.

He stared up at the smoke hole, watching dust motes drift down. He listened to the sounds coming from outside—quiet voices talking, spoons scraping cast iron skillets, people shuffling by in moccasins. How had this happened? Was he back in time again? Did he have two wives? It wasn't uncommon for a Ute to have two wives, but it was rare for a white woman to share a husband with an Indian one. Especially a Swinomish one.

As he watched, he noticed fish swimming through the dust motes, like salmon in a vertical stream. As they swam, they spun faster and faster, creating their own current. Fish swimming through air. Wives sharing his bed. What was happening?

As the hide door flapped open, Whale poked her head in. She swam around and around, filling the tepee with water. He tried to scream, but instead gulped in water.

"Victor," a woman's voice whispered.

"What?" He swam toward wakefulness like a fish rising to the surface. As he opened his eyes, he saw dim light coming through the window, water streaming down its glass, and Adele standing beside him in pajamas and a bathrobe.

"Wake up," she said. "You're dreaming."

"Oh." He pulled the covers up around him, trying to remember if he'd fallen asleep naked. "Where am I?"

"You're at my mom's house, remember? Do you want a salmon omelet?"

Good. We aren't back in time, we aren't in a tepee, and we aren't married, but staying here is like being in an encampment:

lots of togetherness, but little privacy. "I've never had a salmon omelet before, but it sounds good. Where's Eagle?"

"Out in the kitchen with Mom. She's already changed and fed her."

He rubbed his eyes. "Okay, I'm coming. Just give me a minute to dress."

Adele gave his foot a squeeze through the covers. "It'll be ready in ten minutes."

He lay there after she left, listening to rain hammer on the roof. Feeling Mouse nudge his hand, he smiled and rubbed her ears. *Good. She's Mouse, not Whale, and the room isn't filling with water. Dreams could be the window to the soul or the window to a nightmare, and having both Kate and Adele for wives would be a definite nightmare.*

During breakfast he discovered he liked salmon omelets and onion bagels slathered with cream cheese. Willie called to cancel because he'd caught a cold and they couldn't ride in such a storm, but he invited Victor back up for another visit. After they finished eating, he rose from the table and helped Vi carry dishes to the sink.

"Thanks for your hospitality," he said to her. "I enjoyed staying here."

"Come again," she said, grasping his hands. "You could help with the shellfish harvest next weekend or the one after. Bring your girlfriend and Eagle, and stay over."

"Maybe we will. Thanks." He smiled at Adele. "I'm glad I came."

"Me, too. On your way home, you should stop and see the tulip fields."

"Okay. I caught a glimpse of them when I drove in yesterday."

After that he'd packed, said goodbye, and driven off, but had forgotten to call Kate. He remembered twenty minutes later when he parked on a country road and lowered a window to stare at the tulips he'd rushed by yesterday. There were thousands of brilliant blossoms: fuchia and yellow, white and pink, purple and crimson. The sea of color went on for miles, and hundreds of people were out in the rain in the midst of it. Some were workers trudging through the fields in rubber boots, cutting the flowers and tying them into bundles; others were tourists, wandering around in their rain gear. A flock of white geese with black-tipped wings flew overhead, honking and honking. Victor resumed driving, but before turning onto the interstate, he stopped at a roadside market and bought a dozen tulips for Kate.

As he drove south through the congested traffic, Little Eagle dozed in the back seat and Mouse dozed on his lap. He thought of the Indians he'd met this weekend and how good it felt to be included by a tribe again. It wasn't his tribe, of course, but he'd felt welcomed, and he needed that. He resolved to return for more visits and to enter that all-tribal art show.

By the time he reached the Tulalip casino, the rain had slackened to a steady drizzle. He didn't have a cell phone, and couldn't find a working pay phone, so he couldn't call Kate. He decided he should buy one of those infernal things and learn to use it. After changing the baby and grabbing more coffee, he buckled her in and set off again.

CHAPTER NINE

During breakfast that morning at a restaurant, Kate and Mark had watched the drizzle stop and the skies clear. They'd driven to a store and bought plants, dug out the remains of last year's annuals, and revamped Kate's flower beds. Now, after three hours of steady gardening, they were covered with mud and eager to take showers.

"Looks great, Katydid," Mark said, swiping a muddy finger across her cheek. "I really like those dangly pink ones."

"The bleeding hearts?" she asked, dabbing his nose with mud. "I like them, too. They're perennials, so they'll come back next year, like the ferns." She wouldn't be here to enjoy them, but the new owners would. "Thanks for helping me," she said, trudging to the wall spigot. She hosed mud off her rubber Wellingtons, shovel, trowels, and hands.

"You're welcome," he said, stretching his arms overhead. "I could really use a shower now, so thanks for telling me to bring a change of clothes. I think we can still catch that movie." He went to the back door and kicked off his muddy boots.

"Go take your shower first, and I'll start making that lunch I promised you."

"Thanks." He stepped inside, careful not to brush against the furniture, and crossed the dining room to reach the stairs.

Setting her boots on the rubber mat outside to dry, Kate headed into the kitchen and pulled out sandwich makings as the upstairs shower came on. Sandwiches and apples weren't much of a reward for a morning's work, but it was the best she could do at short notice. She decided to shed her wet, dirty clothes for her sweats in the dryer while Mark was still showering. Padding into the adjacent laundry room, she filled the sink with water and swished in soap, stripped off her socks and tee-shirt, and tossed them in. She was peeling off her muddy jeans when she heard the garage door open and close.

"Kate?" Victor called.

"I'm in here, in the laundry room!"

Victor ambled in with Little Eagle. "Hi, gorgeous," he said, handing her a bunch of tulips. "Greetings from up north. Sorry I forgot to call, but I couldn't find a phone."

"Thanks," she said. "They're beautiful. You really should get a cell."

"I know I should," he said, setting down the baby's carrier. "What're you doing in here half naked?"

"Getting out of these filthy clothes," she said, adding her jeans to the sudsy water. "Mark came over this morning and helped me plant those flower beds. It was drizzling earlier, so we both got pretty muddy."

"You didn't have to ask Mark; I told you I'd do it. I like you without clothes," he said as he hugged her. "I missed you."

"I missed you, too. You're home early. So, you didn't go riding?"

"No. Willie caught a cold and it was pouring up there, but he invited me to come another time. Is somebody upstairs?" he asked, pulling away. "I hear water running."

"Mark's taking a shower." She grabbed her sweats from the dryer and put them on.

A door opened upstairs, and Mark called down, "Where are the towels?"

"In the hall closet!" she yelled.

Victor frowned. "Why is Mark taking a shower here?"

"I told you, we got muddy planting. And we were going to a movie afterward."

"Are you doing this because I stayed over with Adele last night?"

"Doing what? What do you mean? You didn't *sleep* with her, did you?"

"No," he snapped, "and Mark's not sleeping with you, either." He bolted out of the laundry, across the living room, and up the stairs.

"Victor, wait!" she said, tearing after him. Reaching the upstairs landing, she saw Mark wrapping a towel around his waist and glancing up just as Victor punched him. He slumped down against the wall, gripping his face as blood oozed through his fingers.

"Get out!" Victor yelled, his fists clenched. "Stay away from my Kate!"

"Stop!" she cried, kneeling down beside Mark.

Mark groaned. "Damn. I think he broke my nose."

"I'll break more than that!" Victor snarled. "Get out of my house!"

Kate glared at Victor. "What'd you hit him for? I told you nothing happened!"

"But it could've! You were both practically naked!"

"Oh, shut up!" Kate leapt up to grab a washcloth from the shower. "Try pinching your nose to stop the bleeding," she told Mark as she gave him the washcloth. "I'll drive you to the clinic if you really think it's broken."

"Damn, it hurts," Mark said. "I think you'd better."

"Don't baby him, Kate," Victor muttered. "He doesn't deserve it."

"Shut up and help me," she said. "Go get a cold pack from the freezer, wrap it in a towel, and bring it up here. We've got to stop this bleeding."

"Get it yourself," Victor said, crossing his arms.

"Victor, please!"

"No."

"Then get out! I don't want you here! This is *my* house, remember?"

"Fine," he said, turning to leave, "if that's what you want."

Kate forced herself to wait beside Mark while Victor stomped downstairs and through the living room, then opened and closed the garage door, and drove off. "Be right back," she said. Running downstairs, she wrapped a cold pack in a dish towel, ran back upstairs, and dropped to her knees beside Mark. "I'm so sorry," she said, pressing the towel against his nose.

"Victor's an asshole," he mumbled. "I don't know what you see in him."

When the bleeding finally subsided, they got dressed and hurried off to the clinic. While a doctor tended to Mark, Kate paced back and forth in the waiting area, wondering where the hell Victor had gone. He shouldn't have hit Mark, but she shouldn't have kicked him out, either. He had nowhere else to go, and he didn't have a cell phone. She had no way to contact him.

———————

"I won't apologize," Victor muttered to Little Eagle as he drove his car around the neighborhood. "*He* should apologize to *me*." He'd been foolish enough to believe a woman like Kate could love a poor Indian with very little money and a baby. He'd given up his tribe for her, traveled through time for her, and now she'd evidently chosen Mark over him—Mark, the rich guy with his expensive house on the lake and exotic vacations.

He hadn't unpacked his car since the trip up north, so he still had some of Little Eagle's baby things. He'd need to return to Kate's house for the rest if they had to leave for good, but for now he was driving around in another drizzle, wasting gas and getting hungry. Driving to an Ivar's cafe, he pulled over and parked. He'd have a big bowl of clam chowder, which would stave off his hunger while he got this crisis sorted out.

———————

After bringing Mark back to her house later that evening so she could care for him, Kate led him into the kitchen. Putting Mark's tepid ice pack in the freezer, she grabbed another one and wrapped it up. "Here you go," she said, handing it over. Mark's nose was broken, his face was mottled with bruises, and both eyes were almost swollen shut. There was no sign of Victor, and it had been hours. Where the hell had he gone?

"How do you feel?" she asked Mark.

"Groggy," he said, slumping back against the counter.

"That's from the painkillers, and you don't get any more of those until bedtime. That's part of the reason I brought you home because you'll be groggy for a while. Are you thirsty?" she asked, reaching into a cabinet for a glass.

"Yeah," he said, "and hungry, too."

"No wonder, we haven't eaten since breakfast." She filled the glass with water and handed it to him. "Do you want me to make a pizza?"

He drained his glass and nodded. "Pizza sounds great."

"Good," she said, pulling a plain cheese pizza out of the freezer. "I'll add some ham and pineapple to this and whip up a salad. You should stay home tomorrow. You know that, don't you?"

Mark was leaning against the counter with his eyes closed.

"Mark," she said, poking his chest.

"What?" he asked, opening his swollen eyes.

"Don't be a martyr. Call the sub-office. You should stay home tomorrow."

"No, I shouldn't. I'm running a make-up lab in earth science, and some of the kids need it to beef up their semester grades. I can't expect a sub to run a lab for me."

"So request Alex when you call. She just got her certification, she knows science, and she needs the work." Grabbing the wall phone, she dialed the number and handed it to Mark.

"Fine," he said, "you talked me into it. But Alex had better be available." He waited for the recording to come on, left a detailed message, and hung up.

"Come on in here," Kate said, guiding him to the couch in the living room. "Lie down and rest while I make dinner."

"Kate?" he asked, easing back against the pillows.

"What?"

He reached out and clutched her hand. "You know I love you, don't you?"

Please don't say that. "Don't be silly, Mark. That's the drugs talking."

"No, it's not. I've loved you for years, but I couldn't say it while Jon was alive and you were still married. Before he died, he asked me to take care of you. I could, you know."

She felt her heart begin to pound. "Be quiet now. Go to sleep."

"Okay," he mumbled, and closed his eyes.

As Kate watched Mark drift away, she wished he hadn't told her how he felt. It complicated her life, and her life was already too complicated. She went to the sliding door and gazed out at her newly-planted flower beds. Had Victor really left her? After what he'd done, she wasn't sure she wanted him back just yet, but she was worried about where he'd gone. She sighed and returned to the kitchen.

———————

Adjusting his binoculars, Victor sat in his car and peered across the street through the fading evening light. Mark sat inside the house with Kate, eating with her at the dining room table. Victor could go in and confront him, or maybe apologize, but he couldn't decide which because he wasn't sure what had happened. He couldn't bring himself to apologize if he wasn't wrong, and if he confronted Mark in front of Kate, she'd get even angrier. He could march right in there as though nothing had happened, but something *had* happened, hadn't it? He'd punched her friend, possibly her lover, and she'd kicked Victor out of her house. Had she kicked Little Eagle out, too? Had she stopped loving both of them?

The baby gurgled in her carrier, her poopy diaper stinking up the car. She needed to be changed, and they both needed a place to stay tonight. It was getting late now, too late to drive back up to Vi's house, and he didn't even have a phone to call her. He wanted to go inside and go to bed, and he wanted Kate back, but only if she wanted him. By the way she and Mark were acting together, it looked like she wanted him instead.

There was enough light in the dining room for Victor to see what was happening. He watched Kate pour herself a glass of wine while the scumbag sat there eating pizza, his face bruised and his eyes puffy. *Good*, Victor thought. If Mark was feeling bad enough, he might stay away from Kate, but he didn't appear to be doing so now. He appeared to be settling in.

Victor had some money with him, but the rest was inside the house, so he doubted he had enough on him for a motel room. He knew Adele was still up north, but maybe she'd let them stay at her apartment if he could reach her. He'd been there before, and it wasn't far away. Putting down his binoculars, he started the engine and drove off to find a payphone to call Adele. There had to be one somewhere.

———————

Upstairs, Mouse huddled on the bed against Cisco, enjoying his warmth. She'd been cold since yesterday when she'd fallen into the sea, and she hadn't yet gotten all of her strength back. Changing into a whale had worn her out, the long drive home had tired her more, and hearing her people argue this afternoon had exhausted her even further. Victor had taken the baby away, and Mouse was worried, but Cisco's steady purring reassured her. The man Victor had fought with was downstairs now with Kate, which disturbed Mouse, since she didn't trust him. She could change form again to scare him off, but she was just too weary. She needed to rest and build up her strength first.

———————

Kate had let Mark stay overnight in her guest bedroom since he'd been too drugged up to drive, and with his eyes so swollen, he couldn't see well enough to drive anyway. Letting him sleep in, Kate slipped off to school early and met Alex before class.

"Thanks for covering at such short notice," Kate said. "It's tough subbing at the end of the year because the kids are so squirrelly, but I'm sure you can handle it."

"No problem," Alex said. "I'm glad I could help. What's wrong with Mark?"

Kate blew out a sigh. "Basically, Victor came home unexpectedly and found Mark naked, assumed we were fooling around, and broke his nose."

Alex's eyebrows arched. "No kidding! *Were* you fooling around?"

"Of course not, you idiot. You know I love Victor."

"Okay, I get that, but why was Mark naked?"

"Because he'd helped me plant flowerbeds and we were both filthy, so he'd taken a shower and was about to dress. When Victor came home, Mark was calling downstairs for a towel and I was in the laundry room, peeling off my own clothes."

"That's weird," Alex said. "Guess I can see why Victor jumped to conclusions."

Kate shrugged. "Yeah, but it hurts that he didn't trust me." A bell rang, and she added, "We'd better get going; class is about to start. Do you have any questions?"

"No," Alex said, studying the lab Mark had left for her, "this looks pretty straightforward. You know I'm looking for a job, so if anything opens up, tell me."

"I will," Kate said. She was tempted to tell Alex she'd be leaving soon herself, but none of her friends knew that, and something stopped her. Until now she'd been sure she wanted to quit and move away, but after what happened yesterday she felt plagued by uncertainty. Victor clearly didn't trust her, and Kate wasn't sure she trusted him. Where was he now, back up north with Adele? It seemed unlikely, but possible. She yawned. "Sorry, I had a rough night. I'm two doors down if you need me. Have a good morning, Alex, and I'll see you at lunch." She headed for her classroom, determined to focus on her students. With only six weeks left before the end of school, every day counted.

———————

Victor awoke stiff and grouchy after a restless night on Adele's sofa bed. He hadn't slept well, and Little Eagle hadn't either, but apparently Adele's roommate Maria had slept just fine. He could hear her singing in the kitchen as she made breakfast and set the table. At least one of them was wide-awake and cheerful.

He began to wake up as he plowed through a hearty breakfast of scrambled eggs, toast, orange juice, and coffee. After Maria left for her job at a pottery studio, he washed the dishes, keeping an eye on the time. He'd slip into the house after Kate left for school, grab the rest of their things, and decide what to do.

When he arrived home, he was stunned to find Mark's car still parked out front. She'd taken him in, evidently, but were they sleeping in now and skipping work? Getting out of his car, he peeked in the garage window and saw Kate's car was gone. *Good.* She'd gone to school, but where was Mark? Returning to the car to retrieve Little Eagle, he carried her to the house, unlocked the front door, and tiptoed in. Creeping upstairs, he heard snoring coming from the guest bedroom, so he opened the door and discovered Mark sleeping. He hovered on the second-story landing, holding the baby and weighing his options. He still loved Kate, but now he didn't trust her. *Why is Mark still here?*

Entering their bedroom, he saw the remnants of their former life—their clothes in the closet, their pajamas on the back of the door, their books resting on the nightstand. Kate's bed was neatly made, but that didn't mean she hadn't shared it. Victor had tried hard to blend into her world, but now he must admit he didn't belong here. He must admit she preferred Mark. Victor glanced at Mouse, huddled on the bed beside Cisco.

"It's time to go home, Mouse," he said.

She blinked and crept toward him.

———————

Throughout the day Kate had felt burdened by a sense of loneliness. While she could still teach, she hadn't taught well, and while she could still answer questions, she hadn't answered them completely. She felt confused and disjointed, like a part of her was unraveling, but she chalked it up to fatigue and her argument with Victor. At lunch she called to check on Mark—he'd slept all morning and was feeling a little better. After she finished teaching, she prepared for tomorrow's classes and headed home. When she arrived Mark was reading on the couch, his nose already turning a mottled burgundy.

"Hi," he said, glancing up from a book. "How'd Alex do?"

Kate set down her tote bag. "She did great, and the kids behaved themselves. I brought some of those labs home so you can grade them if you're feeling up to it." It felt weird having Mark waiting at home for her, instead of Victor.

"Good," he said. "I'll grade some later. Feel like going for an amble around the block? Just a little one, 'cause I'm still wobbly, but I need to get some fresh air."

"Sure," she said, heading toward the stairs. "Let me change first." As she entered the bedroom, she glanced at her machine, but there was no message from Victor. Not surprising, since he didn't own a phone, but he could've found a payphone. She was hanging up her slacks when it hit her: his clothes and shoes were gone. She spun around: his books and pajamas were gone, and the baby's things. She ran into the den where he painted, her heart pounding. All of his art supplies were missing. Mouse was missing.

Feeling her heart clench, she ran back to the bedroom. She found a note on her dresser, a piece of folded sketching paper addressed to her with a paper clip holding it closed. As she opened it, she realized he'd never written to her before. He'd never had to.

Kate,

By the time you get this, I'll be far away. I've tried to fit in here, but I don't belong in your world. It's clear you've chosen Mark, so I must leave. I'm taking Little Eagle home. This handprint is her good-bye wave to you. I will always love you.

Victor

At the bottom of the page was a tiny handprint traced in red crayon. Clutching the note to her chest, Kate felt her knees buckle as she sank to the floor and felt the tears begin to come.

Victor had left her.

CHAPTER TEN

By late afternoon Victor had made a decent start on his journey. After leaving Kate's house, he'd studied a map to figure out how to get to the ocean since he was determined to see it before he left the West Coast. He'd stopped to buy provisions and a baby backpack for Little Eagle and driven south along I-5 through Washington's interior.

Victor's heart ached for Kate, but he was heading home to his people, and they would help smooth the jagged edges of his grief. Caring for Little Eagle would give his life purpose, and he would somehow learn to live with this hole in his heart. He drove with Mouse beside him and the baby behind him, waving at the rush of trees she glimpsed through the window. Washington state had so many trees, much too many to get a decent view. After several tedious hours, he turned west, drove through more trees to the coast, and found a campground near the ocean. At the entrance kiosk, he paid the extra money for a camping structure called a yurt and drove around the loop to find it. Leaving his car, he unlocked the yurt's door, laid out his sleeping bag, and surveyed the strange, round dwelling. Relocking the door, he put the baby into her new backpack and followed the sound of the surf to the ocean.

He crested a dune and saw the vast expanse of water, and it nearly took his breath away. As he walked along the shore in the muted evening sunlight, he watched the waves rolling in and out, kicked off his shoes and felt the sand between his toes. Seagulls cried overhead, diving and plunging into the ocean. The wind cuffed him like a playful friend. As each wave departed to begin its journey back to deeper water, little rivulets formed at his bare feet. Little crabs scuttled here and there across the sand. Eventually the sun sunk lower in the sky, becoming a misshapen golden egg dangling on the horizon. As he watched, it slipped lower and lower, flamed to a brilliant crimson, and slipped down beneath the surface.

He closed his eyes. Surrounded by the twilight, the pounding surf filled his ears like a lullaby. This ocean was alive, and its breathing soothed the pain in his aching heart.

———————

After walking with Mark, Kate was relieved to watch him drive away so she could think more clearly. Victor had left her without a goodbye kiss, without a chance to say goodbye to Little Eagle. *To hell with him!* she thought as she changed the sheets Mark had slept in. "Let him go!" she muttered as she ate her lonely dinner. To pass the time she graded papers and did laundry, but as she started the washing machine she could see how things might've looked to Victor when he came home—her standing there in the laundry room, practically naked, and Mark calling from upstairs, completely naked.

After grading until her eyes ached, she went to bed but tossed and turned for over an hour. It was after ten when she swallowed her pride and called Adele.

"Hello?" Adele said.

"It's Kate. Sorry to call so late, but is Victor there?"

"No, he's not. He stayed in my apartment last night, but he left this morning."

Wonderful, so he'd stayed with her last night. I drove him into Adele's arms. "Do you have any idea where he might've gone?"

"No. So, he's not with you?"

Her stomach tightened. "No. We had a big argument."

"I heard about that. Maybe he's gone out to the coast. My roommate gave him the names of some campgrounds near Long Beach and Astoria. Sorry, that's all I know."

"I'm sure he'll call eventually. Thanks, Adele. Again, I'm sorry to call so late."

"That's okay, I wasn't asleep yet. 'Night, Kate."

" 'Night." She sat in bed petting Cisco, acutely aware of her loneliness. Victor was gone, and he wasn't coming back. She felt torn into tiny pieces.

———————

Mouse settled in on the sleeping bag next to Victor, listening to the comforting sound of his heartbeat. It was warm inside this strange tent, with the heater thrumming on the wall and the ocean pounding on the nearby beach. Mouse was learning to love the ocean and its playful wind. When they'd gone walking earlier, it had threatened to blow her tiny body off the edge of the world, but Victor had sheltered her beneath his jacket. He'd protected her like she'd protected him, so she felt safe here. She curled up on her side and went to sleep.

———————

They stayed three days and nights by the ocean. Invigorated by the sea air and the open vistas, Victor walked the beach for hours, carrying the baby on his back while Mouse changed into a gull and flew above them. When he grew tired, he spread a blanket on the sand and sketched while the baby slept, or he just sat staring at the waves. He slept when he was tired and ate when he was hungry. He savored the solitude, as the campground was almost deserted during the week and few people were out walking. Aside from the constant pain of missing Kate, his sojourn at the sea was a fine one.

The yurt had its own heat and electricity, so it was cozy, and he cooked meals on his camping stove. It had a couch to sit on, a table to eat on, and a bunk with a mattress to lie on. It was like a large, round tepee without a smoke hole, except it was taller, wider, and made of heavy vinyl. He had to get used to tepees again; he had to get used to dwellings smaller than houses.

On his third and final morning, Victor took a last walk on the beach to say goodbye to the amazing ocean. He cradled Little Eagle in his arms and took a long, warm shower in the bathroom. After packing up their things, he swept out the yurt with the broom, dropped the key in the box by the campground entrance, and drove off. He intended to drive east along the Columbia River through the section he and Kate had bypassed weeks ago. Spotting a payphone, he was tempted to call her but was afraid he'd lose his nerve and go running back to her. If she loved Mark now, nothing he could say would make things right again; nothing he could say would make her love him. He drove east along the mighty river—in and out of forests, past a bustling lumber mill, past a noisy city. He drove on and on, gripping the steering wheel, putting more distance between them.

———————

Over the past three days since Victor left, Kate had gone to work to keep sane, eaten to keep her strength up, and slept very little. After teaching all day, she took long walks or did chores to wear herself out, but as tired as she got, she still couldn't sleep. She'd lie there for hours, yearning for Victor. When that got old, she'd drag herself out of bed to make toast and warm milk, but when she tried to sleep again, she couldn't. Usually in the wee hours she'd drop off and dream of him. He'd be walking along a beach, lying in a tent, or driving away from her, his car receding into the foggy distance. When she awoke, she was sobbing, aching to hold him. As she slogged through each interminable day, she'd wonder where he was and what he was doing. Hoping against hope, she would will him to find a payphone and call, but he never did. When she was at work, she managed to maintain a sense of normalcy, but at home she wandered through the house, talking aloud to him.

"I'm sorry I kicked you out," she'd say. "I miss you. Come back to me." Or, she'd regret her suspicions about Adele and say, "You said you didn't sleep with her, but I didn't believe you, and I'm sorry. I need to hear from you. Find a phone and call me."

When Mark returned to school two days after the fight, his face mottled with angry bruises, she avoided him. She couldn't tell him she still loved Victor because saying it would hurt too much. She could see he was confused by her avoidance since he hadn't done anything wrong. He'd only come over to help her plant those damn flowers.

By the third day after Victor left, she'd started pretending he was away on a camping trip, enjoying the ocean and doing artwork. For all she knew, he was, and he'd be back by this weekend with several new sketches and stories to tell. She tried to pretend he'd return, but in her heart she knew it wouldn't happen. In her heart she knew he'd really left her.

—————————

Colorado City — 1863

Sometimes late at night, when the saloon was quiet and she was weary, Doozie would dream about the future she'd passed up for this dump. When she scowled at the sink full of dirty glasses to wash and the filthy floor that needed sweeping, she felt like a damn fool. In the cave before he'd left, Victor had offered to spirit her away to the future time, but she'd turned him down to stay here and run this infernal saloon.

She could hire a boy to do these chores since her wounded shoulder still pained her, but she could manage well enough, and she felt it prudent to save the money. Besides, she figured the more she took charge the more customers regarded her as the owner, not just one of the girls. Cash had gotten tighter since they'd buried Homer, as his funeral had cost a bundle and the girls had begged the day off to go to it. She also needed a new piano since the old one's pieces littered the meadow where that bastard Blackstone had shot it up and murdered Homer.

That meadow, dotted with wildflowers and Homer's red blood. That cave, where she'd expected to die but had awakened to the Utes tending her. She hoped Victor had made it through the passage to Kate since a love like theirs was something to live for.

As she took a kettle from the wood stove and poured scalding water into the sink full of dirty glasses, she wondered what that future time was really like. Did Kate live in a proper house with a picket fence and running water? Did she have a fine horse and a passel of fine friends? When Kate was teaching her to read, she'd said she taught girls her age, but Doozie was no girl. While only sixteen, she was a struggling saloon-keep and grieving widow, not some girlish ninny. If she'd gone to the future, would folks guess she'd been a whore?

Pumping cold water into the sink, she added soap and swished it into suds. She removed her sling and started washing glasses, scanning the room as she worked. The girls sashayed around the gaming tables, cruising for business while gamblers tugged on their beers. Two old codgers played a quiet game of chess. This was her life now, and while it was a mite pitiful, she was determined to make it better. It would take time, but she had plenty of that; it would take money, but she could earn it. Seeing a dandy reading a broadsheet, she resolved to practice her reading tonight—if she wasn't too exhausted.

———————

When Victor reached the cut-off in eastern Oregon for the northern route to Yellowstone, he realized he should check the weather before deciding whether to go there. While he was eager to see the park, he wouldn't camp there if it was still wintry, and early May could still be wintry that far north. Pulling into a café for dinner, he hauled Little Eagle to the bathroom to change her. When he emerged, he saw a young man pecking away on his laptop at a nearby table.

"Hi," Victor said, setting the baby's carrier down at the next table.

The young man glanced at him and smiled. "How's it going?"

"Good. May I ask you a favor?"

"Shoot."

"Could you check the weather up in Yellowstone? I'm considering going camping up there for a few days."

"No problem," he said, bending his head to the task.

A waitress sauntered over and handed him a menu. "Cute baby."

"Thanks," he said. "If I give you a bottle of her formula, could you heat it up?"

"Sure. I'll do that when you order. Today's special is chicken enchiladas, but I'll give you a few minutes to study the menu."

The young man peered at Victor over his wire-rimmed glasses. "The weather in Yellowstone sucks. It's dropping into the twenties tonight, and they're predicting more snow this week. I wouldn't camp up there in the spring even if it did get warmer since the grizzlies will be coming out of hibernation soon and they'll be cranky."

Victor knew this, of course, but seeing grizzlies was one of the reasons he wanted to go there. He'd seen Bear intimidate black bears, but he didn't know how she behaved around grizzlies. It would be interesting to watch, but it was too cold to take the baby camping. He wiped the spit off her chin and took her bottle out of his pack. "Thanks for checking. Guess I won't be going, but I'll buy you a piece of pie for helping me."

"That's nice, dude. Thanks."

The waitress headed over. "All set?"

"I'll take the special," Victor said, handing her the bottle. "Thanks for heating this up for me. She likes it lukewarm. What kind of pie do you have?"

"We've got Dutch apple, boysenberry, lemon meringue, cherry, and pecan."

"I'll take Dutch apple, heated, with a scoop of vanilla, and coffee with cream later. Give my friend here whatever kind of pie he wants."

He smiled. "A slice of pecan with a scoop of vanilla, please."

"Be right back," she said, smiling at the baby until she giggled.

"I'm Victor," he said, extending his hand to the young man.

"I'm Daniel," he said, shaking it.

Pulling a jar of applesauce from his pack, Victor unscrewed it and offered a spoonful to Little Eagle. She lunged at it, apparently ravenous. Soon the waitress returned with their food, and they ate as evening light streamed through the window. Victor decided to drive on until he found a campground.

———————

By the end of the week Kate was sleep-deprived, depressed, and lonely, so when Mark invited her to a T.G.I.F. party, she jumped at the chance, despite the fact she'd been avoiding him. She needed the company, and spending time with her friends would cheer her up. When she arrived they were playing disc golf in the backyard, so she went out and joined them. Jake was looking for his disc in some Oregon grape shrubs down by the dock. Thirty feet away Ben nodded to Kate, threw his red disc toward a canvas basket attached to metal legs, and walked after it.

Mark smiled as she approached him. "You've been avoiding me, Katydid."

She noticed his broken nose had turned an ugly greenish-yellow. "I know, and I'm sorry. I'm just so embarrassed about what Victor did to you."

"That doesn't make sense," Mark said as he threw his green disc. "Oops, too far left. If you're embarrassed you should be comforting me, not avoiding me."

"Maybe it doesn't make sense, but I was also confused by some things you said at my house." Kate threw her disc, watched it sail across the lawn, and turned to study him.

He laughed. "I probably said a lot of weird things while I was taking those drugs, but I don't remember much. Let's forget it and just enjoy being out here."

Does he really not remember, or is he just trying to cover up that he said he loved me? Either way, he's prepared to drop it, so I should, too. "I'm okay with that."

"Good."

Jake emerged from the bushes and grinned. "Found it!"

Mark walked to his disc, picked it up, and tossed it again. "In!" he said as it went into the basket.

Kate retrieved her own disc and watched a boat cruise by, its sails billowing in the chilly wind. She belonged here with her friends, and she belonged in the Northwest; perhaps she'd been stupid to consider leaving. She saw Alex strolling from the house.

"Hey, girlfriend," Alex said, walking up to her. "How've you been?"

"Terrible," Kate muttered. "Victor left me. It's been a horrible week."

She touched her shoulder. "Why didn't you call me?"

Kate shrugged. "I was so depressed I didn't want to talk to anyone. I kept hoping he'd apologize for punching Mark and come crawling back. He left on Sunday after I kicked him out, but I didn't really think he'd *stay* gone."

"I'm so sorry," Alex said, tossing her disc. "How can I help?"

"Just be here for me. Just listen."

"Okay," Alex said as they both walked across the lawn. "I can do that."

They played on as storm clouds began blowing in. When it started raining thirty minutes later, they moved inside and started happy hour.

———————

Colorado City—1863

Doozie snapped awake in her bedroom. She'd drifted off while reading last night, and some peculiar noise had just awakened her. Leaning forward in her rocker, she pulled the curtain aside and peered out the window into the darkness, but could see nothing strange in the yard. It was late and all the girls and their men had gone to bed, so it was quiet. She could hear nothing strange either, but she knew what she was listening for.

Blackstone.

Buster had told her he'd spotted him last week while on a supply run just south of here. She'd been dreading Blackstone's return since he'd be out for vengeance because she'd shot him. After the Utes had escorted her home from the cave, they'd headed up the pass to their summer camp in South Park, so they couldn't defend her now. Victor was gone in the future, her precious Homer was gone forever, and she was stuck here with no protector.

So she'd have to protect herself. Letting the curtain drop, Doozie rose from the rocker and winced as she drew on her shawl, careful of her injured shoulder. Clutching her pistol in her right hand and the lamp in her left, she unlocked the bedroom door, slipped out into the saloon, and began making her nightly rounds. The bar looked tidy with the floor swept and spread with fresh sawdust, with the chairs tucked beneath their battered tables. She tiptoed around, silent as a ghost in her lavender nightgown.

Holding the lamp as high as she could, she searched the room but saw nothing. She climbed the stairs, and the hallway stretched ahead, empty and desolate, all of its doors shut tight. As she crept along, the floorboards creaked, and she grew wary. It wouldn't do to wake the sleepers. Reaching the end of the hallway, she stood by the door and listened, but heard nothing. She eased it open and stared outside, scanning the yard and the way to the outhouse, but she saw nothing. She closed the door and bolted it.

As she tiptoed back, she heard snores wafting from the rooms and recalled her nights as a whore. She'd never go back to that, she'd promised herself; she'd die first. Descending the stairs, she crossed the saloon and searched the kitchen but saw nothing. Returning to her bedroom, she locked the door and leaned against it. Sleep eluded her.

———————

As the car whizzed down the highway, Mouse passed the long days dozing or playing with Little Eagle or staring out the window at the blurry world. It amazed her that the outside world moved, and the inside one didn't. It also amazed her that Victor had left Kate behind; it disturbed her that they'd parted company. When she'd first met Kate, long ago in the past, Mouse's jealousy had flared into a firestorm, but now she cared for her. She seemed a good mate for Victor, and Mouse missed her.

When Mouse dangled her tail in front of the baby, she was pleased to see her reach for it. The child was discovering her world and learning quickly. It was unfortunate she'd lost her mother, and now she'd lost Kate, her second mother. An important bond had been severed twice, and while Victor did his best, he'd never take the place of a mother.

Perching on the baby's carrier, Mouse watched Little Eagle's eyes droop and slowly close. Mouse turned and studied Victor, so silent and so sad. Throughout the days they'd been traveling, he'd said little to her or the baby. Sometimes he muttered to himself as he drove, gripping the wheel and guiding the car onward. Sometimes he even wept. Mouse sensed his heart was very troubled. As they traveled she noticed the air was growing thinner and the stars were growing clearer. Because of this and other signs, Mouse suspected they were going home.

The baby cried out in her sleep, balled her hands into fists, and settled back into a troubled slumber. During some of her feedings, she fussed and lunged for the bottle, but yanked back in pain when she got it. Mouse suspected she was cutting teeth, but Victor was puzzled. Finally, a woman at one of the campgrounds gave him a potion to rub on Little Eagle's gums to dull the pain. Since then she'd quieted, and they'd all slept better.

When they returned home to the mountains, perhaps they'd also return to the past. Mouse could change back into Bear again and relinquish her other forms. Yet she'd changed into these forms to help her people, and she would continue to do so.

"You can't love him," Victor said suddenly. "You love *me*. You belong with me."

Mouse scurried up onto his shoulder. She would help him remember the good things. She would chant songs he could hear only in his heart—songs of the mountains, of the wild places, of their long-lost home. As she began to do this, he sighed and relaxed.

———————

Victor's days passed like troubled dreams, tumbling together into a kaleidoscope of images, thoughts, and feelings. As his trip home stretched into weeks, forests blended into prairies and prairies blended into mountains, but all were colorless without Kate. He drove trancelike for hours, but Mouse's presence calmed him. Little Eagle's teething had quieted since he began rubbing her gums with the woman's potion, so when she did cry, he suspected she was missing Kate.

To relax in the evenings, he would hike the trails around the various campgrounds. With the baby in her backpack, he hiked into forests in some places, and across rocks and sand in others. The sun had been merciless today in this desert, so they would set off later, after dinner.

A breeze came up as the sun sank lower, and the rocks surrendered their warmth. Passing beneath a long stone arch, he studied it and climbed higher. He reached a precipice and watched the sun set over the desert, feeling the peace of its great vastness. Gripping the rough sandstone, he eased down onto the trail and hiked on. The moon rose, casting its light on bizarre shapes. He passed through time and silence, through coolness and warmth, through emptiness and fullness. He heard crickets chirring, water trickling, and bats flying. Setting Little Eagle down, he stretched out on a slab of rock, feeling its warmth rise up into him. The stars glittered above him. The moon inched across the sky.

With a rush of fur, Mouse changed into Mountain Lion and bounded off. As a cloud passed over the moon, Victor clicked on his headlight and continued on.

CHAPTER ELEVEN

Colorado City — 1863

Doozie was busy tending bar as a slow stream of customers drifted in during the lazy hours of late afternoon. Dressed in her favorite yellow dress, she wore the silver and turquoise earrings Homer had given her on their wedding day, and combs in her uplifted hair. She liked to imagine that wearing her hair up lent her an air of respectability, but mainly she just fancied it. She'd made fresh coffee and pickled eggs for her customers, and had set out platters of beef, slices of rye bread, and sweet butter. Folks liked having provisions laid out on the bar to eat, and she only charged two bits for a whole plateful.

As she poured a round of beers, she scanned the room. She picked out a few ranchers playing cards by the window, a couple of shopkeepers nursing their whiskeys, and some volunteer soldiers at a nearby table discussing the latest grim news from South Park. It seemed another victim had been murdered by the bandits. Doozie picked up her tray and headed for the soldiers' table, catching more snatches of their conversation.

"Poor devil was out working his claim near Cottage Grove," one soldier said as Doozie drew near. "They killed and robbed him. Could be Seceeshers, but nobody knows."

"Here's yer beers, fellas," she said, setting their drinks down on the table.

"Thanks, Doozie," portly Albert said as he paid her. "You're such a purdy sight in that yeller dress with those stylish earrings. Are you sure you've given up whoring?" He winked at her with a bloodshot eye.

"You know damn well I'm quit of it, Albert," she said as she collected her money, "so don't even try. Elmer, I need ten cents."

Elmer blushed through his muttonchops and handed it over. "Seems like our Albert's forgotten his manners, Dooz. Don't pay him no mind."

"I won't," she muttered, and hurried off. Every day customers would flirt with her; it seemed like becoming a widow had made her more desirable than she'd ever been as a whore. Doozie suspected they wanted her money more than her, as the saloon made a tidy profit. As she tended her customers, she caught snippets of their conversation.

"I'm hoping my shorthorns fetch a good price this year," one of the ranchers said. "I've been grazing them out east in all that tall grass."

"Ain't you scared o' Arapaho, Richard?" his friend asked. "They hunt out there."

"No," Richard said, shaking his head. "'Cuz I ain't seen them out there lately."

"More whiskey?" Doozie asked, eyeing Richard's empty glass.

He looked up, startled to see her serving drinks. "Where's Homer?"

His friend elbowed him. "Don't you remember, Richard? Homer got kilt a few weeks back, and this gal's Doozie, his widow. She owns the place now, so behave yerself."

"Beg yer pardon, ma'am," Richard said. "Yes'm, I'd like another whiskey."

"Fill mine up, too," his friend said.

Hurrying to fetch the bottle, Doozie glanced at the empty space where the piano had once been. She'd ordered another one from St. Louis and expected it to arrive in a few months; a piano would cheer up the place and draw in more customers. Thinking of this reminded her of Kate, but she shoved her from her mind, grabbed the whiskey bottle, and hustled back to the ranchers. As she poured their drinks, she felt someone's eyes on her. She turned slowly to her left. Blackstone stood out on the porch just ten feet away, glaring at her through the open window. Her pulse quickened.

"There's yer whiskey," she said to the ranchers, and snatched up their coins. She strode to the window and hissed at Blackstone, "Git outta here you son-of-a-bitch! I never want to see you again!"

"Is that so?" Blackstone asked, leering at her. "I'm afraid you *will* see me again since I'm back in town now. How interesting to find you alive, and in such an alluring dress. It goes nicely with that sling you're wearing. Is that where I shot you, in your shoulder?"

"Shut up!" she muttered. "You should be hung for murderin' my Homer!"

Blackstone shrugged. "Actually, I think Charlie's bullet killed your Homer, but even if you did try to charge me with murder, no one would believe a lowly whore."

"I ain't a whore!" she exclaimed, her heart pounding. "Now, clear out!"

He chuckled. "You'll always be a whore, Doozie. Always."

"No, I won't, but you'll always be a murderer!"

Richard had been watching from his table. He rose from his chair and ambled over. "Something wrong here?"

"I don't want this bastard hangin' 'round here," she snapped.

"You heard the lady," Richard said. "Move along. You're not welcome here."

Blackstone glared at them and stormed off.

"Thanks, Richard," Doozie said. "I'm much obliged."

"My pleasure," he said, tipping his hat. "Glad I could help."

Doozie darted toward the kitchen, trying to calm her pounding heart.

———————

Two weeks had passed, and Victor had seen much during his travels, but now it was time to go home—to his real home, back in the past. Since leaving Seattle, he'd seen the ocean, explored several parks, and camped at many fine places between Oregon and home.

Now that he was back in Colorado, he considered visiting Lily and Ivan to say goodbye, but by now Kate would've told them he'd left her, so he thought it better to avoid them. He'd slipped into their house to retrieve his pack and rifle one day when they were gone, then returned to the homeless shelter to stay and ask Luis for a favor.

"Can you drop us off to go camping about twenty miles north of here?" he'd asked Luis that night. "And can you keep my car for a while?"

"Why don't you just park it at the trailhead?" Luis had asked.

"There's no trailhead, just a road, and there's no official campsite, so abandoning it would arouse suspicion."

Luis had glanced at Little Eagle, who was starting to fuss. "Camping with a teething baby? Man, that's a hassle. How long will you be gone for?"

Victor hesitated, considering what to tell him. "I don't know yet; a couple of days. I'll call you when I come out." He laughed. "If the wolves eat me, you can keep my car."

"How are you going to call me?" Luis asked. "You don't have a phone."

"Don't worry, I'll find one. If I don't call, assume I'm still camping." *And I'll be far away.*

"Okay, Victor, I'll do it. I'm off the day after tomorrow, so I'll take you then."

Now, two days later, Victor waved to Luis and felt a twinge of loneliness as he watched him drive away. He took Mouse from his pocket, readied his gear, and prepared to set off. He strapped Little Eagle in her small pack to his front and his big pack to his back. By the time he was done, Mouse had changed to Bear. Picking up his rifle, he entered the forest and headed for the mesa, Bear padding along beside him.

It was early in May, and not yet the solstice, so he hoped Bear's presence would open the passage. As he hiked through the sun-dappled forest, he smiled at the baby, and she smiled back. She was growing fast, and he was eager to introduce her to her people while she was still little. As he continued walking, he heard chorus frogs chirring in a nearby pond. Breaking through the trees into the meadow he spotted hundreds of multicolored wildflowers and said their names aloud as he identified them: springbeauty and sand lilies, larkspur and golden banner, chokecherries and asters. Kate had taught him all these names, and it pained him to see them without her. He crossed the meadow, reentered the forest, and climbed the trail to the mesa.

When he finally reached the top, he shed his big pack and sat on a rock to rest, enjoying the view as Little Eagle dozed on his chest and Bear sat on her haunches beside him. The meadow lay below with its undulating grasses, the foothills rising above it and the higher peaks looming in the distance. He thought of Kate and wondered what she was doing. This was a weekday, so she'd be busy teaching, grading papers, or talking with other teachers. She might even be chatting with that bastard, Mark. He sighed, heaved his pack back on, and set off again.

When they reached the cave, Bear slumped at the entrance and Victor settled in beside her. He fed the baby lukewarm formula from her bottle, wondering how their journey through the passage would be. He'd run through in terror the first time, with Bear chasing him, but had passed through quietly the two other times. He wished it would happen quietly, for Little Eagle's sake.

Victor considered what he'd lose or gain by going through the passage. He'd gain his tribe, obviously, but would lose his freedom when they were eventually imprisoned on a reservation. Despite this, he felt that returning to his own time was the better choice. He began to sing in his native language, bidding goodbye to all he'd miss here—his friends, plenty of art supplies, comfortable dwellings with indoor plumbing and electricity.

Finally, he sang goodbye to Kate. He sang to their love and love-making, to their friendship and adventures, to their dream of raising Little Eagle and growing old together. Those dreams were gone now and would be forever.

He sat beside Bear with his eyes closed, waiting for the passage to open.

————————

Colorado City—1863

"Buster, kin you stay here sometimes at night?" Doozie asked. "Jist when yer in town? I need protection from Blackstone. I kin offer you room and board, but no money."

Buster tugged on his beer, looking doubtful. "Maybe sometimes, if you throw in free beer. But if I git an order to haul freight I gotta grab it, 'cuz I gotta make my livin'."

"Fair nuff," she said. "But you gotta stay sober 'cuz you cain't protect me if yer sloppy drunk. Blackstone was here oncst, an' he'll be back. Snakes like him don't give up easy."

"All right," Buster said. "But where'll I sleep, Dooz, out back in my wagon?"

"That wouldn't help, you bein' out there. I cain't spare you one o' the girl's rooms as they's needed fer customers, an' I cain't have you sprawled out on the floor durin' business hours. I'll haul a bedtick into the kitchen, an' you kin sleep there."

"Sounds nice an' cozy," he said. "I'd fancy sleepin' in yer kitchen."

"Help yerself to any food. Yer job is to hang around and keep yer eyes open."

Buster nodded, solemn as a judge. "You betcha, boss lady. I kin do that."

Doozie laughed. "Now *that's* something', me bein' yer boss." With Buster hanging around, she felt a little more protected.

Just a little.

————————

Victor awoke, aware of someone watching him, but it was only Bear. The sun had sunk lower in the sky, and its rays were throwing long shadows through the ponderosas. Heaving herself up, Bear cast a wistful glance into the forest, turned, and lumbered into the cave. As she approached the back wall, it began to tremble. Dirt and pebbles cascaded from the ceiling. A fissure appeared, and Bear stood near it, waiting. When the fissure widened, Victor strapped on the baby, his headlight, and his pack. As the earth thundered open, Bear climbed through the jagged hole and disappeared. Clicking his headlight on, Victor grabbed his gun and followed her down the rumbling passage.

A vicious cold gripped them in the darkness. Little Eagle began to whimper.

"Hush, Little One," he said, wrapping an arm around her. "Don't be afraid. We're going home now." Outside the thin beam cast by his headlight, they were surrounded by the feral darkness. He kept his eyes on Bear as she led them downward into the passage. As he descended, he felt something grabbing at him, trying to pull him back, and he was almost tempted to *go* back. Back to Kate and all she meant to him; back to the future and all it held for him. But he shook free and trudged onward through the darkness.

The earth groaned and shuddered. A wind howled up from the bottom of the cave, carrying dust and biting cold. Little Eagle was wailing now, so he clutched her against him, covering her face against the choking dust. His gun grew heavier, and he was tempted to drop it, as he couldn't remember why he needed it. He heard his people chanting, calling him home, far away at first, but growing closer. Suddenly the cold ceased and the wind slackened and the dust settled.

He saw Bear down below him, backlit by daylight, and he knew they'd made it through the passage. Emerging into the lower cave, he stood there shaking, a headache clawing at his skull. Within a fog of weariness, he saw a rush of fur as Bear changed to Woman—kind and strong, gentle and powerful, bathed in silvery light. She took his gun and laid it down. She loosened his packs and eased them off. She made a fire.

He heard it crackling in his dreams.

———————

Kate felt a punch in her chest as the air left her lungs, and she stumbled on the trail she was hiking. As she slumped to the ground, she felt her heart ache, and she knew Victor had gone through the passage. He was far away from her now, and he'd left her world forever. She turned and faced eastward, toward Colorado.

"No!" she cried. "Come back!" She waited for a while but felt nothing, nothing to indicate that he was still in the passage and could turn around if he'd heard her. Peering through the forest, she tried to picture the cave, the rocks, the pines. She tried to imagine him sprawled on the ground in the lower cave, resting, taking ibuprofen for the inevitable headache. Little Eagle would be resting with him. Bear would stay and guard them.

"Come back!" she cried again, and started sobbing.

———————

Colorado Front Range—1863

Hours had passed, or maybe days. Victor awakened in the cave with a nagging headache. Moonlight streamed through the entrance. The fire had burned down to embers, but he didn't remember building it. Little Eagle was sleeping beside him. Bear was gone.

He eased up onto his side, felt a wave of dizziness and the grip of hunger. Fumbling in his pack, he found an energy bar, ate it, and chased it down with water. Getting to his feet, he emerged from the cave and saw the familiar meadow, its rippling grasses bathed in moonlight. He glimpsed Bear moving through the grasses and stumbled toward her.

"Thank you, my friend," he said as he reached her. "Thank you for guiding us."

She gave out a growl and continued walking.

Victor walked beside her, his fingers brushing the hip-high grasses, grateful to be home again. The air was cleaner here; the land was wilder; the moon was bigger and brighter. He belonged here in his own time, and so did Little Eagle, but now he had to find a way to reach his people in South Park. Taking the stage wouldn't work since the drivers wouldn't transport Indians, and South Park was too far to walk with all this gear and the baby. Tomorrow morning he'd strap his pack on and hike the eight miles north to his friend Jeremiah's. Jeremiah would lend him a horse.

Victor closed his eyes and listened to the rustling grasses. Being here was good; being here was very good. All that was missing was Kate.

———————

Colorado Front Range—1863

After bidding Jeremiah goodbye the next day, Victor saddled his borrowed horse, packed his belongings into saddlebags, shoved his rifle into its sheath, and set off south along the foothills for Colorado City. He intended to visit Doozie before heading up Ute Pass to South Park. Losing her husband would've been sad enough; losing her time-traveling friend would've compounded her sadness. Perhaps news of Kate would cheer her up.

As he rode, Little Eagle dozed in her pack, giving off little snores. He was aware of how odd a Ute brave must look with a baby strapped to his chest, but he saw no other riders, so he needn't be embarrassed. Bear trotted beside them, sometimes disappearing into the trees, and the day passed like a dream—the sky a robin's egg blue with scudding white clouds, the meadows bursting with wildflowers. When he stopped at the lake on the divide to water the horse, he remembered stopping here with Kate and grew sad. As the sun sank lower, he turned into a canyon to make camp by a creek. The day eased into twilight as he built a fire and cooked dinner: warmed-up formula for Little Eagle and leftover venison for himself. The moon rose. The stars winked on. Bear slipped off to hunt.

He rose at dawn, ate a cold breakfast of biscuits and salt pork, and continued on. By late afternoon he'd arrived at the deserted Ute encampment near town. The ground was scarred by dozens of fire rings, lodgepole tracks, and hoof prints—mute testimony to a thriving community that had moved on. Feeling lonely for company, he fed the baby and headed for Doozie's.

When he arrived she was slicing bread in her kitchen, her left shoulder in a sling.

"That looks delicious," he said through the open window. "Can I have some?"

"Victor!" she cried, rushing to the door and yanking it open. "What're you doin' here? Where's Kate?" She pulled both of them inside and hugged them.

"Kate didn't come with me. She stayed in her own time."

She pulled away. "Why? What happened?"

He shrugged. "It's a long story."

"I got plenty o' time."

"If you must know, another man came between us."

"But that's jist shameful!" Doozie said. "I know you were her true love."

"Guess I wasn't, really, but Kate was mine. It's in the past now, and I need to forget her. I brought Little Eagle with me, though." He eased her out of her pack.

"Give 'er here," she said, cradling the baby in her good arm. "I might steal 'er."

He laughed. "Sorry, but you can't. We're headed up to South Park."

She shot him a glance. "Kin you stay with me for a piece? Buster's beddin' down here in the kitchen as a protection from Blackstone. That scoundrel's been pesterin' me."

"Blackstone's back?" Victor said. "I'm sorry to hear that." He looked around the kitchen. "I could maybe stay a night, but it'll be cramped here with the three of us."

"The baby kin sleep with me," she said. "That'll save a little space."

"I'll consider it." He glanced at the bedtick propped against the wall, trying to imagine sharing it with the grizzled freighter. Buster probably snored like a bear and belched alcohol fumes. "How's your shoulder?"

"Gettin' better, but it still pains me. Take the baby back. I gotta finish this."

He took Little Eagle as Doozie returned to her task. "Can I get a meal here?"

"Of course you can," she said, finishing slicing the bread. "Jist make yerself comfy, an' I'll fix you a plate. Be right back." She grabbed the plate of bread slices and hurried out.

———————

Colorado City—1863

Victor stayed in the kitchen while Doozie scurried back and forth serving drinks and replenishing the food on the bar. It was odd to think of Doozie running her own business, yet she seemed capable enough and worked hard. Before this, he'd only been inside the saloon once, when he'd eaten lunch here with Kate, Rising Moon, and Prairie Flower. Homer had been alive then; it felt strange to have him gone now.

During the afternoon and evening, he'd tended the baby, read the *Rocky Mountain News*, sliced slabs of venison and beef for the bar platters, washed dishes, and talked with Doozie. Now he stared out the kitchen window at the crimson sunset, listening to the sounds of the saloon as it flared to life. Men's voices rose and fell in conversation. The girls laughed and flirted. Doozie chatted with her customers. He heard glasses chinking, chairs scraping, someone plinking on a banjo. *Doozie's place was successful. Good for her.*

With the clientele getting drunker as the evening wore on, Victor was careful to avoid trouble. Some customers would be eager to pick a fight with any Indian, yet he was here to protect Doozie, so he needed to be visible. Leaving Little Eagle dozing in a laundry basket, he slipped outside to visit the outhouse. He passed Homer's disheveled wagon with its bullet holes and mangled piano and the barn with its cow, two mules, and single mare. He saw some men hanging around smoking and talking, but they didn't hassle him.

As he emerged from the outhouse, Buster drove his wagon into the yard. "Victor!" Buster cried. "Ain't seen you in a fair piece."

"I've been traveling, Buster. How've you been?"

"I been workin', but I jist hit a slow spell, so I'm beddin' down here for a bit to help out Doozie." He eased down from the wagon and began unhitching his oxen.

Victor nodded. "She told me Blackstone's back."

"Yep," Buster said. "That snake's been slitherin' around her again."

"Doozie invited me to stay here a while, too, so we'll be sharing that bedtick."

Buster's face lit up with smiles. "Well, now, ain't that dandy? We kin visit and you kin tell me all about yer travels. I'll just finish up here and be in presently."

"Okay," Victor said, turning to go inside. "See you later." He guessed he could tolerate sleeping with Buster for one night.

But just one.

Colorado City—1863

Victor had expected to stay up late, but the saloon had quieted early, and it was barely eleven when he joined the others in the bar. All the customers had left, Little Eagle was asleep in Doozie's bedroom, and some of the girls were playing cards with Buster.

"Victor," Doozie said as she washed some dirty glasses, "tell me all about Kate."

He swallowed his beer. "She's a teacher so she's always busy, but when she's not doing that, she's fixing up her house so she can sell it and move back to Colorado."

She frowned. "Think she'll git over that other fella and come here to join you?"

"No, Doozie. I told you, we broke up. I'm sure she'll be staying in the future."

"That's a shame to toss good love away like that. It jist ain't right."

He sighed. "Breaking up wasn't *my* idea. Can't we talk about something else?"

"Fine," she muttered. "Suit yerself. Does she live in a grand house?"

Across the room, a girl laughed and slapped Buster. "You dirty old thing!"

Victor paused, trying to decide how to describe Kate's home. "It's not a grand house, exactly, but it's bigger than most around here. It has two stories, central heat, two bedrooms, a den, running water, two inside bathrooms, and a two-car garage."

Doozie stared at him. "Two inside bathrooms? With tubs? And, what's a garage?"

He smiled. "There's one tub upstairs, and one downstairs. A garage is like a barn for her car, and a car is like a modern carriage."

Doozie's eyebrows arched. "She's got inside plumbin', central heat, a carriage and horses? Blazes, our Kate's high-falutin'! No wonder she fancies the future."

He shook his head. "She doesn't have horses, Dooz. A car is a horseless carriage with an engine, a type of machine that hasn't been invented yet."

She scowled at him. "Yer lyin'."

"No, I'm not. The future has many conveniences."

She fell silent for a while. "And I reckon she's got lots o' friends?"

"Yes," he said, nodding. "One of them is the man she left me for."

"I'll be damned," she said, frowning. "Is he richer than you, or handsomer?"

Victor sipped his beer. "He's not handsomer, but he's richer. He's a teacher, but I think he's got other money too because his house is bigger and fancier than Kate's."

"Hellfire," she muttered, setting the last glass on the draining board. She drained the sink, pulled herself a beer, and came around the bar. "I'm damn sorry to hear that, Victor. Come an' sit with me fer a piece." She took his arm and drew him over to a table.

"What's Seattle like?" she asked, slumping into a chair and putting her feet up.

He sat down beside her. "It's a beautiful city, with lots of water around it, and many of the people who live there have boats. It's noisy, though, and very busy."

Doozie's face lit up. "I wouldn't mind seeing *that*. Big cities got lots of frolics."

"You didn't want to come with me, remember? I asked you."

"I remember," she said, sipping her beer. "I wouldn't fit in there anyways."

"I didn't fit in there, either. But you'd probably like the frolics."

Buster laughed and stood up from the gaming table. "Sorry, ladies, but you lost. I'll collect my winnin's another time. 'Night." As the girls headed upstairs, he ambled over to Victor and Doozie. "I'm plumb tuckered out. Reckon we oughta lay out that bedtick?"

"Let me finish my drink," Victor said, turning to Doozie. "Kate felt terrible that she had to leave you behind. Many times she wished she'd dragged you up the passage."

Doozie sipped her beer. "But she couldn't, 'cuz she had to git that baby out. I got shot an' fell, an' she probably thought I was dead anyway."

"She *did* think you were dead; that's partly why she left you. When I told her you were alive, she was thrilled, but she felt really sorry that she didn't bid you a proper goodbye."

"She said that? Land sakes, I miss her. Kate was my good friend."

"She still is." Victor drained his glass and stood up. "I'm ready for bed now."

"Me, too," she said, finishing her beer. Setting their glasses on the bar, she led them into the kitchen, opened a closet, and took out some blankets. "Here," she said, handing them over. "'Night, boys. Hope you sleep well."

"'Night," they both said. After setting up the mattress, the men removed their boots. Victor blew out the lamp, and they settled in for the night.

Victor lay there for a while, listening to the crickets chirring through the open window. "'Night, Buster."

But Buster was already asleep.

———————

Colorado City—1863

Victor snapped awake. Buster wasn't snoring beside him, so that hadn't wakened him, and Little Eagle wasn't crying in the next room, so that wasn't it either. Rising from the bedtick, he went to the window and peered out. The moon was up, casting its glow upon the yard, lighting up the barn, water trough, and outhouse. He saw nothing unusual, but couldn't shake the feeling that someone was out there, so he pulled on his boots, went outside to relieve himself, and crouched beside the barn, listening and watching.

A shadow crept across the yard, holding a dim shielded light.

Victor sucked in a breath.

The shadow uncovered a lantern and tossed it through Doozie's bedroom window.

"Hey!" Victor yelled, launching himself at the shadow. He grabbed the figure and tried to hold it, but it slipped away and ran off.

Back at the window, flames were engulfing the curtains. "Fire!" he shouted. "Doozie, get out!" Dashing to the trough, he filled a bucket with water, ran back to the window, and hurled its contents. Through the flames, he saw Doozie grab a pitcher and toss water on the burning curtains. Buster rushed into the bedroom, snatching Little Eagle as she started screaming.

"Are you okay?" Victor shouted.

"We're fine!" Doozie cried, slapping the flames with a blanket. "More water!"

Rushing back to the trough, Victor scooped up water and ran back to douse the flames as Buster carried the baby outside. "You're okay now," Victor said, dropping the bucket and taking Little Eagle. "I've got you. You're safe." She kept screaming as Buster grabbed the bucket and ran for more water.

Doozie emerged and stared at the smoldering curtains. "Who coulda done this? How long you been outside, Victor? Did you see who it was? Was it Blackstone?"

"I came out and saw someone throw a lantern through the window," Victor said, jiggling Little Eagle. "I tried to grab him, but I didn't really see him. He ran off too fast."

"We coulda died," she wailed. "What tipped you off, Victor?"

"I woke up with a bad feeling, so I came out here and saw him."

"Thanks," she said, kissing his cheek. "Yer my hero."

"You're welcome," he said, noticing Doozie's drenched nightgown clinging to her body. He turned away and began to pace, trying to calm the baby. "I doubt he'll be back tonight, but we should take turns keeping watch out here. I'll take the first one."

"All right," Doozie said. "That smoke and kerosene stinks awful, don't it?"

"It does," he said. Above them, one of the girls raised a window and poked her head out. "What's all the commotion?"

"Some bastard tried to burn us out, Bridgette!" Doozie called up to her.

"Damn his eyes! Did you catch him?"

"No, he run off. But Victor and Buster helped me put the fire out."

"Well, thanks! One of you fellas is welcome to share my bed if you like."

"I jist might do that," Buster said, breaking into a grin.

Victor continued pacing. "We should tell the sheriff about this fire."

Doozie snorted. "Why'd he care? I usedta be a whore, so my word ain't worth much, an' yer an Injun, which is even worse. But in my opinion, that asswipe Blackstone done it."

Victor shrugged. "I told you, Dooz, I didn't see who did it. He felt wiry when I grabbed him, though, and Blackstone's wiry. And his height was about right."

"I agree with Doozie," Buster said, setting the bucket down next to the water trough. "Blackstone's too smart to do it hisself, but he coulda ordered it done."

"Damn right he coulda," Doozie muttered, "an' he hates me enough to do it, too. 'Scuse me, gents, I gotta git outta these wet duds. Be right back." She headed inside.

As Victor watched, Doozie lit a lamp in the kitchen and carried it into her bedroom. Little Eagle sniffled, finally quiet. "Hush, little one," he whispered. "No more crying."

Buster stood beside him. "Yer doin' a right fine job with that young'un, Victor."

"Thanks, but I'm sure you'd do the same with your own child if you had one."

"I might aim to, but I don't know if I could. Carin' for a child's mighty tricky."

"Not all that tricky," he said, kissing Little Eagle's downy head. "You just love them and try to do what's best for them." *Had bringing the baby back here been the right thing? She could've burned to death tonight.* He cringed at the thought and held her closer.

Doozie returned fully dressed, carrying three glasses and a bottle of whiskey. "Let's have us a drink," she said, handing out their glasses. "We deserve it."

Victor took a glass and stared at the rough-hewn building. "If this place had gone up in flames, those women upstairs would've been trapped and burned to death."

"There's stairs on the side o' the building," Doozie said, pointing. "Some coulda got out that way, but others woulda died. Whoever done this is a murderer, but I don't fancy talkin' 'bout it no more. Let's jist drink our whiskey an' be glad we're alive."

Victor held out his glass. "You acted fast. I'm thankful to you for Eagle's safety."

"Yer sure welcome," she said, pouring whiskey into their glasses.

"I swear, Dooz," Buster said. "I'm right proud of the way you handled yerself tonight. You done good throwin' that pitcher o' water on them curtains." He chinked his glass against hers. "Here's a toast to our Doozie."

"Cheers!" she said.

"Cheers," Victor said, sipping his whiskey as he cradled the baby. "Buster, can I sit out here in your wagon and keep watch for the next few hours?"

"Yep. There's feed sacks in the back you kin lay on. Reckon I'll take Bridgette up on her offer to share her bed. 'Night, all." He gulped his whiskey down and hurried in.

"I'll bring out some blankets and sit with you," Doozie said. "If you don't mind."

"Not at all," Victor said. "I'd enjoy your company."

As Doozie went back inside, Victor stared up at the moon, wondering what Kate was doing. Was she sleeping soundly in her bed or lying awake, thinking of him? When Doozie returned with the blankets, they climbed into the wagon and settled in.

"Penny fer yer thoughts," Doozie said, pulling her blanket around her shoulders.

"Don't want to talk about it."

"Yer thinkin' 'bout our Kate then, I kin tell. You never shoulda left 'er."

"I *told* you..." he began, but stopped as something brushed across his head. "Look," he said, pointing up at a soaring shadow. "Hawk's up there."

"So? We git lots o' hawks 'round here."

Victor smiled. "I remember now. A bird flew at the kitchen window earlier. That's what woke me up."

"And?"

"Did Kate ever tell you about Bear?"

"The magical one? Sure." Her eyebrows arched. "Oh! That's *her*?"

"That's her," he said, nodding. "She woke me up to warn me."

"I swear!" Doozie cried, watching Hawk's silhouette fly across the moon.

"I should've known," he muttered. "She came back to protect us."

Doozie huddled in her blanket. "I'm gonna rest my eyes now, jist fer a minute."

"Go ahead, Dooz. I'll wake you."

"I swear," she mumbled as she drifted off.

The hours passed. Gradually the sky lightened.

CHAPTER TWELVE

Kate sat in the teachers' lounge eating her tuna fish sandwich, feeling isolated as conversations buzzed around her. Across the table from her, Mark prattled on about a kayaking trip he was planning, and Alex listened as she ate cafeteria tacos next to him.

"Do you two want to go?" Mark asked. "I could try to book a campsite at Deception Pass State Park. The weather's supposed to be clear this weekend."

"I'd like to," Alex said, "but I can't. Maybe another time."

"Not this weekend," Kate said. "I have too many chores." Deception Pass was near where Victor had met Adele for that fundraiser, and Kate couldn't face going there yet.

"Why do you have so many chores?" Mark asked, digging into his tacos.

Kate swallowed a bite of sandwich and washed it down with iced tea. *It's another month until school lets out, and a week after that until the summer solstice. If I hustle, I can finish my chores and list the house, go kayaking with Mark and Alex, and still make it to the cave on time. I can't believe I'm actually considering going to Colorado for the solstice.* "I need to finish some chores because I'm thinking of listing my house." She braced herself for their reaction as she reached for her apple.

"What?" Mark exclaimed.

"You're selling your house?" Alex asked, frowning. "Why?"

Kate shrugged. "Ivan and Lily claim they're getting too old to run their antique business, so they offered to give it to me and let me live there. When I was back there, I realized they're not getting any younger, and I'd like to spend more time with them." *Which was only part of the reason for moving, but they didn't need to know more just now.*

"That's the first I've heard of *that*," Alex said. "You'd leave your teaching job?"

"Well, yeah, I'd have to. Sorry, I didn't mean to spring it on you. So that's why I have plenty of chores to do. Want to come over and help me on Saturday, Alex? I'll feed you."

"I'm pet-sitting this weekend," Alex said, "but if you help me exercise their horses, I can come for a few hours. I can't believe you're going to move away, Kate."

Mark frowned. "How could you leave us, Katydid? Your whole life is here."

"I just need to do something different. Maybe my house won't even sell."

"Are you kidding?" Alex said. "Houses around here are selling like crazy."

"I don't want you to move," Mark said, "but I'll come and help you. Maybe we could go camping together another time."

"Thanks," Kate said, pleased by his offer. "If you could prep the downstairs bathroom for painting, I can start on the windows. I should also shampoo the rugs, but I won't have time to do that this weekend. I have a bunch of grading to do."

"I'll prep the bathroom," Mark said.

"I'll help wash windows," Alex said. "You should get the carpets steam-cleaned."

"Thanks, that's a good idea. How does pizza and a salad sound for dinner?"

Mark nodded. "Throw in some beer and dessert, and you're on."

Alex stood up. "I've got to go teach. What time do you want us on Saturday?"

"How's ten o'clock sound?"

"Sounds good," Alex said, grabbing her tray and heading out the door.

Kate felt a twinge of guilt as she watched her friend hurry out. *If I tell Alex why I'm planning on going to Colorado for the solstice, she'll try to talk me out of it, but I have to tell her.* "See you," she said to Mark, and left the lounge. When she reached her classroom, she stood at the window and closed her eyes, trying to imagine what Victor was doing. If the sensation she'd felt was true, it'd been three days since he'd gone through the passage. Once he left the cave, had he strapped on his pack and just started walking, or had he found a horse to ride? Did he and Little Eagle even miss her?

Victor had left her. Did she have no pride, chasing after him? Did she think she'd just slip through the passage, make up with him, and bring him back? This would be no simple weekend trip; it would be a difficult journey to another century. She missed him terribly, but this scheme of hers was crazy. Maybe she *should* let Alex talk her out of it.

The bell rang, and her students streamed in. She smiled and turned to face them.

"Pop quiz," she snapped. "Put everything away except your pencils."

They moaned, but buckled down to work.

———————

That evening Kate steeled herself and called Lily. She answered on the second ring.

"Hi, Katie! Thanks for sending the flowers. The lilies are especially lovely."

"You're welcome," Kate said. "Happy belated Mother's Day. Sorry I didn't call, but I was busy and it got too late, and I just... " *I didn't want to call because it was my first Mother's Day as a mother, but Little Eagle was gone and I was too depressed.*

"That's all right, honey. Ivan took me out to dinner and a movie and we didn't get home 'til late anyway, so we just went to bed. Your mother sent flowers, too."

"I called her this morning," Kate said. "But I just got her machine." She stared out her bedroom window and watched the rain. "So, is anything new with you?"

"Not really. We're just maintaining the business and taking care of Ivan. We've seen lots of wildflowers on our walks lately. How are you, and how's that baby?"

So, she doesn't know, Kate thought, *which means Victor hasn't been there to get his things or to say goodbye.* "Little Eagle's as sweet as she ever was."

"And Victor?"

"Fine," she lied. "He's out walking right now." They talked for half an hour until Lily excused herself.

"Have to turn in now, honey," she said, "it's getting late. Thanks for calling."

"Take care, Lily. Bye."

"'Night, Katie."

Kate turned off the phone and glanced out the window. It was pouring out there now, which matched her mood. "Damn," she muttered, and dragged off to take a shower.

———————

A few days later, Kate was riding horses on a trail above Lake Washington with Alex. A raft of storm clouds drifted overhead. A few kayaks and sailboats moved across the water.

"I'm going to Colorado for a while," Kate said. "Can you watch Cisco for me?"

"Sure, I'd be happy to. When are you going?"

"Right after school's out," she said, watching a sailboat tack into the wind. "I'm going to see Lily and Ivan, among other things."

"Makes sense, since you're thinking of moving back. How's Ivan doing?"

"Really well. He's been doing a lot of walking."

"Good, I'm glad to hear that. What are the 'other things' you need to do?"

"Don't get mad at me, but I have to take care of something."

Alex shot her a look. "Oh, no. You're not going back to look for Victor, are you?"

"I have to. I love him, and I didn't get to tell him that before he left."

"You're out of your mind! The man *left* you! You need to get on with your life."

"I can't do that without trying to find him because it's my fault he left. I have to tell him there's nothing going on between Mark and me and try to bring him back."

"But how will you find him? He could be anywhere."

"First I need to find out *when* he is. I have a pretty good idea from a note he left."

"What?" she cried, reining in her horse. "You're going back to the past?"

"Yes," Kate said, slowing to a stop. "But I have to wait a month for the solstice since that's when the passage will open. Lower your voice; you're spooking the horses."

Alex scowled. "But it's too dangerous, Kate! You're talking about a trip back to 1863 like it's a ride on the Bainbridge Island ferry! Aren't you scared?"

"A little, but I have to do it. Don't you get it?"

"No, I don't," she said, petting her horse to calm it. "I can't believe you're even considering this."

"Come on, Alex. Don't hate me for this."

"I don't hate you. I love you, but I'm worried sick about you. Can't you see that?"

Kate leaned over and gripped her arm. "But can't you also see I have to do this?"

Alex jerked her arm away. "No, I can't. You have to chase after some Indian from another century who dumped you? It's dangerous! You know you'll be going to a town full of lonely miners, bandits, killers, and who knows what else?"

"Colorado City won't have many miners in the summer—they go back up to South Park to work their claims. Besides, I don't intend to live in town very long. I intend to look for Victor."

Alex frowned. "And how do you intend to do that? On foot?"

"I'm not sure, exactly; I haven't figured it out yet. If I'm lucky enough to get through the passage I could hike to Jeremiah's, rest up, and buy one of his horses."

"Okay," she said, nudging her horse forward, "who's Jeremiah?"

"He and his wife own a roadhouse," Kate said, coaxing her horse into a walk. "The stage stops there, and they serve meals to travelers and rent out rooms."

"At least that part makes sense. How far is his place from the cave?"

"I don't know. Six or seven miles, I guess. Or maybe I could hike to Jeremiah's, take the stage into town, and buy a horse there. I left some gold dust and 1860's money at Lily and Ivan's." Kate glanced over at Alex. "I'm sorry to worry you. I realize how crazy this must sound."

"I can't believe we're talking about this as if it's real."

"It *is* real. It's as real as any dream that comes true or any idea that comes to life."

"But if you have to wait for the solstice, how will you know if Victor's gone back already? Can't you just head him off at the cave and catch him before he goes through?"

Kate smiled. "That would be a lot easier, but I'm pretty sure he's already gone through."

"But how could he, if the solstice hasn't happened yet?"

"Because for one thing I *felt* him leave a few days ago, and for another, Bear's with him. Victor claims she can force the passage open."

"You're kidding."

"No, I'm not," Kate said. "Remember how she changed into a hawk that time? She's got these powers, and we think she can open the passage whenever she wants to."

"That's amazing. So nothing I can say will stop you from going?"

"Nothing."

Alex blew out a sigh. "Okay, I give up. Just promise me you'll be careful."

"I promise." *Living in the past demands constant vigilance.*

"And promise me you'll come back in a month."

"I can't promise that. Time travel doesn't work that way. It's unpredictable." *I can't tell her I might be stuck in the past for much longer since she'll worry even more.*

Alex rode along the trail for a while in silence, considering this. "Okay, then. I'll have to trust you're making the right decision, but I have a favor to ask before you go."

"Shoot."

"My landlord's raising my rent June first, and I can't afford to live there anymore. Since I'll have to move out anyway, can you let me stay at your house for a month or so until I find a new place?"

"No problem," Kate said. "But if I list it please keep the house tidy so prospective buyers can come through and look at it. Okay?"

"Okay. There's just one more thing."

"What now?"

"You spent a lot of time on horseback in the past, right?"

"Right. I had my own horse back there, and she was awesome."

Alex sat up in her saddle and peered ahead. "So show me your stuff. There's a meadow up there and no pedestrians on the trail. Let's race to the end of it."

Kate grinned. "You're on, sucker. Go!"

CHAPTER THIRTEEN

Pikes Peak Region — 1863

It had been many days since Bear guided her people through the passage. She'd stayed in her bear form until the night they'd spent in town at the young woman's house when she'd shifted into Hawk to get a bird's eye view. She enjoyed flying and learned much by doing so. That night she'd spotted the man with the fire and warned Victor.

Now they were in the mountains west of town and heading higher, up to where people were scarce and dwellings were few. Bear felt freer in this wild country, less confined by the trappings of civilization. She missed Kate and sensed that Victor missed her too; it felt wrong for them to be apart. She'd seen him sorrowful before, but never this sorrowful. He carried his sadness deep inside, a wounded man with a heavy burden.

His borrowed horse plodded on, wary of Bear and shying away from her. On their first day out, Victor's noisy friend with the wagon had tagged along, but he'd gone off elsewhere, and now they were alone. At night Victor and the baby camped while Bear guarded them. During the daytime Bear slipped into the trees when strangers approached, for they would shoot her if they saw her.

Night was fast approaching now, and they entered a copse of trees beside a creek. Victor set up a flimsy cloth shelter, staked it out, and laid out their sleeping things, then shook out a feathery cocoon and placed it inside the shelter. He unpacked the horse, led it to water, and fed Little Eagle. He kindled a flame in a metal thing and heated food. When it grew dark, they crawled into the shelter while Bear lay there, listening to him weeping. If she could only speak, Bear would tell him she sensed Kate would come. After Victor quieted and began snoring, Bear padded off to hunt, circling back often to check on their safety. Mountain lions and wolves prowled around here, and common bears that could attack her people. Bear must protect them from these predators.

Scenting a rabbit, Bear bounded after it and caught it. As she savored her kill, the moon rose over the mountain and lit up the valley. Returning to camp, Bear settled in for the night, her ears and nose attuned to any danger. The creek scrambled over its rocks.

———————

Pikes Peak Region—1863

In Victor's dreams a wolf howled. The mountains were cold at night, but the wolf's howls made them seem even colder. The moon shone through his tent, trying to wake him, but he dove down deeper. A dream brought Kate back to him...

She was facing him, silvered by the moonlight, her horse beside her. He reached out to catch her hands, but she drew them back. "You don't love me," she murmured.

"I do love you," he answered, "but you drove me away. I would've stayed with you forever." He tried to embrace her, but she mounted her horse and rode off.

He wept.

———————

South Park, Colorado—1863

The day dawned bright and clear, and by afternoon Victor had reached the heart of South Park. Ascending a hill to get a view, he dismounted, basking in the brilliant day with its blue sky and scudding clouds. He shrugged off the baby's pack and took out a bottle with formula, leaned against a boulder, and began to feed her. As she sucked on her bottle, Victor spotted two figures riding toward them a couple of hundred yards away, their images shimmering in the warm summer air. He grabbed his rifle and pulled it closer. As the men approached and passed below, he could see they were Mexicans, and heavily armed. One glanced up, spied him sitting there, and raised his hat in greeting. Victor waved and watched them ride away north, across rolling hills studded with wildflowers. Within minutes they disappeared.

Victor continued feeding the baby as he watched antelope graze on a nearby hill. According to a paper he'd read at the saloon, it was early July now, so he'd been away in the future less than a month. The grasses had grown tall here in Bayou Salado, and his people would be hunting the plentiful game. When Little Eagle finished eating, he propped her up on his shoulder and burped her, laid her down on a blanket, and joined her in a rest. Cicadas chirred. A breeze rustled the grasses. Suddenly, he heard gunshots. He sat up and dug in his pack for his binoculars. He saw whorls of dust off to the north. *Could the riders he'd seen be attacking someone? Could that dust be from their fleeing horses?*

Returning from a foray, Bear slumped down beside him, sniffed the baby, and growled. Little Eagle's diaper needed to be changed, evidently, although it seemed like Victor had just changed it. When he found his people, he'd get a woman to perform these chores, and his life would be simpler. He changed Little Eagle, strapped her onto his chest, and set off riding. As he rode he sang softly to her in Ute. He knew a few songs in English but no lullabies, and the ones he knew weren't appropriate for children. After a time he came upon a man muttering to himself and driving a wagon pulled by a team of oxen.

"Good day," Victor said, riding up beside him.

The man jumped, but relaxed when he saw Victor holding Little Eagle. "Good day," he said. "I just had a scare a little while ago, my friend, so I'm a tad jumpy. Two Mexicans shot at me."

Victor studied him. "Are you wounded? I see no blood."

"No, I'm not," he said, breaking into a nervous grin. He pulled a thick wad of papers from his pocket and held it up to show Victor. "These papers stopped the bullet from piercing my chest. As a copy of Mr. Lincoln's Emancipation Proclamation is among them, I suppose I can thank the great man for my life."

Victor had read about this proclamation. "You were lucky. Did you get a good look at them?"

"I did," he said, replacing the papers. "I suspect they're the bandits who've been terrorizing innocent people all these weeks. I'm on my way to Fairplay now to report it."

Victor remembered Kate had told him about the bandits; about how they'd almost killed her and Buster. "I think I saw them earlier. Were they heavily armed?"

The man nodded. "They had a fair arsenal. My name's Metcalf, by the way. Pleased to meet you. You speak good English—for an Injun."

"Thank you." He realized he probably spoke better English than most Indians alive now. "My name is Victor Manyhorses. Have you seen any Utes camped nearby?"

Metcalf turned and pointed. "Just east of here. Are they your people?"

"Yes," he said. "I've been looking for them. Will you be safe on your own now?"

"I think so, my friend. Those bandits went north, and I'm heading west." He slapped the reins against his oxen. "Farewell, Victor. Safe journey."

"Farewell." Victor turned his horse and trotted east. As he covered the distance, he felt the sun on his skin, the wind in his braids, and his horse's strength beneath him. When he approached the encampment, he felt his pulse quicken. He heard the sentries sound the alarm, and grinned as he broke into a gallop. Within minutes he was surrounded by his tribesmen — slapping his thighs, grasping his hands, laughing and talking in a joyous Ute cacophony. As he dismounted he saw his brother-in-law Rising Moon running toward him.

"My friend," Victor said, hugging him. "I've come home again."

"Why are you speaking English?" Rising Moon asked, drawing back to cuff his shoulder. "Don't you remember Ute anymore? Are you home for good this time?"

Victor laughed. "Of course I remember my own language," he replied in Ute. "And yes, I'm home for good. I've brought this little one home to meet her people." He saw his mother-in-law Mourning Dove pushing through the crowd with her arms outstretched, grinning like a silver-haired madwoman.

"Welcome home," she said, embracing him. "I'm glad you've returned to us. Is this who I think it is?" she asked, reaching for Little Eagle.

"It is," he said, slipping off the baby's pack and handing her over. "Meet your great-granddaughter, Little Eagle."

"Ahhhh," she said, holding her up. "I like her name. We're going to have some fine times together, little one. What's this strange contraption you've got her in?"

"It's a baby carrier I brought from the future."

Mourning Dove scowled. "It's ugly! Doesn't she have her own cradleboard?" Little Eagle frowned at her great-grandmother, whimpered, and reached for Victor.

"She did, but I had to leave it behind." In his eagerness to avoid Ivan and Lily, he'd forgotten to get it from their house. "Jiggle her to calm her."

"I know how to care for a baby," she chided, jiggling Eagle. "We'll just have to make her another cradleboard. Victor, we'll talk later. Come little one, let's show you off." She ambled away.

Victor turned to Rising Moon. "As much as I love my granddaughter, I'm relieved to hand her over. Caring for a baby is a lot of work."

"I know. That's why we let the women do it. Didn't Kate come with you?"

"No."

Rising Moon studied him. "Is she coming soon?"

"No," he said, feeling his heart sink. "She stayed behind in the future."

"I see," his friend said, leading him into camp. "You'll stay with us, of course, until we can set up your own tepee. Prairie Flower will be glad to see you." The men walked past several tepees to the horse corral where Laughing Brook greeted them.

"Victor, you're back!" the boy said, opening the corral's brush gate. "I'll groom your horse while you go see Milagro. He really missed you. I can hear him now."

"Thank you," Victor said, handing over the reins. Hearing his horse whinny from another corral, he turned and hurried toward it. As he came closer, Milagro whinnied again and pushed through the other horses to reach him. By the time Victor got there, Milagro was pressing against the brush fence, snorting and tossing his head.

"I missed you, too, my friend," Victor said, rubbing his forehead. He slipped into the corral and ran his hands over the big buckskin. "He's in good shape," he said to Rising Moon as he approached.

"He is, but he was frantic when you disappeared. I had a hard time leading him away when we left the cave. He kept screaming and pulling, trying to turn back. He wouldn't let anyone else ride him. Laughing Brook tried once, and got bucked off for his troubles."

"I'm sorry I had to leave you behind," Victor said, stroking Milagro's ears. "I'm finished with travels where I can't take you." He threw one arm around the horse's neck and leaned against his chest, feeling Milagro's big heart beat against him.

Finally, he pulled away. "I've been riding all day and I'm hungry, my friend. I'll come back after dinner and take you for a ride." He eased out of the corral.

Milagro whinnied and tossed his head.

"I'll be back," Victor said. "I promise."

"Come," Rising Moon said. He turned and led Victor to his tepee. Lifting the hide flap, he leaned in and said, "Prairie Flower, look who I've brought home."

Victor could see his sister-in-law inside, nursing her baby.

"Victor!" she gasped. "You came back!"

"I did," he said, coming inside to squat down and hug her. "I brought Mountain Flower's baby."

Prairie Flower's brown eyes widened. "I must see her! Where is she?"

He sat down beside her on a bison robe. "Your mother kidnapped her. She's showing her off around camp."

"But which way did they go?" she asked, starting to get up. "I want to see her."

"No more questions," Rising Moon said, pouring water from an earthen jug into a gourd. "Let him rest from his journey." He handed Victor the gourd. "Drink."

Victor sipped the water, pure and sweet. He lay back and closed his eyes. He'd brought his granddaughter home to her people, and they were safe. He could relax now.

CHAPTER FOURTEEN

The next few weeks swept by in a blur as Kate finished the school year, graded papers, helped Alex move in, finished getting the house ready, and put it on the market. She'd spent the weekend before her trip kayaking with Mark and Alex; she'd even visited Adele in La Conner to make peace with her.

Now Kate was flying over the Rockies and peering down at the forested mountains, remembering the last time she'd flown into Denver three months ago. Back then, Ivan had just had a heart attack and she'd rushed home to see him; now he was mended and getting strong again. As she sipped a Styrofoam cup of tea, she made a mental list of the supplies she'd brought to take back to 1863—extra batteries for her cell phone so she could take pictures, two paperbacks, binoculars, a headlight, and plenty of ibuprofen. When she got to Lily and Ivan's she would grab a tent and Ivan's old rucksack from the barn, a sleeping bag or blanket, along with the pistol she'd gotten in the past, a knife, her gold dust and antique money, and some matches. She'd bought more 1860s money on eBay for ten times its face-value, so she was set financially, but there were two things she hadn't decided yet: whether to disguise herself as a man again in 1863—and whether to tell Lily and Ivan she was going there. They'd worry, and it might give Ivan another heart attack, so maybe she'd just slip away without telling them and hope she'd return the next day like she had before.

As the plane neared Denver, Kate handed her empty cup to the attendant and put up her tray table. She watched the foothills yield to suburbs and a tangle of highways. As they approached the terminal's white-peaked roof, she realized it resembled a cluster of huge tents and wished Victor could see it from the air. Hearing the plane's wheels drop, she straightened her seatback and prepared to meet her grandparents.

————————

On the drive home, when Lily and Ivan asked her why she'd come now instead of waiting until she sold her house, Kate had told them she missed them and didn't want to wait that long. Now she was sitting on the deck sipping a beer and playing Scrabble with Ivan. It was a perfect June afternoon with the chokecherries blooming, hummingbirds zinging in to sip from the feeders, and deer grazing out in the meadow.

"So, Katie girl," Ivan said, drawing some tiles. "How long are you here for?"

"A week or two," she said, laying down the word *chasm*. "I bought a one-way ticket, so I'm open." *That's if everything goes well, and I don't get stuck in the past.*

Ivan sipped his beer. "That's a nice long visit, but won't you miss Victor?"

"Of course I will," she said, watching hummingbirds buzz the feeder. "But I wanted to see you." She sipped her beer and drew more tiles.

Ivan laid down *moody* for a double word score. "We're glad you came, honey. What do you want to do while you're here?"

"Just hang out, mostly," she said. "You know how exhausted I get at the end of the school year, so I'll catch up on my sleep first before helping you and Lily with the business. We could even go through the barn." *So I can look for that camping gear.*

Ivan snorted. "Haven't gone through that musty old barn in years. Did Victor tell you he slept out there sometimes when the weather was nasty?"

"Yeah, he did," she said, laying down *drought*.

"Damn, a triple word score," Ivan muttered. "It was a bit disconcerting to learn that rogue had been using our barn and house all that time."

"I'll bet it was, but he's not a rogue, Ivan. He was a big help in Seattle, but I think I shackled him with too many chores. He also took care of the baby while I taught."

Ivan pulled on his beer and put down *trace*. "Why shouldn't he? I took care of you when you were a baby, and she *is* his granddaughter. I miss that feisty little princess."

"I miss her already, too. You look good, Ivan. Healthy."

"I feel good. I've been taking care of myself. We should go for a walk later."

"I'd love a walk. I've been sitting all day. We could go back into the meadow and look for those Preble's mice."

Overhearing her, Lily came out onto the deck and sat beside Kate. "I was back there the other day and saw some baby mice! Thanks to Victor, they're thriving. By the way, Ivan, we're having bison burgers for dinner so you need to fire up the grill."

"Okay," he said. "Katie wants to help with the business while she's here; maybe even go through the barn. What do you think of that, Lil?"

"I think she's gone batty," Lily said. "That barn's a mess. There are plenty of other things we need help with, honey. Why rummage through that old barn?"

Kate shrugged. "Because I want to keep busy. I also want to look through the camping gear since I might go camping while I'm here." She finished her beer.

Lily studied her for a minute. "We can tackle the barn if you want, but that won't fix your problem, Katie."

"What do you mean?" she asked, feeling her stomach clench.

"You've broken up with Victor, haven't you?"

She watched the hummingbirds for a minute, trying to decide how much to tell her. "Not really. At least I don't think so. We just needed some time apart, that's all."

"Dammit!" Ivan snapped. "He hurt you, didn't he? I warned him not to!"

"Hush, Ivan," Lily said. "What happened? Is he still in Seattle?"

"He doesn't deserve you," Ivan grumbled.

Kate felt her eyes fill with tears. "I have no idea where he is. He left a note saying he's going home and took off with Eagle weeks ago." She started crying.

Lily touched her hand. "I'm sorry, honey. Tell me what happened."

Taking a deep breath, Kate launched into an abbreviated version of their story, relieved to be finally telling them. "So," she said, drying her eyes on a napkin as she finished, "it was partly my fault and partly his fault, but I'm sure we still love each other. I just have to find him and tell him so. She blew her nose into the moist napkin. "Can I have another beer and some chips, please? I'm suddenly ravenous."

"I'll go start the grill," Ivan muttered. He stood up and hurried off.

"You can stay as long as you want, honey," Lily said, hugging her. "You don't have to move back here for us, you know. Are you sure you want to leave Seattle?"

"I'm not sure of anything except that I need to find him. Alex is staying in my house for a while so she can keep it clean for prospective buyers. She said if Victor and I do break up it might be too traumatic for me to quit my job and move, too." She almost choked on the words *break up*.

Lily pulled away. "Alex could be right, and you can consider that, but first things first. We need to get some food into you, and after dinner we'll go for a nice walk. It'll do you good to get out. I'll get you more beer and chips. Be right back." She ducked inside.

Alone on the deck, Kate thought about her plans. She might only be gone a day or two, but what if she died back there in the past and they didn't know what happened? Even if she was only gone a short time, they would still worry, and the solstice was only two days away. She'd have to tell them everything.

Over dinner she did.

––––––––

Two evenings later Kate hiked through the meadow, her muscles aching under her heavy pack, with Ivan and Lily hiking beside her. She'd finally won them over about her scheme to return to 1863, and while they were worried, they seemed to understand. During the last two days they'd helped her organize the camping gear, buy food, and plan her journey. While they'd balked at the pistol she retrieved from her bedroom closet, they acknowledged she might need it. They'd tracked down more antique money, Ivan's old rucksack, and vintage clothes for her to take. She'd decided to go disguised as a man again since she felt it was safer. She'd left the tent behind, and opted for a light wool blanket instead of a modern sleeping bag to avoid drawing attention to herself.

"What a beautiful evening," Lily said as she walked beside her. "It's a good night to travel, if you must go." Ivan walked on in silence. They'd insisted on coming to the meadow to see her off, but Kate would hike up to the mesa alone. They'd promised not to follow.

"Maybe I'll only be gone a day or two," Kate said, "like the last time."

"Maybe," Ivan said. "But even if you manage to get through the passage, how do you know you'll arrive at the *right* time? Did you ever think of that?"

She had, but she'd gotten back before. "I've got the 1863 penny Lily gave me, so maybe it'll serve as a talisman, and it'll be the solstice tonight, so I should be fine." She didn't know how the passage knew *when* to take people to; how it worked was a mystery to her. It was like some ravenous creature, swallowing people up and spitting them out some*when* else. She might end up in the eighteen-twenties, or far in the future, but she refused to worry about it now.

"Do you have your phone?" Ivan asked, trudging along.

"Yep," she said. "It's charged and I've got extra batteries. I'll take pictures so I can show you when I get back." She buzzed with excitement despite the danger ahead.

Lily glanced at her. "At least try to call us like you did the last time, so we'll know you got there safely. That'll be a comfort."

"What do you mean *try to call*?" Ivan asked.

"My phone worked in the past the last time," Kate explained, "but just once. I called that first night from Jeremiah's barn and just heard static, but Lily somehow got my message. It was kind of amazing because I lost reception after that. I could take pictures without reception, of course, but I couldn't make calls. Then the batteries gave out."

Ivan sighed. "Damn. So we won't be able to communicate."

Kate shook her head. "Probably not."

They continued on, and when they reached the base of the mesa they stopped.

"Okay," Kate said. "This is where I leave you." Her pulse began to race. *I'm leaving them, and I might never see them again.*

Lily's eyes filled with tears. "Katie, honey."

Her heart sank. "You promised you wouldn't cry, Lily."

"I'm sorry," she said, and kissed her. She pulled back and brushed her tears away.

Ivan drew her into a hug. "Take care, Katie girl," he said, patting her shoulder. "We'll be with you in spirit." He kissed her cheek and stepped back.

"Be careful," Lily said. "And please try to call."

"I will. Let's not say goodbye, though, let's just say farewell. I'll be back soon."

"I love you, honey," Lily said. "Farewell."

Ivan nodded. "Farewell, Katie. Love you."

"Love you, too." Blinking back tears, Kate turned and headed up the trail into the forest. As she trudged up and up, she fell into a steady rhythm. The evening was warm, and soon she was sweating. When she reached the top, she shrugged off her pack, wiped her forehead, and gulped some water. She imagined Lily and Ivan walking home, and was thankful she couldn't see their sorrowful faces. After resting, she continued on.

When she reached the cave, it was as she remembered. A few sticks of wood lay by the fire ring, but she wouldn't need a fire tonight. The rock wall at the back of the cave was solid, but that should change in a few hours. Shedding her pack, she sat down at the entrance and unwrapped a granola bar. *Am I doing the right thing, or is this crazy? I could get stuck in the wrong time, get raped, or even killed.*

The sun was setting, the clouds flaring orange and crimson. Somewhere across time, Victor might be watching this same sunset. She had to try to find him.

Kate ate her snack and settled in to wait for the solstice.

———————

As the hours passed, Kate paced near the entrance in the twilight, then returned to the cave and sat down, clicked on her headlight, and read a book. She must have dozed off because she awoke in darkness with the earth rumbling and the cave sizzling with electricity. She clicked on her headlight and saw the passage opening into a four-foot-wide gaping hole. Shrugging into her pack, she took a huge breath and let it out, trying to still her pounding heart. "I can do this," she muttered, shining her headlight into the hole. "This is it. I'm going." She crawled through the opening and down the other side.

As she descended the steep passage, the earth shuddered and groaned like a restless animal, blowing its cold breath against her. "I can do this," she repeated. She continued down and down, skirted a rock pile, turned a bend, and descended further. Her pulse raced, and she almost stumbled, but she felt the ground level off as she emerged into the lower cave. She slipped her pack off and stood there, trembling. Kneeling down, she poked her head out of the entrance, saw the moonlit meadow, and inhaled the fresh night air. Feeling her head begin to pound, she took some ibuprofen and laid out her blanket. As she wrapped herself in it, she felt the familiar exhaustion from the time travel weigh her down. She closed her eyes and began to drop off. A wolf howled out in the meadow. Sleep engulfed her.

———————

Colorado Front Range—1863

Rising from sleep was like ascending through warm rippling water. As Kate swam up through its layers, she became aware of several sounds—a woodpecker's hammering, an elk's bugling, a blackbird's trilling. Opening her eyes she glimpsed daylight seeping through the entrance before falling back to sleep. By the time she woke again and went outside, it was almost noon. Her headache was better, but it would take days for it to completely go away; she was tired but not exhausted like she was last night. She inhaled a deep breath, let it out, and saw a herd of elk grazing in the distance. She'd never seen elk here before, the grasses were higher, and the creek was bigger—all signs she might be in the past.

After building a small fire, she made instant oatmeal and coffee and took out one of Lily's cranberry scones. As she sat at the cave entrance eating breakfast, she wondered when she should set off and which way she should go—north or south. Jeremiah's was about seven miles north so she could hike there in a long day, but Colorado City was about twenty miles south so that would take longer and she'd have to camp. The stage road was just over the rise, but she didn't know which days it ran in which direction. She could just strap on her pack, hike over there, and hope it showed up.

After eating she ambled to the creek and knelt down to wash her dishes but felt a wave of dizziness as she stood up. "Nope," she told herself, "not today. I need more rest before setting off." She walked back to the cave and went to sleep.

———————

Colorado Front Range—1863

Kate slept most of the day, got up around dusk and strolled around the meadow, cooked backpacker chili for dinner, and soon fell back to sleep. The next morning she packed up her gear and headed for the stage road, determined to walk all the way to Jeremiah's if she had to. If the stagecoach came along, she'd board it, but if it didn't and she got tired, she'd camp tonight and continue on tomorrow. She paced herself as she trudged across the meadow, stopping often. As she crested the rise, she spotted bighorn sheep grazing on the opposite hillside and remembered Victor had told her he'd been hunting bighorns here when Bear startled him and chased him into the cave years ago. *So that confirms I've returned to the past. Hopefully, I'm also in the right time. I'll find out soon.* She saw storm clouds lumbering in from the north, their bellies heavy with rain, and decided to rest in the ponderosas on the opposite hillside and keep an eye on the weather. If a stagecoach came she'd flag it down; if it didn't she'd start walking. Reaching the trees, she shed her pack and stretched as she noticed four horsemen riding toward her. Taking out her binoculars, Kate watched the riders come closer, searching for tracks as they hunted. *Arapaho*, she realized, as she saw their long hair and painted faces. *If they spot these bighorns behind me, they'll ride over here to hunt them and find me.* A cold fear settled in her gut as she watched them continue on.

When they spotted the sheep, the Arapaho dismounted, hobbled their horses, and started creeping toward their prey. Feeling a tickle in her nose, Kate pinched it to try to stifle a sneeze, but the Arapaho heard it and saw her. As her heart pounded, she watched them creep toward her. The bighorns spooked and bolted uphill. The braves stopped forty feet away and turned north. Thunder rumbled in the distance.

Not thunder, Kate realized, *there's a stagecoach coming, thank God.* The braves dashed for their horses, mounted, and tore off as a stagecoach came over a hill and headed toward her. She fumbled her pack on and rushed from the trees, waving her arms and shouting, "Stop!"

The driver reigned in his horses and stopped. "Need a ride?"

"Yes," she gasped. "Are you headed to Colorado City?"

"Yessir. I don't have any room inside, but I kin fit you up top." Several people peered out from the stagecoach at her—one a pinched-faced man wearing wire-rimmed glasses, one a young blond woman in a blue dress and hat, and one a child about five years old.

"On top would be fine," Kate said, taking off her rucksack.

Climbing down from his seat, the driver spat out a yellowish wad of phlegm. "Let me help you." He hoisted the rucksack onto the roof, strapped it down, and grinned at her. "Climb aboard, friend."

Kate climbed up, held on, and braced herself.

"Giddy-up!" the driver cried.

With a sudden jolt, they were off.

————————

Colorado City—1863

Several bone-jarring hours later the stagecoach lurched into town, its horses lathered and weary, its passengers sore and hungry. Kate's butt hurt from sitting and her hands hurt from gripping. As the driver stopped in front of a familiar hotel, Kate tried to remember what it looked like inside from the last time she'd been here.

As she climbed down off the stagecoach, she realized she had to stay somewhere, and the hotel was as good as any. Her old cabin was close by and she'd brought its key, but it was probably dirty, and she didn't want to stay with Doozie. She stretched, heard her joints crack, and thought her spine might need a major realignment.

As the driver unloaded the luggage and helped the other riders, Kate stared down the dusty street at the saloon and decided to go see Doozie later. When the driver tossed her rucksack down on the sidewalk, she propped it up against the wall. Going into the dimly-lit hotel, Kate inhaled the delicious scents of biscuits, stew, and cooked apples. A harried-looking woman was setting the table with mismatched plates and glasses.

"Need a bed?" the woman asked.

Kate nodded. "I'd like a private room if you have it."

"Yer in luck," she said. "We got one."

A teenaged boy appeared at her side. "Want a hand with yer bag?"

"I'd like to look at the room first," Kate said.

The boy led her out of the hotel and up the outside stairs, into a large room partitioned off by sheets of canvas. Through a space between them, Kate saw a man and woman dozing on blankets with a baby dozing between them. Another man sat in the next cloth cubicle polishing his boots as a woman knitted beside him.

"There's plenty of space here if you want to sleep on the floor," the boy said, "and down here's yer private room." Passing three closed doors, he showed her a little room with a lumpy double bed covered with a weathered quilt, a chest of drawers with a wash basin and pitcher, and a window overlooking a yard. "It's two dollars fer a place in the bed, but you might have to share it if another traveler comes in later." He smiled, revealing a gap in his front teeth. "That price includes mama's fine supper and breakfast. The privy's out yonder, and yer honey pot's under the bed. Want the room?"

"It's clean and cozy," Kate said. "I'll take it."

"Thank you, sir," the boy said. "I'll bring up yer gear. Supper's at six."

Kate smiled as she watched him stride away. He'd called her *sir*, so her disguise must be working. She'd clean up and rest a bit and go to Doozie's after supper.

———————

Colorado City—1863

When she strolled into the saloon a few hours later, the place was noisy and the crowd was boisterous. Spying Doozie hauling a tray of drinks to a table, Kate stood off to the side and waited for her to notice her. Men played cards, drank, and devoured the bar food as women cruised the room like sharks seeking prey, decked out in cheap jewelry and brash colors. Glasses chinked. People burst into laughter. A scrawny man played a lively tune on a fiddle.

"Here's yer beers, gents," Doozie said to some men as she set down their glasses. "That'll be ten cents each." Decked out in a bold yellow dress with turquoise earrings, she propped a hand on her hip and tapped her boot, determined to get her money. After she did, she wheeled around and spotted Kate.

Doozie looked stunned for a second. "Balls, Kate!" she cried, hugging her. "Yer back!"

"I am," she whispered, "but don't blow my cover. Call me Mac, remember?"

"All right, Mac, but you startled me! It's so damn good to see you!"

Kate grinned as she savored the sight of the girl. "It's great to see you, Dooz, and I like your hair up like that with those pretty combs. Your place is booming."

"Business is brisk, an' my fiddle-player lures 'em in. I started wearing my hair like this to look more respectable. Glad you fancy it." She gripped Kate's hands. "How long you here for? Are you stayin' this time? I been missin' you somethin' fierce, Mac."

"I've been missing you, too," Kate said, squeezing Doozie's hands.

"Come over here," Doozie said, leading her to the bar. "I cain't visit with you right now 'cuz it's so busy, but I kin sure offer you some food."

"Thanks, Dooz, but I ate at my hotel. I booked a room there."

Her blond eyebrows arched. "I swear, Mac, a hotel gits mighty pricey! You kin put up here if you want. Buster's sleepin' on a bedtick in the kitchen. My bedroom's right next to it, an' yer welcome to share it, but it was burnt in a fire and I ain't got a proper winda' put in yet." She laughed. "You know we git powerful rowdy and stay up late, so bunk where you want."

Kate remembered those late nights from when she worked here as a piano player. "Thanks for the offer, but the hotel's fine for now. I might clean up my cabin and stay there a few days, but I intend to go up to South Park to look for Victor. He's gone up there, hasn't he?"

"Yep. Thank heaven you came back to git 'im. He misses you somethin' fierce."

Kate's heart leapt. *Victor misses me.* "I can't tell you how much I've missed him. And you said Buster's staying here?"

"He is, 'til I find somebody permanent. I gotta hire a man fer protection 'cuz Blackstone's back in town. He tried to burn my place down a few days ago. He woulda, too, if it hadn't been fer Victor." A customer caught her eye and held up three fingers.

"Blackstone's back?" Kate asked. "I was hoping he was dead."

"Nope," Doozie said, darting behind the bar to grab some glasses. "He's alive, damn his eyes. Fancy a beer on the house? You kin settle in at yonder table."

"I'd love a beer," Kate said. "Is Buster around tonight?"

"Not yet." Doozie pulled some beers, set them on a tray, and slid one across the bar to Kate. "He went to the sawmill this morning to fetch some lumber, but he oughta be back this evenin'." She grinned. "He'll sure be glad to see you, Mac."

"What's today's date, Dooz? I need to know."

"It's July 16, 1863, silly. Gotta hustle now, Mac. There's cards on that table if you wanna play solitaire, and a paper to read." She turned and hurried off.

Kate watched the card players, drinkers, and working girls. She'd made it back to the right time, and she was standing in Doozie's saloon like she'd never left. Breaking into a grin, she grabbed her beer and headed for the table to read the paper.

CHAPTER FIFTEEN

Victor crept up a hill above a herd of bison a hundred yards distant, the sun warming his bare back, the wind blowing his scent away from the animals, feeling more alive than he had in months. With Rising Moon on one side and the war chief Running Deer on the other, Victor once again felt like he belonged.

Reaching the top, the men peered down through the tall grasses and watched the herd graze below, keeping their bodies low and their breathing shallow. A change of wind could betray them, or a horse's whinny, sending the massive beasts stampeding off. Like silent ghosts they eased back down the hill, mounted their horses, and cocked their rifles. Nodding to each other, they launched their horses at the herd, Milagro in the lead.

Shots exploded and several bison fell. The others thundered off, eyes wild and rolling, plunging through the grasses—running, running. As the beasts disappeared in a cloud of dust, Victor and Milagro galloped across the trampled grasses to where Victor's fallen bison lay—eyes open, bleeding, still alive.

Jumping from Milagro, Victor crouched beside the beast and drew his knife. "Thank you, my brother, for relinquishing your life." The huge eyes rolled toward him in terror; the huge chest heaved. Shoving his knife beneath the shaggy hide, Victor pierced the animal's heart and watched its blood ooze out. The bison shuddered and grew still. Its eyes lost their luster.

"Thank you, my friend." Victor closed his own eyes and savored the moment, his heart pounding with the thrill of it. He smelled the metallic scent of blood, the pungent scent of sweat, and the rich scent of earth.

I'm finally fully alive, and I'm finally home again.

—————————

A warm wind blew Hawk above the grasses, hillsides, hunters, and fallen bison. She soared on thermals, rising up and up with their heat and energy, using them to push her higher and higher. Beneath her the hunters knelt beside their bison, chewing on the still-warm hearts as the women hurried toward them to begin butchering.

Hawk watched Victor as he glanced up and saw her. Watched the horse named Milagro paw the earth. Watched the retreating herd pound through the grasses, sending up clouds of dust. She had remained with Victor and Little Eagle for many days, hiding as Bear in the forests, flying as Hawk through the mountain air, sleeping as Mouse in Victor's snug tepee.

Now she senses that it's time to go; someone else she loves needs her. Rising higher, she soars above Victor, letting the thermals carry her off to the east.

She soars; she rests; she hunts. Stopping during the day's heat, she lands on a shady aspen branch, tucks her head under her wing, and dozes. She dreams Hawk-dreams of soaring and catching mice, Mouse-dreams of nibbling paintbrush blossoms and darting down holes, Bear-dreams of chasing deer and stalking coyotes. Within her dreams she sees a familiar form and trots toward it; hears a familiar voice and listens to it; feels a familiar hand and nudges under it. It's Kate's slender form, her lovely voice, her gentle hand. She's come through the passage to this time and is now somewhere east of here.

Hawk snapped awake from her nap and lifted off, rising over the mountains and meadows. During her journey she spies the bison grazing, the stream winding, the antelope running, the coyotes playing, the wolves hunting, the deer nibbling, the flowers blooming, the grasses waving, the aspen fluttering, the woodpeckers hammering, the hummingbirds whirring, the elk bugling, the mountain lion stalking. She sees all these as she flies east, feeling the day wane and the air cool. As the sun sets, the shadows lengthen and the thermals lose their energy. Darkness falls. Hawk flies on.

During the night she hunts again, sleeps again, dreams again. A delicious river of scents and sounds flows through her dreams. Sometime before morning she awakens, spreads her wings, and continues on.

Hawk searches.

— — — — — — —

After a night spent in the lumpy bed at the hotel, Kate felt amazingly well-rested. The beer had helped relax her, along with the irrational belief that she was safe behind her unlocked door. She was surprised she'd slept so well with so many people nearby snoring, sneezing, and coughing. *What a slumbering cacophony.*

The chamber pot stank. She nudged it further under the bed, dressed, and checked her appearance in the mirror. "I look quite respectable," she said, studying her blue homemade shirt and gray loose-fitting trousers. "Time for breakfast."

The dining room bustled with hungry travelers. The long table was loaded with platters of steaming eggs and sausages, biscuits, and butter. Jugs of milk and pots of coffee were set at either end. Kate found a seat on a wooden bench between a stout, weary-looking matron and a young woman nursing an infant.

"Hope my baby didn't keep you up last night," the mother said, her freckled face etched with fatigue. "He's teething, so he's a bit cross."

"No, he didn't," Kate said. As she scooped eggs and sausages onto her plate, she wondered how Little Eagle was doing, whether she was eating more solid food. "Pass the biscuits, please." She sipped her coffee, wincing at the taste. "This coffee tastes strange."

"It's roasted grain," the matron muttered. "It's impossible to get real coffee during this infernal war."

Doozie can get real coffee, Kate thought. *She's a wonder.* She smiled as she buttered a warm biscuit. She longed to take Doozie back with her, but she had things to do first.

After breakfast she paid the innkeeper for another night, grabbed her rucksack, and ambled along the wooden sidewalk to check out the town. Things had improved since she was last here a month ago: a couple of dilapidated structures had been cleared away, broken windows had been replaced, and some of the broken fences had been mended. A few people waved as she passed, glancing up from chopping wood or tending kitchen gardens. Log cabins squatted among frame houses, barns, and outbuildings. Horses stood tied to hitching posts, their tails swishing away flies as wagons and buckboards rumbled by. Kate passed a blacksmith's, a barrel-maker's, two mercantiles, a bakery, three saloons, and a livery. When she strolled past Doozie's place, it was shuttered and dark; Kate suspected those inside were still sleeping off the night's labors.

A lanky young man strode out of a mercantile and began sweeping the sidewalk.

"Abner?" Kate asked. "Remember me?"

His face lit up with smiles. "I swan, Mac! How've you been keeping yourself?"

"Very well," she said, smiling. On her last visit, she'd been impressed with Abner's youthful energy and good manners. He'd given Prairie Flower a good trade for her deerskins and was friendly to the Utes. "I heard the Utes have left for South Park."

"Oh, yes," he said. "Hunting's better up there in summer, and it's much cooler."

"I hope to go up there myself soon. Well, take care."

"Good day," he said, and continued sweeping.

Kate sauntered off. About ten minutes later, she arrived at her cabin, saw the rough-hewn logs chinked with crumbling mud, and inserted the key into the rusty padlock. She shoved the heavy door open, revealing the plank floor, the plank table with a wash basin, and the cast iron woodstove. She set down her pack and studied the tiny window with its dirty pane, and the wooden bed with its straw mattress, tattered quilt, and bison robe. As she moved closer, Kate saw the quilt and robe were riddled with holes and littered with mouse droppings.

"What a mess," she said. Propping the door open, she dragged the robe and quilt outside. The tick mattress came apart in dusty tatters but no mice emerged from its remnants. She wouldn't bother to buy new bedding; she'd just fold up her blanket and sleep on the wooden frame. As she grabbed a broom and swept the droppings off the floor, she began to whistle.

"Well, now," a man's voice said from the doorway. "Welcome home."

Her heart stopped. *I know that voice.* Gripping the broom like a weapon, she turned and faced Blackstone. "Get out of here!"

He stood there, smirking, his left arm cradled in a sling. "But I just got here, MacKenzie. Aren't you going to invite me into your humble palace?"

Kate began to tremble. Her loaded gun was in her pack across the room. "I *said* get out."

He inched closer.

She clutched the broom against her chest. "Stay back, asshole."

He grabbed the broom with his good arm and shoved her against the wall. She gasped as he pushed the handle against her throat to cut off her air. "I should kill you for shooting me and murdering Charlie," he snarled. "How'd you get out of that cave? Where'd you go?"

Kate couldn't breathe. Stars exploded behind her eyelids. Feeling his sling against her skin, she grabbed his bad arm and yanked it.

"Damn!" he cried, releasing the broom and stumbling backward.

She gulped in a huge breath, lunged forward, and whacked him with the broom.

He tripped over a chair and fell to the floor.

"Get out!" she yelled, and whacked him again. Lunging for her pack, she pulled out her gun, cocked it, and thrust it at him.

"You little pissant! Damn you!" Blackstone scrambled to his feet and bolted out.

Kate rushed to the door and watched him stumble off. She was back in the past now, with all its dangers, so she'd have to be more careful; she'd have to remember to keep her gun handy. As she watched Blackstone disappear around the corner, she felt her hands begin to shake and set the gun down. She'd held a gun on him several times before, and each time she'd ached to kill him. What bothered her most wasn't that she wanted to take his life, it was that she felt she had a right to. She paced back and forth trying to calm herself.

She fished inside her pack for the matches. Going outside, she lit the pile of discarded bedding. As she watched it burn, she imagined Blackstone burning with it and felt a morbid satisfaction.

After a while Kate poked at the dwindling flames, making a mental list of where things stood. Blackstone hated her, and she hated him, so she was in grave danger. She had to find Victor, talk Doozie into coming with them, and get the hell out of here.

———————

Victor lay in the grass, digesting his breakfast and listening to the stream. Aspen leaves fluttered overhead, casting a dappled shade. Milagro grazed a few feet away. His sister-in-law Prairie Flower squatted nearby, slicing bison meat into strips and hanging them on a rack to dry. Her sleeping son hung from a ponderosa in his cradleboard; Little Eagle slept in an adjacent tree. His mother-in-law Mourning Dove was helping slice bison meat, as was Badger Woman, the widow he'd rescued from the Arapaho when he'd been in the past the last time. Since he'd returned, she'd followed him around like a puppy. A very lonely and love-sick puppy.

She owed Victor her life and longed to please him, but he didn't want her as a lover. He wanted no woman yet. Soon his people would pressure him to take another wife to be a mother to Little Eagle, but he wouldn't pick Badger Woman. Her ugly scar bothered him, although he knew it shouldn't. When he looked at her, he didn't see her sparkling eyes, her kind smile, or her grateful heart—he saw the pink scar tissue in the middle of her face where her nose had been before the Arapaho cut it off to shame her.

Another female flirted with him, too, but she was just a girl. At fourteen, Soaring Falcon was the daughter of Running Deer, their war chief. An accomplished horsewoman and tireless worker, she was over by her family's tepee cutting bison strips and casting him flirtatious glances. Victor sighed. He'd been happy with his people before, and he was sure he could be happy again—as soon as his heart healed. Perhaps another woman could help it heal, but he just wasn't ready yet. For now he was content to lie by this stream and listen to it babble.

When Little Eagle awoke and started fussing, he leaned up on one elbow and waved at her. Although his tribeswomen cared for her, he often helped, which confused them. They weren't accustomed to a Ute brave tending a child, but he was used to doing it. When the soft rabbit fur in her cradleboard got soiled, he sometimes changed it. When he wasn't off hunting, he often played with her, took her on walks, and fed her porridge. Since Prairie Flower was nursing her own child she insisted on nursing her niece, too.

The baby began crying in earnest, waving her arms at him from her perch in the ponderosa, squirming to escape. She disliked being confined to her cradleboard for long. She enjoyed the comfort of her modern carrier so he often used it when he took her walking, although its odd appearance prompted many comments. Scrambling to his feet, he hurried over, eased her from her cradleboard, and patted her naked bottom.

"It's okay, little one, I've got you," he said as her cries tapered off.

"Does her rabbit fur need changing?" Prairie Flower asked.

"No," he said, reaching inside the cradleboard to feel it. "It's still dry, but I think she's hungry."

"Wait," she said, putting down her knife. She settled in against a boulder and stretched out her arms. "Give her here."

"All right," Victor said. "But after she eats, I want to take her walking." He laid her in Prairie Flower's lap and watched her begin to nurse. He was glad he'd returned, glad his granddaughter was being cared for by her people, but sometimes he missed the comfortable trappings of the future. Amid the staggering beauty of this mountain park, he sometimes missed having a studio to

paint in and a comfy chair to read in. Of course, he also missed...
But no, he refused to think about *her*.

"I'll be back," he said, heading for the nearest cooking fire. "I'm
hungry, too."

———————

As the morning passed, Kate's mood improved when she
realized she'd probably scared Blackstone away for a while. She
tidied up the cabin and decided it would do for however long she
needed it. She hauled water from a nearby creek and cleaned the
window and the table. Around noon she went to the saloon,
hoping for a hearty lunch. She found the place empty, except for
Doozie.

"O' course you kin eat here," she said, setting food on the bar.
"I'd be hurt if you didn't. Help yerself while I make another pot of
coffee and git that old fart Buster up. He got in after you left last
night." She hustled for the kitchen.

"Thanks," Kate said, reaching for a plate. As she loaded it up
with roast beef and rye bread, she noticed a buxom young
redhead creeping downstairs, gripping the banister like a lifeline,
obviously hung-over.

"Hey, Mac," she said, joining her at the bar. "How have you
been keeping yourself? I haven't seen you in a fair piece." She
pecked Kate on the cheek.

Kate was startled by the kiss but remembered the girls thought
she was a man, and a gay one at that. "Hey, Bridgette. I got in last
night, but I guess you were busy."

She smiled and wiped the sleep from her eyes. "You could say
that, darlin'. An old flame showed up, randy as a rutting bull, and
we screwed like hell-on-fire." She poured a cup of coffee, added a
generous dollop of cream and three teaspoonsful of sugar, took a
sip, and sighed. "Lord, I needed this. I'm afflicted with a wee
headache from too much drink. I was up 'til all hours, but the
blessed fool paid for my loving like a prince of Ireland." She
plucked two pickled eggs from a jar, set them on a saucer, and
turned her bloodshot eyes on Kate. "Sorry, but I'm not much for
conversation in the morning."

"I hate to tell you, Bridgette, but it's past noon already."

"No need to shout, Mac," she said, clutching her forehead.
"Leave me be 'til I sip my wee coffee." Gripping her breakfast she
shuffled to a table and slumped into a chair.

Kate slathered butter on her bread and stole a glance at the weary woman, sipping coffee in her plain yellow dress. She knew Bridgette had been a maid back East and had been raped by the bullwhacker leading her wagon train out west. All of the girls had horrible reasons why they'd ended up here, and she felt sorry for them. She knew she couldn't help all of them, but maybe she could help just one. She put some roast beef on a slice of bread, added tomatoes and mustard, and covered it with another slice.

Doozie returned and chided Kate. "What the hell you doin' with my fixins'?"

Kate grinned. "Making a sandwich. People eat these all the time in the future."

Doozie set the fresh pot of coffee down and hugged her. "I don't care what yer doin', as long as yer here. Welcome back, blood sister. We got some catchin' up to do. Come eat with me at yonder table and we'll talk a while."

———————

After lunch and an enthusiastic reunion with Buster, he drove Kate north of town in his wagon, passing two ranchers herding cattle near the deserted Ute encampment. It looked much the same, with its fire rings, stone tepee circles, and empty horse corrals, but it felt lonely and abandoned to Kate.

"It seems so ghostly here without people," she said, looking around. "Could you take me up to the Utes in South Park next time you go?"

Buster spit out a wad of tobacco. "I reckon so. I got a load o' lumber needs haulin' up there, and I'd fancy yer company, but you oughta buy a mount first."

"The Utes probably have my Lady Grey at their encampment. It doesn't make sense to buy another horse if I have a perfectly good one already."

He shrugged. "Suit yerself, but the Utes might not have yer horse. Be right back. Gotta take care o' bus'ness." He jumped from the wagon and disappeared into a stand of scrub oak.

Easing down from the wagon, Kate strolled to the abandoned corral and rested her hands on the brush gate. She could almost hear the horses whinny; almost see Lady Grey trotting up to greet her. A hawk cried overhead, and she looked up to watch it. Something about it seemed familiar as it spiraled downward in diminishing circles. It cried again as it flew toward Kate and landed on a nearby slab of rock.

"Well, I'll be darned," Kate said, sitting beside her. "About time you showed up."

Hawk settled her feathers and studied her with piercing gold eyes.

Kate stroked her wing. "Smart bird. Beautiful bird. Where's Victor?"

Hawk closed her eyes and seemed to sigh.

Buster emerged from the trees and stood there, dumbstruck. "I swear, Mac. You're awful close to that bird."

"This bird and I have a history. Remember that bear we saw at Harrison's cabin?"

"You mean the one that spooked them bandits? Course I remember. Why?"

"Because this hawk is her, in another form. She's a shapeshifter."

He laughed. "Whaddya take me fer, Mac?"

"What do you mean? Haven't you ever heard of shapeshifters?"

"Course I have, but I don't cotton to that kind o' lore. I got 'nuff trouble dealin' with survivin'."

Hawk expanded her wings and screeched at him.

"I'll be damned," he said. "Never seen nothin' like it. Listen, Mac, I got some supplies to fetch afore I go to South Park, but I oughta be ready in a couple o' days."

"Good," Kate said. "I'd like to come, but first I want to talk to Sheriff Trask. I need to tell him Blackstone murdered Homer and attacked me in my cabin this morning."

Buster nodded. "I'll go with you since I promised Doozie I'd accuse that asswipe Blackstone o' conspirin' to set her place on fire."

"Do you have any proof?" she asked, stroking Hawk's head.

"No, but it's the kinda thing he *would* do, don'tcha see? I need to apprize our good sheriff o' Blackstone's true nature. I got some money, in case he needs convincin'."

"You mean like a bribe?"

"O' course. Everybody's got his price, an' I know some lawmen take 'em."

Kate shook her head. "Yeah, but a bribe? I'm not sure that's wise. I'm not even sure it'll do any good to tell him. Remember, he went along with Blackstone's decision to hang Angelina's husband." She remembered Jeremiah's cook, now a grieving widow.

"It were the people's decision, Mac. That's what happens to horse thieves."

"But don't you remember?" Kate asked. "A rancher came forward later to clear Luis of all the charges. Trask and Blackstone hung an innocent man!"

Buster shrugged. "Be that as it may, that's how things is done around here. Doozie has a stake in accusin' Blackstone, so she should come with us. She told me she tried to accuse him before of killin' Homer, but the sheriff didn't pay her no mind."

"That's awful," Kate said. "Let's go this afternoon before the saloon gets busy."

"All right." As he watched the ranchers herd their cattle, his gaze rose to the top of the mesa behind them. "Look," he said, pointing. "We got company. See 'em?"

Kate shielded her eyes to look. Six figures sat on their horses, silhouetted against a clear blue sky. "I see them, but hold on." Retrieving her pack from the wagon, she pulled out her binoculars and glassed the ridgeline. "Looks like Arapaho. I saw a hunting party north of here just a few days ago. Wonder what they're doing here?"

"Don't know, but I don't like it. They's awful close." As the ranchers spotted the Indians, they spurred their horses and began moving their cattle toward town.

Buster frowned. "Could be a war party. People are scared 'nuff around here without *them* showin' up."

"Why?" Kate asked. "What happened?"

"You ain't heard? Course not, you been gone. A family was murdered northeast of here—both parents an' two younguns. Parents was mutilated somethin' horrible. We better git back to town, quick."

They climbed into the wagon and hurried off. By the time they returned to town, others had raised the alarm.

———————

Sheriff Trask was devouring a plate of fried chicken and biscuits when Kate, Doozie, and Buster strode into his office an hour later. "Can I help you folks?" he asked, licking grease off his fingers.

Kate took a deep breath in and let it out. "We want to report several crimes."

"All right." Trask wiped his mouth with a kerchief and leaned back in his chair. "What crimes are they, where and when did they happen, and who committed them?"

"Blackstone committed at least two of them," Kate said. "We're not sure about the third, but we have our suspicions."

The sheriff frowned. "Blackstone, our circuit judge?"

"Yes," Kate said, feeling her stomach clench as she thought of him. "He murdered Homer the saloon-keep a few weeks ago on the stage road north of here, we suspect he conspired to set Doozie's saloon on fire last week, and he assaulted me in my cabin just this morning."

Trask bit into a biscuit "You sure took your time reporting a murder. Why?"

"I've been traveling," Kate said, "and I just got back."

"I tried to tell you before," Doozie snapped, "but you wouldn't listen to me."

The sheriff chewed his biscuit. "Now, Doozie, it's not that I didn't listen, I just needed more time to investigate. Tell me what happened this morning, Mac."

"Blackstone rammed a broom handle against my throat and tried to strangle me."

Trask coughed on his biscuit, cleared his throat, and took a sip of coffee. "I see. Did you witness the other crimes you're accusing him of?"

"I witnessed Homer's murder," Kate said, "but not the arson attempt."

Doozie lunged forward. "I seen 'im shoot Homer with my own eyes! He tried to kill me an' Mac that day, an' coulda burnt down my whole place with that fire!"

Trask sipped his coffee. "Did anyone else witness these crimes?"

"I was alone in my cabin," Kate said, "so no one else saw him attack me."

"I seen the fire myself," Buster said. "That place coulda gone up like a tinderbox, Sheriff. Plenty o' women coulda died that night if we hadna put it out."

Trask nodded. "But did you actually *see* who started it?"

"No," Buster said, "but I think Blackstone done it, or put somebody up to it."

The sheriff's eyes narrowed. "Did anyone else see Homer's murder?"

"Victor Manyhorses," Kate said. "You could ask him, but he's up in South Park."

"The Ute?" Trask said. "I don't give much credence to Injun witnesses."

"Well you should," Kate said. "He was there, and saw the whole thing."

"Listen, Mac," Trask said, rising from his chair. "I'll investigate this when I have time, but I have more pressing matters to deal with now. You've probably heard a war party was sighted north of town this morning, and a report just came from Denver that hostiles are conspiring to attack every settlement near here. Concerning Blackstone, these are serious accusations, as he's an upstanding member of our community, and it's your word against his. He's a respected circuit judge, but Doozie's a whore..."

"I ain't a whore no more," Doozie interjected. "I own the place now."

"... and Buster's an itinerant freighter," Trask continued, "and you're just a barroom piano player."

"We know that," Buster said, pulling a leather pouch from his pocket. "That's why I reckoned you might need some financial help with yer investigatin'."

Trask scowled. "Is that what I think it is?"

Buster dangled the pouch in front of him. "Fer investigatin' expenses."

"Get out!" Trask growled, shoving the pouch away. "I don't take bribes!"

"I'm powerful sorry," Buster said, shrinking back, "but I heard some sheriffs do."

"Well I don't, so get the hell out!"

They hurried out, putting some distance between themselves and the sheriff's office. The street was clogged with frantic travelers on horseback and mules, searching for provisions and a place to stay. Settlers were driving wagons crammed with families and stacked with belongings, with goats and cows trailing along behind them. "Maybe we shouldn't have bothered," Kate said, stopping to catch her breath in front of the livery.

"I told you he wouldn't listen," Doozie muttered. "Not to the likes of us."

"Oh, he listened," Kate said. "He just didn't like what he heard."

Buster tucked the pouch back into his pocket. "Don't give up jist yet, he might change his mind. He did say he'd look into it."

"He might," Kate said, "but don't get your hopes up. If he's as tight with Blackstone as I think he is, he'll tell him we accused him, and that'll piss him off. What's going on?" she asked, staring at the bustling street. "Why are all these people in town?"

"They's comin' in fer safety," Buster said. "Folks is fortin' up an' gittin' ready fer that attack, an' cuttin' logs to build a barricade to hide behind afore the Injuns come."

"Really?" she asked. "Where's it going to go?"

"Around yer hotel, Mac," he said, pointing at it.

Buster was right. Men in wagons and buckboards were hauling fresh-cut logs into town, lugging them down the street and unloading them in front of Kate's hotel.

"Reckon I'll git my oxen hitched up and help 'em," Buster said. "I'll come by an' check on you later, Dooz. You got 'nuff provisions?"

"I doubt it," she said. "I got to hustle to lay in more. We're bound to be busy, an' who knows how long we'll be holed up. Yer welcome to come stay with us, Mac."

Kate shook her head. "I'll stay at my hotel since I've already paid for the night. How many hostiles do they say might be coming?" Her heart began to pound.

"Don't rightly know," Buster said, hawking up a brownish wad. "Folks say the messenger told the sheriff there could be hundreds, so take care, friends." He hurried off.

Hundreds? It was one thing to see a small scouting party, quite another to be attacked by hundreds. "Do you think we'll be safe in town?"

Doozie shrugged. "Cain't know fer sure, but we kin hope."

As Kate peered at her hotel, she saw men stacking logs. "All these people will never fit behind one barricade."

"No," Doozie said, "but many of the women and children will. My girls won't be welcome there, but we kin board up the windas and hole up in my place jist fine."

Kate saw the steady resolve in Doozie's hazel eyes. "Aren't you afraid?"

"Course I am, but I been through it before. I guess you ain't."

"No," Kate said, "never. But I guess I'm about to."

———————

Throughout the afternoon Kate helped Doozie buy provisions until supplies ran out. They bought three hams and eight strings of sausages from the butcher, snagged six loaves of bread from the bakery, and bartered a miner a kerosene lantern for a sack of pinto beans.

"Aren't you afraid to go up the pass now with all these hostiles around?" Kate asked the miner as he handed her the beans from the back of his wagon.

"Nope," he said, snapping his reins. "Might be safer up there. If those Injuns are attacking down here, they'll be too busy to go up the pass to fight Utes in South Park."

"Good point," Kate said, watching him rumble off. "Maybe we should go there."

"Not jist yet, Mac," Doozie said. "I want to come with you and Buster when you go, but I need to git ready. It were Homer's dream to open a saloon in the diggin's fer the miners, an' he left me a claim I could work, too. That could fetch me a tidy sum."

"Run a saloon plus work a mining claim?" Kate asked as she followed her across the street. "You'd work yourself to death doing both, and what about your place here?"

"I'd hire a man to work the claim," she said, opening the door to her saloon. "Bridgette could run this place. Let's git these provisions put away in the kitchen." As they passed through the main room, they saw business was already brisk. Several patrons were drinking and gambling, Bridgette was serving drinks, the girls were circling the tables, and the fiddler was tuning his fiddle. As they entered the kitchen, Kate noticed several homey touches—red checked curtains hung in the windows, a red ceramic lantern dangled from the ceiling, clean dishes and cups were neatly stacked in the cupboard. An open door led to a room off the kitchen. "Is that your bedroom in there?"

Doozie took the beans from her and put them in the pantry. "Yep, that's it. Like I told you, I got my big winda boarded up, but I still got that little one. It still smells a tad smoky, but I scrubbed the burnt floorboards and pitched out the ruint curtains."

As Kate looked into the bedroom, she saw a double brass bed with a patchwork quilt, and a rocking chair. A small wooden table topped with a kerosene lamp and a primer she'd given Doozie sat by a boarded-up window. "It smells more like soap than smoke. Have you been keeping up with your reading?"

Doozie picked up a knife and started slicing a ham, setting the slices on a large platter with a flowery border. "I read ever' chance I git when I'm not too weary."

Kate joined her at the table. "I'm proud of you, Dooz. You were a quick learner to begin with, and you've kept it up. Not many students would do as well in such isolation."

"I aim to better myself, Mac, and readin's one way to do it. Damn, that hurts." She set down her knife and gripped her shoulder. "My shoulder still pains me sometimes, but it's healin'. Could you finish slicin' this ham whilst I make a pot o' coffee?"

"Of course," she said, taking up the knife. "How can you get real coffee beans when everyone else is using roasted grain?"

Doozie smiled. "I got my ways."

"I'll bet you do," Kate said. She noticed a lumpy-looking mattress tucked behind the cupboard. "Is that Buster's bedtick?"

"It is," Doozie said, pouring some of the precious coffee beans into a grinder. "If you quit the hotel an' come here, he might invite you to share it, but don't. He snores like a grizzly."

"Don't worry, I won't," Kate said as she sliced the ham. "I remember he snores from when we camped out in South Park a while ago when I was here before. Speaking of the hotel, I should get back for supper. I paid for it, so I may as well eat it."

"Suit yerself," Doozie said, turning the grinder with her good arm. "But it'll be crowded there, with all them extra folks in town."

"I hadn't thought of that," Kate said, setting the last slice of ham on the platter.

"You could sleep with me in my bedroom, but Buster might think we's lovers. Did he ever suspect you was a woman when you traveled up to South Park?"

"No, I don't think so. Like I said, we camped out, plus I kept all my clothes on." *Except for the time the bandits made me strip, but they'd already knocked Buster out.*

Doozie straightened a vase of wildflowers on the table. "Or I might jist find you another bedtick to sleep in. Put that plate o' ham on the bar on yer way out, Mac."

"Bye," Kate said, picking up the platter and heading out. "I might come back later."

Doozie flashed her a smile. "You do that."

When Kate reached her hotel, she saw men setting logs on end in the ground close together to completely encircle the building. It looked like the skeleton of a fort, with a large protective enclosure. Portholes had been notched into the logs at intervals for shooting weapons. As she went inside, she saw the dining room was crowded with more travelers, some sitting shoulder to shoulder at the table and some standing. Kate found a seat next to the young mother she'd met that morning.

"Hello again," the woman said as she jiggled her baby. "I forgot my manners this morning and failed to introduce myself. I'm Daisy, and this here is little Horace. My husband is out working on the barricade."

"My name's Mackenzie," Kate said, smiling at Daisy, "but you can call me Mac. I'm pleased to meet you, but I wish we could've met under better circumstances." As she reached for a plate, she wondered how long their food would last if they were besieged for some time.

"I must apologize for tonight's meal," the innkeeper said as she appeared with pitchers of milk and water. "With this attack comin', I must make our supplies last, so we're having beef dodger to make what meat I have stretch a bit further."

Kate glanced down at the plate of corncakes filled with minced beef. "Don't apologize, I like beef dodger." She hadn't had it since her last journey to the past, at Jeremiah's roadhouse.

"We must do what we can under this siege," the innkeeper added.

At this sobering thought, the fifteen or so guests passed dishes to each other until everyone had filled their plates with dodger, green beans, and biscuits. They ate in relative silence, their utensils clinking against their plates while their hostess refilled their glasses. From outside came the sounds of men working on the barricade. Occasionally men came inside to drink glasses of milk or water and went back out to continue working. Two men and a woman finished eating and hurried out to help.

"My husband and I were headed up to Fairplay to help run my aunt's hotel when we learned of the attack," Daisy said. "My aunt's with child, and needs our assistance."

Kate nodded as she savored her dodger. "So you've decided to wait a while?"

"We have," she said. "We're just lucky we found a place on the floor here."

While I have a comfy bed in a room to myself, Kate thought. She considered trading places with Daisy but doubted she'd sleep well surrounded by so many strangers.

"I think that's wise," a hefty, bald-headed man said. "I was going up to the diggin's myself to sell my wares, and intended to stop over in Fairplay." He reached for another biscuit, slathered it with butter, and popped half of it into his chubby mouth.

"What do you sell, sir?" their hostess asked, refilling his milk glass.

"Sewing machines," he said. "Needles, thread, scissors, and other sundries."

"Wares like that oughtta sell to womenfolk," she said, "but there aren't many women in the diggin's. Settlers' wives will buy 'em in town, though." She grabbed two pots of grain coffee from the stove and set them down on the table.

"Precisely," the man answered. "Thus the journey to Fairplay." Wiping his mouth with a napkin, he belched and nodded to the innkeeper. "Name's Ebediah Watson."

"Agnes Cooper," she said with a nod. "Pleased to make yer acquaintance." She glanced over at her teenaged helper. "My boy's name is Ned." Ned lifted two pies off the windowsill and carried them over to the table, then returned for two more. "If yer ready," Agnes said, "I'll cut these pies fer dessert."

"I'm most definitely ready," Ebediah replied. "Is there a Mr. Cooper, ma'am?"

"Not anymore. I've been a widow these past two years, so it's just me an' my Ned now." Agnes started cutting the pies and passing the pieces around.

As Kate finished her dodger, she watched Ebediah chomping his biscuit, Daisy sipping her milk as she cradled her baby, and an older couple whispering to each other. Although she'd enjoyed staying at the hotel, she was suddenly weary of so many people and craved the privacy of her room where she could read the copy of *Journey to the Center of the Earth* she had brought from the future.

The pies were a tasty shoofly-like molasses and the grain coffee was passable. Afterwards Ned and Agnes cleared the table and started washing dishes while their guests went their separate ways. Some hurried outside to help build the barricade, others went upstairs, while others went out back to check on their animals. After a stop at the privy, Kate headed upstairs to her room but was stunned to find it occupied.

"Well, hello," Ebediah said, sitting on the bed with his waistcoat unbuttoned and his shoes off. "Looks like we're roommates. Agnes rented me the other half of your bed."

No way, Kate thought, trying to regain her composure until she remembered what Ned had told her when she rented the room: "You might have to share it if another traveler comes in later." She inhaled a breath and let it out, scanning the room to see if anything was missing. Her pack was still leaning against the wall with her blanket strapped to it, and her jacket was still hanging on a hook. It was common for travelers of the same sex to share a bed, and while Kate was glad her disguise was working so well, she couldn't stay here with Ebediah. She couldn't stay alone in her cabin either, not with Blackstone around, so there was only one option left—she'd have to stay with Doozie.

"Actually, I've been invited by some friends to stay with them," she said. She squatted next to her pack, shouldered into it, and heaved herself up.

"Suit yourself," the trader said, leaning back and closing his eyes.

Grabbing her jacket, Kate hurried from the room and out through the partitioned sleeping area, passing Daisy nursing her baby behind a curtain.

————————

A half-hour later Kate set her pack down on the floor of Doozie's bedroom, grateful for the privacy. Through the thin walls, she could hear the saloon coming to life, with its spirited conversations, raucous laughter, and lively fiddle music. Lighting the kerosene lamp, she settled into the rocker and started reading, but suddenly remembered she'd broken her promise to call Lily and Ivan. It'd been three whole days since she'd come through the passage and she'd promised to call them as soon as she got here. "Damn," she muttered, getting up to pull her phone from her pack. She couldn't get a signal, so she left, passed through the kitchen, and went out into the deserted yard.

Great, she thought, glaring at the screen, *still no signal*. But there wouldn't be since there was no cell phone tower here. As Kate watched the sun set behind Pikes Peak, she remembered she hadn't gotten a signal the last time she called from the past, but Lily still had gotten her message. She punched in their number and heard a barrage of static.

"Lily and Ivan," she began, pacing back and forth, "it's me, Katie. I'm so sorry I forgot to call, but I made it through the passage safely." She heard silence for a second, and a crescendo of more static. "I took the stage into Colorado City, and I'm staying with a friend." *I can't tell them I'm staying with Doozie because they'll worry about me sleeping in a saloon.*

"I haven't found Victor yet because he's gone up to South Park, but I'm hoping to get up there soon. I'm just waiting until..." *Until what? Until the hostiles decided whether or not to attack? Until the sheriff arrests Blackstone and it's safe to travel without him stalking me?* She heard dead air and more static. "I've got to go now," she added, feeling her heart tug, "but please don't worry. I love you. Bye." Kate shut off the phone and clutched it to her chest, hoping they'd get some comfort from her belated message—if they even got it.

The outhouse door slammed open and Buster appeared, fumbling with his buttons and gaping at her. "Who ya talkin' to? An' what's that contraption yer holdin'?"

Kate let out a sigh, suddenly weary of all her deceptions. This was Buster, her friend, whom she'd trusted with her life. He deserved to know the truth. "It's a phone," she said, "a device we use in the future. I was using it to call my grandparents."

"What d'ya mean, the future?" he asked, sauntering over to have a look. "An' why'd ya jist call yerself Katie? That's a woman's name."

"I'll tell you," she said, "but you're going to want a drink first."

CHAPTER SIXTEEN

Kate got two beers from Doozie at the bar, carried them into the kitchen, and settled in at the table to tell Buster the truth. He took it well, considering, but needed a shot of whiskey to help him swallow it. He paced back and forth, trying to grasp it all as Kate studied the latest newspaper.

"So you been a woman all this time?" he asked, peering out the window into the darkness.

"Yep," she said, glancing at a stagecoach timetable. "I've been one all my life."

"I swear. Even when we was campin' up there in South Park last spring?"

"Uh-huh." She set the paper down and gave him her full attention.

"Even when we was captured by them Mexicans who kilt my friend Harrison?"

"Yes." She remembered how Buster had been out cold when they'd ordered her to undress, which was why he hadn't seen her naked, thank God. Kate could still see Harrison lying dead in the snow and Buster lying beside him. "When I undressed, they were shocked to see I was a woman. That's when Bear showed up and chased them off."

"Hellfire," he said, reaching for the whiskey bottle. "Does Doozie know?"

Kate nodded. "Doozie knows, but the girls just think I'm gay."

"Gay?" he said, looking puzzled for a second. "You mean, light on yer feet?"

"You got it. Doozie also knows I came from the future, so when I leave here, I'll try to convince her to come back with me. She'd have a better life there."

"Doozie, in the future? I swear, woman, you cain't mess with her life like that." He poured himself a shot of whiskey and drank it. "So, why'd you come back here?"

"I'm in love with Victor, but we had a fight in the future. I came back to get him."

"Tarnation, Mac! Yer in love with an Injun?" He shook the empty whiskey bottle. "I cain't take no more o' these revelations without more whiskey." He turned to leave.

"Before you go, promise me you won't tell anyone. Let's keep it our secret."

"I wouldn't dare tell yer secrets; folks'd think me crazy." He wandered out into the saloon.

Going into Doozie's bedroom, Kate settled into the rocker and read for hours before stretching out on the bed and dropping off to sleep.

Now she was lying awake in the wee hours, wondering what had awakened her. Springs were creaking above her, so at least one of the girls was working, and Buster was snoring on his mattress. Kate rose from the bed and tiptoed into the kitchen, eased past Buster and glanced out the window. Doozie was out there alone, clutching a shawl to her chest and staring at the moon.

"Doozie!" she whispered as she opened the door. "Get back in here."

"But it's such a lovely night, Mac. Listen to them crickets chirpin'."

Kate crept out and stood beside her. "Aren't you afraid of being out here alone?"

She let out a sigh. "No, I ain't. I felt cooped up inside an' needed some air. 'Sides, I heard somethin' out here, so hush up an' listen." She stared into the night.

As Kate listened she heard animal cries coming from the mesa east of town and others coming from somewhere closer. "I hear them. What are they?"

"Hush," Doozie snapped. "It's them Injuns talkin' to each other."

As the cries continued, Kate peered into the moonlight. "What're they saying?"

"Don't know," she said, "but I suspect it ain't no good."

"They's communicatin' with each other," Buster said, hitching up his suspenders as he ambled toward them. "Seems like they'd be quieter if they was aimin' to attack us."

Lights began to come on in some of the neighboring houses. From the saloon's upstairs windows came the sound of talking. By the light of the moon, Kate could see men patrolling the unfinished barricade. She saw a figure in the shadows and gasped. "Is that an Indian?"

Bear stepped into the moonlight and started moving toward her.

"Gawd," Buster muttered. "It's yer bear. Keep that creature away from me."

"Let me see it," Doozie said, leaning closer. "Damn, it's big, ain't it?"

"Bear's a *she*, not an *it*," Kate said as Bear grunted and sat on her haunches.

Suddenly the door burst open at the top of the stairs on the second floor and a man and a woman bumbled out, laughing and cussing.

"I swear," Doozie said. "Them two could wake the dead with their carryin' on."

The woman laughed and pulled away. "'Night. I'll see you in my dreams."

"Goodnight, my lovely," the man answered as he turned and headed down the stairs. He swore as he grabbed the railing to steady himself, stumbled to the bottom, and hurried off.

The woman caught sight of Doozie and darted inside.

"Hellfire," Doozie muttered. "If I ain't mistaken, that was Bridgette with that bastard Blackstone, after I warned her not to let him in! I'm gonna give that tart a piece o' my mind!" She stormed off across the yard.

"Poor Bridgette," Buster said, watching Doozie hustle up the stairs. "She's always had a weakness fer Blackstone, but I couldn't tell if that was him, could you?"

"Not really," Kate said. "I couldn't see his face well enough."

Doozie reached the landing and pulled on the door, but it was apparently locked. "Open this right now!" she snapped. The door creaked open, and she slipped in. Through the open windows, they could hear Doozie and Bridgette arguing.

"Guess we'd better get back inside," Kate said, turning to go. "With all this commotion, the Indians will hear us, if they're still around."

"Oh, they's still around, all right," Buster said, following her in. When they got into the kitchen, he buttoned his shirt, snatched up his rifle, and put on his hat.

"Where're you going?" Kate asked.

"To keep watch at the barricade. I signed up fer a shift. Lock the door after me."

Kate locked the door and stood staring out the window, realizing how flimsy this house was. Anyone could jimmy the lock, break the window, or bust in the door. Once again she was struck by how precarious life was here, by how people could die from any number of causes. It was dangerous here, no matter how blasé Doozie appeared.

"I was dead wrong," Doozie said, returning through the saloon into the kitchen. "That was some other fella, not Blackstone, but that half-wit Bridgette thinks he's gonna marry her." She glared at the empty whiskey bottle and tossed it into a rubbish bin. "She showed me a brooch he gave 'er with a big showy garnet. I swear, a brooch!"

"Did you apologize?" Kate asked, easing into a chair. *Doozie may be wide awake despite the late hour, and Buster has gone to keep watch, but I'm exhausted.*

"I did. I told 'er respectable fellas don't marry girls like 'er, but she laughed at me an' claimed he loves 'er. The only man loved me enough to marry me was my poor Homer. I need Bridgette, Mac, she's my right hand. I don't want 'er to go off an' git hitched. She lures the customers in an' kin work the bar, too."

Kate studied her. Doozie wasn't a whore anymore, but she was a madam, and she profited from other women's whoring. "Bridgette deserves to get married if she's found someone, Dooz. Maybe you should pursue another line of work."

"An' what line o' work would that be, pray tell?"

"If you came back with me and went to school, you could make a better future."

"I doubt that," she muttered. "I ain't young enough fer school no more, an' I ain't got no other kind o' future ahead o' me. Mine's tied to this saloon Homer left me."

"What do you mean, you're not young enough?" Kate asked. "Sixteen isn't old."

Doozie shot her a look. "I'm older than dirt, an' I seen too much in my lifetime. I got a toothache, too, an' that don't help." She ran her fingers through her long blond tresses, combing out its tangles. "We oughta git some more sleep, Mac. Mornin' 'll come soon enough, with all its troubles." She turned and went into her bedroom.

Kate followed her. As she collapsed into bed, she felt her muscles relax. Doozie deserved so much more than this, and if there was any justice in this world, Kate was going to help her get it.

––––––––

The hostile Indians left as suddenly as they'd appeared. By mid-morning the next day, scouts confirmed they'd abandoned their camp atop the mesa. Scouts also came across a traveler who'd been partially scalped before other travelers scared the Indians off; a woman sewed the shaken man's scalp back on. During their short-lived siege, the hostiles raided several surrounding farms and ranches—stealing stock, trampling crops, and burning buildings. Within hours those settlers who'd fled to town days ago were headed back home again, glad to be alive and determined to start over.

Doozie's place was virtually abandoned by late afternoon but for a few old men swapping gossip and nursing their beers. Grabbing a bottle of whiskey from behind the bar, she took a sip, swished it around in her mouth, and spat it out. "Got a sore tooth," she explained to Kate as she stood beside her, washing glasses. "I think it's time to git ready to go up to South Park, don't you?"

Kate nodded. "Absolutely. I've got some pills you can use for the pain in your tooth."

"Maybe later. I got plenty o' provisions to take with us, but I need to git Bridgette to mind the place whilst I'm gone." She laughed. "If she ain't runnin' off to git hitched, that is. I'll talk to her if you go find Buster an' ask 'im when he kin leave."

Kate found Buster buying supplies at Abner's mercantile. "I kin be ready in two days," Buster said, carrying a small barrel of nails to his wagon. "I gotta git Harrison a proper tombstone, an' another stone I promised fer someone else, an' the fella who chisels 'em cain't do it 'til tomorrow."

"A tombstone," Kate said. "That's good of you."

"I wanted to do it. His folks sent me money when I wrote 'em he'd passed, an' I chipped in my part. It's the least I kin do fer my old friend Harrison."

"Okay," Kate said. "See you later at Doozie's."

———————

Two days later they packed their gear onto Buster's wagon and headed up Ute Pass shortly after dawn. By eight o'clock the pass was already jammed with several wagons and horsemen heading west. Kate rode a chestnut mare she'd rented from the livery, Doozie rode her own mare, and Buster leaned forward in the front seat of his wagon, negotiating his oxen up the precipitous trail. Hawk flew overhead, glancing down as she followed them.

They plodded on, the morning sun warming their skin, Fountain Creek plunging down beside them. As the hours passed, they climbed higher and the air got cooler. By noon the pass opened up into a meadow where travelers had stopped to rest.

After watering their animals at the creek, the three of them spread out their lunch in the shade of an aspen grove.

"I fixed beef sandwiches," Doozie said, laying them out on squares of brown paper, "jist the way Mac likes 'em. An' I brung pickled eggs and cider."

"I'll swap some o' my venison jerky fer that cider," Buster said.

"Here," Doozie said, handing him a jar and taking the jerky.

They ate in silence, savoring the peace, listening to the patter of conversation drifting over from the other travelers. Hawk perched in a nearby ponderosa.

"Ouch!" Doozie said, touching her cheek. "I think I jist broke my tooth."

"Is it the same one that's been bothering you?" Kate asked.

"Yep," she said, spitting a chunk of it into her palm. "Damn."

Buster belched. "They got a dentist in Fairplay who's usually sober."

Doozie shook her head. "Not likely to go to one. I'm fearful o' dentists."

"Suit yerself," he said, "but a sore tooth is a hindrance."

After lunch they continued on as clouds began to move in. By late afternoon the temperature had dropped twenty degrees, the sky was spitting rain, and a chilly wind was blowing. When it started thundering, Kate and Doozie wanted to stop and set up camp.

"No need," Buster yelled into the wind. "Harrison's cabin's jist up ahead."

Thunder rumbled. Lightning flashed across the leaden sky. It began to hail—huge marble-sized pellets coming down in icy sheets.

"Ouch!" Doozie cried. "That hurts! An' our horses is gettin' spooked."

Whipping his oxen into a trot, Buster steered his wagon along the slick road, up a hill, and into the ponderosas. "Here we are," he said, stopping beside a lean-to barn. "Let's tend to the animals an' git inside that cabin there."

Kate and Doozie dismounted and led their horses into the barn as Buster unhitched his oxen. "I swear," he said, leading them in, "there's still hay here. Surprised the varmints didn't git it after all these weeks." He tossed some to the animals as Kate and Doozie wiped down their horses. After they finished, they hurried inside the cabin, then started a fire in the stove with wood stacked nearby. Hail hammered the roof.

Doozie looked around the tiny cabin. "Where's yer friend Harrison?"

Buster sighed and pointed out the window. "Out yonder in the yard, that's his grave covered with rocks. Mexican bandits kilt 'im right in front o' me an' Mac."

Doozie nodded. "I remember now, you told me."

"It was awful," Kate said. "They made him strip naked, march around in the snow in his bare feet, and shot him in cold blood."

"It's gettin' late an' we's tuckered out," Buster said, sinking into the only chair. "We oughta spend the night here. You ladies take the bed, an' I'll take the floor. When that stove heats up, we kin make us some supper. I seen some rice we kin eat."

Doozie groaned. "My tooth pains me, Mac. Gimme some o' them brown pills."

"Okay," she said, taking some ibuprofen from her pack and handing them to her.

"Thanks." Doozie popped them into her mouth and chased them down with water.

As they waited for the stove to heat, Kate remembered she hadn't taken any photos yet, so she pulled her phone from her pack. "You two get over by the window and I'll take your picture."

"What's that thing?" Doozie asked, staring at it.

Buster laughed. "It's her contraption from the future that folks talk on. An' it's a camera, too? "

"Yes," Kate said, motioning them to the window. "Go stand there and smile." Walking over to the light, they leaned against each other and grinned foolishly.

"There," she said, taking their picture and holding up the phone so they could see it. "See?"

"Blazes!" Doozie said, gaping at the image.

"I'll be damned," Buster muttered.

The hailstorm eventually passed, leaving the air cold and the evening sky a muted blue. They cooked rice on the stove, fried slices of ham in an iron skillet, and ate peppermints for dessert. As the sun began to set, they lit a lantern, played cards, and sipped whiskey. It began to rain again, a soothing, steady drizzle. Later, they crawled into their respective beds, sleeping like the dead in the dead man's cabin.

———————

Badger Woman had much to tell Victor about his daughter, so he tried not to stare at her pinkish splotch of a nose as they talked. They'd spent hours together that afternoon before the storm came up, talking about Mountain Flower's harsh life in the Arapaho camp. Badger Woman was eager to tell him what she could remember, despite the Ute taboo against speaking of the dead.

"She never gave up," Badger Woman said, leaning over her cooking fire. "Not even when they beat her. Your daughter was a courageous woman." The storm had passed, the sky was clearing, and a few stars peeked through the tattered clouds.

Victor's heart sank. "They beat her, even when she was pregnant?"

Badger Woman shot him a sorrowful look. "Not so much then, but more after Little Eagle was born." She touched the scar on her face. "Look what those demons did to me. No, don't. I know you find me disgusting." She sighed and stirred her bison stew.

He looked away, at the stew pot. "You're not disgusting, but I admit your nose is difficult to look at. I'm skilled at leatherwork and could make you a patch to cover it."

She smiled. "A leather patch would get caked with snot. Metal would be better."

"I'm no tinker, and where would I get metal, anyway?" *Silly woman. Vain woman. I'm trying to help, and she's suggesting metal?*

"Maybe in one of the mining camps," she urged, dishing out a bowl of stew. "Those miners dig such things out of the ground. We could go tomorrow and look for some if you like. Here," she said, handing him the stew. "Eat. You look famished."

"Not tomorrow," he said, taking the wooden bowl. "I'm going hunting tomorrow, but I'll consider it." Badger Woman was an excellent cook, and he never passed up a chance to eat her food. Her stew was tasty, the best he'd had in camp, and he wondered what she'd added to make it so. He could've learned some cooking tricks from her, but he remembered Ute braves didn't cook. He kept quiet and ate the delicious stew.

———————

The next morning they clustered around Harrison's grave, regarding the new granite tombstone. Blooming columbines bobbed in a gentle breeze. Hawk perched nearby, watching and waiting. Buster dabbed at his rheumy eyes and bowed his head to pray: "Harrison, I hope this stone keeps you company during the lonely nights. I wish you happiness in the afterlife. Be well, my friend." He raised his head. "Well, that's that."

They resumed their journey under a sky as blue as a robin's egg and saw few people except for an occasional miner trudging by with his overburdened mule. Once Kate thought she glimpsed Indians spying on them from a distant hill, but decided it was a trick of the shimmering summer light. Buster taunted her with thoughts of marauding Arapaho, but she refused to believe him.

"Stop it," she snapped. "You're just trying to scare me."

"They's around," he said. "They come up here to fight Utes an' hunt. Ain't seen 'em yet, though." He craned forward in his seat, urging his oxen onward. "Should be in Fairplay by tonight if we push it, or we could jist camp outside of town."

"Let's camp," Kate said. "Okay, Dooz?"

"That's fine," she said, riding up next to her. "With 'nuff whiskey, I'll sleep as good as I did last night. My tooth still pains me, though, so I might have to visit that dentist."

Within the windswept vastness of South Park, Kate saw hundreds of wildflowers—flaming Indian paintbrush, purple lupines, golden banner, and showy daisies. They rumbled along the lumpy trail for hours as Hawk flew overhead, sometimes veering off to hunt prairie dogs. As the sun sank lower, they made camp, laid out Buster's bison robe next to the fire and the women's blankets in Doozie's tent, and made supper. They sat around the crackling campfire, eating and sipping whiskey as alpenglow tinted the snow-clad mountains. Stars winked on, pinpricks of light in an ebony sky. Wolves howled in the distance. Hawk changed to Bear and slumped down nearby, watching and guarding.

They crawled into their beds and slept.

Bear continued watching.

———————

Victor had resisted going to Fairplay, but Badger Woman was so kind that he allowed himself to be coerced into going in exchange for more of her cooking. Rising Moon and Prairie Flower had decided to come with them to trade pelts, so he wouldn't be trapped alone with the widow's eager flirting. They'd already ridden for hours, but it was a fine day and he had nothing better to do. Milagro pranced along, nipping at the other horses, eager to run. Little Eagle dozed on Badger Woman's back while

Prairie Flower's baby dozed on hers. Badger Woman chattered on, clearly excited about getting a new nose.

"But we might not find a metalsmith," Victor cautioned her.

"We will," she answered, riding beside him on her sorrel pony. "I dreamed of it."

"Perhaps, but he might not want to trade with Indians. I'll meet you on that ridge up there," he said as he loosened Milagro's reins and felt him lunge forward. When they reached the ridge, he slowed Milagro to a trot. As he stopped to survey the land, he spied two riders about a mile away charging a wagon and shooting. He drew out his monocular and peered through it.

———————

"Git down!" Buster yelled, grabbing his rifle as he dove under his wagon. "It's them Mexicans!" Kate and Doozie leapt from their horses, scrambled down beside him, and drew out their pistols. The horses tore off.

"You okay, Buster?" Kate asked, ducking behind a wheel as a bullet whizzed by.

"I ain't hit," he said, firing at the bandits. "I cain't believe them sons o' bitches found us agin." He fired at them as they rode by, screaming like banshees.

Kate fired at one bandit as he yelled and veered off. Another fired at her and missed, but his bullet exploded a sack of flour on the wagon, showering them with white dust. Doozie swore and crawled on her belly to get a better shot. Buster wriggled to the other side of the wagon and fired his rifle as the bandits circled around.

From somewhere on her right more shots rang out, and Kate turned to see a rider plunging off a ridge, shrieking and firing as he rode toward them. One bandit fired at him, yelled to his companion, and galloped off. The other bandit fired again and retreated.

The lone rider chased the bandits off in a cloud of dust before turning and riding back. As he approached, Kate crawled out from behind the wheel and smiled as she recognized him. He came closer, dismounted, and walked toward her. *Victor's here in front of me*, she thought, aching to hold him.

"You came back," he said, raising his hand to touch her, and dropping it. He glanced at Buster and Doozie, then back to Kate.

She shrugged. "I was in the neighborhood." She brushed flour off both of them. "I already told them we're lovers, so we can..."

"Great," he said, pulling her into an embrace.

Kate relaxed as she felt Victor's arms envelop her. Suddenly he was kissing her, and his kisses lasted forever, but not nearly long enough. When they finished they drew apart and stood there, grinning at each other.

"I'll be damned," Buster said, brushing himself off as he walked over. He stared at them and shook his head. "You two are crazy fer lovin' each other, but I reckon that's yer bus'ness. Thanks fer rescuin' us, Victor. What're you doin' out here all alone?"

Victor pointed to the ridge where the others were watching from their horses. "I'm not alone, but I was riding ahead and spotted you. My friends and I are going to Fairplay to do some business." He waved to the others, and they started towards him.

"Good," Buster said. "We're goin' to Fairplay, too. We kin ride together."

Doozie rushed over and hugged Victor, leaving flour on his buckskin shirt. She perched on her toes and kissed his cheek. "Thanks, Victor! Glad to see you two back together."

"You're welcome," he said. "What are you doing out here?"

"Looking for you, of course," Kate said as she saw Milagro inching toward her. "I missed you. Bear's around here somewhere... there she is." She pointed at Hawk circling overhead. "Hi, you big baby," she said to Milagro as she buried her face in his mane and stroked his neck.

Victor glanced up at Hawk. "I wondered where she went. She's been with you?"

"For days," Kate said, hugging Milagro. "Good boy. I missed you, too."

Buster shook his head. "I don't subscribe to yer drivel 'bout magical animals, but thanks fer comin' to our aid, Victor. Let's git goin'. I gotta git these supplies to Fairplay." He brushed flour off his pants and climbed up aboard his wagon.

"How long have you been back?" Victor asked Kate.

"Just a few days—ever since the solstice," she answered.

"How are Ivan and Lily?"

"They're fine, but they didn't want me to come here." Kate's pulse quickened as she watched the Utes ride closer. "Is that Rising Moon and Prairie Flower?"

"Yes," Victor said, "and that's Badger Woman with them, the captive I rescued."

"And is that baby on her back who I think it is?"

He smiled. "Yes, that's Little Eagle."

"I can't wait," she said, her heart pounding. She started running toward them.

———————

During their journey to Fairplay, they spotted a herd of bison, several antelope, and one dead miner. He lay sprawled by his placer claim, his chest a bloody mess, surrounded by cawing crows and stripped of his clothing. His burro stood nearby, its saddlebags torn and empty. When it saw them, it pulled on its tether and began to bray.

"Bet it was them Mexicans," Buster said. "They rode at us from this direction, an' this looks like their handiwork. They like to prey on folks in the middle o' nowhere. His gun's missin' and his saddlebags is empty, so I reckon they robbed the poor bastard."

The burro continued braying.

"Shut up, you cantankerous beast," Buster muttered, descending from the wagon. Plucking a handful of grain from a sack, he hurried over to the burro and fed him. "Here, little fella, stop yer squawkin'." The burro gobbled up the grain and nuzzled Buster.

Victor dismounted and waved his hands to scare the crows away. "We should bury him here, or take his body into Fairplay so someone can identify him."

Buster sighed. "All right. Let's wrap 'im up in that sheet o' canvas and strap 'im to that lumber there. Come on, help me." They tied the body onto the wagon and set off.

As they were riding into Fairplay they saw a man running from a group of horsemen. "Help!" he cried. He was barefoot, his feet were bloody, and he was clearly terrified. Another man opened the door of a nearby house. "Come inside here!" he yelled, and beckoned him in.

The riders rode up. "Hand him over," one shouted. "He could be one of them!"

"No!" someone cried from the house. "You've got no proof he's a killer!"

Buster drove his wagon closer. "Ain't my business, but who're you after?"

"Bandits!" one rider snapped. "They're killing folks all over South Park!"

Buster spat a wad into the dust. "We was jist attacked by Mexican bandits, not two hours ago, and he weren't one o' them, so let 'im go. Y'all a posse?"

"We're the Colorado Volunteers," another man said, "and we're searching the Park to apprehend these murderers." He dismounted and strode to the house, talked to someone inside, and returned. "We'd be obliged if you'd provide us with the bandits' description."

"I kin do that," Buster said. "They's Mexicans, like I said, one barely twenty and the other maybe thirty-five. They's got a vendetta against white folks and say their Holy Virgin wants us dead. They's wearin' decent clothes and they's heavily armed, with fine Spanish saddles and silver bridles. "

"Thanks," the Volunteer said, turning to the others. "Let's go." As the posse rode off, the men who'd been hiding emerged from the house. The runner looked around and limped away on bloody feet, and the one who'd helped him rushed over to shake Buster's hand. "I'm Father Dyer," he said. "Pleased to meet you, and thank you for saving an innocent man's life."

"Buster P. Carmody," he said. "I heard about you. Yer that itinerant preacher."

"Yes, I am," he said, smiling. "Welcome to Fairplay." He stared at the body tied to the wagon. "Who do you have here?"

Buster shrugged. "Don't know. Found the poor devil out by his claim with 'is chest blasted open. We thought somebody here in town might know 'im."

"Too bad," Dyer said. "Let's take him to the undertaker. We'll unwrap him and spread the word. Follow me." He set off walking up the street and they followed.

————————

Within an hour they'd dropped off the body, found Doozie her dentist and Badger Woman her metalsmith, who both turned out to be the same man—the local barber. As they entered the barbershop, its proprietor was shaving someone in the next room while singing an Italian aria. Kate and Victor sat beside each other on a bench in the anteroom, and she could feel him wanting her. Badger Woman studied a human-hair wreath mounted in a glass frame as Little Eagle cooed in her carrier. Prairie Flower and Rising Moon left to go trade their pelts.

"I ain't so sure 'bout this," Doozie said, studying several frightening-looking instruments hanging in a glass case. "Maybe my tooth don't hurt all that much."

"Suit yerself," Buster said, peering at the case. "Wonder what *that* one's fer?"

"Don't know," Doozie muttered, "an' I don't wanna know."

As the singing stopped in the next room, a dandy ambled past them and out the door. The white-coated barber appeared, drying his hands on a linen towel. He looked friendly, passably clean, and reasonably intelligent. "Need help, folks?" he asked.

"Can you fashion a metal nose for this woman?" Victor asked.

He studied Badger Woman. "I can do that. I've made a few noses. I'll need someone else's nose to copy from and an hour or two of her time."

"Good, but we'll wait," Victor said. "Take care of her first," he added, nodding to Doozie.

The barber smiled at Doozie. "And you, miss?"

Doozie glared at him. "You smell o' whiskey. You been drinkin'?"

He shrugged. "Just a smidgen, no more than usual. What can I do for you?"

"Nothin'," she said, turning to go. "I cain't abide a drunk dentist. I'm leavin'."

"Wait," Kate said. She got up, went to Doozie, and reached for her jaw.

"Don't, Mac," she said, wincing and ducking away from her. "It hurts."

"Just what I thought," Kate said. "We're staying, and you're letting this dentist help you. He seems capable enough, despite his whiskey breath. Can I watch, sir?"

"If it's all right with my patient."

"Fine," Doozie said. "If I die you can haul my body out afterwards and bury it."

"I will," Kate said, patting her hand. "Now get your butt back there."

Buster left to deliver his lumber; Victor and Badger Woman left to find Prairie Flower. Doozie followed the dentist into the back room and slumped into the chair while Kate stood beside it. The room was so small she barely had enough room to stand.

"Open up," the dentist said, selecting an instrument from a covered jar. "Does that hurt?" he asked, probing carefully in her mouth.

Doozie gripped the chair. "Hellfire! Course it hurts!"

The dentist nodded. "That thing's rotten, miss. It must come out or it'll cause no end of trouble." He reached for a bottle of whiskey. "Ready?"

She blanched. "Ain't you got nothin' stronger?"

He drew back and studied her. "Of course I do, but you need to trust me. Since you inquired, I'll be using chloroform and morphine in a tincture of aconite with some alcohol." He removed the cork from the whiskey with a genteel flair. "Take a swig of this first, and it'll relax you. Don't want you jumping out of my chair now, do we?" He poured Doozie a shot and handed it to her, then poured himself one and chugged it.

Careful, Kate thought. *Don't drink too much. That's my friend you've got there.*

Doozie downed the whiskey. "Not bad. Now gimme that morphine."

After mixing the drugs in a spotless beaker, the dentist plucked forceps from a jar, moistened wads of cotton in the mixture, and gently rubbed them against Doozie's gums. Minutes later, she sprawled in the chair, a stupid grin on her face. "I'm ready. Let 'er rip."

"My name's Walter," the dentist said. "Walter Atchison. Pleased to meet you. You shouldn't feel much, miss, until afterward, and I'll give you something for the pain." He bent over her and started singing.

———————

After Kate led the wobbly Doozie off to the nearest hotel, Victor and his two tribeswomen moved into the back room and the dentist set to work. Walter made a cast of Prairie Flower's nose, melted tin into the mold, and fashioned a two-tiered covering, singing all the while. Impressed to hear Victor was an artist, he'd handed him a tool and let him embellish the nose with arrow designs. He then threaded turquoise ribbons through the holes he'd punched on both sides, held it up for approval, and tied it onto Badger Woman's face.

"There, my dear," he said, waving his hands with a flourish. "Do you like it?"

She studied herself in the looking glass, turning this way and that like an excited girl before a dance. "Tell him I like my new nose," she said, smiling. "I will be proud to wear it, and I am no longer ashamed to show my face. Thank you, Victor, I am grateful."

Victor had to admit that Walter had done a superb job of craftsmanship on Badger Woman's nose. "She loves it," he translated to Walter and turned back to her. "You're welcome," he added. "Consider it my payment for tending Little Eagle and for helping me find my daughter." Badger Woman had been transformed. Instead of an ugly pink scar with gaping nostril holes, she now owned a tasteful adornment. With any luck, she might find another husband and stop pestering him. "How much do we owe you?" he asked Walter, drawing out his leather pouch. After settling on a fair price, they weighed out some gold dust onto Walter's scales, shook hands, and parted company.

They all stood there afterward in front of the barber shop, trying to decide what to do next. Prairie Flower and Rising Moon had traded their pelts, so had little reason to linger in town, and Badger Woman was eager to return to camp and show off, but Victor was reluctant to leave without Kate. He felt drawn to the hotel across the street where she'd taken Doozie and longed to be with Kate, but this was 1863, so he couldn't openly share a bed with her. A curtain parted in one of the hotel windows, and Kate waved down at him. He must go to her. Surely they could find a place to be alone.

CHAPTER SEVENTEEN

Kate left Doozie to sleep and joined Victor and the others. They explored the town together while waiting for Buster to return from his deliveries. They walked to the mercantile where Badger Woman traded her beadwork for four enameled spoons and a mirror with which to admire her new nose. As they were resting on benches in front of Walter's shop, he came out and invited them next door to his place for chilled dandelion tea and cookies.

Victor settled in under a cottonwood in Walter's backyard, took Little Eagle out of her carrier, and laid her down on a blanket.

"Thanks," he said, sipping from a glass Walter handed him. "Good tea. I haven't had any this good since I left Mac's place." He nodded at Kate, who sat down on the blanket and dangled a ribbon above the baby's chubby hand. *Kate came back for me.*

"Where was that?" Walter handed glasses to Prairie Flower and Rising Moon.

"Thank you," Rising Moon said, raising his glass as Prairie Flower smiled.

"I used to live in Seattle," Kate answered, "but I've moved back here now."

"Good," Rising Moon said, nodding sagely. "You *should* live here."

"Is that so?" Walter said, handing some tea to Badger Woman. "You've been to Seattle, Victor? I've always meant to go there. How did you get there?"

Ooops, Victor thought, almost gagging on his molasses cookie. He couldn't claim he'd gone by train because there *was* no train yet from Denver to Seattle, and of course he couldn't say he'd driven. He chewed while he considered how to answer.

Kate touched Eagle's fist and smiled as the baby gripped her finger. "No, not in Seattle. We had tea down in Colorado City."

Which we did, a few months ago. She covered my mistake and didn't lie. I can't abide lying.

"I see," Walter said, leaning against a tree and biting into a cookie. "Is Colorado City where you learned such good English, Victor?"

"I learned most of it around Taos where I lived when I was younger, but I practice whenever I can. I'm good with languages."

"Evidently," Walter said. "It's incredible, really. And you're an artist, too. You have many skills."

"Thanks," Victor said, reaching for another cookie. "I'd show you my work, but it's at the encampment. I could bring it another time." He turned to Kate. "When I told Walter I was an artist, he let me embellish Badger Woman's metal nose with decorative arrows. She could call herself Arrow Nose now." When he translated this into Ute, Badger Woman laughed.

"I'll consider that," she said, peering into her mirror.

"Here you be!" Buster said as he joined them in the yard. "I reckoned I'd find you here since you weren't at the shop." He snatched the last cookie from a plate and plopped down on the grass. "I delivered all o' my goods, so I kin relax now." He bit into his cookie. "Delicious, Walt, per usual. Is yer missus still away in St. Louis?"

"Yes, but she'll be coming home soon. You fancy some of this dandelion tea?"

"I would," Buster said, reaching for the pitcher. "Got any more cookies?"

"Of course. I'll go get them and a glass." Walter ambled toward his house.

"What'll you do now, Buster?" Kate asked. "Stay here in town?"

"Fer tonight, I reckon," he said, gulping tea from the pitcher. "I might take a nap right here in the shade, mebbe wander over to the saloon later fer a meal and some cards. I sometimes stay with Walt when I'm in Fairplay, so mebbe I'll invite myself."

Kate nudged Victor. "Are you going back to the encampment tonight?"

"We planned to," he said, "but I won't go without you. It's a couple of hours' ride, so we'd need to leave soon before it gets too late." He nudged her with his elbow.

"I need to stay with Doozie until she feels better," she said. "Maybe the others can go back, and you could stay here with Buster tonight so I could spend time with you."

Rising Moon rolled his eyes. "You two are like lovesick youngsters."

Buster shook his head. "I swear, Mac, this is dangerous! An Injun with a white woman? You could git kilt fer that, Victor! So, I reckon yer friends know yer courtin'?"

"These friends do," he said, "except for Badger Woman. Looks like she knows about us now, though," he added, noticing her scowl. "I suspect she's jealous since she's figured out Mac's a woman. She's been flirting with me for weeks now."

"Great," Kate muttered. "Just what I need, another rival. Do all single women have to fall in love with you? I'll stay with Doozie at the hotel tonight, but if she's feeling better tomorrow is there anywhere we could camp that's close to town but, you know…private?"

Buster pursed his lips as he thought. "Most anywhere, jist go outside o' town a ways. Why do you…oh! Lordy, Mac, cain't you wait 'til yer back in the encampment?"

Kate blushed as she glanced at Victor. "We haven't seen each other for weeks, Buster. You can't blame us for wanting to be together."

"I reckon not," he mumbled. "I could ask Walt if Victor kin stay here, I guess."

"I know of a secluded hot spring nearby," Victor said. "We could camp there tomorrow night if Doozie's feeling better and go home the next day. How's that sound?"

"It sounds perfect," Kate said as she got up. "I need to go check on Doozie now."

"I'll walk you to the hotel," Victor said.

———————

Doozie groaned, turned over on her side, and groaned again. *She was in a meadow full of spring flowers, a meadow she hadn't seen since childhood. Her mongrel puppy ran toward her and nuzzled her hand, but that puppy had died long ago.* She opened her eyes and saw Kate stroking her hand. She was sitting in a chair beside the bed, haloed by soft lamplight.

"Kate," she murmured. Pain shot through her jaw and pulsed around her head. "Lordy, it hurts."

"I'm sorry," Kate said, pouring a liquid into a glass of water and stirring it around, the spoon clattering, clattering. "Here, drink this. It's time for more of your medicine." She helped her sit up and drink the bitter mixture, fluffed up her pillows, and eased her back down against them.

"Don't leave me."

Kate smiled. "Don't worry, I won't. I've been here all night. I told the innkeeper you're my sister so I could tend you. She wouldn't let me stay in your room otherwise."

Doozie nodded, but winced as that made her jaw throb. She could feel the morphine she'd just drank start to ease her pain. "Did I sleep a long while?"

"Hours," Kate said, wiping Doozie's forehead. "It's the middle of the night now. I brought up some chicken broth for you at suppertime, but you were out, so I ate it."

Doozie chuckled, as this struck her as funny. "Chicken broth would be dandy. Wisht I had some." *She felt her body floating up to the ceiling and watched the flowers on the wallpaper as she passed them by.* "I'm floating," she said, and chuckled again.

"That's the morphine. We'll switch to ibuprofen tomorrow if you're ready. I don't want you getting hooked on this stuff." She lay something cold against Doozie's cheek.

"*Cold*," Doozie said, and shivered.

"It's just a cold, wet cloth, Dooz, like I gave you earlier. It helps with the swelling."

Kate's words turned to bubbles with tiny symbols inside, pink and blue and green and yellow. The symbols became the letters, the sounds became the words, and the bubbles carried them through the air to her ears. "Pretty bubbles," Doozie whispered.

Kate smiled again. "Just sleep, Dooz. You're doing fine. I'll be right here." She settled into a chair and picked up a book.

As Doozie let her eyes close, the bubbles floated around her. Maybe all she had to do was catch them, and they would help her read. She reached out for them.

———————

A door slammed. Someone laughed out in the hallway. Footsteps descended the stairs. Kate stretched, worked the kinks out of her back, and unraveled herself from the overstuffed chair where she'd spent the night. It was morning, and sunlight was streaming through the lace curtains. The hotel was coming to life.

Doozie was still asleep, her face tranquil under the spell of the morphine, the damp cloth leaving a wet spot on her pillow. Lying there with her arms outstretched and her blond hair tousled, she looked like any sixteen-year-old sleeping off an injury...except that girls her age shouldn't have to get a rotten tooth pulled out by an inebriated barber.

Going to the wash basin, Kate poured water from the pitcher and began to wash herself. By the time she'd re-bound her chest and put on clean underwear, Doozie was awake.

"Mornin'," she said, yawning. "Must be a bother to bind yer chest like that."

"Yeah, it is," Kate said, pulling a clean shirt out of her pack. "But I have to do it to keep up my disguise. I'm not *that* well-endowed, but someone could notice, and I don't want to risk that. How do you feel?" She put on her shirt and buttoned it.

Doozie yawned again and propped herself up against the pillows. "Still hurts, but it ain't gnawin' on me like it done last night. I had the strangest dreams, though." Shoving the covers off, she swung her slender legs over the side of the bed and sat there, swaying. "Whoa. I'm powerful dizzy, Kate."

"Be careful," she said. "Let me help you up so you can use the chamber pot."

"I'd be right grateful. The room's spinnin' like a whirligig."

After helping Doozie relieve herself, Kate sat her down in the chair, propped her feet up on the stool, and covered her with a blanket. "Ready for some food yet?"

"Yep, I'm starved. Some oatmeal an' coffee would be dandy if they got it."

"I'm sure they do. If you're all right here by yourself, I'll go down and get us both some breakfast." Kate combed her hair out and tied it back in a ponytail. Be right back."

She returned twenty minutes later with a tray full of food. "I've got a pot of coffee, two bowls of oatmeal, sausages, and toast. The hotelkeeper must have your talent for finding real coffee these days," she said as she closed the door.

Doozie opened her sleepy eyes and smiled. "I swear, Kate. You'll spoil me."

During breakfast, Kate explained her plan to go camping later with Victor if Doozie felt better. As she stood at the window and ate her oatmeal, she saw him sitting on a bench in front of Walter's shop. He was sketching, gathering a circle of curious onlookers. "I'll only go if you're comfortable with me being away all night," Kate added. "I could ask Buster to look in on you and give you your medicine. I'm sure he'd do that."

"I'm sure he would, an' I'm sure you oughtta go to them hot springs. You an' Victor deserve to git away by yerselves. I'll be fine if you jist leave me my potion."

"Okay, but after we eat, let's see how you do with just ibuprofen. I'd feel much better leaving you with Buster if you're not taking morphine."

Doozie laughed. "Half the girls I know take a bit o' morphine at times."

I can believe it, Kate thought. "I'm sure they do, but I don't want you taking it unless you absolutely need it. I won't be going 'til this afternoon, so I can see how you do. I booked the room for another night, so you can stay here and rest."

"Like I said, Kate, you'll spoil me." She set her empty bowl down on the tray and tried to sip her coffee, but it dribbled down the side of her mouth. "I believe I'm done eatin'. My jaw's startin' to pain me, an' I'd like to git back into that soft bed agin."

"Okay, I'll help you." After giving Doozie some ibuprofen, Kate helped her into bed. In a little while, she'd go talk to Buster.

———————

Steaming water soaked into her pores, relaxing all of her aching muscles. The sun was setting, casting a pinkish glow through the rising steam, lighting up the suspended particles of moisture. The other Utes had returned to the encampment, and Kate and Victor were alone in the hot springs.

"Mmmm," Kate murmured. "This is paradise."

Victor pulled her closer and nibbled her ear. "I've wanted to bring you here for a long time, ever since we first made love in the cave." He ran his tongue around one of her nipples, then the other.

She raised his head and kissed him, tasting the salt on his lips, and moved her hips against his until she felt him harden. "That seems like eons ago."

He slid his hands around her buttocks and began massaging them. "It seems like only yesterday. You came all the way back for me, Kate. I can barely believe that."

She felt his skin against hers, hot and slippery. "I can barely believe it myself, but here I am." She moved her tongue inside his mouth and kissed him again.

His hands gripped her buttocks as he eased inside her. They floated together, all salty lips and slippery muscles as the water suspended them, their bodies becoming one body. Waves of pleasure burst through her, again and again, as they slid against each other. Afterwards, she hauled herself out onto a rock and lay there, breathing in the fresh summer air.

"God," she murmured. "I've missed you."

He hauled himself up beside her. "And I've missed you."

"And not just for the sex," she said, throwing her leg over his.

"No," he said, rubbing his heel along her calf, "but I missed that, too."

As they lay there, they watched the stars wink on and listened to the creek rush by. Bear slumped down a few feet away and rested her head on her paws.

"Now that you're back, are you staying?" he asked.

She felt a breeze caress her skin. "I don't know, I don't have a plan. I just knew I had to find you to tell you I still love you. You left so suddenly after we argued."

He rolled against her and kissed her. "I almost called you from Oregon before I drove back, but my pride wouldn't let me. I wanted to find out if you loved Mark more than me before I went through the passage, but I was afraid to hear the answer."

"I wish you *would've* called," she said, touching his cheek. "You could've saved us both a trip. Mark's a good friend, but I don't love him, and I told him so before I came here. He was crushed, the poor guy. Alex was mad at me at first, but she got over it."

He eased up on an elbow. "Why would she be mad at you about Mark?"

"Not about Mark; because she's worried about me. She said if I'm going to fall in love, a guy from my own time would be better than some Indian from another century."

He stroked her wet hair, spreading it out along the rock. "Imagine that."

She studied his wet body in the moonlight. "She wanted me to promise her I'd be back in a month before she'd agree to watch Cisco."

His eyebrows shot up. "Did you?"

"No. I told her time travel doesn't work that way, and you can't predict it."

"No kidding. *Are* you planning to try to go back in a month?"

"No, I told you, I don't have a plan. I'm getting chilled. Let's go back in."

They slipped back into the steaming water. Bear watched them as they again made love in the steaming hot springs.

———————

The next day they broke camp and returned to Fairplay to check on Doozie. Leaving Victor in front of Walter's shop, Kate went into the hotel and trotted upstairs.

"Doozie?" she said, knocking on her door. "Are you decent? It's Mac."

"Come in," she said.

"Hi, there," Kate said as she walked in. Doozie was sitting up in bed, reading a book and sipping a cup of tea. Buster sat in the chair beside her, reading the latest broadsheet. "Looks like a library. How's our patient?"

Doozie shrugged. "Not bad. I'm still sore, but yer little brown pills worked, an' I slept like a babe last night. Buster's a mighty fine nurse."

"Good," Kate said. "Think you'd be able to ride to the encampment with us?"

"Mebbe, if I take my time an' rest along the way, but why would I want to?"

"Just to visit and spend some time with us. You could rest there while you recover."

Doozie thought for a minute. "Might be a nice visit. You reckon we could stay there a few days?"

Kate nodded. "Victor said we'd all be welcome. You and I could share your little tent, if nothing bigger is available, since they all know I'm a woman anyway. They just had a bison hunt, so there's plenty of food, and it'll be good to see everyone again, except for Growling Thunder, the medicine man. He despises me."

"Do we need to fret about the bastard?" Doozie asked.

"No. The war chief likes me, so Growling Thunder wouldn't dare harm me."

"I want to find Homer's claim first," Doozie said. "That's partly why I come up here."

"I know where it is," Buster said. "Homer showed me on a map, an' it's right next to mine. I got an errand to do there, so I kin take you. Then I might go on with you to the encampment."

"All right then, but since we're payin' fer this room, I'd fancy a bath first."

"I'll help you take one," Kate said, "but first I'll go tell Victor we're going."

After Doozie had her bath, they treated themselves to a meal in the hotel's dining room, paid their bill, and left. Doozie and Kate rode a little ways behind the others.

"So, was yer visit to the hot springs all you hoped fer?" Doozie grinned.

"It was," Kate said, smiling to herself. "It was a beautiful night and the hot springs felt wonderful. Everything was perfect."

Doozie guided her mare around a prairie-dog hole as another prairie dog barked a sharp warning from twenty feet away. "An' everything's good twixt you two lovebirds?"

"It's great, Dooz. We still love each other, and I'm glad I came back."

"I swear," she said, and sighed. "I'm happy fer you. You deserve yer happiness."

As they rode the bright sun beat down on the undulating hills and the blooming wildflowers. After a while Buster steered his wagon into a clearing with a magnificent view of the higher peaks. A log cabin nestled in an aspen grove dotted with columbines. A discarded mining sluice lay beside a rushing stream.

"Gotta stop here fer a piece," he said, jumping down from the wagon. "This here's my old place. Lend me a hand, Victor." They wrestled a burlap-covered bundle from the back of his wagon and carried it to a rock-filled crevice in a nearby hill. "Now," Buster said, "let's put it right in front here." He unwrapped the bundle revealing a carved granite headstone. He and Victor began chipping away at the rocky earth with a pick and shovel.

When the stone was seated, Kate moved closer to read its inscription: "Here lies Soars on the Wind, beloved wife of Buster P. Carmody. Born during the month of elk bugling, 1844, died July 30th, 1862. Our unborn babe died with her. May their spirits find peace." A soaring bird was etched on the tombstone.

"I'm so sorry, Buster," Kate said. "I didn't know you had a wife."

Tears streamed down his grizzled face. "I did, a Ute girl. Died almost a year ago."

"What happened?" she asked, touching his arm. "If you don't mind my asking."

He blew his nose into a kerchief. "I was in town that mornin' at the assay office, so I don't rightly know. I worked a claim in them days, so I'd gone off to git my samples assayed. When I come back, she was lyin' dead over yonder by them flowers, her body pierced with arrows, her purdy hair scalped, her new buckskin dress ripped all to hell."

"Who killed her?" Victor asked.

Buster shook his head. "The Arapaho, I reckon, judgin' by the arrows, but I never found out fer sure. I know Utes like to be buried in crevices an' caves under a passel o' rocks, so I done her that courtesy, but I wish her loved ones coulda come to say good-bye. I bought this stone to keep her comp'ny, and to honor her memory."

"It's a fine stone," Victor said, "and I'm sure she'll like the soaring bird. I was away when she died, but I heard of her death. I didn't know her. Where was she from?"

"Down by Taos. I jist wish her people coulda come to sing her on her journey, but I didn't have time to git word to 'em."

Victor sighed. "I will sing for her." As he closed his eyes, a mournful keening poured out of him, rising up and up through the afternoon stillness. Then all was silent.

"I thank you, my friend," Buster said. "They's gone to their rest now. If yer sure I'd be welcome at the camp I'll go with you. I got goods to trade, an' I'd druther not stay here alone."

"Of course you can come," Victor said. "Many of my people know you."

"I'll ride on with you, then." Buster pointed into the aspen. "That's Homer's claim jist over there, Dooz. Come on, I'll show you." He walked fifty yards up the stream, and they followed. "We bought 'em together, you see, an' our land shared this stream."

"We woulda been neighbors," Doozie said. "Is there much gold in yer claim?"

Buster shrugged. "A little, but I didn't git rich on it. Don't know 'bout yers."

"No, you wouldn't." Doozie studied the rocky land and the stream.

"We should get going," Victor said, "if Doozie's ready."

She nodded. "I'm ready."

They mounted up and headed for the encampment.

———————

As they approached the camp, scouts called out warnings, women glanced up from their work, and dozens of eyes watched them ride closer. Doozie cast a frightened look at Kate as they confronted the sea of strange faces.

"I kin stay in my wagon," Buster told Victor. "Jist tell me where to set up."

"You can set up over there by the creek, next to that stand of aspen."

"All right," he said, "see you later." He drove off.

They dismounted at the edge of camp and stood holding their horses as Rising Moon strode toward them. "Welcome back, Kate!" he said when he reached them.

Kate smiled and touched his shoulder. "Thank you, it's good to be back. This is my friend, Doozie. She wants to stay here with us for a few days."

"Welcome," Rising Moon said. "Will you both stay with me and Prairie Flower?"

"Maybe," Kate said, and turned to Victor. "Where're you staying?"

"With him, of course," Victor answered. "There's room for you and Doozie in their tepee, but the babies wake us up at night, and Rising Moon snores."

"I do *not*," he said, cuffing Victor's shoulder.

"Yes, you do," Kate said. "I've shared your tepee before. Thanks for the offer, but Doozie and I were hoping for a little more privacy."

"I have a tent I could lend you, but it's not very big," Victor said.

Rising Moon pointed across camp. "Your old tepee's set up over by the creek, but Badger Woman's using it. Maybe she'd share it with you, or move to another tepee."

"It wouldn't be right to ask her to move out," Kate said. *And if she's jealous of me, she won't want me there. But I'd rather not sleep in Doozie's cramped tent.* She paused for a minute, wondering what to do. "I'll ask if we can stay with her, and if not, we'll just pitch Doozie's tent. Buster has all our gear on his wagon."

Rising Moon nodded. "All right, but you must join us for our evening meal."

"We will," she said, turning to Victor. "Let's go see Lady Grey now."

"Come on," he said, leading them off along the camp's perimeter. "She's been awfully cranky since you left." As they approached the corral, three boys ran out and took their horses. "Laughing Brook!" Kate exclaimed to one, ruffling his hair.

He flashed Kate a smile and greeted her in Ute.

In the corral, Lady Grey spotted her, whinnied, and shoved through the other horses.

"Do you want Laughing Brook to saddle her for you?" Victor asked.

"No," she said, watching her horse hurry toward her. "Just bring me a bridle. I can't leave her in here, now that she's seen me, and I want to walk her." As Grey reached the brush fence, Kate reached over it and hugged her. "I've missed you, my beauty."

Grey pressed against the fence and nuzzled her.

"I'm sorry I left you," she said, rubbing the horse's soft forehead. "But I couldn't take you with me." Laughing Brook returned, put a bridle on Grey, and opened the gate to let her out. She nudged against Kate, almost pushing her over.

"I remember this horse," Doozie said. "You won her in a race, didn't you?"

"Yes. I had to race Growling Thunder for her, but I won. He'll never forgive me for that." As she led her horse off around the edge of camp, she saw Badger Woman up ahead, rising from her cooking fire to greet them. "Ask if we could share her tepee tonight, Victor, and if she's jealous of me. I won't stay with her if she's jealous."

He translated, and Badger Woman answered him. "She says this tepee is the tribe's gift to you for saving Laughing Brook's life, so you and Doozie should stay here. She'd be grateful if you let her stay with you until tomorrow, when she'll move, but she doesn't have any extra blankets or bison robes. And yes, she was jealous at first, but now she can see that you love me." The squat middle-aged woman smiled sheepishly at Kate, her hands propped on her ample hips, the afternoon sun reflecting on her new metal nose covering.

"Good," Kate said. "Tell her thank you, and we have bedding in the wagon."

Victor translated and listened carefully as Badger Woman added something. He stared across camp. "She just told me Ouray's here visiting relatives. I must go see him."

Kate followed his gaze as Lady Grey nudged her, begging a ride. "Go, and I'll find you later. Maybe I will take her out for a ride."

"I'll meet up with you at supper." Victor headed off.

Doozie sighed. "I need a rest, Kate, an' more o' them pills. I'm tuckered out."

"Okay," Kate said, beckoning to Buster. "Let's get settled, so you can lie down."

———————

Victor had never seen his friend so sorrowful. As they sat around Rising Moon's campfire after supper, he watched Ouray's demeanor as he met Doozie. Even while downcast, he was courteous; even in grief, he was a gracious ambassador for his people.

"I'm pleased to meet you," he said to Doozie. "Buster and Kate, I'm glad to see you again. Victor tells me you've been away for a while. I'm sorry my wife isn't with me to greet you, but she didn't go hunting with me this time. I thank the stars for that." He sighed and turned to Victor. "I dread telling her about Paron. His own mother died, and Chipeta loved him like her own child."

"Yes, she did," Victor said. "Can I tell them what happened?"

Ouray nodded and stared at the fire. "Go ahead. I can't bear to."

He inhaled a deep breath and let it out. "While Ouray was on a hunting trip northeast of Denver three weeks ago, the Sioux attacked the Utes' camp. They stole half of their horses, killed three braves, and captured Ouray's five-year-old son Paron. When

Ouray discovered Paron was missing he tried to pursue his captors, but there were a hundred Sioux and only thirty Ute warriors. They were greatly outnumbered, so they had to return to their camp to protect the others."

"They attacked at night, so we couldn't tell who they were," Ouray added. "But we killed one of their warriors, and he was wearing a peculiar type of shirt worn only by the Sioux. Later I met a Mexican who trades with them. He said Friday has Paron now."

"That devil," Victor muttered. He turned to the others and explained, "Friday's an Arapaho chief, an especially cruel one. I'm sorry, my friend," he added as he turned back to Ouray. "I've felt the pain of losing a child. I often worry about losing my Little Eagle."

Ouray shot Victor an anguished look. "Last spring you told me you'd read in a book that Paron would be stolen, but I refused to believe you. Now I wish I had."

"What could you have done?" Victor asked. "Kept him in camp all the time under Chipeta's skirts and never taken him anywhere? That's no life for a spirited Ute boy."

"Did the white man's book say I found him?" Ouray asked.

Victor paused as he considered lying. He couldn't tell Ouray the book said that when he finally found Paron, the boy refused to acknowledge him as his father; he had to give him some hope. "One book claimed you found him years later among the Arapaho, so don't give up. They also claimed you and Chipeta would adopt three other children."

"*Years* later?" he asked. "This is hard news, Victor."

"Yes, it is, but at least it said you'd find him. Will you stay with us for a while?"

He shrugged. "Just a few days. We must return home to the western mountains, and I must tell this sad news to Chipeta." He sighed and turned to Kate. "Victor says you returned from the future. Why did you come back, and how long will you stay this time?"

"I traveled back to find Victor," Kate said. "He came to the future to live with me, but he didn't feel like he belonged there. To be honest, I'm not sure I belong here either, and I don't know how long I'm staying. That depends on a lot of things."

Victor watched Kate as she spoke while staring at the flames. *So, Kate truly doesn't know how long she'll stay. Will she return to her own time, or stay in mine?* He reached for a piece of cornbread.

"I see," Ouray said, leaning against a saddle. "Victor, where's your little one?"

"I hear her crying now," he said as Prairie Flower rose from her seat and went into her tepee. "She'll bring her out. You won't believe how much she's grown since the last time you saw her."

They sat there late into the evening, talking around the fire. At one point Victor saw Growling Thunder hovering a short distance away, glaring at them, but he slunk away into the shadows.

— — — — — — —

The next day Victor helped Badger Woman move her things from Kate's tepee into his mother-in-law's, so she could live with her. When he saw how small and battered Doozie's tent was, he helped her set up his modern one. His tribesmen had become so accustomed to his outlandish possessions from the future they'd almost stopped chiding him about them. Besides, with the afternoon showers so prevalent, Doozie deserved a rain fly, and his tent had one. As they worked, Buster was dozing in his wagon about fifty feet away, and Kate was standing by her tepee taking pictures with her phone of the encampment and Little Eagle.

"You an' Kate oughtta share her tepee," Doozie said to Victor as they staked out the tent. "You two lovebirds need yer privacy, an' I'll be safe here in this fancy tent 'tween you and Buster."

"Thanks, Dooz," Victor said, pounding the final stake into the ground with a rock. He longed to spend another night with Kate without any chaperones. He unzipped the tent's screen door and held it open. "There, it's ready for you."

Doozie gasped. "What made that strange sound?"

"It's a new-fangled gadget from the future that's used instead of buttons," Victor explained.

"I swear. What won't they think of next?" Doozie returned to the tepee, grabbed her things, and tossed them into the tent as Kate ambled over and took her picture.

"You should be careful about taking pictures, Kate," Victor said, frowning. "Some of my people might think you're trying to steal their spirit."

"You're right," she said, putting her phone away. "I'm sorry. I didn't think anyone here would recognize my phone as a camera. I promised to take some back for Lily and Ivan, and I got carried away."

"That's okay," Victor said. "Let's zip the tent back up now," he added to Doozie as he showed her how, "so the bugs won't get in. What do you ladies want to do today?"

Doozie thought for a minute. "I'd like you to show me 'round camp fer starters."

"Okay," he said. "We could go for a ride later, too, if you want."

"Sounds good," Kate said, loading Little Eagle's carrier onto her back. "The baby's gotten so much bigger than when you left, and she can do so much more now. She's gotten really good at holding her head steady and rolling over. Okay, let's go."

After they roused Buster, Victor escorted his friends around camp, pausing at tepees to talk, sampling food people offered, translating conversations between Ute and English.

As they were talking with one family, they heard a woman scream behind them.

"Stop!" she cried in Ute. "No!"

They all turned to see Growling Thunder beating a young Ute woman with a leather quirt about fifteen feet away. She was curled beside him in a ball, whimpering.

Kate turned to Victor. "Stop him! He's hurting her!"

"She's one of his wives," he said, "and I'm sorry to say he's allowed to beat her."

"That's jist awful," Doozie said as the man raised his quirt again.

Before Victor could stop her, Kate rushed over and grabbed the quirt from the medicine man's hand. "No!"

He spun around and glared at her. "You!" he hissed. "Witch!"

"Did he just call me a name?" she asked Victor.

"He just called you a witch."

"I'm not!" she snapped, flicking the quirt at Growling Thunder's face.

"Eeyih!" The medicine man raised his hand to his bleeding cheek. "I'll punish you for this, witch."

"No, Kate," Victor said, yanking the quirt away from her. "You can't interfere in this."

"I can't let him beat her. What did she do to deserve it?"

Victor frowned at Growling Thunder and asked him.

"This worthless woman burned my breakfast," he spat out.

As Victor translated Growling Thunder's complaint, he noticed a small crowd was beginning to gather. "Just walk away, Kate, and stop interfering. You're causing him to lose face, and he'll hate you for that."

"He already hates me," she fumed, "and this is barbaric."

Victor nodded. "Yes, it is, especially in *your* time. But unfortunately we're not in your time, and it's *our* way." He reluctantly handed the quirt back to Growling Thunder.

"Screw your ways," Kate muttered, pointing her finger at the medicine man. "Tell the pig the sun will darken tomorrow as punishment for beating his wife."

"What are you talking about?" Victor asked, staring at her.

"I read about a solar eclipse in a settler's journal I found in Lily's things. It happened on July 30th, and I remember the date because that's Ivan's birthday. Today's July 29th, so it'll happen tomorrow."

"You're sure about this?" he asked. The crowd was pressing closer, watching them.

"Yes, I'm sure. Tell him."

It might not hurt to take the medicine man down a peg, Victor thought, *and he might even stop beating his wives*. "Okay, but if you're wrong, this will cause us no end of trouble." He turned to Growling Thunder and relayed the message in Ute.

People in the crowd gasped. Growling Thunder laughed. "You cannot know this," he snapped.

"It will happen," Victor said, "because Kate says it will. She can see the future."

Growling Thunder lunged forward and raised his quirt at Kate. "Tell your witch lover she will suffer for this."

Victor pushed him away. "Don't threaten her, or you'll have me to deal with. And she's *not* a witch."

"She *is*," the medicine man snarled, then turned, grabbed his wife's arm, and dragged her into their tepee. The crowd dispersed, muttering amongst themselves.

"Let's move on," Victor said, beckoning Kate away. "I hope you're right about this."

"I'm sure I am," she said. "That pompous bastard deserves to be frightened."

They continued walking around camp. Stopping at Mourning Dove's tepee, Victor sampled a piece of elk jerky and said to her, "Kate you already know, of course, but this is Buster and Doozie. Meet my former mother-in-law, Mourning Dove," he added to the others in English.

Mourning Dove's bright brown eyes lit up when she saw Little Eagle. As the older woman smiled, Victor noticed the gap in her teeth and the gray in her long hair, but her gaze was clear and steady. In her early fifties, Mourning Dove was still strong and capable, and she was still a good healer. "Want some jerky, Dooz?" Victor asked.

"No!" she snapped. "I broke my tooth on jerky, but I'd fancy some o' that nice soft cornbread."

"I'd fancy some o' that, too," Buster said, smiling as he raised his floppy slouch hat. "Yer bread looks delicious, ma'am. Mind if I have a smidgeon?"

Mourning Dove glanced up at Victor. "What does Blue Eyes say?"

"He says your cornbread looks delicious, and he'd like to have some."

"Oh, he would, would he?" She cut a slice of cornbread. "Tell him he has beautiful eyes, and he's not bad looking, but he smells like whiskey." She set the slice on a tin plate, drizzled a bit of honey onto it from a honeycomb, and handed it to him.

"Stop flirting," Victor said. "Buster's a wanderer, so he'd seldom be home to keep you warm at night, and he's a hearty drinker. Doozie would like some cornbread, too."

Mourning Dove prepared more cornbread with honey and handed it to Doozie. "Welcome to my camp. Sit down and visit." Badger Woman emerged from the tepee and smiled at them.

"So this is who she moved in with," Kate said. "I didn't realize."

Victor shrugged. "It makes sense since they're both widows, and get along well enough. We can stay and visit if you like, but we shouldn't linger if you want to go riding. As you know, it often rains later in the afternoon."

"I ain't goin' ridin'," Buster said. "I'm gonna stay in camp an' do some tradin'."

Kate adjusted Eagle's carrier on her shoulders. "Ask Mourning Dove if she'll watch the baby while we go riding."

He translated this.

"I will," Mourning Dove said. "So your white lover will allow me to watch my own granddaughter? How *kind* she is, although she's returned to steal your heart away."

"Be nice," Victor cautioned. "Eagle's lucky to have so many people who love her, and Kate loves her like her own daughter." He turned to her. "She said she'd like to watch her."

Kate shed Eagle's carrier and handed it over. "Uh-huh. I'll bet that's not all she said."

"It's not, but I really think she's starting to like you."

Kate laughed. "I doubt it, but that would be encouraging."

"Maybe not *like* you exactly," he said, "but she respects you for saving Laughing Brook from the lightning sickness. You earned a lot of points for that last spring."

"Whatever. I'll take any points I can get."

"*Whatever*," Buster said. "I 'member you like to say that." He and Doozie finished eating their cornbread, licked their fingers, and handed back their tin plates.

"Thanks, ma'am," Doozie said to Mourning Dove, then whispered to Victor, "Kate says she's a healer. Ask 'er if she kin help me."

"Thank you," Buster said, bowing to Mourning Dove. "That was scrumptious."

She smiled. "He's handsome, for a white man, and courteous," she said to Victor. "I like his silly hat and blue eyes, as they make him look mischievous. Is he married?"

"He's a widower," Victor said. "He's already had one Ute wife."

"Old women can't be choosy. If he's had one Ute wife, he could have another."

"You're shameless," he said. "Could you look at Doozie's sore mouth later?"

"Of course," Mourning Dove said. "Later."

———————

The three of them left the encampment and rode off across the prairies, through seas of three-foot-high waving grasses. Hawk flew overhead for a while, then disappeared in another direction.

"Let's rest here," Victor said, stopping by a creek flowing through a stand of aspen. "Doozie looks spent." They dismounted and hobbled their horses.

"Sit down and close your eyes," he said to both of them. "I want to take you on an adventure."

"Is this some kind of touchy-feely thing?" Kate asked.

"I don't know about that, but it's an Indian thing." He reclined against an aspen and watched the others settle in. "Now, close your eyes and listen. What do you hear?"

Doozie groaned. "I don't know 'bout this kinda thing. I cain't..."

"Yes you can," he said. "Please close them."

"All right, but only 'cuz I'm so weary." After stretching out under a tree, she added, "I hear them horses munchin' an' them prairie dogs barkin'."

"I hear cicadas chirring," Kate began, "and a red-winged blackbird singing."

Victor closed his own eyes. "I hear the creek trickling and a hawk crying."

"Aspen leaves fluttering," Kate added. "Grasses rustling."

"Listen to the earth breathe," Victor continued. "Listen to its creatures."

"All them sounds!" Doozie said. "I always thought South Park were empty."

"No," he said. "It's full of life. Now open your eyes and tell me what you see."

Kate opened hers. "I see hundreds of wildflowers...Indian paintbrush, larkspur, harebells...mountain bluebells and scarlet gilia...columbines and cinquefoil."

Doozie stretched her arms behind her head and looked around. "I see a purdy blue sky an' high fluffy clouds. Tall grasses movin' like waves. Little bushes with red berries. Hawk comin' back to us, perchin' in that tree over there."

Victor nodded. "I see vast rolling prairies and mountains with dazzling snowfields. I see a ribbon of creek glinting in the afternoon sunshine. I see the land of my people as it's existed across the ages, with Utes riding horses, hunting bison, and setting up tepees. I see them curing hides and fashioning beadwork; making love and having babies and raising children. I know all of this will end within my lifetime when we're forced onto reservations, but I intend to live free in this land as long as I can."

"That was beautiful," Kate said, casting him a worried look. "But what do you mean?"

Hawk flew down and perched beside him. "It means I'll stay as long as I can. I don't know how long that'll be." *If she's worried about me wanting to stay here forever, she could be right.*

———————

Later that night Victor and Kate lay in her tepee after making love and watched a small crackling fire. Doozie was asleep in the tent; the baby was with Prairie Flower.

"I want to stay here forever," she said, curling up next to him.

"You can't, my love," he said, pulling his sleeping bag over their nakedness. "After a while you'd miss your modern conveniences, and besides, you're not a Ute."

"I know. I was just kidding. But I love being here with you now."

"Me, too," he said, kissing her. "But I want to remind you not to take pictures of people without their permission. I've heard grumbling about you stealing their spirits."

"I told you earlier I was sorry. Who's been grumbling?"

"A few of the older people, but mostly Growling Thunder. He already thinks you're a witch because of the time-traveling and your threat earlier today, so you shouldn't provoke him further."

"That old windbag. I didn't take any pictures of him, so how did he find out?"

"Someone must've told him, maybe our war chief Running Deer's daughter. She likes me, so she's probably jealous, but it could've been anyone. Only take pictures of people you trust, and only if you ask their permission first. Growling Thunder may be a windbag, but he's dangerous because he hates you, so be careful."

"I will," she said, easing from the sleeping bag. "Geez, *another* jealous woman." She crawled to her pack and pulled out an energy bar. "I'm starving. Want some of this?"

"No, I'm full. Prairie Flower stuffed us tonight. How could you still be hungry?"

"I don't know, but I've been ravenous lately. Maybe I'm pregnant." She bit into the bar. "This isn't bad, but I wish it was a piece of double fudge chocolate cake."

He leaned up on one elbow and grinned. "Do you think you *could* be pregnant? We were apart almost two months, and we've only been together here twice, but it's surely possible. It would be amazing if you're pregnant!"

"I could be. I missed my period last month, but I chalked it up to the stress of your leaving. Chocolate cake with French vanilla ice cream…" *If I let him think I'm pregnant he'll probably come back with me, but I don't think I am.*

"If you stayed here, you'd miss things like fancy desserts and flush toilets."

"Don't mention toilets. I'm already afraid to go outside to pee tonight, with all your talk about Growling Thunder. Is he still pissed off that I won Grey in that race?"

Victor nodded. "He is. Running Deer told me he tried to buy her back after you left here, but he wouldn't sell her since she's yours. He told me something else, too."

"What's that?" She finished her snack and covered up with the sleeping bag.

"He thinks Growling Thunder told Blackstone where the cave was weeks ago, and that's where he and Charlie were going when they attacked Doozie and Homer that day."

She stared at him. "He told Blackstone where to find us so he could kill us? That's frightening. I didn't realize they knew each other."

"They do, evidently. And another thing—when we were in Fairplay, I heard Blackstone's coming there soon to serve as a circuit judge. So, please be more careful around here. You're safe with me or one of our friends, but don't go out alone, okay?"

"Sorry. I already went riding alone yesterday when you went off to talk to Ouray before supper. Blackstone, damn! I thought I'd gotten away from that asshole."

"Not yet," he said, frowning. "Promise me you won't do that again."

"I promise."

"I know you crave your freedom," he said, stroking her hair. "That's one of the many things I love about you." He shoved the sleeping bag off them, pulled her closer, and kissed her. "Are you still hungry?"

"Maybe ... what do you have for me?"

"Something delicious, if you're still hungry." He stroked her breasts.

She felt his tongue on her nipples. "Yes," she murmured. "I'm still hungry."

CHAPTER EIGHTEEN

By mid-morning the next day, Mourning Dove had examined Doozie's mouth, mixed together a potion of herbs for her to drink, and was massaging her wounded shoulder with an aromatic salve. Doozie lay on a blanket outside her tent, listening to the creek as she drifted off. Victor sat nearby, drawing as he translated.

"She said your tooth will be fine in a few days if you rest and drink her potions," Victor said. "But she's more concerned about your shoulder. She said the salve and her massages will help, but you shouldn't lift anything heavy for a while."

Doozie chuckled. "Tell her I 'preciate her help, an' I been tryin' to be careful, but I gotta run my business. I gotta lift trays o' food an' carry drinks an' such."

Victor translated, and Mourning Dove replied. "She asked what kind of business you run, and I told her. She said you should get some help, or find another type of work."

Doozie chuckled again. "Cain't do that, as saloon work's all I know. Least I don't have to whore no more, that's even tougher." She listened to him translate this as Mourning Dove massaged her shoulder. *This is real nice*, she thought, *lying in the shade and being cared for*. The creek made a joyful sound as it trickled by, and the aspen leaves fluttered overhead.

Victor cleared his throat. "She says a sweet girl like you shouldn't work in such a rough place in your condition. She says you should catch a good man and get married."

She thinks I'm a sweet girl. Let her. I've worked hard all my life, and a hurt shoulder won't stop me. As the leaves shifted in a breeze, the dappled sun warmed her face. "What's she mean *in my condition*?"

"She says she saw you throwing up this morning and thinks you're pregnant."

"I suspect I might be. Tell 'er I had a good man oncst, but he died."

"I did, but she said you should find another one to take care of you. She says turn onto your stomach, so she can rub your shoulder's other side."

As Doozie turned over and settled into her blanket, she felt Mourning Dove's strong hands soothe her aching muscles. This must be what it feels like to have a mother, she thought—someone to care for you. Not a husband old enough to be your father, and not an older whore, but a mother. She'd left home and her own mother years ago. As she drifted off again, she wanted to lie here forever and never have to worry. That would suit her just fine. She heard footsteps and opened her eyes to see Kate walking toward them.

Kate squatted down beside her and asked, "Is she helping?"

"Like a miracle. She's got good potions an' powerful hands, but she's bossy."

"Yeah, she's like that, but she's a good healer. Victor," Kate added, "could we go find Running Deer's daughter? I want to ask her if she ratted on me about taking those pictures."

"Okay." he said, "Just let me add a few more touches to this drawing."

"I'll be stayin' right here," Doozie murmured.

"Okay," Kate said. "I'll come find you afterward for your reading lesson."

———————

They stood by Running Deer's tepee later, talking to the war chief, his wife Raven, and their daughter Soaring Falcon. "Turns out she *did* tell Growling Thunder about the pictures," Victor said. "I told her not to speak badly of you again, and Raven made her promise. She told her daughter that pictures don't steal spirits, you're not a witch, and I belong to you, so I can't be with her."

Kate nodded as the girl shot her a sullen look. She doubted Soaring Falcon really believed she'd stolen her spirit, but she was only fourteen, and insanely jealous. She wanted Victor for herself, evidently, and couldn't stand for this white woman to have him. "I hope scolding her helps," she said, "but she's a lovesick teenager and I've taken her man, so who knows what she'll do. Tell her I'll send her picture away if she wants." Taking out her phone, she showed her the image and pretended to delete it. She wouldn't *really* delete it, as she wanted to show it to Lily and Ivan someday. "There, it's gone."

Soaring Falcon's eyes grew wide as she muttered a phrase in Ute.

"She wants to know where it went," Victor said.

Kate shrugged. "Tell the little snitch it's in the cloud, or wherever." As Victor translated this, Kate looked toward Growling Thunder's camp, about forty feet away. The ugly medicine man squatted beside his tepee, chiding his wives as they cooked at his campfire.

"I told her that it no longer exists," Victor said.

"Good," Kate said. She noticed the light beginning to dim. "Oh, my God!" she exclaimed, glancing up at the sun. "It's happening! The eclipse!"

Victor looked up. "You're right!"

"Don't look at it!" she cried. "And tell the others not to either. They'll burn their retinas."

As Victor translated the warning into Ute, all around them people glanced up, then down, suddenly fearful. While they passed Kate's warning around in frightened murmurs, the moon slowly cast its shadow across the earth. The sky grew dimmer and dimmer. The murmurs grew louder and louder. As they all watched each other, Kate found Victor's hand and squeezed it.

She inhaled and slowly exhaled, feeling her heart leap into her throat. Would these people blame her for this frightening event? Would they think her a witch? Kate could see many of them staring at her, awestruck. Growling Thunder glared at her from his camp.

Kate blew out a breath. "This is amazing, but I might've made a serious mistake about predicting it."

"How so?" Victor asked. "You were right about the date."

"I was, thank God, but Growling Thunder *really* hates me now."

"I'm sure he does, but like you said, he hated you anyway."

"He did," she said, turning to go. "Let's find Doozie, so I can see if she's okay." She nodded goodbye to Running Deer's family.

Over the next hour or so, the moon seemed to gobble up the sun, then slowly spit it back out again.

———————

The next few days passed like a tranquil summer dream, their time spent resting and tending to Doozie, visiting friends around the encampment, reading, and riding horses. Much to Kate's relief, Growling Thunder had left, and no one seemed to know where he'd gone. Ouray left with his tribesmen to return home to the western mountains, after asking Victor to help translate at any upcoming future treaty talks. Although Victor didn't promise to help, he said he'd consider it.

Kate soon discovered she wasn't pregnant which eliminated the possibility of using that to lure Victor back to the future. Since Doozie still hadn't gotten her period and she'd thrown up the day before, she was convinced she was pregnant. Kate couldn't imagine a worse environment for a pregnant girl than a smoky, rowdy saloon, but Doozie was determined to keep on working.

"Maybe it's time to start up that new place," she told Kate one morning over breakfast. "Maybe I kin leave the saloon business behind an' jist run a hotel."

"Hotels are a lot of work, too, Dooz, but I'd agree with your decision to leave the saloon behind. It's no place to raise a baby." Kate shook a gourd rattle in front of Little Eagle; she squealed with delight and reached for it.

"Plenty o' women done it. Bridgette had a young'un herself oncest."

"She did?" Kate asked, smiling at Little Eagle. "What happened to it?"

Doozie shrugged. "She couldn't work an' care fer it, so she shipped it off to her sister in St. Louis, an' sends her money most every month."

Kate picked the baby up and hugged her. "Well, see? She couldn't work in a saloon and raise her baby."

"I'd wanna raise my own child, anyways. Don't got no sister, 'cept fer you, Kate." Doozie gazed across the creek to where Buster was tending his oxen. "Maybe Mourning Dove were right 'bout me catchin' myself a man. Buster's always been sweet on me, so maybe he'd marry me." She sighed and rubbed her tiny belly.

Kate snorted. "Buster? He's old enough to be your father!"

"So was Homer, but I loved 'im. I don't mind his age, long as he's good to me."

Kate glanced over at Buster. "He's a kind man and makes a decent living, but wouldn't you rather marry someone closer to your own age for a change?"

"I reckon so, but where'm I gonna find a good one? Folks in town know I been a whore, an' the only fellas I meet wander into my saloon. Who else would marry me?"

Kate sighed. "I see what you mean, but you're not even sure you're pregnant yet."

"I think I am. I ain't got my courses yet, and it's been over a month since I lay with my poor Homer. 'Sides, I heaved my guts out agin this mornin'."

"Let's not talk about this now. Let's just sit here by the creek and enjoy the day."

"I mean to enjoy the day, all right, but Buster's invited us to go fishin'. Says he fancies a bit o' trout, an' knows a good stream not far from here. He kin share my horse, so he don't have to drive his wagon, an' we kin have us a little picnic."

"Sounds great," Kate said, jiggling Little Eagle. "I could use a break from camp, and I promised Victor I wouldn't go out riding alone. Let's clean up these dishes and leave him a note. He's gone off hunting with Rising Moon."

————————

Two hours later they were sitting together on a blanket in the shade of some aspen beside a rushing stream. Buster had wandered off upstream a half-hour earlier in search of quieter pools to fish. Little Eagle lay in front of them, reaching for a ribbon that Doozie dangled above her. Kate was reading a newspaper from the previous week.

"She's grown up a bunch since I first met 'er a few weeks ago," Doozie said. "Cain't wait 'til I git my own little one."

"Yeah, they grow like weeds," Kate said, skimming an article about the latest Civil War battles back East.

"But first, I gotta catch a husband," Doozie added. "Buster might do."

Kate glanced up from the broadsheet. "So, still thinking about Buster, eh? That's why you wanted to come, to flirt with him? You did a fine job of it holding onto him on the way here."

"You cain't fault me fer tryin', Kate, and we was sharin' my horse. I come to flirt, sure, but I hankered to git outta camp, too, jist like you did."

"Buster doesn't have a proper home. Even if you caught him, where would you live?'

"He's got that log cabin. We could live there an' work the diggin's."

"But his wife's buried near that cabin," Kate said, watching the turbulent water. "Do you really think he'd want to live there with you?"

"Meybe. It's a dandy little place, an' we could make us a good life there."

"You deserve your dreams, Dooz, but you'd be bored as hell living way out there." She set her paper down and pointed to a bird dipping in the noisy stream. "Look at that water ouzel diving for bugs in that current."

"Water ouzel?" she asked, leaning forward to look. "We call that bird a *dipper*. Mmmph!" She stopped as someone covered her mouth and grabbed her from behind.

Suddenly a hand clamped over Kate's mouth too, and a vise-like arm gripped her chest. As she struggled she saw Doozie struggling beside her. Little Eagle started to cry.

"Be still," a man's voice snapped behind her, "and I won't kill the baby. If you struggle, I'll shoot it."

No! Kate thought, her skin crawling. *That voice!* She smelled nicotine on the man's fingers and the scent of hair oil. As she stopped struggling and tried to breathe, the arm gripping her chest loosened.

"No screaming," he snarled, "and I'll let you go."

She groaned and nodded.

"Good," he said, and released her. He came around to face her, and she saw it was Blackstone, pointing a gun at her chest. "Shut that baby up," he said. "We've got us some captives, don't we, friend?"

As she turned to see who he was talking to, Kate was horrified to see Growling Thunder holding the still-struggling Doozie. "Let her go, asshole," she muttered and crawled to Little Eagle. "Hush, honey."

The medicine man snickered and released his captive. "No screams."

Doozie glanced at Kate, turned back to him, and shook her head. "No screams."

Kate considered their situation. Any minute now Buster could come wandering back into this deadly trap—if he was still alive, that is. She glanced upstream for any sign of him but saw none. *Good*, she thought. *Maybe they haven't seen him.*

Blackstone sneered at her. "Growling Thunder claims you're a woman, MacKenzie, which makes our current situation *much* more interesting." He leaned forward and lifted her chin. "Amazing. All this time and I never guessed it."

She jerked her head back, wondering how far away Buster was. If she could reach the pistol in her pack and get off a shot, he might hear it above the noise of the stream and come back to help them. "How did you find us?" she asked.

"My Ute informant here came and got me," Blackstone said. "I pay him handsomely to watch you. I speak a little Ute and he speaks a little English, so we understand each other."

"Asshole," Kate snarled again. She picked up Little Eagle to try to calm her.

"Now, that's no talk for a lady," Blackstone said, his cold, gray eyes narrowing. "But I misspoke, since you're not a lady, are you?

Let's have some fun, shall we? Keep that baby calm, and you girls take off your clothes. Doozie, you go first."

"No!" she snapped. "I won't!"

Blackstone pointed his gun at Little Eagle and cocked it. "You *will*, or this baby dies. Do it."

Growling Thunder eased his quirt from his belt and began flicking it at Doozie, drawing a bead of blood from her cheek.

"Ow! Stop it!" she cried, holding up her hands.

Blackstone smiled. "Doozie, get undressed and let Growling Thunder take his pleasure first. I'll follow after him, and then we'll start on MacKenzie."

As Doozie glared at him, she unbuttoned her skirt and let it fall, then removed her bloomers. "I hate you!" she muttered as Growling Thunder took off his leggings.

"I know," Blackstone said. "Keep going."

She unbuttoned her blouse and camisole, tossed them onto her skirt, and stood there with her fists clenched—completely naked except for her boots. "You'll burn in hell fer this, Blackstone."

"I doubt it," he said. "I don't believe in hell."

Growling Thunder leered at Doozie and began strolling around her, flicking his quirt at her arms, breasts, and thighs. She began to tremble as blood beaded on her skin. A whimper escaped her lips.

As Little Eagle began crying again Kate held her closer, her heart pounding against her rib cage. If she and Doozie refused them, they'd hurt the baby, but they were going to hurt them all anyway. Hell, they'd probably kill them. If they were going to die, they should try to survive, no matter the consequences. "I need to get her bottle to calm her," she said, inching toward her pack. "It's right over there." *And my gun's inside it.*

"No tricks, MacKenzie," Blackstone said. "Just get the bottle and shut her up."

She had a chance, but just a tiny one.

"On second thought," he said, "tell me where it is, and I'll get it."

Now she had *no* chance.

Growling Thunder shoved Doozie to the ground and pried her legs apart.

She looked at Kate and began to sob.

———————

Victor and Rising Moon had hunted all morning with nothing to show for it. As they rode along under the midday sun, Victor glanced at his friend and pointed to a nearby butte. "Let's rest the horses and hike up there to look around."

They hobbled the horses and began to climb, Hawk circling overhead. As they crested the hill, they saw nine or ten Indians with horses in a valley below, and dropped to the ground. Victor pulled his binoculars from his pack and saw a brave lifting a bloody scalp from a lifeless Ute. "Arapaho," he whispered, his anger rising, "and I can see they've killed our scout." He handed the binoculars to Rising Moon.

"We have to warn the others in camp," his friend said, glassing the scene. "We'll try to slip away without them seeing us, but they'll have a clear view of us down that valley."

"We have to try," Victor said. "Let's go."

They crept down the hill, freed the horses, and mounted. "Get ready," Victor said, pulling his rifle from its scabbard. They skirted the base of the hill and rode into the valley that would lead them home. Victor glanced back to see if they were being followed and saw some of the Arapaho pointing at them and mounting their horses. Suddenly a shot rang out about a mile ahead of them. Hawk screeched and flew off toward it.

"Something's happening up there," Victor called to his friend as they rode on. He heard another shot, then a woman's scream, and a baby yowling. "That's Eagle and Kate!" he cried, spurring Milagro onward. They galloped off toward them.

———————

Blackstone yelled and dropped his pistol, his right hand shattered where Buster had just shot him. Kate rushed to grab his pistol as he fell to his knees and started screaming.

"Git away from them women!" Buster shouted from the willows by the creek.

Growling Thunder fired his pistol toward Buster.

"Gawd, my ear! That damn Injun shot it!" Buster swore. He wiped the blood from his eyes, took aim, and shot Growling Thunder in the thigh as he fired again. "Doozie, run!"

"Eeyih!" As the Indian fell and dropped his gun, Doozie lunged for it.

"Keep back, Blackstone, or I'll shoot!" Kate said. She lay the baby down on the blanket. "Keep Growling Thunder covered, Dooz."

"I got 'im," she said, rising to her feet and cocking the gun.

Blackstone was kneeling in front of Kate, his face contorted in pain. "You don't have the guts to kill me, MacKenzie. If you did, you would've done it already."

"Don't tempt me," Kate muttered, her hands shaking as they held the pistol. "I'll kill you if I have to. Buster, are you okay?"

"No, I ain't!" he said, emerging from the willows. "That bastard shot my ear off! Lord, Doozie! Did he rape you? I'll kill 'im if he did."

"No, but he was 'bout to!"

"I said stay back, Blackstone!" Kate cried as he grabbed for her.

Doozie spun and shot him in the leg.

Blackstone slumped to the ground. "Bitch!"

"Bastard!" Doozie said. "Stay down, or I'll shoot you agin."

Buster stumbled over to Kate, blood streaming down his neck. "Is my ear gone? Tell me the truth, now."

Kate studied the bloody pulp where his ear should be, but it was dangling by a strip of shredded tissue. "Looks like it, but it's hard to see with all this blood. Give me your kerchief, and I'll wrap it up for you. If we can get to a doctor quick, maybe he can reattach it." *Could they do such things in this time?*

Doozie cocked her head and listened. "Someone's comin'—I hear horses. An' there's yer hawk, Kate," she added, pointing above them. Hawk descended with her talons outstretched, diving at Growling Thunder. He screamed and raised his hands to ward her off.

Kate bound Buster's ear to his head, tied the kerchief tight, and watched it soak with blood. "There. That's the best I can do." She stood and stared at the approaching riders. "Look," she said, waving her arms at them. "Victor's coming with another brave! But wait..." A cloud of dust rose in the distance behind them. "Someone's chasing them." As the men came closer, Rising Moon waved to her and veered off across the prairie.

Victor pounded up and reined in Milagro. "What happened?" he asked as he caught sight of Doozie and Buster. "What are you doing here?"

"Blackstone and Growling Thunder attacked us," Kate said, "but Buster shot them. Why did Rising Moon ride away?"

"An Arapaho war party's after us," Victor explained, "so Rising Moon's heading for camp to warn the others. We've got to get out of here!"

Kate pointed to Blackstone and Growling Thunder. "What about them?"

"Leave them. Think you can ride, Buster?"

"O' course. I'll git the horses." Buster darted off into the willows. Doozie fumbled into her clothes.

Kate's heart pounded as she watched the approaching dust cloud. She buckled the baby into her carrier and shouldered it. "Are we heading for the camp, too?"

"No, it's too far," Victor said, watching the riders. "There's a cave about a mile from here where we can hide."

"Hide in a cave? What if they trap us inside?"

"It's a death cave. They'll be afraid to attack us once we're inside."

"Don't leave us here," Blackstone begged, struggling to sit up. "They'll kill us."

"Shut up!" Buster said as he led the horses over. "You deserve to die."

As Kate took Lady Grey's reins and mounted, she heard shots and war cries. "Grab my pack, Dooz, and climb up behind Victor. Hurry!"

"They've seen us!" Victor yelled, firing his rifle at the riders. "Go!" Shots zinged by, barely missing them.

Then they were galloping off, racing across the stream, up the far bank, and out across the prairie. Soon a hill loomed ahead, coming closer and closer, with a thicket of scrub oaks, burial mounds, and a narrow crevice in a rocky bluff.

Kate felt a pain in her arm and cried out, "I'm hit!"

"Keep going!" Victor yelled. "We're almost there!" He slowed down to ride through the oaks and they followed him, riding through the crevice into a large cave. "We should be safe now," Victor said as they dismounted and led their horses further in. "They'll be too afraid to come closer." They heard a few more shots and angry war cries.

Kate stared at the blood soaking her shirt as pain shot through her upper arm. "Damn, it hurts! I've got some bandages and ointment in my pack, Dooz, plus that morphine we have left. Could you find them, please?"

Victor eased Little Eagle's carrier off Kate's shoulders and set it down beside her. "Let me see." Unbuttoning her shirt, he pulled a kerchief from his pocket, dabbed at the blood, and studied her arm. "It's not too bad; the bullet passed through. We'll have to clean it up, but you'll be fine."

"Okay," she groaned as Little Eagle started crying. "Was the baby hit?"

"No," Victor said, "she's fine."

Kate nodded and stroked the baby's head. "Good. Quiet, little one. I'm right here."

"Got 'em," Doozie said, holding up the vial of morphine and some packets of bandages. "They're big 'uns, so they should...oh, no!" Her eyes grew wide as Buster slumped to the ground beside his horse. "Buster's fallin'!"

Victor hurried over and knelt beside him. "He's been shot in the back."

Buster groaned. "Look at it, would ya?"

Victor pulled Buster's blood-soaked shirt away from his body. "I think the bullet's still in there. I can try to dig it out with my knife."

"I'd 'ppreciate that, but I kin wait. Tend to MacKenzie first."

"No," Victor said, rising to his feet. "Your wound's worse, so we'll fix you up before Kate. Doozie, bring those supplies over here."

"I'm comin'," she said, hurrying over to kneel beside Buster.

"I can wait," Kate said. "Glad I still have some morphine, but I *do* feel a little faint." She felt her knees buckle and crumpled down against the rock wall. "I smell smoke. Do you smell smoke?"

Victor sniffed the air and frowned. "Yes, and I hope it's not what I think it is." He went to the entrance and peered out as a bullet zinged by. "Damn them!" he said, ducking back. "They're setting fires to smoke us out. Hawk's out there, diving at them. Hope they don't shoot her."

"Good for Hawk," Kate said, reaching over to comfort Little Eagle. She could hear the Arapaho shouting and Hawk shrieking. Smoke began drifting in. "What can we do?"

"Just sit tight," he said, returning to her side. "If we try to ride through them, they'll mow us down. We'll have to wait here until they leave, or until my people come to rescue us. If we have to, we can go deeper into the cave, but we should tend your wounds while we still have this light from the entrance. I have my headlight, but the batteries are getting low."

Kate nodded. "I have mine, too. Do you think anyone will come to help us?"

"They will if Rising Moon got through to them. I told him where we'd be going."

"We got some food an' water left," Doozie said, "so we kin last a bit. I'm ready over here, Victor." She'd laid the supplies out on a kerchief.

"Just rest," Victor said to Kate, patting her shoulder. "Keep the baby calm, and I'll be right back." He went over to Buster.

Kate sat there in a fog as they began to work on Buster. She heard the Arapaho breaking limbs outside. She saw the smoky light from the entrance and their skittish horses huddling together. She let her eyes close.

Suddenly Victor was stripping her shirt off, and he and Doozie were kneeling beside her, studying her wound. "I'll clean 'er up if you hold 'er," Doozie said.

"Okay," he said, holding up a bottle of whiskey. "Drink some of this, Kate."

She took a sip and winced. "God, that's awful."

"Take another one," he said.

She did, and handed the bottle back. "Damn, it hurts." Pain radiated through her arm and shoulder, making her nauseous.

Doozie nodded to Victor. "Hold her arm still, and I'll pour whiskey on it. Kate, this'll smart a little. Ready?"

"Ready," she said, taking a deep breath. But the whiskey burned like fire. "Shit!"

"Easy, love," Victor said, gripping her arm.

"Dammit!" Kate sucked in another breath, and let it out. "Hurry up!"

"Hold on," he said, "you're doing great. Brave girl."

"Shut up," she snapped, and bit her lip against the pain.

"Hold still," Doozie said, blowing on Kate's skin to dry it. "I'm gonna lay these bandages on yer wound now, an' this here ointment."

As she laid the moistened bandages against her, Kate felt a soothing coolness.

"I'm gonna pull it snug now with this fancy white tape. Nearly done, my friend."

Kate felt tape pricking each side of her wound, slowly pulling the hole closed.

"There," Doozie said. "Done. You kin let 'er go, Victor."

As he released her, Kate leaned back against him, relieved to feel his arms around her. "Thanks, Dooz, you did great."

"Yer welcome. I jist patched you up, is all. It ain't like I had to cut you open like Victor did Buster." Ripping a strip of her skirt off, she wrapped it around Kate's arm and helped her put her shirt on, then handed her a flask of water. "Here's some morphine."

Kate gulped it down. *My eyes are just so heavy.* "I'm so tired."

Victor kissed her and passed her to Doozie. "I've got to go keep watch. Just rest now. If you need more morphine, we can give you some." He eased away and stood up.

She shook her head. "Give it to Buster. Did you get his bullet out?"

"No," he said. "I couldn't. We dressed his wound and gave him morphine."

"That's too bad." She looked over at Buster, passed out on the hard ground, his wound bound with another piece of Doozie's skirt.

Victor went to the entrance and looked out. "We'll need to move deeper into the cave if this smoke gets worse, but first you and Buster need to rest. Lean back against Doozie, and let that morphine start to work."

The scent of smoke drifted in. Hawk appeared and perched beside her.

"Hey there," Kate mumbled. She leaned back and drifted off.

———————

After leaving Kate to rest, Hawk left the cave, flying over the Arapaho stoking the fires outside its entrance. She headed to the place where her people had left the evil men. As she approached the aspen grove, she could hear frantic screams.

Three of the Arapaho must have stopped here when the war party chased her people to the cave and had bound the white man and medicine man to some trees. She could see them struggling against their bindings as the Arapaho cut into their bodies and pulled out strands of their guts.

These men would die, and they would die soon.

Hawk veered off.

CHAPTER NINETEEN

Kate heard Victor calling in the distance and horses whinnying. The scent of smoke hung in the air.

"Wake up," Victor said, jostling her. "We have to move now."

"What's happening?" Kate asked. She saw the horses huddled together, their eyes wide with terror, and Bear sitting beside her. "She changed shape again."

"Yes," he said. "The smoke's getting worse, so we have to go deeper into the cave. Come on, I'll help you up." He held out his hand.

Kate leaned forward and winced as pain shot through her arm. "Damn!"

Victor pulled her to her feet and steadied her. "How do you feel?"

"It hurts, but I can handle it."

"Good." He put his headlight on, gave one to Kate, and handed over her pack. "I'll take the baby—you can carry your pack with your good arm."

"Okay." She started coughing as she slung it over her arm. "This smoke's awful."

"Put this on," Doozie said, handing her a damp kerchief. "It'll help." She and Buster were wearing kerchiefs and holding the horses. Buster was bent over with pain. Behind them the cave narrowed into a dark passage.

Kate squinted into the dimness. "Is that passage big enough for the horses?"

Victor clicked on his headlight. "I hope so." He shrugged on Little Eagle's carrier and turned to face them. "This cave is Na-gun-tu-wip, where departed spirits cross over to the other side, so we'll see and hear some frightening things. Steel yourselves."

I know he's leading us away from danger, but what other dangers lie ahead? Kate tied on her kerchief, clicked on the headlight, and took Grey's reins from Doozie.

"I'll go first," Victor said, "and Kate can go last. That way we'll have light at both ends." He tied on a kerchief and reached for Milagro. "Ready?"

They all nodded.

Victor stepped forward leading Milagro; Bear nudged in front of him and padded off. As they entered the passage, Kate could feel it luring them deeper. The horses' hooves scraped along the rough trail. A wolf howled in the distance. An owl hooted.

"What's that?" Doozie asked, her voice shaking.

"Guardians of the death cave," Victor said.

As another wolf howled, the path began descending, winding down and down into the earth. An owl flew over, grazing their heads with its wings, and still they descended. As the smoke lessened, they pulled down their kerchiefs to inhale fresher air coming up from below, but Buster's breathing became labored, and Kate could hear him wheezing. "Are you all right, Buster?" she asked.

"No," he rasped. "I cain't breathe. My chest hurts somethin' fierce." He slowed to a stop and bent over, coughing. When he caught his breath, they resumed walking. After an eternity of plodding through the darkness, the passage opened up into a huge cavern, with hundreds of tiny flickering lights illuminating its vastness. Buster slumped to the ground and began coughing again.

Kate dropped Grey's reins and sank to her knees beside him. "Lean against me," she said. In the glow of her headlight, she saw flecks of blood speckling his shirt.

He leaned against her shoulder, clutching his kerchief to his mouth and wheezing. "I'm done fer. Reckon that damn bullet nicked a lung."

Doozie knelt beside him and took his hand.

"I love you, Dooz," he wheezed. "I woulda married you."

"I woulda married you, too," she said, stroking his cheek. "Fight, Buster. Don't give up."

Suddenly he shuddered and breathed out a ragged sigh. His eyes relinquished their light.

"He's gone," Doozie whispered, and closed his eyes.

Kate looked at the stocky little freighter's weathered face and remembered the adventures they'd had together. She felt the weight of his body against her shoulder and felt the tears begin to come. Kate and Doozie lowered Buster to the ground.

Victor lifted the baby from her carrier and came to stand beside them.

They heard a stirring of wind and saw a narrow spine of rock spanning a chasm of swirling mist. A slender figure appeared on the other side, shrouded in a dun-colored robe, its face hidden beneath a hood.

"You must go back," it said, holding up one hand. "It is not your time to die."

Victor pointed to Buster. "Our friend has passed. May we bury him here under a rock mound?"

The spirit nodded. "Bury him quickly and return to the land of the living."

"Death waits for us outside," Victor said. "May we linger until it passes?"

"No," it said. "This is a death cave. If you stay here, you will perish."

Suddenly Bear roared. The baby whimpered. The horses shrieked and bolted off. As Bear's roars echoed throughout the cavern, she began changing. Within seconds she became a towering Woman, her weathered face alive with light, her long hair a silver halo. "These are my people," she thundered, "and I've guided them through many dangers. Allow them to remain here until this danger passes." She stood at the edge of the chasm, glaring at the spirit. Moments passed as she waited for an answer.

Finally, the spirit spoke. "Very well. I will grant them this favor to honor you, and I will summon a guide for their friend." It turned and watched as a Ute woman emerged from the shadows, glowing faintly and moving swiftly. She stopped at the edge of the chasm.

Buster's spirit rose from his body, lifting up and drifting toward her.

"My love," the Ute woman said, opening her arms. "It brings me joy to see you again. I long to hold you and lead you home. Cross this bridge and come to me."

"Soars on the Wind," Buster breathed, "my beloved wife."

"Come," she said, beckoning. "I will meet you in the middle." She began gliding across the bridge toward him.

Buster set off, drifting across the narrow bridge until he reached the middle.

"Shed your bloody things," his wife said. "You no longer need them."

He peeled them off, tossing them into the chasm, and stood naked. His body was young again, whole and unharmed, with no traces of wounds or blood.

"Now," Soars on the Wind said, "it is time to go." She took Buster's hand and led him across the chasm. Bending to pick up a bundle of sage, she crushed it in her hands and blew its scent to the others watching from the other side. "Remember your friend when you smell this," she said to them, "and be glad you knew him." The couple turned and disappeared into the shadows.

"You may linger here until the danger passes," the cloaked spirit said. Then it faded away.

"You must rest now," Bear Woman said, pointing to a mossy spot by a small waterfall lit by flickering lights. "Lie down there and dream peaceful dreams. I will tend the horses and wake you when it's time to go."

They settled in on the soft moss. As Kate lay listening to the trickling water, she reached for Victor's hand and began to relax. She watched Bear Woman survey the cavern, her gray eyes alert, her silver hair floating around her.

Kate closed her eyes and slipped into a deep sleep.

———————

Kate emerged from darkness into sunlight, flanked by Doozie and Victor carrying Little Eagle. Bear Woman strode ahead, leading them through fields of wildflowers, up and down gentle hills. The scent of sage perfumed the summer air.

"Where are we going?" Kate asked, hurrying to keep up.

"To a place your heart is choosing," Bear Woman answered. "Home."

Kate smiled and continued walking.

———————

Victor adjusted the baby's carrier on his back and walked beside Kate, listening to Bear Woman answering her question.

Home, *she had said,* to a place your heart is choosing. *His heart was choosing a place of safety where they could all live together.*

As he walked he was filled with a deep sense of peace.

———————

Doozie's heart was choosing to follow Kate wherever and whenever she went, for she knew Kate would love her and care for her. Doozie was finished with struggling for no useful purpose. She was ready for a new life.

———————

Bear Woman woke them. "We must go now."

Victor sat up and yawned as the others awoke around him. The waterfall trickled, the horses waited, and the lights still flickered around the cavern. Bear Woman was changing back to Bear again, her hands thickening into paws, her skin bristling with fur.

He stretched and glanced at Little Eagle yawning beside him. "I feel like I've been asleep for hours, and I had the most peaceful dream. But I have a headache."

"I had a nice dream, too, but now I have a *horrible* headache," Kate said as she sat up and rubbed her temples. "And, unfortunately, we're out of ibuprofen."

Doozie rose to her knees. "I had me a dream, but I cain't remember what it was. I got a powerful headache, too."

"Come on, Little One," Victor crooned to the baby as he shouldered her carrier.

Bear lumbered to the passage and turned to wait for them. They clicked on their headlights, gathered their horses, and followed her up and up. A wolf howled, but it was far away; an owl hooted, but they could barely hear it. As they ascended, the darkness began to lighten and the air grew fresher. Finally, they reached the upper cave and emerged into the sunlight.

"I don't smell smoke anymore," Kate said.

"I don't either," Victor said. He peered into the trees but saw no sign of Arapaho. "It looks clear. Let's go." As they led the horses through the oaks, he saw no traces of fire. *That's odd,* he thought as he mounted Milagro.

As they rode back to camp, Victor noticed the grasses were shorter and the very air felt somehow different. Soon they found the camp, or what was left of it. There were no tepees or people, only abandoned fire rings. The stream still flowed, but it was much smaller. The ponderosas framing the clearing were much taller. The site was obviously deserted and had been for a long time. He dismounted and stood there, listening.

The others dismounted and stood beside him. "Where are they?" Kate asked.

"Gone," he said. "I suspect they've been gone for many years." His heart ached for the loss of his people. Once again he felt adrift like when he'd traveled before. As he thought of losing Rising Moon and all the others, he felt his eyes fill with tears.

Kate touched his hand. "What could've happened?"

He glanced at Bear, sitting beside him. "I think Bear brought us through the death cave, and we time-traveled."

"But how?" she asked. "It wasn't *our* cave, the one we usually pass through."

He sighed. "I suspect many caves are portals. Ours is one, and that cave must be another." He surveyed the rolling prairie with its waving grasses; he listened to the sighing wind with its hidden secrets. "I think our time in the past was over, and we're meant to be here now. I just wish I knew when *now* is." He took off the baby's carrier and set it down.

"Baa!" Little Eagle chortled as Bear nuzzled her.

Doozie had been staring at the old encampment, but now turned to stare at him. "I swear, Victor. We're in the future time?"

"I'm sure of it. I think our hearts chose it as we slept."

She gasped and shot him a smile.

Kate picked a rusty stake out of the dirt and held it up to him. "Look, I think this is from your tent." She glanced around and picked up another. "Do you hear that noise?" she asked, turning toward the south. "It's coming from over there."

"I hear something," Victor said, raising his binoculars. "Might be an engine." He glassed the valley south of them and saw a truck barreling down a road, some telephone poles, and a scatter of antelope. As he passed the binoculars to Kate, he caught the scent of sage and thought of Soars on the Wind's words: *Remember him when you smell this and be glad you knew him.* He was glad he'd known his lost friends, but he was ready to return to the future.

Suddenly Kate's phone rang. She dug it out of her pack and answered it. "Lily, is that you?" Her eyes widened as she listened. "When *are* we?"

Victor's pulse quickened as he watched her face light up with joy.

Kate beamed at Doozie and pulled her into a hug. "Welcome to your new life, Dooz. We're back in my time." She turned to Victor and asked, "Are you okay with this?"

"Yes," he said, studying Bear. "I think Bear protects her people, and she brought us here because she knew this is what we really wanted. This is where we belong."

Kate kissed him. "I think so, too. Lily," she said to her grandmother, "we're somewhere in South Park, and we'll be at your house as soon as we can. It might take us a few days, though." She paused as she listened. "Love you, too." She turned off her phone and smiled at him. "Let's go."

As they mounted their horses and set off, Bear trotted ahead of them. Victor could imagine all the hills and valleys they'd have to travel to Ivan and Lily's, but he knew they would make it.

He knew Bear would lead them home.

THE END

ACKNOWLEDGMENTS

Writing is a solitary endeavor, but when the time comes to give my book to readers, I'm privileged to have several outstanding people to help me. I'm extremely grateful to my friend and editor Roger Ward, who went through countless decisions with me and guided me through the publishing process with infinite patience. As with my first book, this one wouldn't have been printed without his efforts. Once again, I'm indebted to my friend Harriet Halbig, who read the entire manuscript, coaxed me off the ledge when I needed it, and gave me valuable encouragement and feedback. My sister Cathy McDonald made this arduous journey with me a second time—combing through every phrase and scene—helping me grow as a writer with her extensive comments and edits. For this I thank her with all my heart and for being my Northwest expert on many aspects of life in that fascinating part of the country. My friend and hiking buddy Su Ketchmark patiently accepted my excuses of why I had to write instead of hike, gave me general feedback, and took the author photo. I'm grateful to my fellow writer Sharon Gerdes who read through the manuscript and contributed many excellent study guide questions. My friend Sophia De La Mora was my baby-whisperer, providing valuable advice on what infants Little Eagle's age eat, get carried in, and act like. My friend Lynn Roth crafted the bookmarks. I'm grateful to my readers, who asked for more stories about the characters they'd come to love. Finally, I'm deeply thankful to my husband Jim, who walked with me every step of the way, listened to countless scenarios, read several versions, drew the map, and brought me back from the dark places where I sometimes wandered. I couldn't have done this without him.

AUTHOR'S NOTES

This is a work of fiction, but I've tried to be culturally sensitive and historically accurate. Any mistakes or inaccuracies are my own.

The Yakama Nation Museum (http://yakamamuseum.com) that Victor and Kate visited on their way to Seattle is in Toppenish, Washington, and is one of the oldest Native American museums in the United States. They have a large exhibit about Celilo Falls, an important tribal fishing area on the Columbia River and the site of the oldest continuously inhabited community in North America (15,000 years). Artifacts from the original village site of Celilo indicate trade goods came from as far away as Alaska, the Great Plains, and the Southwestern United States. In 1957, the falls were flooded by the construction of The Dalles Dam.

East of Vantage, Washington, high above the Columbia River and Interstate 90, is the sculpture of fifteen life-size horses galloping across a ridge that Kate showed Victor. Called *Grandfather Cuts Loose the Ponies* (or the Wild Horse Monument), it commemorates the wild horses that once roamed the area.

Although just one bike officer appears in the scene where Adele's purse is stolen, the Seattle bike police usually travel in pairs. From http://www.seattle.gov/police/units/bike_patrol.htm and another site: "The Seattle police bike squads, which started as a two-man experiment in 1987, have become a key factor in discouraging downtown drug crime. Seattle is 'generally credited with spurring the modern renaissance of police cycling,' said Maureen Baker, executive director of the International Police Mountain Bike Assn."

The Swinomish Indian Tribal Community (www.swinomish.org), which Adele and her family belong to, consists of peoples descended from several Coast Salish tribes that originally lived in the area. The Salish Sea is a term used for the extensive network of saltwater waterways between the mainland and Vancouver Island in northwestern Washington and southwestern British Columbia.

There are yurts at many state park campgrounds along the Washington and Oregon coasts that resemble large, squat, conical-shaped tepees. Unlike primitive tepees, they come with basic furniture, screened-in windows, and electricity.

For thousands of years, the Ute tribe has lived in Colorado and Utah, as well as parts of New Mexico and Arizona. They were organized into a loose confederation of seven bands—Mouache, Capote, Weeminuche, Tabeguache (or Uncompahgre), Grand River, Yampa, and Uintah—each with their own shamans, chiefs, and territories. Their territories sometimes overlapped, depending on seasonal food-gathering and hunting.

While most of my characters are fictional, some actually existed, like the following:

Father Dyer was a self-ordained, itinerant Methodist preacher who ministered to residents of isolated mining camps and towns in Colorado, including Fairplay. Because he was often entrusted to carry mail, and often in winter, he was also known as the "snowshoe itinerant."

Ouray was born in 1833 near Taos, New Mexico, the son of a Jicarilla Apache father and Tabeguache Ute mother. Since this area was populated by Native Americans, Anglos, and Mexicans, he learned to speak several languages. When Ouray was a teenager, his parents rejoined the rest of the Tabeguache band in western Colorado, leaving him and his brother to be raised by a relatively wealthy Spanish couple. The boys received a decent education and a better life than many of their contemporaries, but they earned their keep by working on the couple's hacienda and tending their sheep herds. Ouray joined his parents' band when he was seventeen and eventually became a sub-chief.

Once gold was discovered in Colorado in 1859, settlers streamed into the state, and the government had to decide what to do with the resident Native Americans. Ouray was hired as an interpreter and treaty negotiator; in 1863, he was part of a delegation of Utes who visited Washington, DC. Ouray evidently distinguished himself there, for he was later recognized as "Chief of the Utes," although he wasn't a particularly powerful chief and he hadn't been chosen by the Utes to represent them. While he became their main negotiator and made other trips to Washington, many of his actions were controversial. Ouray strove to represent the Utes and evidently believed negotiating with the government was the best way to protect their interests, but he became disillusioned by treaty-breaking. Ouray's son Paron was captured by the Sioux in 1863, then captured by or traded to the Arapaho who raised him. When a young man suspected to be Paron was located years later, he refused to acknowledge his heritage, and never rejoined the Ute tribe.

The Hispanic bandits who terrorized whites in South Park were real. Brother Felipe and Vivian Espinosa launched a seven-month killing spree between March and October of 1863. Felipe was a penitente who had visions of the Virgin Mary telling him to kill gringos; the brothers' hatred was evidently fueled by indignities their family had endured previously. Beginning in the San Luis Valley of Colorado, their rampage spread to Cañon City, Little Fountain Creek (near Colorado City), Ute Pass, South Park, Red Hill, and Fairplay. When Vivian was killed, Felipe escaped and later convinced his nephew Vincente to join him and the spree continued. After the bandits were killed, a diary was found in Felipe's pocket describing the murders. The Espinosas claimed they murdered thirty-two gringos, but only twelve deaths were verified.

Colorado City (now known as Old Colorado City) emerged as a supply town to the South Park gold fields in 1859, before Colorado Springs existed. Within a month after it was established, one hundred and fifty wagons passed through and headed up precipitous Ute Pass, and many gold-seekers chose this free route instead of the toll road out of Denver. By the winter of 1860, the new town boasted eight women and three hundred men residents. The Utes made their winter camp nearby in the Garden of the Gods and were evidently peaceful neighbors.

The Indian threat which prompted the settlers to abandon their homes and "fort up" in Colorado City actually occurred, but in the summer of 1864, not 1863 as in the book. Over a period of several months beforehand, plains Indians had attacked wagon trains, stolen horses, acquired ammunition, and threatened settlements along the Front Range. On June 20, all four members of the Hungate family were murdered by hostile Indians forty miles northeast of Colorado City. Several other assaults occurred, and Governor Evans sent messengers warning residents of a massive impending attack by Cheyenne and Arapaho. With the Civil War raging, only about three hundred men of all ages were left in El Paso County, and only a volunteer militia. Within days of the governor's messengers, all ranches were abandoned, and people near Colorado City flooded into town for protection. A fort was built around the Amway Hotel. During the next month or two, all of the women and children stayed in the fort at night while mounted men patrolled the area east of town. Although small bands of Indians appeared, the threatened raid was a failure because the settlers had been warned, and the hostiles returned to their camps. (*Memories of a Lifetime the Pikes Peak Region* by Irving Howbert, 1925, and other resources.)

The Rocky Mountain News was a daily newspaper published in Denver from April 23, 1859, until Feb. 27, 2009. It was also known as a "broadsheet." I enjoyed many hours reading older editions on microfilm in the library at Colorado College in Colorado Springs while researching this book.

Having an infected tooth in the Old West was serious business. Many medicines used for dentistry contained acids, abrasive substances, alcohol, and narcotics like cocaine, heroin, or morphine. Extraction was the treatment of choice and could be performed by barbers, dentists, blacksmiths, druggists, physicians, or anyone with a good pair of tongs. Native Americans used various herbs, roots, or grasses, placing concoctions on the painful area as an analgesic salve.

(http://bustlesandspurs.blogspot.com/2010/05/old-west-dentistry.html)

According to numerous references, the last grizzly in Colorado was killed in 1979 by a big-game outfitter in the San Juan Mountains. However, the bear's necropsy revealed she might have borne cubs, indicating the possible presence of a male and surviving cubs in the area. Occasionally outfitters, hikers, and bear biologists find new evidence, and sightings persist, including a creditable one in 2006 near Independence Pass, but the Great Bear is now listed as extinct in Colorado. Our wilderness is less wild because of the grizzly's absence, and I wanted to bring one home to Colorado in my stories.

Some of the book's locations are modeled on the Palmer Divide where I live, which has its own unique flora, fauna, geology, and weather. It's not unusual to have temperatures in the sixties in January, or a two-foot snowfall that breaks tree limbs in October. I've lived here for decades, and despite several wildfires and increasing urbanization, this place is still beautiful, and I still love it.

SELECTED READINGS

Aldridge, Dorothy. *Historic Colorado City: Town of the Future.* Colorado Springs: Little London Press, 1996.

Anderson, John Wesley. *Ute Indian Prayer Trees of the Pikes Peak Region.* Colorado Springs: Old Colorado City Historical Society, 2015.

Auer, Tom. *Chronicles of Colorado.* Niwot: Roberts Rinehart Publishers, 1993.

Craighead, John J. and Frank C. Jr. *A Field Guide to Rocky Mountain Wildflowers.* Boston: Houghton Mifflin Company, 1963.

Gray, Mary Taylor. *The Guide to Colorado Birds.* Englewood: Westcliffe Publishers, 1998.

Howbert, Irving. *Memories of a Lifetime in the Pike's Peak Region.* New York and London: G.P. Putnam's Sons, 1925.

Jefferson, James, Delaney, Robert W., and Thompson, Gregory C. *The Southern Utes: A Tribal History.* Salt Lake City: University of Utah Press, 1972.

Jones, Stephen R. and Cushman, Ruth Carol. *Colorado Nature Almanac: A Month-By-Month Guide to Wildlife & Wild Places.* Boulder: Pruett Publishing Company, 1998.

Marr, Josephine Lowell. *Douglas County: A Historical Journey.* Gunnison: B & B Printers, 1983.

Marsh, Charles S. *People of the Shining Mountains.* Boulder: Pruett Publishing Company, 1982.

McConnell, Virginia. *Bayou Salado: The Story of South Park.* Chicago: The Swallow Press, Inc., 1966.

Mills, Enos. *The Grizzly: Our Greatest Wild Animal.* Boston and New York: Houghton Mifflin Company, 1919.

Murray, John, ed. *The Great Bear: Contemporary Writings on the Grizzly.* Anchorage and Seattle: Alaska Northwest Books, 1992.

Peterson, Roger Tory. *A Field Guide to Western Birds.* Boston: Houghton Mifflin Company, 1961.

Pettit, Jan. *Utes: The Mountain People.* Colorado Springs: Century One Press, 1982.

Rockwell, David. *Giving Voice to Bear: North American Indian Rituals, Myths, and Images of the Bear.* Niwot: Roberts Rinehart Publishers, 1991.

Rockwell, Wilson. *The Utes, a Forgotten People.* Ouray: Western Reflections, Inc., 1998.

Shepard, Paul and Sanders, Barry. *The Sacred Paw: The Bear in Nature, Myth, and Literature.* New York: Arkana/Viking Penguin, 1992.

Smith, Anne M. *Ute Tales.* Salt Lake City: University of Utah Press, 1992.

Smith, P. David. *Ouray: Chief of the Utes.* Ridgway: Wayfinder Press, 1990.

Swinomish Indian Tribal Community. *13 Moons: The 13 Lunar Phases, and How They Guide the Swinomish People.* La Conner: Swinomish Office of Planning and Tribal Development, 2006.

Whitney, Stephen. *Western Forests.* New York: Alfred A. Knopf, 1992.

Wroth, William, ed. *Ute Indian Arts & Culture: from Prehistory to the New Millennium.* Colorado Springs: Colorado Springs Fine Arts Center, 2000.

Wyss, Thelma Hatch. *Bear Dancer: The Story of a Ute Girl.* New York: Simon & Schuster, 2005.

READING GROUP DISCUSSION QUESTIONS

1. Sawatzki begins the sequel shortly before the first book ended. How did you feel about this? Why do you think she chose to do this?

2. Which do you think would be more difficult, for someone from the present to adjust to life in 1863, or for someone from 1863 to adjust to modern times? What would be the easiest adjustment, and what would be the biggest challenge for each?

3. After passing through the tunnel into another time, Victor and Kate experience headaches. How realistic is the time travel experience? Why do you think the tunnel opens during the solstice?

4. Victor is a Ute from the Tabeguache band of Utes. Who do you consider to be your tribe? How closely do you associate with individuals with a similar heritage?

5. Kate and Victor have very different expectations about parenting roles for a new baby. How well does Victor adapt as a caregiver for Little Eagle? Which has been the biggest driver of changes in parenting roles—culture or time?

6. As the book progresses, we learn that Bear is a shapeshifter. When did you first suspect that Bear could change forms? Did any of the forms surprise you? Bear thinks, "Deep inside, she was still Bear." What traits did Bear maintain through her many forms?

7. Victor says that most whites fear grizzlies and want to exterminate them, but natives are taught to respect Earth's creatures. How has our attitude toward animals changed, and what is being done currently to preserve Colorado animal species from extinction?

8. How did the discovery of gold in the Rockies affect white man's encroachment on Indian territories?

9. Kate was less than totally forthright with Victor about her relationship with Mark. She certainly didn't tell Mark that she had fallen in love with Victor. Whose fault was it that Victor became jealous of Mark? When caught in a love triangle, is honesty the best policy?

10. When Doozie inherits the saloon, she stops working as a prostitute and shifts to the role of saloon manager and madam. Albert asks her, "Are you sure you've given up whoring?" And she says, "You know damn well I'm quit of it." What were the financial prospects for a young unmarried woman in the 1860s, and what would you have done if you were in her shoes?

11. Kate uses her phone to take photos in the past. Victor warns her that his people might think that the photos are stealing their spirits. What have been the greatest technological achievements of the past 150 years, and how have they changed our perception of humans' role in the world?

12. How did you feel about the way the story ended? Did you expect Kate and Victor to stay together or each end up in their own world?

Diane Sawatzki sitting on a Ute Prayer Tree
La Foret, Black Forest, Colorado
Photograph by Su Ketchmark

Diane Sawatzki earned a bachelor's degree in biology from the University of Colorado. She's been a park naturalist, nuclear medicine technologist, secondary science and math teacher, and freelance writer. While researching and writing video scripts for historical documentaries, she developed a keen interest in local history, and a tale of frontier Colorado began to emerge. The result was her first novel, *Once Upon Another Time*, a time-travel historical adventure set in the Pikes Peak region in 1863. A librarian with the Pikes Peak Library District, Diane lives with her husband near Palmer Lake, Colorado, in the foothills of the Rocky Mountains north of Colorado Springs. *Manyhorses Traveling* is Diane's second novel and is the sequel to *Once Upon Another Time*.

Visit our website at www.palmerdivideproductions.com

Photo courtesy of Pixabay.com

Made in the USA
San Bernardino, CA
17 November 2017